Black Shadows

Simon Swift

A Wild Wolf Publication

Published by Wild Wolf Publishing in 2011

Copyright © 2011 Simon Swift

First print

ISBN: 978-1-907954-08-5

www.wildwolfpublishing.com

Black Shadows has been a labour of love. There are far too many people to thank. The dedications are easy...

To Sarah, the love of my life.

To Harvey, the most amazing boy in the world.

And to Ruby, my little princess.

Praise for Black Shadows

"Black Shadows is Raymond Chandler or James Ellroy reinvented for the 21st century. There's a real authenticity about the period; the setting – New York in the 1940s - the characters – all coming together in a detective story that really hits the heights.
From the dramatic opening onwards, the reader is hooked. It's a proven formula: a wisecracking detective, exotic female characters and shady gangsters, but here everything works so well."
Jake Barton, bestselling crime author of *Burn Baby Burn*

"Black Shadows is a tightly written piece of noir fiction, inviting obvious comparisons to Raymond Chandler and Dashiell Hammett."
HarperCollins

"The setting, the wisecracks, the gangster element, the upright but flawed detective falling for the beautiful woman - what's there not to like?"
Gerry McCullough, author of *Belfast Girls*

"It is one of the best NY stories I've read. LOVE LOVE that opening - the mention of the shooting and the visual of the bloody steak. Not-so-subtle brilliance."
Elizabeth Lindberg, New York actress, playwright and author of *Dionysus* and *Out of Sync*

"Excellent read. One of the best detective stories I've read. Great characters and a very good plot. The pace is fast and really holds your interest. This one is well worth reading. I highly recommend it."
John Harold McCoy, author of *Bramwell Valley*

"If you fancy being drawn into the world of film noir, slick private eyes and femme fatales, this is the book for you. Here's lookin at you, kid."
Catherine Chisnall, author of *Surfacing* and *Descending*

I would like to thank JP Noel, possibly the greatest cover artist in the world. I owe you a huge debt of thanks, buddy. Very soon, Errol Black will be coming to an island near you with a crate of beer under his arm!

I would also like to thank all the amazing people that have contributed in making Black Shadows the fantastic book that it is today. It wasn't always this good! There is a whole army of you angels out there. You know who you are, and I tip my hat to you all.

Prologue

23 October 1935
Newark, New Jersey

When the shooting started, I was tucking into a nice, bloody porterhouse steak. A generous portion of mashed potatoes, string beans and turnip accompanied it, swimming in the tasty juices from the meat. A half empty bottle of claret stood in the middle of the table and a basket full of bread rolls sat at the edge. Three other men were eating; Terry Shadow was on my right, a small, wiry Irishman faced me, and Dyke Spanner was next to him.

The first few shots took us by surprise, but as they were not meant for us it did not really matter. A small man dressed in a brown suit was firing a pistol, but it was his partner, a larger, angrier, uglier man that was doing the damage, pumping the room full of shotgun blasts. Three of their intended targets were sitting in the far corner, and were all badly hurt in the opening exchange.

Dyke Spanner turned the table on its end, sending the plates of food crashing to the floor, before firing a volley of shots in the general direction of the mayhem. The wine survived, snatched by Terry Shadow seconds before, who was now drinking it straight from the bottle. We all cowered behind the table as it started to splinter before us, firing the odd shot back in the direction from where they came.

"Stop firing that fuckin' gun," shouted Terry in between gulps. "They're not here for us."

He was right. The intended hit was taking a piss in the bathroom. He was shot eight times; suffering mortal wounds to the abdomen, but amazingly didn't die for another 23 hours. The others all joined him in the death roll, as did Terry Shadow only moments after he scolded Dyke Spanner and myself. He died with a third of a bottle of claret in his hand and two clean gunshots to his head.

The moment Terry died I knew that it would change everything. There was no guarantee I would walk out of here alive. In fact, the chances were looking slimmer by the second, as all four of the killers' targets were now approaching their end. But if I were to survive, my whole life as operative for The Shadow Man Detective Agency would be different.

Terry Shadow was the founder, owner and overall supremo of The Shadow Man Detective Agency. We averaged thirty cases a week, from debt collecting to missing persons. By far the most popular, however, was mob work. We did everything for the wise guys except pull the trigger. It didn't matter if it was surveillance; tailing future hits, recovery; finding frisky treasurers that tended to go walkabout, or troubleshooting; which just about covered most things. If it paid, we did it. But most often it was security.

New York was full of would-be gangsters. There were regional mobs everywhere, all with their own tribal territories controlling protection rackets, narcotics, gambling and women. Everybody wanted a piece. It was these guys that we dealt with most. Transporting a name safely was a quick and well-rewarded job, even if the risks were supposedly high. Luckily the mobs tended to leave outsiders alone, which made my life a lot easier. We only lost one man in three years and didn't discriminate, working for anybody who paid well. New York wasn't short of those.

The bank balance swelled, but all our reputations suffered. Some weeks we pulled in twenty grand clear and all went home happy. It couldn't go on forever. Don't get me wrong, I didn't particularly like what we were doing, but it wasn't my conscience that got the better of me. After all, I was only following orders. It had to end sometime. I would never spend all the money anyway, and although I had a reputation as a mob hanger-on I was hardly one of the boys. With Terry dead, the end was in sight. I decided right there and then, as bullets fizzed around my ears and blood splashed all over the carpet, that enough was enough.

It was the silence that broke my thoughts. A faint patter of footsteps, the slamming of a door, and then nothing. I checked myself over and to my surprise I was not hurt. The table was nothing more than firewood, there was broken glass and pints of blood splattered all over the floor, but I was in one piece. I looked over at Dyke Spanner and his smile told me that he too was unhurt. Our third dining acquaintance was gone.

The peace was broken by a stocky, heavy-set man, bleeding desperately from the middle, stumbling out of the bathroom. He had a smoking cigar between his teeth and a rather disheveled fedora in one hand. In the other shaking hand he held a gun, which he raised and pointed at every man in the room before lowering it and swearing resignedly to himself.

Of the other three targeted men, one was unconscious, one was absent and the other groaned aloud in a pool of his own blood. Dyke tapped me on the shoulder and said, "Errol, we should go. We don't want to be caught up in any of this. Let's get the boss to a hospital and scram."

I nodded watching in amazement as the man embraced his unconscious friend before leaping to his feet and pointing at me. "Kid, come here."

I looked at Dyke and he shrugged.

"I said come here," repeated the dying man, more in hope than authority.

I holstered my weapon and walked through the debris to the man. The only other survivor had staggered his way through to the main tavern and could now be heard ringing for medical assistance. We all knew it would be too late. Dyke stayed nearby.

Up close he looked exactly the same as in all the news pictures. Although he was physically a small man, he still exuded an aura that a dying man should not be able to hold. His deep-set eyes were wild and darted around, even though he was talking to me and I was close enough to smell his breath. He was sucking a peppermint but he still smelled distinctly of death. His nose was crooked and had been broken many times, his chin square, his ears large but unobtrusive and his lips thin and colourless. He looked like a man I had seen many times and yet he was a man I had only just set my eyes upon.

"Come on Rolly," urged Dyke Spanner.

The last words of Arthur Flegenheimer have since been the subject of much myth and speculation. There are many pages of transcript from an official stenographer, which formed the basis of Bill Burroughs's 1969 story. To me, most of it was the nonsense of a dying man, a proud, powerful and incredibly vicious, but nevertheless a dying man. The last words he uttered to me may or may not have been similar nonsense. When he finished talking about gloves, Hitler and the trouble with Jews he looked at me square in the eyes and said, "Think big, son, think big. And whatever you do steer clear of the wise guys, they'll kill you!" and he patted me several times on the back.

Before I could reply, Dyke Spanner grabbed me by the shoulder and hauled me out of there. "The cops are here we gotta go," is all he said.

So I cleaned my hands of the mob, refused all offers, however handsome, and kept to the private stuff. With Terry gone it was now Errol Christopher Black who was the boss. It wasn't fear of dying, most mobsters died on the job that was a fact, but I had lost fear years ago. I simply decided that it wasn't for me anymore and took my low-life standards elsewhere.

Dyke Spanner refused to follow.

Chapter One – The start of something big
Manhattan 1945

I smoked my second to last Lucky, watching the smoke spiraling up, glowing a mournful purple in the sporadic neon from the avenue below, before pouring myself a large Remy Martin and resting my feet on the desk. It looked like being a long evening.

The Black & Wentz Detective Agency sign had lost its shine. Once a handsome, glimmering piece of brass, offering hope and enthusiasm to the many clients who knocked reluctantly on the heavy, wooden door, it was now nothing more than a dull old sign, nailed to a dirty, creaking door that led into a small, cluttered office. Over the years there were fewer and fewer people that would see it.

Inside, the dullness evaporated as soon as the blinds were lifted. The view from my window was fantastic, you could see right over Midtown Manhattan. We were on the 31st floor facing the Empire State Building, a shining beacon of American Architecture, with a great view over the city; the sleaze and the millions of nameless people battling to win the perpetual rat race. I shared this office with my partner Hermeez Wentz and our trusty secretary Ava Jameson, who were both out, probably at home with their feet up and the zzzs rapidly approaching.

I drained the Remy, lit my last Lucky and got ready to hit the paperwork. My first day back from a long vacation had been uneventful, and the pile of bills, which had been growing over the last few weeks, was still goading me from the desk in the corner.

Then suddenly She entered the scene. I should have felt it immediately. She had trouble written all over her beautiful face. Sure she caught me at a bad time, I was tired, bored and my resolve was weakening. I was always a sucker for a good mystery and a good looker. She didn't disappoint on either score.

She had long, dark brown hair, straight down to her shoulders with curls at the end. She was wearing a classy, black evening gown that revealed just enough to accentuate her curvy figure without cheapening the effect, with a tiny, red cardigan, buttoned only at the neck. A delicate gold watch and a sparkling diamond ring were the only jewelry on show. The ring was on the wrong finger, unless you were her fiancé, and was very tasteful; a single diamond mounted on a simple gold band. Her face was dominated by her dark, piercing eyes that at first appeared to be too large, but when they looked at you could only be described as beautiful. She had a small, pixie nose and full lips, painted red that seemed to move in slow motion as she spoke.

She cast a stunningly beautiful silhouette on the frosted glass door and then came in and intrigued me. Sitting with her long, tanned legs crossed and a cigarette glowing from between her lips, this is what she told me...

"I'm so pleased that you are here, Mr. Black," she said in a timid, girlish voice with a slight trace of an accent. I couldn't quite place it but it was European, possibly Italian.

"You're lucky that I am. I've been away a while."

"I don't feel very lucky right now," she said. "In fact, Mr. Black, I am in a terrible muddle, I really am."

She looked at me all the time she was talking, blushing slightly as I held her gaze.

"I'm sorry, Miss...."

"Claudia, my name is Claudia."

"Claudia. Why don't you take a drink and we'll see if I can help you."

I took out another glass and poured her a healthy shot of cognac, watching her curiously as she tentatively took hold of the tumbler and gulped the drink, before coughing embarrassedly. I chuckled and re-filled my own.

"Here, take this." I handed her my handkerchief and she held it to her mouth before smiling. The smile could have come right from the gods.

"I am sorry Mr. Black, what must you think of me? I really am in the most terrible mess. I'm absolutely at the end of my tether."

"Take your time sweetheart, there's no rush. When you're ready why don't you tell me all about it?"

"You're very kind." She jabbed out a hand and rested it on my own. It was warm and felt soft, like a velvet glove on a block of firewood. She removed the hand and started fiddling in her dinky, black shoulder bag. She pulled out a small block of lipstick and a pair of black, lacy panties and handed them over to me.

"I've sensed that something is not right for quite a while now. I'm not some silly, paranoid little girl you understand, but when I found these it was just too much."

I smiled at Claudia and looked right into her big, puppy eyes. A single tear rolled down her cheek, which she quickly dabbed away with my handkerchief.

"I take it that these are not yours," I said, businesslike.

She shook her head and said, "If only they were, Mr. Black, then I wouldn't be here now. No, I am afraid I don't wear this brand of lip stick and the...they are certainly not mine." She took a deep breath. "I found them in the trouser pocket of my dearest George. When I was doing the laundry of course, I wouldn't otherwise go through his things, although..." Her sentence petered out and she looked blankly out of the window with a confused look on her face.

"They could of course be a gift. Maybe you have a birthday or a special date in the not too distant future?"

Claudia shivered and shook her head. She picked up the lipstick and screwed off the top, the colour stick was worn nearly all the way down. She took the panties in her hand and made a fist. "They could not be for me, Mr. Black. They smell of...a woman."

"Your dearest George, is that your boyfriend, Claudia?"

She turned to me and smiled. "Not my boyfriend, Mr. Black, my fiancé. We are soon to be married and we will have the most wonderful ceremony with a huge reception and a marquee with bouquet after bouquet of sweet smelling flowers. So far he has been unable to afford a wedding ring. George does not yet earn very much money, but soon we will live in a big house and I will have a large, golden ring."

I nodded and waited for her to continue. She sat there for a good three minutes almost enjoying the silence, as I was enjoying watching her in it. All of a sudden she flushed again and apologized before continuing the story.

"I don't really believe it is true, but she's been pestering me for weeks now and when I found these things I..." she paused, "well, I guess I just want to know really. George is very secretive. He never tells me things unless he thinks that it is necessary that I need to know. Now I think I really do need to know."

"Okay Miss..."

"Claudia."

"Claudia, I think I'm getting the picture. You want me to put a tail on George for a while, make sure he's behaving himself?"

She looked down at her hands and fiddled with her bag, before looking up eyes ablaze and nodded. "Yes, Mr. Black, I do. I will pay you handsomely for the task. This may not seem like a big deal to you but to me...you see George is my life. I cannot bear to think of him...well you do know what I mean, you are a man of the world. Just do whatever it is that you have to do, and then my mind will be at ease." She pulled a purse out of her bag and leafed out a one hundred dollar bill. I didn't even blink as she handed it over but the alarm bells were going off in my head. They were put to bed by a return of that seemingly innocent, angelic smile and a flutter of her long lashes.

"We reside together in a small house in the East Village." She gave me the address and directions to get there. "Tomorrow evening George is out on a business meeting. Maybe that would be a good time to start the..."

"Yes, it probably would," I interrupted to save her the pain. "What I need is a good description and a few details, it won't take a minute." I opened the drawer and pulled out a fresh pad of paper and a pencil.

"George works very hard," she said slowly, avoiding my gaze. "He has a good job down in Battery Park...taking people over on the ferry."

"The Staten Island Ferry?"

"No, to see the statue. He's hoping to get lessons to captain the vessel, that's what his business meeting is all about. He would make a great captain."

"I'm sure he would. And a description."

"Yes, of course. He's thirty-eight years old, a little over six feet tall with short, blond hair. His eyes are blue and he has lovely thick eyebrows, a shade darker than his hair colour. He is very softly spoken and very gentle, a true gentleman which I am sure you are aware, Mr. Black, makes him very attractive to the ladies."

I smiled and gently shook my head.

"Tomorrow, he will be wearing his best navy blue suit with a red handkerchief in his breast pocket. He will be meeting the shipping committee for a meal at a creperie in Chelsea and then going on for a drink at the Dragon Bar in Chinatown. I overheard him arrange it on the telephone. I do not know when to expect him home. He has told me not to wait up."

I took it all down and put the pad away. "That should be all I need Claudia. The job shouldn't be too difficult, but if you think of anything else that may help. It's probably better for you if I don't call you so why don't you call back here in a couple of days and I'll give you a progress report."

"You are very kind, you really are."

She looked a little sad, but her voice held firm, "Please Mr. Black, this means a lot to me. Please take the job personally and take it seriously. To me this really is a big deal."

Those were the last words she said with her slow motion mouth before she leaned over the desk, kissed me softly on the cheek and left the office. All of a sudden the sign looked shiny again.

It was the start of something big...

Chapter Two – Watching

There is no greater evocative symbol of America than the cherished lady. Raising the torch of liberty with one hand and clutching a stone tablet in the other. She has become an icon of everything that is American, a colossal figure standing proudly over the New York Harbor. The fact that she was sculpted, designed and mainly financed by Frenchmen and not Americans is not the biggest surprise to first time visitors; it is the realization that this fantastic piece of architecture is not the huge figure they expect it to be. At only 151 feet one inch tall from base to torch, The Statue of Liberty is actually disappointingly small.

The hundreds of people queuing inside Castle Clinton, for tickets to take them across the Liberty Island Ferry, were obviously not too disappointed. I was sitting on a rather creaky wooden bench around the edge of the old fort, chewing on a pastrami-on-rye, watching the hordes handing over their cash excitedly, awaiting a dalliance with the old girl. The sun was shining warmly and the water was looking calm.

The time was now just after midday and the lunchtime rush was beginning. George Ferriby had just finished his morning shift on the ferry and was heading out of Battery Park towards the Financial District. I finished off my sandwich and stood up to follow him.

I had started the surveillance a little after seven o clock the same morning, waiting patiently outside the small house on East 5th Street until George appeared. He was dressed casually in black slacks, polished boots and a large overcoat. Under the coat, the collar of his Liberty Island blazer poked out and he kept a pair of thick gloves in the pockets, which he wore for a while and then returned.

We walked west along 5th Street until it hit Bowery and then headed due south, through Little Italy, Chinatown and into the Financial district. George walked briskly without looking around him; I followed on the other side of the street keeping one hundred yards apart. It took thirty minutes to arrive at Battery Park. A quick coffee and muffin, at a diner across from the fort, and George went to work, ferrying people by the hundreds across to Liberty Island. He worked diligently and quietly for the next four hours barely uttering another word, stopping only to smile at the pretty ladies and take photographs if asked.

Ava Jameson had been more than a little surprised to see me at six thirty, when she unlocked the office door and hung up her coat and hat.

"Let me pour you a coffee and then come and give me a big hug," I said, and smiled at her, my arms open wide.

She turned in surprise, flashed me a lovely smile and then rushed into my arms, hugging me warmly. "Oh Errol, you're back. I've missed you. Did you have a good time?" she asked, wriggling free and then putting a hand on my cheek.

"It was a nice break. I'm glad to be back but missing it already. Look at you princess you look fantastic."

Ava blushed and shrugged her shoulders, enjoying the compliment.

She had been secretary for the Black & Wentz Detective Agency for three years now. She had always been pretty, but when she first joined us was nothing more than a girl; twenty-two years of age, painfully shy but a genius at running an office. Since then she had matured immensely, her confidence had grown and her beauty had flourished. No longer did she wear conservative, plain sweaters and long, over the knee skirts, but attractive, figure showing attire that not only looked classy and sexy, but very adult. Now, she was truly a woman, but would always be my girl.

She was tall, nearly six foot, with long, straight legs and a firm backside that she always claimed was too big. Her hair was shoulder length, dark brown and wavy. Although not classically beautiful, her face was pretty; she had big, green eyes that were always quite heavily made up with dark eyeliner, a medium-sized, well-shaped nose and soft-boned cheeks. Her mouth was wide with thin lips, which she painted soft pastel colours.

"I'm afraid business is still very slow," she sighed. "Hermeez said it's going to have to pick up soon or we'll all be out of jobs."

"Well my little sweetheart, it already has. Last night a Miss Claudia, surname unknown, came in and hired me. It's nothing big, just a simple surveillance detail, although she pays well and she pays cash." I handed over the hundred dollars as well as a fresh cup of coffee.

Ava's eyes widened as she took the money. She took a small sip of her coffee and put the cash away in her log book. "I hope you've not taken to mugging rich, old ladies whilst you've been away," she said, and sat down smiling.

"She's not old," I said. "And I don't get the impression that she's rich either. In fact she seemed a little mysterious." I shrugged. "Who cares, if she pays promptly she can be as damn mysterious as she likes. I've written down the details on the pad, which is in the tray."

I finished off my coffee, leaned over Ava and gave her a little peck on the cheek. "I'm afraid I'm going to have to love you and leave you. Tell Hermeez that I said hello and I hope to see him for a drink a little later in the day."

"Oh, Errol, before you rush off. Dyke has been calling every day since you left. He wouldn't leave a message, not even with Hermeez, but he looked like he might be in trouble."

"You told him I was away?"

"I simply told him that you were unavailable and that I would pass on the message."

"Okay, I'll deal with it."

Ava frowned and then said, "Did Margaret have a good time? I bet she's lovely and tanned."

She said it coolly then immediately looked like she wished she hadn't. "I'm sorry, Errol, you don't have to answer that. Look I'm just so pleased that you're back."

"Me too, sweetheart. Look, I gotta go."

"And Errol, keep in touch. I haven't seen you for three weeks."

I had arrived at the Ferriby household just in time to catch a glimpse of Claudia kiss George on the doorstep and then close the door. I had decided that it would be a better idea to start the job a little earlier than she had suggested. It would not

18

only give me a good chance to study the subject better, but maybe also allay any nagging doubts about the case in general. Claudia had left a surprisingly indelible mark on me. She had given me almost nothing to go on, but left an unmistaken sense of mystique. I knew she wasn't telling me everything, that things ran a lot deeper than what she was letting on. They always did. But I was prepared to play it her way and not probe too deep.

I stood on the sidewalk and gazed along the street, at the tall buildings, the lary neon signs, the people all shuffling along aimlessly. George Ferriby headed north up Broadway, took a left turning onto Liberty Street and another left onto Greenwich Street. We were in the heart of the financial district, a place teeming with suited professionals all carrying an umbrella in one hand and a briefcase in the other. Billions of dollars of business was done every day of the year in this relatively small area.

Ferriby ducked into a restaurant on the corner. I followed him in a minute later, handed my coat and hat to the attendant and waited to be seated. The place was small and cosy; it was an open room with several alcoves and large pot plants to give privacy. The lighting was dimmed and soft, jazz music gave a relaxing background. At the far end there was a bar, the rest of the room was filled with small dining tables, most of which were full.

I managed to get a table three away from Ferriby, who was sitting across from a beautiful, redhead. She was drinking red wine and her face was smiling even though her eyes were not. I could not catch what they were saying to each other, but she laughed at his every word. Whereas Ferriby was obviously enjoying displaying his immense humorous talents I got a feeling the lady was a little less genuine, playing along a little.

I too ordered a carafe of red wine, and observed my subject as inconspicuously as possible. They both had soup and a roll, followed by a Caesar salad, but were not really interested in the food. Ferriby enjoyed making the lady laugh, and she never tired of performing to order. Thirty minutes into the rendezvous the redhead put a hand on Ferriby's, very tenderly and he held it in his own before kissing it softly. They then finished their wine,

19

looked around the restaurant and stood. Their lips only met briefly and the lady left, leaving Ferriby to sit on his own for another five minutes before he too left.

I followed him back to the ferry and he simply got back on with his work. His shift would go on for another four hours, I had earlier checked at the office, which was always advertising for ship hand vacancies.

Back at the restaurant, the bartender was very forthcoming.

"Georgy Ferriby, sure I remember. He comes here most days." He looked at his watch and pulled a face as if contemplating nuclear physics. "Usually about lunchtime, maybe between twelve and one."

"And the lady?"

The bartender smiled and tapped his nose with his right index finger. "Wasn't she something?" He whistled through his teeth and gave me a filthy smile. "What I could do with a lady like that."

"Do you know what she's called?" I asked. "Is she Ferriby's wife?"

The bartender found that thought funny. He laughed out loud and shook his head. "Oh no, Georgy's not married, my friend. I don't think he's what you would call the marrying type. No, he's too fond of the ladies. He must have brought, oh maybe four, five different girls here over the last year. No, that fine figure of fresh meat wasn't his wife, although I'd gladly make her mine I don't mind telling you."

I nodded as enthusiastically as I could as the bartender guffawed at his own inanity. In spite of his boorishness he was proving a useful character witness and it would be careless to alienate him just yet.

"How long has George worked down on the ferries?" I asked.

He shrugged. "As far as I know he's only helping out a friend. You gotta appreciate we're not best buddies or anythings. I mean I do hear the odd bit here and there but..." The pause was long enough for me to hand over another five bucks, which was grabbed lightening fast and shoved down the front of the big man's apron.

"Well," he said and moved his head closer to mine, which was already close enough although a well skilled driver could manoeurve the Staten Island Ferry between us. "Well, I heard that Georgy is into a bit of buying and selling, you know what I mean?"

"Nope. Care to elaborate."

"I don't want to say anything, but..." he looked from side to side, "diamonds is what I hear. Brings 'em in from the Continent. Now it sure has been nice talking to you Mr...Mr. whatever your name is, but I got some things I should be doing."

I tipped my hat and left the restaurant.

Whatever George Ferriby was in to was none of my damn business and the more I heard about it the less I wanted it to become my business. The only part I was interested in was the part I was being so handsomely paid to be interested in. In that respect it was looking more and more like sweet Claudia was going to be sadly proven correct. I doubted the assignment would last the week. Tonight would be the meal, where I already had a good idea just who he would be dining with. I would take my camera, get proof of the infidelity and leave it to them. That was the theory, but like all good theories it was full of holes.

Joe's Diner had once been described as the sleaziest joint in the Bronx. That was unfair there were more seedy diners in the Bronx than Chinamen in Peking, and Joe's was by no means the worst. Located only five minutes walk from my own apartment and only a couple of miles from the Yankee's Stadium in the Belmont neighborhood, the small, dingy establishment fails to impress primarily because of its name. The word 'diner' in the title of a place gives the presumptuous idea that beautiful plates of food will be served there; of fresh fruit and salads, of gateaux's and pastries. None of which are on offer at Joe's. Apart from whatever Joe feels like whipping up on any given day, dishes ranging as wide as pastrami sandwiches to Russian Goulash, the diner is a drinking den. A place where locals gather on an evening to drink, play cards and drink some more. The lighting is poor, the tables are old and battered and the bar has several gunshot marks embedded in it. In short, the place has character and is never short of a supporting cast of them drinking from dusk till dawn sitting on its wobbly barstools.

It was on one of those wobbly barstools that I was now sitting. It just so happened Joe was a good friend of mine. He not only provided the worst fare in the district, but somehow managed to accumulate invaluable information on many of his clientele. This place was home to me. It was filthy, smelly, dingy and full of low-lifes. It was my bread and butter. If I had a dime for every case that had been solved thanks to a conversation in Joe's, I'd be a rich man.

"Should I ask you if you had a good time wherever it is that you been?" asked Joe, "or shall I just bring you a cold beer and mind my own goddamn business?"

"Better stick to the beer old buddy."

Joe smiled and pulled out a couple of cold bottles from the refrigerator. He twisted off the caps and wiped the necks down on his apron before handing one over and then taking a long drink from the other. "That's good," he said and patted me on the back. "Good to see you again Errol, you look well."

"Cheers," I said. "You look like you could do with a holiday."

Joe shook his head and took another drink of the beer, finishing the bottle. He was a large man, maybe 250 pounds with a face that you could lose your wallet in. What little hair he had left was a sandy colour, the same as his eyes. Years of drinking and fine living had made the veins split on his large nose making it redder than a ripened beetroot and his smile was littered with blackened teeth. Although he had a reputation as being a bit of a slob, Joe was the opposite he just had the misfortune of turning every fine piece of cloth into a rag. His clothes were always clean and well pressed but for some reason they just looked scruffy on him. It was said he could get a suit cut at the Savoy Guild and still come out looking like he was frightening the birds for a living.

"Who's the punk you brought in with you Eezy?" asked my friend nodding behind me.

22

I took a look over my shoulder where a baby-faced youth, dressed in a pin-striped suit was nursing a cola. He looked away the instant I clocked him, pretending to take an interest in a newspaper.

"I'm not sure," I replied. "He's been with me most of the day. It's nothing to worry about."

"I can make sure he doesn't follow you back out if you like. It's not a problem."

"No thanks Joe, I think I'll leave him there a while longer. See if he gives anything away. Thanks anyway. You could bring me the telephone over here if you don't mind and another of those cold beers."

Joe nodded and went to get the telephone.

Ava answered on the first ring.

"Hello sweetheart, how are you getting on?"

"Errol, it's so nice to hear your voice again so soon. I'm actually getting on really well. I've just this minute got back in the office from a wonderful luncheon down at The Warldorf"

"Hell, I must be paying you well."

"I didn't spend a dime and before you make a jibe I was dining with a lady. Your lady in fact."

"The future Mrs. Ferriby?"

"The very same and you're right she's not old, although she does appear to be rich. The bill came to over my whole week's salary. I felt a little bit guilty actually Errol, I had just spent most of the morning investigating her and she was so nice, I can see why you like her."

"I don't recall saying that I like her."

"Maybe not, but I can tell that you do, and you should. She's lovely."

"Lovely, eh? Tell me more about your digging."

"Well, the house she lives at in the East Village..."

"Yes."

"According to the records, she doesn't live there. That address has been unoccupied for three months. The last owner packed up and left for Alabama in February. I checked with the registry and the real estate agents, the property is on the market right now."

"Anything on the straying would-be husband?"

"Only that he hasn't worked on the ferry for long, a couple of weeks in fact. And he isn't meeting anybody from the company tonight either. Not officially anyhows."

"Ava, as always you have done sterling work? Has anybody else called? Have you seen Hermeez?"

Ava sighed. "No he hasn't been in yet, although I have had his wife on the telephone?"

"His ex-wife."

"Yes. I don't like to gossip but I think she's bleeding him dry. Maybe you should have a chat."

"We'll see about that. I'm going to have to go now but before I do there's just one more thing. I want you to get your pencil handy. There's not much to go on but you might turn something up, you usually do."

I gave as good a description of the young punk that had been tailing me ever since Castle Clinton. Ava was a wonderful artist, she could create an uncanny likeness from the most simplistic of words. She said she would do what she could and hung up the telephone.

Joe took the telephone away and we talked for a while. As I was about to leave, he mentioned that Dyke Spanner had been chasing me down.

"Don't worry, Errol, I didn't tell him anything but it did seem important. Maybe you should look him up."

"That's exactly what I'm going to do," I said, and left the diner.

Chapter Three – Dyke Spanner

He was wearing a blue suit. She was wearing a red evening gown.

I managed to get a table in the corner with a good view of the whole restaurant, a cosy Creperie in Chelsea with dimmed lighting and elaborate drapes. There were candles on the tables and beautiful bunches of freshly, cut, sweet smelling flowers scattered here and there.

I had decided against leaving my camera in the car. Once it became clear that this was not a business meeting at all but the very stuff of Claudia Ferriby's worst nightmare, I chose to keep the camera bag with me at all times. I had no idea where they would be headed after the meal and it would be better to be on foot. I could not risk losing them and having to go through it all again. Shakedowns were certainly not my specialty and at times, I wondered what the hell I was doing. If it hadn't been for the impression the young, nervous Claudia had left on me, or the alluring, encapsulating beauty of the mystery date, I would probably not have gone through with it.

I already had a few shots of the pair together from outside the creperie. The two walking arm in arm, him holding her hand affectionately as she studied the menu. The one little peck on the cheek, which was far from damning but would certainly provide grounds for many an interrogation from a suspicious future wife. If indeed Claudia was to be his wife.

That thought nagged at me throughout the main course. The little digging I had done so far made this far from clear. Ava had not mentioned the matter, yet the bartender I spoke to earlier was adamant. I was starting to think she was nothing more than a jealous girlfriend caught up with the wrong boy.

Watching them together I still got the feeling that George was trying a hell of a lot harder than she was. He was a handsome guy, very smartly dressed who you would have expected to have a beautiful girl on his arm, but he had an edge. He didn't always look comfortable. She, on the other hand, was very much at ease. At times she looked like she was enjoying a rather difficult game that she played confidently and comfortably.

She sometimes appeared to laugh a little too heartily when he wasn't expecting her to and any moment of affection was quickly moved on without upsetting or deterring him.

She was incredible. I found it hard to look at her and not lose myself. At times I forced myself to look away, worried that I was staring too intently and would give the game away. I thanked my luck that the lighting was poor otherwise I might have been rumbled.

The meal lasted for a couple of hours and although I could not hear what they were saying, I was sure it was nothing to do with running the Liberty Island ferry. Nobody joined them, and there were no messages brought to them from late absentees. In fact, the only attention they received was from me, and from the young punk that had been my shadow for most of the day. I had tested him a few times on our foot patrols, simple moves that anyone other than an amateur would pass. He kept with me without problem or obvious irritation. But despite my attempts to get eye contact he never came too close, he simply looked away or turned around and walked in the opposite direction, only to be on my tail again five minutes later.

Earlier in the day, I had lost him briefly and switched the stakes. As soon as he realized I had dumped him he entered a drug store and went right through to a telephone booth at the rear. I watched him make a quick call and hid amongst the toiletries as he exited.

I picked up the receiver and called the operator. "Excuse me Miss I think I have just been cut off."

"I'm extremely sorry, sir. I shall try to reconnect you." There was a pause. "Is the number you require BR 4-3543?"

I smiled. "That is correct," and put my finger on the cradle. Dropping a quarter in the slot, I dialed another number.

"Timmy, it's Errol. I need a favour ... yeah I know but you're a lot better man than I am ... I need an address to go with a telephone number ... No no it's nothing big, nothing big at all ... Good you're a pal Timmy."

26

I read out the number and a minute later Sergeant Timothy Matthews of the NYPD homicide squad gave me an address. I thanked him and hung up the telephone.

From the creperie, I followed George and his sweetheart into the heart of Chelsea, where they caught a cab into Chinatown. Claudia's hearing was proving to be good and five minutes later we were all alighting outside the Dragon Bar, one of Chinatown's most infamous bars. As well as being the location for post meal drinks it was also the local haunt of a certain Dyke Spanner. Tonight I would kill two birds with one stone.

Chinatown was easily the most insular of Manhattan's little microcosms. With over 150 restaurants and hundreds of garment factories, it had a thriving economy of its own. The obvious prosperity of the neighborhood highlighted by the crowded streets, booming diners and beautiful street markets with wonderful displays of shiny squids, trussed up crabs and piles of exotic fruit, vegetables and spices give off an illusion of safety. While it is true that crime was officially very low, there is a more sinister reason than it being a booming area. Extortion and protection were commonplace, as was filthy sweatshops packed with workers often doing seventy or eighty hours a week without any union protection. Everything was controlled by the ruthless Tongs, the Chinese Mafia, which kept the entire goings on in Chinatown in-house.

Chinatown had been Dyke Spanner's home for the last fifteen years. For some damn reason he liked it, and he drank everyday in the same joint. I was curious as to what he wanted to tell me. He was usually a stickler for keeping his business separate from mine. Not one to risk losing a buck, or maybe an arm or a leg, by involving my good self, so if Dyke wanted me, something sure was important. There was an outside chance that it would not be friendly, so I kept my gun warm and my eyes peeled.

Across the street was "Ping's Antique Shop". It was the family business of Weeny Jung Ping, an old friend and accomplice. On entering the Dragon Bar, I was surprised at just how it had changed. It must have been over a year since I had

27

last been in; at that time there was serious consideration as to whether the Dragon should be closed down. There had been a spate of gangland shootings in and around the Bar and it was getting a reputation as a no-go area. The local community was anxious to keep it open and liaised with the authorities to do so which was very rare in Chinatown.

The talks had obviously worked. What used to be a run-down watering hole for unsociables and low-lifes with exclusively Chinese clientele was now a thriving bar with bright, clean decor, new furniture and a wide variety of customers from all over the City. I ordered a beer and took a table in the corner with a good view of the whole bar. George Ferriby and his date were sat on barstools up to the bar and were talking together. The young punk followed me in and took a seat a couple of stools down from them. There was no sign of Dyke.

The evening progressed and the drinks flowed freely. Nobody joined my two subjects and nobody joined the kid. We all simply went about our business each keeping a close eye on the other. It was only when the kid went through the back corridor to the restrooms that I decided to follow him in. Maybe I was bored maybe I was feeling reckless, whatever the reason I followed him through and promptly lost him.

The men's room too was freshly refurbished, but as I wandered through expecting to see the young face on the kid turn to worry or surprise it was me who was surprised. There was nobody there. I took a piss and washed my hands, resigned to more hours of watching the young lovers I was being paid to watch. I was mentally writing a report when my thoughts were brutally interrupted.

The gunshots rang out loud but were soon drowned by the loud music coming from the bar. I finished washing my hands and exited the washroom. To my left was a fire exit that led out to an alleyway that ran down the side of the Dragon Bar. It sounded as if the shooting had come from that direction.

I pulled my weapon from my holster, slung the camera bag over my shoulder and pushed the fire exit door. Hazy, frying fumes blew out of a vent on the side of the building as I walked down the alley. There was an eerie silence penetrating the musky

28

air. The music was now a dull beat and there were no cars or noise at all. I lit up a cigarette and inhaled deeply. As I snapped back the shaft of the lighter, I heard a groan from the end of the alley.

I held my gun close to my chest and peered into the blackness. Dyke Spanner scrambled out with his hand on his chest and blood all over his shirt. I could hear a car speed off in the distance. He smiled at me and collapsed at my feet. I rolled him over and checked his wounds. They were bad.

"Still thinking big Eezy," he mumbled and let out a croaky chuckle.

"Who shot you Dyke?" I asked. "Give me a name."

He simply smiled and looked down at his bleeding chest.

I kneeled down and looked at his dying eyes. "You're going to be alright, Dyke. The ambulance will be on its way. Tell me, what's it all about?"

"Have you been talking, you son of a bitch?" he spat and blood dribbled from his mouth and down his chin.

"About what, Dyke?" I asked, now hearing the sirens in the background. I looked down the alley; there was a small crowd gathering but nobody edged towards us.

"She'll make you smile for a while but then she'll make you cry," he said, but his voice was now distant and fading fast. I asked him again what he meant but he just smiled. Finally he said. "The fuckin' Jew. The fuckin' Jew. Who cares eh?"

Then he died.

I stood up and stepped aside. The crowds of people were closer and the sirens were getting louder. The police would soon arrive and I would talk to them when they did. I went back into the Dragon Bar; music was still blaring out but the punters all looked different. They had all heard the shots. They would know the score. The table where George and the mystery lady had sat was empty. I checked the restrooms but they too were empty. They were gone.

So was the punk.

I sat in the bar thinking. I was sad. Of course I was sad. It wasn't everyday that you saw one of your friends croak right

29

under your nose. Although, let's face it the business we're in, it wasn't all that rare either. Dyke had been a friend, a good friend at times, but he was always chasing the big bucks. Me, I was little more content with whatever came my way, which wasn't too much nowadays, but was always enough to survive on.

I stayed in the bar out of the way for a good few minutes. I hoped that Tim Matthews, a friend of mine in the force, would be here soon. This was his patch so there was a good chance that he would be. I could talk to him. If anything was going down, he'd be sure to let on.

As soon as the police cordons were up I re-approached the scene. A uniformed policeman chewing gum under an enameled sign that read Dragon Street held out an arm. "What do want here, you can't come through."

I gave him a world-weary smile and held out my badge, "I'm Errol Black. Where's Sergeant Timmy Matthews?"

The uniform cockily looked me up and down and then lowered his arm. "Over there," he uttered and I headed back towards the throng. I could see Tim ahead of me supervising the forensics. He saw me coming and met me half way.

"Hello Errol." Tim was a barrel-bellied, small man with a thick-set face and unshaven, ragged look. "When did you arrive? Just before us?" he nodded at the blood on my shirt.

"Yep, I was right here when he staggered out. He died on my toes without even recognizing me. I thought it wouldn't take you boys long, so I'd better hang around and find out the form. What the hell happened Tim?"

"He's got two great big holes in his chest. He didn't have a chance. No witnesses, no clues. Maybe you could tell us something?"

"I didn't even hear the shot. I was simply on my way down to the Dragon for a beer and there he was."

"Dead?"

"Hell, I told you…"

"He was trying to contact you, Eezy. He has been for a while now, he even came to me to try and track you down."

"What did you tell him?"

30

"I told him jack but let's not get into this now the guy's dead. And another thing, when the hell do you just pop down to the Dragon Bar for a beer? There are twenty bars closer to home for Christ's sake. And all better than this godforsaken place. What's going down? Was Dyke in some sort of trouble? Come on, you can tell me. Off the record if that's what you want."

"I'm sorry, Timmy. I don't know anything. I only wish I did. If I find out anything you know I'll be in touch."

"Yeah, when it suits you. What you carrying the camera for, Eezy?"

"I don't have to answer that."

Tim looked me in the eyes doubtfully, let out a deep sigh and smiled. "What case you on, Eezy, you wanna tell me that?"

"Nope," I replied sternly.

"The telephone call this afternoon, what was that about? I did you a favour, Errol the least you can do is give me a little back. Come on, Dyke was a friend to both of us."

"I needed the address for a case I'm on. The case has got absolutely nothing to do with you and nothing to do with Dyke Spanner so you might as well drop it Timmy. You know the rules I don't have to tell you anything about it. In fact I'm not allowed to even if I wanted to."

"Sure you don't but if you don't start soon you will. Come on just help me out a little."

"If you wanna question me, Timmy, you can take me right down to the station and go right ahead."

"You stupid bastard! Are you on any case or are you now too busy fuckin' dead men's wives," he said, but apologized immediately.

I sighed and said that I'd be in touch.

Tim scowled, opening his mouth and then shutting it without a murmur coming out. He cleared his throat noisily, "It's a tough old break. Dyke sure had his number of faults, but he was a good man, at heart. Too good for some punk to fill him full of lead, that's for sure."

"I guess you're right," I replied, not really listening to him. It was clear there was nothing to learn from the police, "I better go and break the news to Mrs. Spanner."

I patted Tim on the shoulder, turned around and was on my way. I could just about hear Tim shouting out for me to watch my way. I would have to do that.

Chapter Four – Marlow

Friend or no friend, when a detective gets killed it's bad for business. The killer thinks he can get away with it and it's bad for detectives everywhere. I stopped over at a public call box. It's either you or me angel. I tossed a dime. Unlucky, you win.

"Precious," I said down the phone to Ava, "bad news, Dyke's been shot...yes, he's dead...I know darling, I know... No I don't know who killed him...I'm afraid you're going to have to break it to Maggie...No I can't, I'm busy chasing bad guys. You've got to do it babe...That's it, good girl, I'll call you. You're a sweetheart, bye."

I replaced the receiver and hailed a cab. On the way there I thought seriously about the developments. I was angry with myself for letting Timmy get to me. Hell, the guy was only doing his job and to be fair to him he had been closer to Dyke than I had for a good number of years. I knew he had a right to be questioning me, what with blood on my shirt but it still got my back up. I guess the fact that all I had got from Dyke was a jumbled rambling of a dead man annoyed me even more. I was now resigned to never finding out just what it was he had wanted me for.

I took the quickest route down St James Place and over the Brooklyn Bridge, but still failed to arrive till gone midnight. The street, the apartment block was on, was deserted. There was nobody around and the place was silent. I paid the cabbie and figured out a plan.

Brooklyn Heights Gardens was an exclusive block of apartments. Unique in this area in its cleanliness, safety and luxury. There were only twelve flats on a hectare of land. Most were on short-term lease or even week-to-week rental. Movie stars, big shots or anyone important that was unfortunate enough to land in Brooklyn stayed there. It was extremely rare that any of my cases would lead me to an area such as Brooklyn Heights Gardens. It seemed times had changed. I would enjoy finding out why...

I managed to bluff my way past the doorman, covering my bloodied shirt with a bunch of flowers from the gardens, and took the elevator up to the tenth floor. Upon reaching the door to the apartment my mind was racing. I ditched the flowers, took out my weapon and knocked on the door. There was no answer. I knocked again and put an ear to the heavy, wooden door. Nothing. Not a peep.

I looked around me and tucked my gun away before knocking on the other two apartment doors on this floor. There were no answers at either of those. Mentally I tossed a coin and smiled at its outcome.

I attempted to pick the lock. No joy. I figured I'd have to force it. There was no one around; the silence was ringing loud in my ears. The door was heavy and thickly polished. It had a little pane of glass -I put my eye to it and peered in. There was a lamplight on the wall and I could see a black leather sofa. I went back ten paces and gave the door the shoulder. It was a stupid thing to do -the door didn't move an inch. All I achieved was a sore shoulder and to make me even madder than I already was. Again I looked around and then kicked in the pane of glass. Using my hat for a glove I knocked through the shards of glass. I was now able to reach in and unbolt the door from the inside. The door easily pushed open.

This was what I called an apartment! It was a large, open-plan, loft style flat with beautiful polished wooden floors throughout. There was an oriental rug in the hallway and several others scattered around the place. The walls were painted a deep crimson and decorated with various pieces of abstract art. There was a famous Kandinsky and a Monet in matching, gold frames. The kitchen was on your immediate left as you entered the apartment and there were two doors at the far end. The rest was living space, with a comfortable looking sofa in the center and a dining area to the right. There was a balcony, which looked out over Manhattan. At this time of night the views would be fantastic.

I must have lost myself a little in the sheer elegance and beauty of the place. For the next thing I knew there was a gun pushing against the back of my head...

"What the hell do you think you are doing?" came the voice of a woman. "Turn around! Slowly," she instructed.

I raised my arms and slowly turned around. I smiled hiding my surprise the best I could.

She was even more beautiful up close. She was still wearing that slinky, red evening gown. She looked a little scared which made her even more beautiful. Her shoulder-length, flaming red hair framed her pale, delicate high-cheek boned face. Her eyes were green and fiery, her lips full and very red, her nose small and perfectly shaped, her cheeks soft. And her trigger finger was ready.

"You don't want to do anything hasty sweetheart," I said and lowered my hands.

"Is that right?" she answered, whilst lowering the gun and forcefully pushing me back onto a sofa.

"Put the gun away. I don't like women holding guns, you never know when they're going to pull the trigger."

"Who are you?" she asked. "You don't look like a burglar? And why have you been following me?"

"The name is Errol Black and I haven't been following you. I-"

She laughed, "You're the Private Investigator? You are the famous Errol Christopher Black. Christ, I had heard you were good."

"So had I. Maybe we both heard wrong."

"So Claudia took my advice. I am pleased about that. However, I don't think my sister is paying you so well to break into my apartment."

Now I was stunned.

I shook my head. "I don't know why the hell your sister is paying me," I said to mask my surprise. "But I sure as hell plan to find out. Come on put the gun away, I'll pay for any damage." I reached for my Private Investigator's license and showed it to the lady.

She took it and smiled. The whole room lit up. She then put the gun on the table and went over to a drinks table by the window.

"Why don't you sit down, Mr. Black..."

"I already am," I said. "And you can call me Errol."

35

"Errol, would you care for a drink? I should introduce myself. My name is Marlow. I can quite confidently say that I am Claudia's best friend in the whole world."

"Pleased to meet you Marlow, I'll take a brandy on the rocks, if I may."

She poured a large one and one for herself and brought them over. I took the drink and kissed the hand that she offered me.

"Are you real sisters?" I asked.

Marlow smiled and took out a cigarette. "Not blood sisters no, although we may as well be we couldn't possibly be closer."

I lit the cigarette for her and lit one for myself. She inhaled deeply and blew out a thick stream of smoke through her vivid red lips. "You must understand this, Errol. Whatever you have seen tonight is not what it seems. I am not in any way involved with George Ferriby."

"I see?"

"Not in any romantic sense, no. George Ferriby is a bad man." She said his name through gritted teeth. "He is a womanizer and a scoundrel. He is involved in so many scams I am surprised he can remember who he had told what. In short he is no good for my dear Claudia."

I took a drink. "I suppose you have told her this."

"So many times, but it makes no difference. Lovely, sweet and beautiful though she is, Claudia is an absolute disaster when men are concerned. She can't see what is in front of her."

"So that's why you put her up to hiring me?"

Marlow finished her cigarette and immediately lit another. She looked me right in the eyes as she smoked it quickly, shivering as she exhaled.

"I didn't expect you to take photographs or do such a thorough surveillance job. I just... I guess I just wanted you to tell her the truth about that scoundrel. Claudia is such a lovely person."

I finished my drink and crunched the ice in the bottom of the glass.

Marlow finished hers and then re-filled them both. She sat next to me on the sofa and sighed. She was close enough for me to feel her warm breath on my cheek. Close enough for me to smell her perfume and musky scent. Close enough to give me a raging hard-on.

"So where do we go from here?" she said and put a hand on my neck, ruffling my hair. "You still haven't told me how you got here. I never let George come here." She looked at me with a puzzled face that I just wanted to kiss. "How did you find my flat, Errol? And just why did you break in? Surely that's not part of the job?"

I tried to compose myself. "My being here has got nothing to do with Claudia."

She looked even more confused and glanced briefly at the gun on the table, but continued to play with my hair, running her long fingers through it and then down my neck.

"It isn't?"

"Tonight has been a bad night," I said, taking her hand in my own and kissing it softly. "A man has been killed. A man, who was a friend of mine. On top of that there has been a real unsavory character tailing me most of the day. I managed to turn the tables on him and he made a telephone call. You want to know where?"

She nodded her head gently but her eyes looked worried.

"Here."

"Oh Errol," she said in a frightened, high-pitched voice and stretched out both her arms to snuggle up to me. I put my drink down and held her. She was trembling when she said, "I may be in great danger. Who is this beast, did he follow you here?"

I gave a short description of the young punk that had followed me and softly stroked her hair. She let me go for a moment and I stood up and walked to the window, pulling the drapes aside and looking down.

"I don't think so. He disappeared tonight about the same time that you and Ferriby vanished."

I watched her nervous face and rejoined her on the sofa. She still looked frightened, but quickly regained her composure,

37

again playing with my hair, stroking my neck, and brushing her body lightly against mine.

"Why would he telephone here?" I asked, but she didn't have an answer. Not a verbal one anyway. Instead of speaking she stood up facing me and reached for the straps of her gown. She pulled it down painfully slowly over her breasts; until they could be held no more and burst free. Her nipples were pink and erect, as big as golf balls, but softer to touch. They invited me to do exactly that.

She slowly wiggled out of her gown, letting it drop first to her knees and then to the wooden floor and before I could move her panties had also gone.

She now stood before me, her milky body, with large, firm breasts facing skyward and long, straight legs with a red, well-pruned pubic patch proudly on display. She took a step forward and straddled me, her breasts an inch from my mouth, begging to be kissed. I gratefully accepted the invitation as her hands did their work, skillfully undressing me until we were both naked and aching with desire.

I lay back and opened my eyes wide, feeling her fingertips, as light as butterflies, brush quickly across my chest, down over my abdomen and then lower. She moved them in circles slowly then quickly, softly then harder until she found what we both wanted her to find and she gripped me tight as she lowered herself down.

I awoke in a huge, king-size bed. It was draped in purple silk sheets, with heart-shaped pillows and a black lace trim. The dame was cuddling up to a rather cute, black cat on the Oriental rug in front of the warming, open fire.

She smiled beautifully at me across the room.

"Sleeping beauty awakes," she said and then let out a throaty laugh. "You must have needed that."

She was right; I had slept better than I could remember. Last night had released all the tension of the day. By the time we moved into the bedroom all we could do was sleep and it was lovely, blissful, deep sleep.

The dame let go of the cat and sat on the edge of the bed.

She was wearing a small silky dressing gown, showing off her impressive curves in all their glory. She reached over and gave me a kiss gently on the lips. The cat instantly stood up and strutted out of the room, sensing that maybe he would soon be a crowd. He stopped at the door, looked at me with his big, sad eyes and then left.

"How about some breakfast, Errol? I cook a mean bacon and eggs," she said, smiling.

"That would be swell, darling," I replied. "Maybe I could take a shower whilst you get it together."

She nodded and left the room. While I was washing myself, I thought back to the situation I was really in. It would have been cute to think that this broad was simply knocked over by my natural charm, but I had my doubts. She quickly turned on the charm when the questions I asked got a little bit difficult. I guessed she was playing for time and for the moment I would allow it. If I could find out about the punk another way and still get to sleep with the beautiful Marlow it was fine by me.

She came back minutes later with two plates of food and we ate breakfast in silence. When we had finished she sat with her back to mine and started to brush her long hair.

"What will you tell Claudia, Errol?" she said without looking around.

"I'll tell her the truth," I said, and waited for her to turn and look at me with those big, puppy eyes. "That her fiancé is a no good son of a bitch. That he is cheating on her now and will continue to do so, regardless of whether he knows she knows it or not. I will offer her my services to give him a good beating if that's what she wants, although I doubt that it is. And when that is all over I will send her my bill and walk back out of her life."

I smiled at Marlow as sweetly as I could. "Unless you invite me back in it."

She smiled warmly at me and walked back to the bed, sitting right by my side. I reached out a hand and she kissed it all over before guiding it between the joins of her dressing gown and to the swell of her breasts. I took a nipple between my fingers and felt it harden. Minutes later we were both naked again and sharing each other intimately.

When we had finished Marlow snuggled up to me, nestling her head in the crook of my arm.

"You know if you are in any kind of trouble I'd be only too willing to help," I said. "You could talk to me about it."

"You're so sweet Errol, you really are," she replied.

"But you don't need my help?"

"No." She paused. "Not yet anyway, but thanks for the offer."

"Just remember it's always there. Now, how about lunch today?"

"I'm sorry, I can't."

She ran her fingers down my chest, softly over my belly and down to my softening penis. "I could make dinner though, why don't I give you a call."

"That would be great darling," and I gave her both my office and home numbers.

I lay back and relaxed as my erection wore off. I thought a little about Dyke, but mostly about Claudia. She wasn't going to like what I was to tell her but I could not do anything about that. It was for the best, I was sure of that much.

I entered my own office block to find Ava busily typing away. She would usually not even look up and acknowledge my arrival, but on this occasion she immediately stopped what she was doing and looked me right in the eyes.

"Anything I need to know, precious?" I asked, pre-emptively.

"Errol, what's going on? That bitch was so hard, as if she didn't even care. No tears, no surprise, nothing-"

"Different people take different things, different ways. You know that, angel. I appreciate you breaking the news, now is there anything I should know, anyone been in here?"

Ava slammed her hands down on the desk and let out a shrill shriek.

40

"You always do this, Errol. You always cut yourself off. Something's going on. Have you ever considered the fact that someone may be able to help you? Maybe you can't do it all on your own?"

I ignored Ava's outburst and proceeded through the outer office and into my inner-sanctum. It wasn't unusual that she would go off like this, and we both got quite used to it. This time, however, she followed me right through, prompting me to look up as I poured myself a Remy Martin.

"Are you and Maggie having an affair?" she asked me right out. Very unlike Ava, no messing about, nothing. A simple, straight question. Of course, she was not to get a simple, straight answer.

"Can you get in touch with the florist, send a nice bouquet to the Spanner household? There probably won't be much of a funeral, but at least we can send our respects."

I sipped at my champagne cognac and put my feet up on the desk.

"Errol, how could you do it? I know what you're like... for God's sake I ought to." she paused a moment, her beautiful face a mace of anguish. "He was your friend, did that mean nothing to you?"

I sighed deeply and finished off the cognac, instantly pouring another. "I don't need this right now. Come on sweetheart, not now. I've just got here, I haven't had much sleep and there's a lot of things I gotta do. Let's drop it, eh?"

At that, Ava left the room and went back to her typing. She returned a few minutes later. Now wearing a more conciliatory, calm look on her face, she held out her hands. I looked up to her and shone out a wide smile.

"Okay, I'm sorry," she offered and sat right on the end of my desk, "Maybe I went a little over the top. I know, it's none of my business, but I do still care, Errol, you know I do."

"Come here precious," I urged and gave a good, friendly hug. "You're the best, you know that. I need you, but I need your support more than anything."

She smiled a little embarrassed and stood back a few paces. "Tim paid you a visit, yesterday afternoon. He brought

41

that new Lieutenant with him. They didn't say much, just that you should keep in touch. I don't know, I got the impression they wanted to suggest something but thought better of it when they arrived. Maybe they wanted to say it face to face."

"Huh, that'd make a change. You told them I was out on business, and didn't have any idea when I'd return?"

"Sure I did."

"Good girl, what time is it?"

Ava looked at her timepiece and sighed, "Five to-"

Before Ava finished her sentence the telephone rang. I waved as Ava left the room, and then picked up the handset.

"Yes."

"Yes. What kinda way it that to answer the telephone. You won't get any business answering yes."

It was Jake Wiseman, my brief. One of the most important people a private detective can possibly know. He's got me out of more scrapes than I cared to remember.

"Jake, I take it you've heard the news?"

"Yeah, I've heard the news alright. I thought I better warn you, that new Lieutenant's been sniffing around. He wants a result on this one. Says he's no longer prepared to right the Dragon off as a no-go area."

"What business is that of mine?"

"Oh, don't worry Errol, he's not implying anything, nothing like that. I think he's more outstretching a hand of compromise, a gesture of goodwill between his boys and yours. He knows as well as I do that if anybody's gonna get to the bottom of this it's gonna be you. He just wants a little co-operation, you know?"

"You know what he can do with his co-operation, Jake? It only works one way and that's not acceptable. Anyway they get in the way, they mess things up. I hope you told him that."

"Sure I did Eezy, sure I did. If that were all it was I wouldn't have even bothered you. I just thought you better know this. If you continue to brush him off and get his back up, he's prepared to dig up some pretty smelly shit."

I sighed. "He's got nothing on me, I'm clean."

"For one, he knows you've been messing around with Maggie Spanner. There are a few unsavory rumors about that, but nothing I can't handle. More importantly, he also knows that your license is coming up for renewal soon. He didn't say anything directly but it appears that he's got some influence in that department, you know what I mean? Any rumors or allegations floating around, however ridiculous and unbelievable they are, they're not gonna be a help."

"Whatever you have to do Jake, sort it out! Get him off my back and keep me clean. I'll sort this mess out as quickly as I can, but I'll do it on my own, certainly without the help of Lieutenant fuckin Beech!"

"I'll do my end, Errol. Don't worry. Just try and keep a low profile, you know. No more walking into homicides, not this close to home not anywhere."

I said goodbye to Jake Wiseman and replaced the handset. I didn't need pressures like this and was feeling a little agitated. I'll show him where to shove his co-operation.

I calmed down a little and wrote out a report for the Claudia/Ferriby case. I took it through to Ava and asked her to drop it off discreetly at the house in the East Village. I would call by myself tonight to answer any questions and help out in any possible evictions, which may happen as a result.

The morning passed by quickly. I did a bit of work from the office, ringing round a few people. I considered the Ferriby case closed and now until something else came up I would spend my time looking into the murder of Detective Dyke Spanner. We argued frequently, sometimes violently. He was a cocky, know-it-all son of a bitch and I guess so was I. Still, we managed to keep in touch, go for a bourbon once in a while. He certainly had his good points; they were just well hidden that was all.

For months it had been quiet at Black & Wentz, not a sniff of business above the usual mundane telephone jobs that barely paid the rent. A couple of weeks ago I was paid a visit from my landlord's "friend". He was concerned that he was being taken for a fool, that I was assuming he was a soft touch. It was only a friendly visit, of course, just to let me know that if I didn't pay up he was going to start breaking a few bones. I sent him packing with a thick lip.

And all the time Dyke was flitting from one job to the next, without a care in the world. A couple of times I'd telephoned him, asked if he had too much on. You know, whether he wanted to pass some of the less exciting, mundane stuff down to me. That wasn't Dyke's way. The way he saw it, he was a public service, not so much in a line of business, but doing a job for the people. Everything given to him he would personally deal with. He would give it the time it deserved and quite happily put his life on the line for the smallest of rewards. He worked very closely with the Feds, flying all over the country, dodging bullets wherever he went.

I hoped his killer would soon be found. In spite of what the police appeared to think, I did not know who had shot him or why. Of course, there was the suspicious kid that had been following me, but that was a flimsy piece of supposition and not something I would bring up without a lot more investigating. I had a few ideas about how I would tackle that.

Marlow kept creeping back into my thoughts. She was a wonderful lay, my first in a while, but just when I thought back to us last night it was not only Marlow who was there but Claudia. I put the thought from my head and had a cigarette.

I decided this was no time to sit on my hands.

I considered the worth of checking out Dyke's office. He was very rarely in it, didn't keep a secretary or have a telephone, and never took notes. Whatever files Dyke Spanner required he kept firmly in his head. Best place for them Eezy, he used to tell me, that way the only person knows what I'm thinking is me. It was worth a try and I would do it tomorrow. Start at the bottom and build up.

I dug out all the contacts he had ever given me, which didn't add up to much, and gave them a call. There was no sign of anything suspicious. Most of them hadn't dealt with him in a long while. He had been on something big, that much seemed clear, and I wasn't going to solve it on the telephone.

Why couldn't he have got in touch with me earlier? It's not as if I've been busy lately. I'd only been out of town a week or so. I wondered about his funeral. The people round here didn't care much for honoring the dead, the most respectful gesture from the residents of our neighborhood would be a graceful throw into the Central Park lake.

Chapter Five – Hermeez Wentz

When it got to midday, it hit me that I hadn't been back home for over twenty-four hours. There was not a great deal of significance in this as there were very few people that knew where I lived - I had always felt it prudent to keep that information in as few hands as possible - but for some reason I felt an urge to make a quick visit back. Was there something there that would help me out? If nothing else I could get some lunch there and freshen up.

I headed back to my flat. I had a hunk of beef in the refrigerator, which would go down great with a beer. It was nearly lunchtime and I was starving. I mixed with the traffic and soon pulled in on the kerb outside my flat. My home was a simple, two bed roomed flat. I was on the ground floor overlooking the lovely garden of colorful flowers that stayed alive right through the Fall.

I opened the door and entered my 'living room' - I called it that because it was the only place where somebody hadn't tried to rub me out. The decor in my flat was simple; there was not much of it - a table to eat from, a sofa to relax on and stacks and stacks of bookshelves on every wall. Each one was brimming with books, many of which I hadn't yet got round to reading. It was how I liked it.

When I got inside the flat I noticed Hermeez Wentz. He was sitting on one of my sofas, with a steaming cup of coffee in one hand and a brimming sandwich in the other. He was a tall, muscular, handsome man with languid, sky blue eyes and dark, almost black, short cropped hair. His nose was small, well sculptured, sitting nicely in the middle of a charming, charismatic face. He was always clean-shaven and well attired, priding himself on an appearance of sophisticated bravura. He looked like a cross between a film star and a gangster and spoke in a charming, soft voice, emphasizing words with his sparkling eyes. It was often said by the ladies that Hermeez gave off an irresistible sensuality, without even trying, that could melt the heart of any lady and dampen the knickers of most. I wouldn't know about that. To me he was simply Hermeez Wentz, my partner and my best friend in the entire world.

Hermeez Wentz had been my longest friend; we had not only grown up together, forming that enigmatic bond that boyhood pals create and adults cannot even hope to understand, but carried it on further into manhood. I had consumed my first beer alongside him, made love for the first time with him doing the same in the next room, a paper-thin wall away, and I had even killed my first human being shoulder to shoulder with him.

"Eezy, you really shouldn't go leaving your windows open. Do you fancy a coffee?" he said and stood up, putting his coffee and food down.

I smiled and we embraced.

"I'd love a coffee," I said. "And I didn't leave the windows open. Is that how you got in?"

Hermeez nodded and passed me a cup. "Yeah but I wasn't the first. Nothing seems to be damaged, or taken. Maybe you should have a look around."

I did exactly that and he was right. There was nothing stolen and apart from the latch on the bathroom window that had been snapped in half, there was no damage. I brushed it off for the moment and we sat down to talk.

"How was the funeral Eezy?" asked Hermeez.

I sighed. "It was difficult for Maggie. She put on a brave face and it helped to have somebody with her but it was still hard."

He nodded. "You still haven't told anybody?"

I shook my head, "Nope. Why the hell should I? They can all think what the hell they want to ... and do. I guess it will be worse now that Dyke's dead."

I studied my friend's face, which reacted exactly like I expected it would, turning from good humour, to shock to exasperation to eventually worry.

"You hadn't heard," I said. "He was killed last night. I was the one that found him."

I told Hermeez how I had stumbled across the dying Dyke Spanner last night. I didn't expect him to be upset; he thought a lot less of Dyke than I did and he wasn't my bosom

47

buddy. He showed the respect that he would show for the death of any acquaintance, he said a little prayer, raised a toast to Dyke Spanner and for the next minute we sat in silence. When he was ready he asked me a little more. I told him what I knew, which was very little and I filled him in on the case that had led me to the Dragon Bar on that fateful night.

"Is there a connection?" he asked.

I shook my head. "I don't think so. If there is, it is not yet evident." I shrugged. "I'll find out in good time."

Hermeez looked surprised. "What do you mean, you'll find out?"

"You know exactly what I mean. You may not have thought much of Dyke..."

"Neither did you Eezy. He was a son of a bitch, and you know it."

I smiled at my buddy. "Either way I'm going to look into it. The police already think I may be involved. And I'm sure they're gonna want to talk to you at some point."

Hermeez narrowed his baby, blue eyes and rubbed his big hands through his hair. He looked agitated and restless. He finished his coffee and put the cup down on the table before sighing deeply and then flashing that killer smile at me. His eyes were smiling too. "Of course you're gonna look into it. Forget I said anything."

Ever since the end of The Shadow Man Detective Agency, Dyke and Hermeez had barely been on speaking terms. Terry Shadow had managed to keep us all happy. We always had money, we always had plenty of work, no matter how dirty it was, and we always had the ladies. Terry was like a father figure and he provided the glue that kept us all together.

When the Agency split right after Terry's death, Dyke decided to go his own separate way. I don't think it was the split that set Dyke and Hermeez at loggerheads, they had not seen eye to eye for a long time, but it was only then that their rivalry took on a more nasty turn. What had started as competitiveness progressing quickly into a simple dislike of each other grew into a hatred between both men.

When Dyke started taking jobs off the Agency it grated. Accounts and contacts that we had nurtured for a long time were wiped out. Hermeez resented the way that Dyke took any job he could get; he had absolutely no scruples for whom he worked, whether it was Outfit, the Feds or simply fleecing an old lady of her savings. As long as it paid, and paid well, Dyke would do it. Hermeez was more honorable and although we took the higher ground we suffered financially for it.

Taking the spoils was not enough for Dyke. He wasn't simply happy that he was driving around in a Murphy Dusenberg, while me and Hermeez were in battered old Fords, that he was wearing exclusive suits, not off the rack rags, or that he was moving office every other month, each time to something bigger and better. No, Dyke could never just enjoy his good fortune he always rubbed it in. Most of the time Hermeez would just take it, after all they had fought before and Dyke always ended up with the bloodier nose, but when it involved the ladies Hermeez would not let it go.

It all came to a head five years ago.

Hermeez Wentz had always had the reputation as a ladies man. He played the life of an eternal bachelor well, romancing several different ladies at any one period of his life. Never did he lie to any of them or promise them anything that he wasn't prepared to uphold. But never did he have the intention of settling down with any of them and making them the first Mrs. Wentz. This was the accepted situation and all parties were aware of the facts. Most would accept it and enjoy playing the game others would reluctantly refuse secretly hoping they could change this most delicious of lotharios. None of them could.

Until Marcia Grey entered the scene.

Marcia was a most beautiful, young girl with long, sandy blonde locks and a sweet, apple-pie face. Her eyes were always alive with such excitement and a passion for life that was rare amongst 1930s New York youngsters. She had a gentle trail of freckles on her soft, smooth cheeks and little dimples at the corner of her mouth, which accentuated when she smiled, and she smiled a lot. Although she was only eighteen and nothing more than a girl she had the body of a lady with large, full, breasts, a pert, rounded bottom and legs that were as long and straight as route 66. She enjoyed showing off her egg timer figure and was doing just that when Hermeez first encountered her.

It was late one Saturday evening, the snow was piling up outside and the temperature was minus 20 when Hermeez and myself entered the Long Legs Club off Broadway for a late drink. We were both tired and cold from a long stakeout that had proven fruitless and were in need of some liquid warmers and a bit of light entertainment. The Long Legs was owned by a friend of ours and provided late night jazz as well as beautiful dancers. The girls were not strippers and never did more than dance, but they were classed as erotic entertainment and had a strong following amongst the late night drinkers.

I bought the drinks, a couple of bourbons, and joined Hermeez at a table in the corner. He finished his drink in one go and accepted another without blinking. His attention was well and truly grabbed by the beautiful girl in a black, two-piece outfit that was larger than a bikini but smaller than a flapper-skirt and body top. She danced gracefully and professionally, never holding eye contact with any of the punters for more than a second or two. Except Hermeez, who she smiled at throughout the routine. We sat and watched the show for the next twenty minutes without speaking. Our glasses kept being refilled but not a word was spoken.

After the routine had finished Hermeez declared that he was going to take the dancer out for a meal. This would contravene the rules of the Long Legs but Hermeez was adamant that he must meet the girl and that he wanted to persuade her to give up the dancing and get a proper job. For the next two weeks we found ourselves frequenting the Long Legs late into the night and enjoying the performance of the young, blonde girl. The more Hermeez raved over her, the more uncomfortable I felt watching, but she was awesome and there were many gentlemen who had to wait a few minutes after she had left until they would stand and go to the bar.

On the seventeenth night, Hermeez got to speak to the girl and found out her name was Marcia. I don't know what they talked about but they immediately struck up a rapport and sure enough she agreed to go out on a date with my irascible partner. Three weeks later, she had given her notice at the Club and moved in with my friend. And five weeks after that they were engaged to be married.

When I spoke to Marcia she always impressed me as a girl who was very clever, yet humble, she knew she was incredibly beautiful yet played that down and she really convinced me that she was truly in love with Hermeez. She always talked about her desire to make it big to be famous as an actress or a singer, although she never really made any strides in either profession, much preferring to join Hermeez on exotic holidays and be looked after, which was her absolute right as his girl. It didn't worry him that she was much, much younger than he was although he once confided in me that her fierce ambition left him uneasy.

This was all forgotten when they were married; a grand occasion with over a hundred guests and myself as best man. They honeymooned in the Bahamas and for the next couple of years were the picture of happiness. It was only when Marcia got her first acting job that it all started to go wrong. She was so excited when she burst into my apartment, where Hermeez and I were having a meeting. She was booked on the next flight to Los Angeles and would start work immediately on a film; it looked like at last she was going to be the star that she had always told us she would be.

Their marriage undoubtedly suffered, with Marcia spending a lot of her time at the other end of the country, and Hermeez often busy when she returned. I can't be one hundred percent sure that he never strayed whilst she was away, although he swears to me that he didn't. She, on the other hand, strayed many times, often sleeping with a casting director at lunchtime and the male lead at dinnertime. She regaled us with her sordid exploits in great detail after an almighty row, when Hermeez had accused her of treating him like a dog and insisted that she would have to give up on her acting to save their marriage. I think his pride was badly bruised because it was the first time that he had truly given himself to a relationship and realized he had never

51

really been in control. He went crazy that night, slinging accusations and giving ultimatums as if she was his ten-year-old daughter, not his beautiful wife. It was then that she hit him with the bombshell and he walked out. At first, I thought that she was drunk and that she had made it all up to hurt him or stun him into shutting up. However, she then made a play for me and I too walked out.

The divorce proceedings began straight away and from the beginning, it was dirty. Hermeez hired an investigator to check out Marcia's activities in LA and she did the same, claiming that it was his unreasonable behavior and his incessant adultery that had led to the breakdown. And so it went on. Although he was hurting he soon slipped back into his old self and it seemed like the whole thing would soon be forgotten and my old buddy would be back. Until the court hearing.

Both parties gave their version of events and it appeared that a satisfactory truth would be hard to find. When Hermeez's detective gave his findings, it looked pretty damning for Marcia and then she unveiled her own secret weapon. Her detective was no other than one of Hermeez's longest associates and one time friend, Dyke Spanner. His testimony was cruel, untrue and final. He knew Hermeez inside out and what he didn't know he made up, convincing the judge that the man was a real low life and deserved to be hanged not simply taken to the financial cleaners. Marcia won a massive pay out and Hermeez and Dyke were forever going to be enemies. To make matters worse, as the courtroom was cleared Dyke sneered at Hermeez and said he only did it for the money, but that he should have done it for free.

"What do you mean," I asked. "You betrayed a friend."

"I didn't really need the money," he laughed. "But boy can she give a mean blowjob."

We both spent the night in the cells. Hermeez swore he would never do business with Spanner again and that he would not be happy until the man was dead.

And now he was dead.
"Ava told me Marcia's back in town."

Hermeez sighed and gave a wry smile. "Yeah, she's back and she wants more money. Money, that at the moment, I don't have. A couple of days and she'll be gone again. Then I will be back with you full time."

"Don't worry about it, take your time."

"You're a buddy, Errol. A couple of days, that's all I need. Did Ava tell you the police are going to question me?"

"No, but I think it's likely, don't you?"

He nodded. "Sure. Maybe you looking into it isn't a bad idea after all."

I agreed and put on another pot of coffee.

Chapter Six – Claudia

The East Village is a better-kept secret than its famous cousin, Greenwich Village. It was early in the twentieth century that it started to attract the very people that first made Greenwich such a fun place to be. The artists, the politicos and the literati all flocked East when the rents started spiraling and the tourists descended on their homes in Greenwich.

I always enjoyed a stroll through this part of Manhattan, feeling a sense of belonging amongst the radical bookshops, offbeat clothes stores and dingy, watering holes. Why the hell, I, of all people, would belong here I don't know, but it felt like home from home. The cafes were always full of would-be writers, the streets awash with musicians and artists and the place so full of life. People would stop you simply to talk, stand at street corners and tell each other stories or just watch the world go by.

It was now after nine thirty in the evening and I was doing just that; watching the world go by. I was sitting in a cafe across the street from Cooper Union, a seven-story building erected in 1859 by a wealthy industrialist. The enormous brownstone building was where Abraham Lincoln started his charge to the White House with his "might makes right" speech in 1860. I thought it was ugly, but then so was old Abraham and he didn't do too badly.

On the way to the East Village I had stopped by at Dyke Spanner's old office in the Bronx. It was a run-down, decrepit building on the edge of the district. Ironic really, the guy lived in Chinatown yet kept an office an hour away.

Nothing.

Not even a chest of drawers.

The door was unlocked so I had a look around. It was a small office with a solid wooden desk and a chair. On the desk was a mug with D.Spanner emblazoned in bright red lettering. The walls were bare and the floor uncarpeted. The only other item in the room without a window was a waste-paper basket. It contained a screwed-up piece of paper. Normal white, drawing paper, without a mark on it. I quickly did a crayon test on it, but nothing showed up.

Typical Dyke Spanner, everything in the head.

I had waited for Marlow for our dinner date but she didn't show. I hung around for over an hour but there was no message, so I ate alone and drank a bottle of red wine alone. By the time I got around to telephoning Ava I was feeling maudlin. She checked the apartment for me and phoned me back. It was empty.

I finished my coffee, feeling a lot fresher and more sober than I was an hour ago, and headed East along St Mark's Place. When I hit Tompkins Square Park I turned south and walked a block before again going east and finding myself right in the heart of the residential Village. Row upon row of old, three or four storey buildings, some of them terraced housing, some converted into fancy apartments, and others stand alone single properties. No two buildings were alike.

I found myself going over the last words Dyke had uttered, inventing meanings for them and then discarding them as absurd. Who did he mean, who would make me smile but then make me cry? Was he talking about Maggie? Hell he knew damn well that she was not going to stay with him after the way he had treated her. Why would he spend his last moments of life telling me such a thing? It just didn't add up. I decided it couldn't be her, it just didn't fit. Maybe the whole diatribe was just the jumbled rambling of a dead man. It sure might as well have been for the good it had done me.

When I approached the house, there was a commotion ringing out. The rest of the street was silent, the flea market providing the only sound, a distant hum in the background. But as I walked up the front path, there was a loud argument in process, the angry sound of a man and the crying, pleading almost of a young girl. Not any young girl, it was Claudia.

I knocked on the door and the shouting temporarily abated. Footsteps padded along the hallway and the door opened slightly. I found myself face to face with a pretty pissed off George Ferriby, his eyes no longer placid and full of romance, were now filled with hate and rage.

I smiled and pushed a foot in the small gap between door and frame. "Good evening," I said, before pushing my head slightly inside the door. "Claudia, are you okay sweetheart," I asked loud enough to carry into the house.

Ferriby caught me unawares, swinging his head forward abruptly. It was a poor attempt at a butt catching me on the forehead instead of rearranging my nose. But it did put me off balance long enough for him to slam the door and once again resume what he had been doing before I arrived. I could faintly hear him shouting accusations at Claudia, calling her a slut and a tramp and her squeals in return.

I didn't knock on the door again. Instead, I kicked it so hard that it was left swinging limply on its hinges before charging through the hallway into the melee. The house was larger than it looked from the outside; the hallway was long with a polished floor and two rooms leading off it to the right, the kitchen was at the end of the house and to the left of the front door was an open stairway. It was there that the noise was coming from.

Ferriby appeared on the first floor landing as I made it to the top of the stairs. He wore a face of incredulity which was soon altered to pain and blood as I swung a couple of right hooks into his nose and cheek. He fell against the wall, holding his bleeding face with his hands. He then became the recipient of a proper head butt, which landed exactly where it was intended and caused him to stumble forward onto his knees. I grabbed him under both armpits and dragged him away from the stairs, throwing him harshly to the floor.

It was then that Claudia came running out of one of the rooms.

"Oh, Mr. Black," she whimpered. "Thank god you are here."

She had tears streaming down her cheeks and was wearing only a small, white nightie, which just covered her panties. It was frilly at the top and hung down off her shoulders and straight from the breasts down. She stepped over her slumped boyfriend and slung both her arms around me, clinging on tightly. I held her firm, stroking her hair and patting her back, unsure where to put my hands but wanting to put them

56

everywhere. I didn't get chance however, as Ferriby was now back on his feet swinging wildly, this time with a knife in his hand. I gently pushed Claudia aside and dodged the blade the best I could in the narrow corridor.

Ferriby lunged forward, I feigned to the left and swung my fist hard, catching him on the chin. He surprised me by lashing out again wildly with the blade and catching me across my front. Pain shot through my midriff and blood seeped out of the cut. I knocked him to the ground with one blow before stumbling myself. This time he stayed down. I hauled him down the steps, careful so not to bang his head and dumped him outside on the sidewalk, closing the door on the way back in.

Claudia ushered me back up the stairs and into a bedroom. The room was big with a large double bed in the center. The walls were painted magnolia and there were fresh flowers in vases all around. Everything was frilly and lacy, very girly and there were cuddly toys and pictures of animals in frames. The furniture was pine and the carpet pink and soft.

I lay out on the bed and Claudia sat across me her skimpy nightie barely concealing her modesty. She ripped open my jacket and began nursing my wound. It was only a small cut, but it was reasonably deep. She expertly managed to stop the bleeding and put a dressing on from her first aid box.

"You poor thing," she said in her beautiful, soft, voice. "Are you all right?"

"Yeah, I'm sure I'll live," I answered, before letting out a laugh. "Just thought I'd come and check you got the report okay. I guess you did."

She managed a smile and wiped her eyes. She looked even more beautiful than the other night. Frightened and vulnerable, but incredibly sexy. With only a thin layer of lace between us and her warm body resting on mine I felt aroused. I shouldn't have I know, my stomach was hurting and I was in lust with another woman but I still got the hard on of a lifetime. I don't know if Claudia felt it or if she just flew back to reality but she flushed red, stood up and covered herself with a gown.

"Look at me I have hardly got any clothes on. What must you think of me," she said, as if she didn't already know.

57

"Would you please excuse me for a moment and I will make myself look more decent."

I didn't think that that was possible but I did anyway.

"Make yourself comfortable in the living room," she said as I reluctantly left the bedroom. "Help yourself to a drink I won't be a minute."

When I got to the bottom of the stairs, I quietly went outside and checked on the place where I had dumped Ferriby. He had gone and there was no sign of him around. I shrugged my shoulders and re-entered the house, going into the first room off the hallway which appeared to be the living room. There was a couple of large, leather sofas dominating the room with an expensive looking oriental rug in front of the them, between them and the open fire, which was blazing away warmly. The floor was wood throughout and the walls were plain, with several pictures hanging in elaborate frames. There was a sideboard with a wireless and a record player on one side and a decanter and glasses on the other. Behind the sofas there was a large window, covered by thick, heavy drapes that came right down to the floor.

I selected a record, a jazz number by Charlie Parker, set it on the player and made myself a drink. There was a small picture on the sideboard of an old man. I picked it up and studied the grainy, black and white image.

"Would you mind pouring me one also?"

It was Claudia. She was now wearing a plain housedress and an oversize sweater. The clothes were large and unflattering but she still managed to look beautiful in them. "I think I could do with one."

I poured her a healthy measure and we both sat down on the big sofa, facing each other with our legs in a yoga position. She had composed herself rather well and applied a fresh coat of makeup, but she was still shaking as she cupped the glass of gin and tonic, sipping it as if it would give her safety and protection.

"I'm sorry that had to happen Claudia," I started, "I didn't intend to cause you any more hurt and heartache than was absolutely necessary, but I always do a proper job. The facts are that George Ferriby is no more than a womanizer and a cheat.

He has been using you for a good while now and would have continued to do so indefinitely." I sighed. "I'm sorry."

Claudia smiled weakly, "I know. I think I have known that for a long time but I just didn't want to admit to it. Tonight I had finally decided to confront him. I wanted to talk, to discuss things, to reason with him but he never gave me the chance."

I pulled a packet of Luckies from my jacket and put one in my mouth. "Do you mind?" I asked, holding my Zippo.

Claudia shook her head. "No. May I also have one?"

I lit one, handed it to her, and then lit another for me. "How do you mean 'he never gave you the chance'?"

She sucked on the cigarette, coughed a little and then exhaled. "Tonight he came home drunk, stinking of perfume and with lipstick all over his face. He made no attempt to hide what he had been up to and then tried to force himself on me. I fought him off the best I could and threw the report in his face. It felt good telling him that I knew exactly what he had been up to and that I had evidence of it, but it just made things worse."

I finished my drink and sighed. "Did he hurt you, physically I mean?"

"No. No he didn't, thanks to you."

She stood up and kissed me softly on the forehead. "Would you like another drink Mr. Black? I'm sure I would."

I nodded. "Yes, that would be nice, but only if you call me Errol. I'm not your employee anymore, the job is finished."

She poured the drinks and sat down. "Yes, the job may be finished but he will be back. That thought fills me with dread." She flushed slightly and put her hand in mine. "I'm sorry I am being rude. How much do I owe you…Errol?"

"The bill's covered. You probably paid me too much already."

"Well if I did, I'm glad. You're worth every cent."

That almost made me blush. I mean almost, what she said next actually did.

"If I paid you some more would you consider staying the night? I'm a little bit scared he may come back. After tonight I'll be alright, but would you consider it?"

All of a sudden, I came over all professional. The truth was that I would have loved to stay overnight but I don't think she was offering what I was wanting and I had to think of Marlow. I steered the conversation flawlessly. "Is there nobody else you could stay with? A friend, perhaps? I would be happy to see you get there safely."

Claudia sat back and sighed. "Normally I would stay with my friend Marlow. She is the most wonderful person in the whole world, Errol, she is beautiful and kind and intelligent. You'd love her, I'm sure."

"But…"

"But she's gone away for a couple of days. I had lunch with her today and she said goodbye. When she comes back we'll have to all meet up."

I smiled. "Yeah we will, that would be swell," I said, but my mind was wandering. If she had gone away this lunchtime, it meant one of two things; either she had no intention of meeting me for dinner and if so what the hell was the other night about, or something had come up, which made me wonder about the kid. When I had mentioned him at her apartment she had put a brave face on it but it was obvious to me she was frightened. Did she know him after all? I wished I had taken Joe's advice and intercepted him earlier when I had had the chance. Now it may be too late.

At least it appeared she had not mentioned my little piece of housebreaking to her friend. Although she wouldn't would she, as it was her that had been the date.

"Is she not dating?" I asked as nonchalantly as I could.

Claudia shook her head. "Not any more. She had been seeing somebody but they split a week or so ago. He was a detective too but he was married and so it was never going to work. She'd love you though, Errol, I'm sure."

The music finished and Claudia got up and put another on. "Another?" she asked holding up her glass.

"Do you mind if I change from gin?" I asked.

"Don't tell me," she began as she headed over to the bar in the corner of the room. "Cognac, straight, no ice?"

I chuckled and nodded as she went ahead and poured the drink.

"My father used to drink cognac. He always said it was a real gentleman's drink. Cognac for the boys and vodka martini for the girls. And bourbon for the wild men."

"He's a wise man."

"How's the stomach?" she asked, handing over the cut glass and joining me on the sofa.

"Oh, a little uncomfortable, but it's holding up. You bandaged me up real good, sweetheart."

For a moment, Claudia wondered off somewhere, staring blankly into space. "He used to call me sweeteart..." she muttered, before coming back to reality. "So Errol, what do you say? Will you stay over and make sure I'm okay. Tomorrow I will be fine I promise."

We stayed up and talked well into the night. Claudia lost more and more of her shyness with each drink. She didn't ever talk in specifics but she liked to remember her childhood and background. She sometimes talked passionately and sometimes sadly but always with great intrigue. In spite of us talking for hours I hardly gleaned any real information on her. She had cut herself off from her family when her father died and now wanted nothing to do with them. She had many fond memories and kept throwing in anecdotes about various names, Mario or Mikey, or Stanley but never gave too much information. She was fascinated by my life and I probably opened up a lot more than I had intended, telling her about the roller coaster life of detective work. As the evening wore into night and the night into morning we got on really well. We listened to many more records, we danced, drank and had a thoroughly good time together.

When the daylight came I gave her lift to the Central Manhattan Library where she had being doing a bit of casual work and headed back to my own apartment, a lot happier than I expected to be and a hell of a lot more frustrated than I wanted to be.

Chapter Seven – Tongs

Depending on whom you believe, the triads originated in mainland China anytime between the first century A.D and the seventeenth century. Their main aim was to overthrow the Manchu Ch'ing dynasty and to restore the Chinese Ming dynasty. These resistance movements were born in the monasteries and used the triangle as their symbol, which represented the blending of Heaven, Earth and Man. Each of these elements are represented by a number which is derived from early Taoist numerology.

There are many myths and legends of battles won and battles lost in the early life of the triad resistance, of fighting monks, betrayals, bloodbaths and audacious victories. Much of these are unsubstantiated or impossible to ever prove. What is clear is that these secret societies that started as semi-religious political organizations, or even forms of trade unions, soon evolved into highly advanced criminal organizations. Underground political resistance soon became usurped by the lure of riches gained through prostitution, money lending, drug dealing and extortion.

In the mid to late nineteenth century, over 100,000 Chinese people migrated from their homeland to the United States, mainly to the west coast where they were used as hard labourers building the great America railroads. As a people the Chinese could hardly have been worse treated by authorities and it is this persecution that contributed to the closed societies that expanded across the nation.

Just like the triads sprung up from adversity in the Orient, the Chinese Americans soon formed their own version, the Tongs. The Tongs were on the surface nothing more than social societies, but underneath a new criminal underworld was forming which would not directly challenge the Mafia as they kept almost exclusively to themselves but would nevertheless ravage the Chinese community for years to come.

I had heard the stories many times from my good friend Weeny Jung Ping. He had an encyclopedic memory of the history of the Chinese people and never tired of telling the tales of old. I was now sitting outside his shop on the corner of Canal and Lafayette streets waiting for him to return from his daily meditation at the Buddhist Temple.

I had intended to pay Weeny a visit from the moment I found the dying Dyke Spanner, and was even keener to do so after I found the note. It had been waiting for me on the doormat to my apartment, folding neatly between the business section of the New York Post. Giving nothing away but saying a great deal it simply said, "Great Antique Sale. Come and see for yourself. Something for everyone."

Weeny Jung Ping had migrated to America as a young boy, settling in New York's Chinatown in the early 1900s. Through no real choice of their own his family were plunged right into the Tong wars that were raging at the time between the Hip Sing Tong, led by the humouressly named Mock Duck and the On Leongs, the existing power led by the so-called Mayor of Chinatown, Tommy Lee. These wars would rage on throughout the early part of the century and lead to the death of many innocent and not so innocent Chinese people.

Weeny was only five at the time and was seventh son of a family of thirteen. By the time he reached his teens the first Tong War was over, thanks to the intermediacy of the Reverend Charles Henry Pankhurst, but almost all of Weeny's family had perished. All that were left were himself, his ageing mother and two of his younger sisters. They would live in relative peace, running their laundry business in Chinatown for the next few years. By 1924 the launderette had gone into the ground and Weeny left home to open up his own antique shop. This was to prove an extremely lucrative and rewarding business over the years and provided Weeny with a good base to pursue other goals.

I first met Weeny Jung Ping through my mentor and former boss Terry Shadow. We had been doing a surveillance job for the better part of a month on behalf of one of the smaller New York gangs. It was the usual stuff, one faction were worried they were being taken for a ride by another and wanted certain members of the posse followed and their movements logged. It was none of our business what this information would eventually

63

lead to and we tried not to think about it, in a way justifying it to ourselves through ignorance.

This time, however, my ignorance was tested to the limit. Some how I had got isolated from the rest of the surveillance detail and found myself alone with a very dangerous mobster as my quarry. I had been following him for miles in and around lower Manhattan and were now deep in the rabbit warrens of Chinatown. I was young and inexperienced and I had not realized that for the last couple of hours the mobster was well aware that he was being followed and wanted to know why. He cast out the line and reeled me in, cornering me in one of the many narrow alleyways.

The cobbled alley was deserted as I edged further into murky darkness. I had not seen my subject for the last few minutes and was wondering to myself if he had escaped my notice, maybe through one of the fire exits that led out to the mist filled alley. I checked on a few of the doorways as I slowly moved down the path but they all seemed solidly closed and I could feel the tension rising. Before I had chance to think about what to do next I found a gun pushing into the back of neck and I turned around to see the mobster smiling a nasty, gap toothed grin.

The next few minutes seemed like some of the longest of my short life; the mobster asked question after question each of which I gave the same answer, "Fuck you!" to which he replied with either a kick to the shins or a slap around the face. Eventually he got so pissed that he kicked me to the ground and cocked his weapon. I was down on my knees looking up right down the long barrel of his Magnum .45 awaiting death with a mixture of fear and resignation when out of the mist came a small, wiry figure that let out a shrill high pitched scream and flew through the air. The gangster was knocked to the ground and the gun disappeared into the blackness. I then felt myself being lifted onto my feet and pulled through a door that had opened from nowhere and to safety.

My saviour had been Weeny Jung Ping who had claimed to have heard the commotion and decided he didn't want a murder outside his business. I never did ask him the real story

64

and he never offered me one but over the next few years we kept in touch and became quite close friends. I became a better detective and Weeny became a little more open about his own secretive world in which he did jobs for a variety of different people, from the feds to the many networks of intelligence agencies around the world.

A small, huddled figure walked past my car and disappeared into the shop. Before I could switch off the engine and get out of the car the figure had reappeared and was sitting in the passenger seat next to me.

"Keep the engine running Eezy, we're going for a little drive."

It was Weeny Jung Ping. He was a small man, maybe only five feet two and can't have weighed more than 130 pounds, with a taut, yellow face and jet black hair that was greased back. His features were very small apart from his lips which were long, thin and colourless, his ears almost too small and his nose thin and smooth. He had grey eyes with long, lazy lashes that made him always look tired but kept the secret of a sharp intelligent mind.

He rested the gun on his lap and smiled warmly as I fired the engine and pulled out onto the main thoroughfare. We were heading north along the Bowery, past Confucius Plaza and up through Little Italy. The street was busy with morning traffic and the sidewalks full of workers and street sellers. Weeny remained silent, lighting a cigarette and putting it between my lips, and then lighting another for himself.

"You're gonna need that," he said as we continued our journey, but didn't add to it as I looked quizzically across at him.

The gun was still ominously placed on his lap. He made no attempt to hide it or to keep it close to his grasp, choosing to just leave it their menacingly. He surely noticed me looking across at it as I didn't try to hide my curiosity but decided against asking him direct. I would find out soon enough. If I knew anything about Weeny Jung Ping it was that he would only tell you what was on his mind when he was ready.

We took a right turn onto east Houston Street and kept going right until we hit FDR drive which was the main street on the east side of Manhattan. The East River Park was to our right and then the murky waters of the East River and beyond that Long Island. Dilapidated warehouses and run down housing estates littered the wasteland that was the northern part of East River Park. Wang directed me into the spider web of narrow lanes that took us into this area.

Normally when I rendezvoused with Weeny Jung Ping I would be 80 percent certain of coming away alive. The 20 percent doubt was not through any fear or suspicion of my friend but the company that he sometimes kept, although even throughout our acquaintance he did always have an edge. To some this edge would be intimidating, frightening even, to others it would be baloney and they would right it off with a shrug of the shoulders and hearty chuckle, sometimes at their peril. I did neither, I was simply aware of its presence.

For some reason, as we meandered further away from the busy part of town where we had met, and into the deserted stretch of the East River Park's worst excesses, I only put my chances at fifty-fifty.

Weeny tapped my shoulder as we reached a battered old building that had long since stopped being any use to anyone. It was three storeys tall and made of uninspiring grey breeze blocks, with boarded up windows and cracked gutterings that were drip drip dripping dank, smelly water. I killed the engine but Weeny shook his head as I started to get out of the car.

He took the gun in his right hand and leant over to me. "Sorry about the cloak and dagger, Eezy, but I gotta take precautions."

I nodded and raised my arms as he padded me down, pulling out my own weapon and emptying the clip before putting it back in my holster.

He lit another pair of cigarettes and took a deep breath. The sun was shining warmly through the windscreen and the temperature was rising…

"Did you read the papers whilst you were away?" he asked.

I shrugged and waited for him to reach into his inside pocket and pull out a piece of newspaper cutting that was folded in half and in half again. He slowly unfolded the cutting and handed it over. It was from the Times, a piece from page eight with the headline, "CHINESE BARTENDER SLAYED AT HOME" I looked at the picture and recognized the dead man, it was the former bartender of the Dragon Bar, Woo Wang.

I thought of Woo Wang. He had been the bartender at the Dragon Bar for as long as I could remember. He was a big, broad-shouldered ex-boxer, with a square jaw and cauliflower ears. Never one to shy away from a confrontation. Many times I had seen him reach for his gun, which was always handy behind the bar. In the old days he used his bulk and strength to dispel any disputes. He was a truly frightening beast of a man, and there were plenty hoodlums who had found themselves tossed from the Dragon Bar. Very few took it any further. If they did they would get a good beating the next time. Woo Wang would give you one chance, first he would be gentle, then he would take offence.

It was after he ejected a crazy one night that he had to up the security. A little guy that wore renaissance hats was a real pain in the ass. He pestered all the ladies and challenged anyone who warned him off. Eventually Wang had to intervene, but the crazy wouldn't go quietly. Standing his ground and opting to trade blows with the ex-fighter like a true maniac. He was of course no match for the monster bartender, but just as he was about to be thrown out he pulled a rod.

At first everybody laughed. It was quite a usual occurrence for some no good punk to pull a rod when he was getting a beating, but then they would leave quietly. Not on this occasion -Woo Wang took one step forward and got a hole in both feet. As he fell to his knees the crazy gave him a big kick in the face and made a quick getaway.

Ever since that nasty confrontation, Wang chose to use the threat of a weapon. It would never be loaded and he would always stay behind the bar. The simple threat would usually be enough.

The newspaper article suggested that it was a disgruntled punter that had committed the murder. I doubted it. There were several people, men and women that had been thrown out by

Woo Wang, but none of them were to blame. I was sure of it. So was Weeny Jung Ping.

"First Woo, and then our mutual acquaintance Dyke Spanner."

"Are you telling me there's a link?" I asked.

Weeny said nothing, simply fluttered his long lashes and smiled.

"I don't know just how well you knew Woo Wang, Errol, but he was a very good friend to me. More than a friend, in fact. He was my eyes and ears at the Dragon Bar. As you know, I have not taken alcohol for ten years now and I have not entered the Dragon Bar for more than three, but the truth remains that it is an extremely useful place to have a contact. Much good information can be gleaned innocently or otherwise from within its grubby interior."

He was right; the Dragon had long been a meeting place of many undesirables making it vital to anyone in the information business. He continued...

"It was Woo that first alerted me to the dealings of Dyke Spanner."

There was an engine in the background. It sounded like a battered old car, growling and spluttering and it was appeared to be getting closer to where we were parked up. Weeny's ears pricked up and he gripped the gun a little tighter.

I watched him, smiling. "Dyke Spanner's dealings?"

"Before he was killed there was no doubt in my mind that Dyke was up to something big. I don't know how big or what exactly it involved but it was a jump into a league in which he did not belong."

I shrugged. "What? Are you talking about something criminal? Are we looking at blackmail, extortion, robbery, what?"

The engine stopped and a car door opened nearby. Weeny took a good look around and raised the gun slowly before resting the barrel on my forehead. He pressed it down hard, cutting into the skin and looked around again, a deadly serious look upon his face.

"I apologize again for the inconvenience, Errol but this may answer a few questions for me. I shall keep talking and you try not to be too nervous okay. I hope very much that I won't have to pull this trigger and if I do so I promise you it will only be in response to a most unlikely betrayal by your good self. Do you follow?"

I nodded. "Carry on! What dealings?"

"Like I said, I don't really know. He was getting involved with a big man very adept at those three examples you have given. A shady character, known as The Coward or rather colloquially, The Portly Gangster. My information suggested that Dyke had something that they wanted, maybe it was illegal maybe it wasn't, whatever the truth he was in no rush to sell."

"Who is this portly gangster? Is he one of the really big boys?"

"Again I am not sure. I thought that maybe you would be able to tell me this information."

"Me?"

"Your name was spoken many times, by both Dyke and the cutout. Woo never saw the portly gangster but he kept a close eye on the meets right from the first time they made contact. Apparently Dyke refused to do business unless you were alongside him, this he insisted upon even though he and the cutout were lovers."

"The cutout was a woman?"

"A very beautiful woman. Although I have long since learned not to trust another man's judgment on the fairer sex."

Weeny relaxed the gun on my forehead a little and smiled reassuringly. There was no sound around us, everything was deadly silent. Weeny sighed and lowered the gun. "Errol, I have to ask. Did you kill Woo Wang?"

"No, I did not," I answered immediately. "Why would you think I did?"

"One night after a shift at the Dragon Bar he was warned off. Presumably by one of the portly gangster's henchmen that had noticed him taking too keen an interest. A real dandy who wouldn't have been out of place in the back street bars of Bangkok, but still a tasty piece of work. He wore bright clothes and had the most terribly greasy black hair. I too have been constantly followed since Woo shared his information with me."

"Weeny, I swear that this has got nothing to do with me. Whatever it is, I sure as hell want to find out, but at the moment I know less than you. That's the truth."

Weeny smiled and threw the gun on the dashboard.

"I am glad that that is the case, Eezy. I always thought that it would be but I am still very pleased." He shrugged and gave me a hug. "Of course I believe you."

I gave a sigh of relief. Weeny had tested me the best way that he knew how. If I had been working against him for this portly gangster then I would have been sure to have a shadow. By putting the gun to my head he was testing my validity as a lone wolf. No guardian angel would have been able to stand by and let him threaten me like that, however cool.

This meeting was not turning out the way I had expected. Even if I hadn't been summoned to a meet, Weeny Jung Ping would have been exactly the next person that I would have wanted to see. Now my curiosity was even more aroused. It was now a good bet that if I could find the portly gangster I would find the killer of Dyke Spanner. And if my name had been as involved as Weeny said that it was, there was a good chance that they would be trying to find me.

"It appears that the next move has been forced upon us, Errol. There can be no question, you have to meet him."

"Maybe you're right, maybe not. If I agree, how do you propose to arrange a meeting with a man that we have no idea where to start looking for?"

"How else but through the cutout? You surely know where to find her."

I looked at my friend and shrugged, "I do?"

He smiled a killer smile. "Sure you do, I watched you come out of her apartment yesterday."

The real estate agency was a small, understated office deep in the back roads of the financial district. There was a large potted plant in the far left corner of the room and little else to take notice of. One large desk was manned by a young, heavily made up brunette, with fake tan and bright red lipstick. She had a desk full of files and a brimming multi-tray system and the walls were covered with pictures of various establishments either for sale or for let. Apart from the springy carpet and the constant ringing of a telephone from somewhere out of sight in the back room there was nothing else of interest.

The assistant smiled and stood as I entered and offered a small, warm hand to shake. I took it in my own and kissed it before sitting down and waiting for her blushing face to regain its composure.

"Good afternoon sir, how may I help you?" she asked in a businesslike tone.

"The house in the East Village, the old, three storey one that's in today's Post, I would like to take it up on an immediate six month lease. I am in rather a hurry, so would like to sign the contract right away. I have a bankers cheque with me now."

The girl smiled as if I had just told her I wanted her to perform advanced brain surgery and started flicking furiously through some files.

"Please excuse me, sir. I will be just a moment," she said, and disappeared through to the back room.

I could hear her talking softly, presumably on the telephone as there was no other sound, apart from her tapping something irritably. I stood up, flicked the sign on the door around so that the closed sign was showing to the outside, and took a quick look at the files she had been perusing. In the third file, I found a picture of the house I was asking after, the house that was still being advertised in the papers as for let. There was a note attached to the photograph of the house, it said...

THIS HOUSE IS NOT FOR GENERAL LEASE. IT HAS BEEN PAID FOR UNTIL MARCH 19. ANY ENQUIRIES SHOULD BE DISCREETLY PUT OFF.

And there was a telephone number at the bottom of the note. I put the file back and waited for the girl to return.

When she returned, five whole minutes later, she was wearing an even more confused look on her orange face and shrugged as if that would answer all my questions. Another two minutes later she added, "I am so sorry, sir. The house in question has already been let. I would be happy to arrange

71

another viewing; would you like to look through some of our brochures?"

"When was the house taken? It is still advertised in today's Post." I tapped the paper for effect.

She cleared her throat nervously. "I am sorry, sir. I am not at liberty to say."

"Okay, thank you very much," I said, smiled graciously and kissed her shaking hand again, before turning around and walking out of the door.

Ava sounded cheerful until I filled her in on the previous night's events. I assured her that I was okay, but asked her to keep a watchful eye on Claudia even though the case was officially closed. She seemed quite happy to do so, telling me again what a wonderful girl she was. I gave her the sketchy details that I had on The Coward and The Portly Gangster and asked her to do some digging. If anyone could prize out some information on him, then Ava could. Before I hung up the telephone, I asked if she had had any luck on the kid.

"If you had asked me that only one hour ago I would have said no," she said in that tone of voice that she took when she was feeling extremely pleased with herself. "I checked out all the usual channels; police records, the various contacts that we have and what seemed like hundreds of bars and clubs. I even specifically tried the gay bars, I don't really know why it was just a hunch."

"Good a reason as any," I said, chuckling to myself at Ava's use of the word.

"But none of them came up with anything."

"Until," I said, playing the game.

"Until an hour ago when a gentleman came wandering into the office. I'm afraid I was busy doing a little tidying up and had left the sketch on my desk in the outer office. When I went back through there was a man, he was holding the sketch and nodding his head. When he saw me he commended me on my drawing skills and said that he hadn't seen that man in years. I said, "You know him?" and he said, "Sure I do. That ma'am is one cold bastard. I didn't know he was back in New York though. Last I saw of him he was lifting shirts in the Far East." I didn't understand that but I laughed anyway, the man seemed to think it was funny and I wanted to get as much out of him as possible."

"Ava, I am sorry to interrupt your story but who was this man, what was he doing wandering into the office?"

"I'm coming to that, Errol. He said his name was Arnold Muchado and he was looking for Hermeez. He said he was an old friend and was just calling in on the off chance. He was ever so nice and he invited me out for lunch, but the best bit is I got the kid's name, it is Audrey Daniels and he's wanted for questioning for a string of crimes. I'm still digging up on him it should be a lot easier now that we have a name."

I agreed with Ava, but I was thinking more about the name Arnold Muchado than that of Daniels. Muchado was notorious in certain circles in New York and he did not simply wander into people's offices on the off chance of anything. He was reputed to be a close associate of "The Mad Hatter" aka Albert Anastasia, the founder and operating head of the national crime syndicate's enforcement arm Murder Inc. He was a loan shark by trade and no doubt paid a great share of his gains into the syndicate's coffers, but was not averse to adding murder and maiming to his list of skills. What could he want with my partner? He surely didn't just want to take him out for a drink; the only places people like Muchado took you for a drink was out in the desert just before they hit you round the back of the head with a baseball bat.

I warned Ava to be careful and not to go to lunch with him, but she took my caution as paternal concern and told me she was a sensible grown up girl. At least she promised me she didn't find him attractive and was merely flattered, although she hadn't decided whether she would go or not. In the meantime she would carry on digging on our friend Daniels and she accepted my decision to send a little extra security round the office block. Finally, I asked her to get in touch with Timmy Matthews and find out as much about the Dyke Spanner investigation as she could. She agreed and reluctantly told me she would do this instead of meeting Muchado for lunch. I put the

73

telephone down thankfully but with a lot more worry than I had picked it up.

It wasn't long before I was heading back to my apartment. I stopped for a bite to eat on the way back. A little place around the corner served a mean porterhouse -bloody as hell with a green salad. It all went fast, swilled down with a nice cool beer. I lit a cigar and picked at the salad, blowing thick smoke rings in between crunching bites of cucumber.

As I polished off the remains of my dinner, I evaluated the previous few days' events. What began as a simple domestic case was looking like turning nasty. I wasn't sure just who was and who wasn't involved and to make matters worse I wasn't sure what it was they were involved in, even if they were involved. If what Weeny Jung Ping told me was correct then Marlow was certainly a hell of a lot more than Claudia's friend, which made the whole thing about Claudia and Ferriby curious. And where the hell was she? I didn't know whether to be worried or angry. I kept thinking maybe Daniels had got his hands on her and she was in some sort of trouble, although she really did seem like a lady that knew just how to take care of herself. The other person I just could not get out of my mind was Claudia. There was no reason to think that she was any more involved in any of this than by the coincidence of the company she kept, but she was a mysterious lady and the puzzle of her house being for let and yet not for let was strange to say the least. I was also worried about my partner and friend, Hermeez Wentz, he didn't look himself today and if Marcia Grey was back in town there was certain to be heartache and trouble for him and that was without the added confusion of an Arnold Muchado on the lookout. In spite of all this, it was becoming clear to me that I must concentrate on Dyke Spanner. Maybe that would be the answer to all of this and if that was the case, I must find the portly gangster as soon as possible and take Weeny Jung Ping's advice. I couldn't help but think I would soon be going the way of my former friend. I put the thought out of my mind and had another steak.

Chapter Eight – Messenger

He was waiting for me at the top of the stairs. Sitting on the landing floor, his face pasty, his hair greasy and black; combed back, cigarette precariously dangling from his thin lips. He was sitting in a pile of butts, an empty packet of Camels torn to shreds. He wore a tight black polo-neck and brown slacks with a spotty cravat around his pale neck. His shoes were brown sandals and he wore blue socks.

Oh, and he was Chinese.

I struggled to hold back a chuckle as I approached. His eyes flickered as he saw me and he straightened out.

"Don't get up if you're comfortable," I said, my hand itchy for the 9mm under my arm.

He got up slowly, eyeing me all the time as he unraveled his spindly body. Not giving to chance I pulled my rod and shoved it in his gut, making him wince and breathe all over me. I held my breath.

"The boss wants to see you," he blurted out.

"Then why doesn't he show his face instead of sending punks like you bothering me?"

The man chuckled to himself. "I'll tell him you said that. He doesn't like his boys being called punks."

He looked me up and down and sneered, "Especially by small time no good detectives."

"I need a name. I don't talk to any punk, and you can tell him that as well if you like. Give me a name and I'll think about it."

"Don't push it Mister, you won't use that and you know it," he nodded at the gun and stepped back, reaching for his own.

I smacked him twice with the revolver, along one side of his head and the back of his neck. He dropped like a sack of potatoes and sat amongst the garbage. His ear was bleeding, but he'd live. I took out his gun and emptied the clip before replacing it. I then pulled out my pen and scribbled a number on his forehead.

Later that evening the telephone rang. Ava had left for home long ago so I answered, "Black."

"Yes indeed, Mr. Black, I am truly honoured. Even if you do slap my boys around."

"If you'd seen how he attires himself you'd have helped me. Whom am I talking to?"

The phone let out a shrill, high-pitched laugh. "My name is unimportant, although I do appear to have gained recognition as the rather uncomplimentary label The Coward, as you have probably guessed. I think perhaps, Mr. Black, that we may have an issue of mutual interest that we should discuss. I propose that we arrange a rendezvous."

"Listen Coward, just say what you gotta say!"

"No more games, sir, please listen carefully. As I am sure you have surmised, I have the dame in my care. She is very frightened and cannot wait to see you again. She will come to no harm as long as there are no shenanigans to be played. If you do as I say I will be happy to release her into your care and we can get on with some business, if not..." he let the sentence hang.

I sighed, "No such thing as an honourable gangster heh? Who says the dame means anything to me? Why don't you just do with her what you gotta do?"

"You surprise me Mister Black, I took you as more of a caring, romantic type of chap. Shall I kill her, shall I?"

I sighed again. "Where's the meet, I'm a busy man," I said as matter-of-factly as I could.

"As I am myself, sir, as I am myself. The sooner we meet the sooner this will all be over."

That's what I feared.

"Do not forget, sir, if you want to, how shall I put it...recommence your little soiree, you'd better do just as I ask. We do not require any heroics, if I smell a rat my patience may run out. I am a reasonable man, I really am."

"Tell that to Dyke Spanner. Where?"

"A short drive, that is all. I'm sure you're a man with a full tank of gas, am I right?"

Who was this guy? I didn't know whether to laugh or cry. I looked dumbly at the telephone and made up my mind.

"If you take the New York State Thruway, keep driving north. For speed you can either choose to stay on Route 87 or if you prefer your outings to be through more picturesque countryside why not jump onto Route 9 which hugs the Hudson River. About fifty miles north of the City you will come to a junction with several possibilities, a little like your twenty first birthday, sir. You can either take a left turning for Kingston or keep going north until you hit Saugerties when you will need to go left. Whichever option you choose you are heading for a small town just within the Catskill Park called Woodstock. There is a bar in Woodstock where we are sure to be uninterrupted. It is called The Wyatt Earp, all the locals will know it if you get lost."

"The Wyatt Earp?"

"Be there. Twelve midnight, Saturday. Oh and Mr. Black, come alone. Remember I have a very good sense of smell, if my nostrils smell rodent my boys will want to play with their guns."

The line clicked dead.

Woodstock was a tiny town that I had only ever been to once. It was a farming area at the foot of the Catskills in the Borscht Belt, which for some reason had become popular amongst artists and writers. There were few hotels, fewer casinos but numerous sleazy bars. There was also a large amount of wasteland; hills, countryside and meadows. A number of wealthy farm owners resided in the area in their own luxurious compounds. The whole Hudson Valley district had a reputation for small time mob activity with several gangs that were too small for the City taking their habits upstate. Like Vegas, all that wasteland provided a good graveyard. It was not too long a drive from the City, but if the next chapter of the mystery was there then that would not matter.

A short drive indeed. Maybe I should forget the whole deal and take what I knew to the police. Timmy Matthews would chew my ass for playing hard ball with him but would soon thank me for the information I could give him. Unless he already had me down as Dyke's killer, which looking at it from his point of view would not be altogether a foolish conclusion. In spite of this, walking away would be the sensible thing to do.

I considered this for the time it took to locate an overnight bag. It would never really be an option. I'm afraid I'm a romantic. If I hear voices crying in the night I go see what the matter is. If I hear a cat meowing on my driveway, I go and get a saucer of milk. It's the nature of the business.

Chapter Nine – Central Park

The Plaza hotel lies at the most southeasterly corner of Central Park, in the Grand Army Plaza, a well preserved, cobbled courtyard at Fifth Avenue and 59th Street. It is a fine old hotel, reminiscent of a grand French Chateau and has rates to match. Not only is it the tops as far as luxury, service and reputation in the whole of New York, it is widely accepted that it is worth every cent. I wouldn't know, I had never been through the doors.

Until now.

I had called ahead and left a message, receiving a courteous reply from the hotel Concierge desk an hour later to say that I was expected around lunchtime. It was now twelve thirty and after admiring the plush lobby and even plusher receptionist for a few moments, I enjoyed ten seconds of high speed elevation and padded my way along the springy carpeted corridor on the top floor. This floor was home to the most executive suites in the establishment and was suitably decorated.

When I reached the Park Suite I knocked on the solid wood door and waited. The door opened and there she was, one arm leaning against its huge frame with a cheeky grin on her face a brimming glass of champagne in her right hand. Her fingers were painted red, her lips were pastel colour and shiny although not as shiny as her eyes, clear blue eyes that literally sparkled.

She didn't say anything, just stood there smiling with her drink dripping on the carpet and her aroma intoxicating me with sex. I shook my head gently and smiled inwardly before taking my hat in one hand and ushering her in with the other. She let out a little giggle, shrugged her shoulders and turned on her heels, taking her firm, round breasts and her soft, warm naked body with her.

Naked, yeah, that's right. I should have been surprised but I was too busy being aroused.

I watched her skip back into the hotel room, looked left to right and then followed her in, making sure the door clicked locked behind me.

"Are you making sure we won't be disturbed?" she asked in her girly, Southern twang. "Why you haven't even said hello yet."

"Hello Marcia," I said, finding myself in a huge suite, amazing in its sheer class and beauty. It really was lavish with ceilings you could fit a set of football posts under and a bed you could fit the whole offence eleven in. The walls were tastefully covered with expensively framed pieces and decorative wall hangings, the thick, springy carpet was the sort of floor covering you just wanted to take off your shoes and socks and let your feet sink into its softness and warmth.

There was more, much more but the fact that I was directly behind a beautiful, naked woman who showed no sign of covering up her perfectly sculptured form, from her large, rounded breasts to her bushy, dark brown triangle of hair between her long, straight legs, was distracting me just a little. For the time being this was fine with me, although she knew she had thrown me wildly off course and I was sure she was enjoying the fact

She giggled again and threw the drink down in one go before throwing herself on an upright chair by the fireside and holding the empty glass out in my direction. "Hello Mister Black, would you mind doing the honours?"

Would I mind indeed? I filled the glass from a bar in the corner of the room and poured myself a coke. It was only just gone midday after all and I needed a moment to gather my thoughts. I did just that and took the drinks over, taking a seat facing Marcia at the side of the black, marble fireplace.

"You look uptight," she said. "I suggest that you rearrange whatever is necessary to make yourself more comfortable. I'll tell you what, why don't you take something off?"

She winked at me but it came out as more of a squint. She wasn't drunk but she was getting there fast.

"Why don't you put some clothes on Marcia, you're not working now," I said, mentally punching myself for my ridiculous professionalism. I was doubtful how long it would last.

Marcia just smiled and opened her legs. She was sat back in the chair directly facing me, not a yard from me, with one arm raised above her head bent at the elbow with her little finger between her lips and her legs spread wide. I couldn't but help look and she knew it.

"You don't really mean that, Mister Black, you always did like looking."

I felt myself flushing and immediately looked away. "And you never tired of being looked at, did you Marcia? Only you couldn't stop at just flaunting yourself, you had to go further and further down the road until you became exactly what you are now."

"And what's that?" she asked, closing her legs and sitting up a little straighter.

"A cheap little tart."

I didn't mean it of course. Marcia had never been cheap. Even when her fledgling film career sunk deeper and deeper and she took to doing soft porn flicks to earn a buck she was still a classy lady. Champagne was always on ice, rich and famous company was never far away and she always looked a million dollars. Whether she had clothes on or not.

"Is that why you came here today, to insult me?" she said with an edge to her voice that was half way between hurt and condescension.

"Well it certainly wasn't to be seduced by you," I replied, keeping my legs tightly crossed and my fedora strategically on my lap.

"No, once was enough for you wasn't it Mister Black."

I sat down again and sighed. "Look I'm sorry I shouldn't have called you a cheap tart. And will you quit calling me Mister Black. It was always Errol, and it still is Errol."

That seemed to lighten the mood. Marcia grinned, not cockily or with even a trace of arrogance, just a natural, incredible smile that would melt the coldest of hearts. I was well and truly thawed already and by the time she widened those baby blue eyes of hers and raised her right hand to her forehead in a mock salute. I was practically cooking. I couldn't help but notice her

81

breasts jiggled as she moved, her nipples were not hard but placid and extremely inviting.

"So... Errol..." she said, "why did you invite yourself to my humble suite, pray tell?"

As she said it, she kicked her toes on the oriental carpet that was the size of a billiard table and certainly worth a great deal more.

I narrowed my eyes and tried looked stern, but from her reaction I most definitely failed. "I don't want you bothering Hermeez. Whatever happened between you two is in the past. You know it took him a while but he's eventually got over you and he doesn't need any trouble from the past."

She crossed her arms, pushing her breasts together and up, and shrugged her shoulders. "Why would I bother Hermeez? As far as I am concerned, Hermeez and I are finished. I simply gave him a call as a courtesy, as he always does when he passes through LA."

"He does?" I said in surprise.

"Sure he does. Sometimes we go for a drink; sometimes a meal and then we go our separate ways and often don't speak until the next time. This can be anything from a month up to a whole year."

I was surprised. As far as I knew, Hermeez had not been in contact with Marcia since the divorce. He had vowed he never wanted to see her again and knowing him the way I do I had believed him. He never even hinted to me that he had been seeing her. But Marcia had no reason to lie about it and I was convinced she was telling the truth.

"What does Arnold think about you meeting up with your ex-husband?" I countered and watched her reaction closely.

She looked puzzled. "Who is Arnold?"

"Arnold Muchado, who else? I hear you have made it to moll at last. Tell me is it just like in the movies?"

Marcia stood up and walked over to the bar, filled her glass and brought me a fresh one, this time with a little rum in the coke. I shrugged and took a sip. She sat back down, crossing her legs, still not a ounce of humility about her nakedness or my obvious erection and smiled again.

"You always were looking out for Hermeez. I wonder if he appreciates it as much as he should. You're a good friend to him Errol, you know that?"

Not as good as I should have been, I thought, as Marcia went on to tell me that she did really love my buddy, that she would always love him and deep down they both knew it, whilst all I could think about was what I would love to do to her again and again and again.

"I do know of an Arnold Muchado," she said eventually. "It's hard to be in the entertainment business and not hear of him. He controls many of the unions you know, some say through money some say through influence, yet we all know he cracks kneecaps and bangs heads together. But that's as far as it goes. I think I may have met him the once although not to talk to, I'm afraid there's lots of pretty girls in Hollywood, even I am nothing special."

She sighed as if the fact really upset her. I'm sure she was being modest, it surely wasn't true.

"If you think that I am some kind of gangster's moll you are wildly mistaken, Errol. If Muchado is involved with Hermeez, which I guess he is by your presence here, even in my rather inebriated state," she nodded at her fast emptying glass, "then it is nothing at all to do with me. But I would appreciate it if you could get him out of it. We may not be married anymore, but I do so want him to stay in one piece."

"You really mean that don't you?" I said.

She sighed and nodded her head. "Yes I do," and then put her head in her hands. When she looked up again she had tears streaming down her cheeks. I passed her my handkerchief and she wiped her eyes.

"Look, I guess I ought to put some clothes on. You really must think that I'm just a stupid child, I'm sorry if I embarrassed you, Errol." She looked at me excitedly. "Maybe we could go for a coffee somewhere."

Ten minutes later, she reappeared wearing a tiny light blue skirt and cardigan to match, made out of a fluffy woolen fabric. She wore garters from the skirt and had plain, brown stockings that would have looked rather mundane on anyone else

83

but on Marcia they managed to look fantastic. She was a lot more humble and if anything it was her that appeared embarrassed, making it all the more unbelievable that only half an hour ago she had rather crudely tried to seduce me with a sordid display of exhibitionism. What was even more unbelievable was that this randy old goat had politely refused, against remarkably physical odds.

I stayed for another half hour.

This time we drank coffee and talked without the mental sparring. It was pleasant enough although I couldn't get her naked image out of my mind. I had forgotten what an interesting and nice girl she was, with the nice bit being the real attribute. This did make me embarrassed, as she talked about her life and loves, dreams and heartbreaks; I realized that she was just a girl, a young girl with a lot of history and lot of problems. She insisted that she would always love Hermeez, and he too would love her but that they could never again live together and that was what hurt. When we again broached the subject of Muchado I promised her that it would be all right and I would not allow Hermeez to get into any trouble. It was a promise I was doubtful that I could keep.

Timmy Matthews was looking at his watch when I arrived. I was over half an hour late when he looked over his shoulder into my smiling face. He stood and shook my hand and we both took a seat on the creaking wooden bench that looked over the western side of the lake in lower Central Park. I had taken a short stroll from The Plaza up through the park, past the zoo, along The Mall and over the Bow Bridge, into The Ramble, where we had arranged to meet last night.

It was supposed to be a clear-the-air talk between two old friends that had not seen eye to eye the other night. Timmy was wearing his usual full length, dirty trench coat, brown suit with half undone tie and a crumpled fedora. He had what looked like egg spilt down the front of his shirt and a pile of butts around his ankles. He looked at me, his craggy face a picture of worry, but managed to raise a smile.

"Hello Timmy," I said. "Sorry I'm late."

84

He shrugged and said, "I'm surprised you showed at all. I hope you're in a better mood than the other night."

"I'm sorry about that too, but you know I don't like being pushed. How's the investigation going, am I still the prime suspect?"

"You're still walking around aren't you, Errol? Have you got anything you want to tell me?"

"Yeah, I didn't kill Dyke Spanner. There you go, I've said it, now if you want to call me a liar we know exactly where we are."

Timmy held out a paw and patted me on the shoulder. "Hey calm down, this is supposed to be friendly, a couple of old friends talking, okay?"

I nodded, "Okay."

And for ten minutes that's exactly what it was; I asked Timmy how his kids were and he told me about little Desmond's home run for the under tens; he asked me how the refurbishments were coming along in the office and what I had planned to do for the Christmas break. We both gave our opinions on the events in Washington and the state of the nation and critical reviews of the Yankees and the Dodgers. He even told me a couple of jokes that were doing the rounds and we had a good belly laugh together before watching with interest as a kingfisher appeared on the lake and gracefully plucked lunch from beneath the murky waters. But inevitably it was not going to stay like this and it was Timmy that led the way…

"Right then, Eezy. Give me an assessment. I've read your statement and I've thrown it away. This is firmly off the record and if you want, it will stay that way I just want your spin on things. First up, who do you think did kill him?"

That was a question.

I smiled and lit up a cigarette. "Possible suspects are numerous. First, you got me; I was at the crime scene, I was seen by various witnesses holding the body and it was fairly common knowledge we didn't see eye to eye. It's all pretty circumstantial but a possibility nonetheless. Only I'm telling you I didn't do it, so you've got that to take into account.

85

"Secondly, there is the delectable Mrs. Margaret Spanner; Again it was well known they were not getting on and here is the added possibility of crime of passion, as you know many murders are committed by spouse's or partners especially when they are, how shall I put it..."

"Unfaithful?"

"Yeah, that will do, unfaithful. Thirdly, there is my partner and your other good friend, Hermeez Wentz, Dyke's sworn enemy ever since his marriage break up. And indeed they were not best pals even when they worked together. Hermeez has been acting a little strange of late, and does not appear to have an alibi. Neither, of course, does Maggie. Fourthly..."

"There's more?"

"Much more, only here is where it starts to get difficult. You see it wasn't any of the first three so the fourth option is very, very important."

I lit up a Lucky and sucked the smoke deep into my lungs before breathing it out into the cleanest air in New York.

"Fourthly, there is the chance that it was someone involved in Dyke's work, whether it is current or previous. As you know he has made many enemies and lost plenty friends, there is always the chance that one of those has come back to get revenge. I think we both agree we can rule out simple random killing, he wasn't robbed and his body was found to be uninterfered with, so that makes it somebody he knew, but if you want a list of names it could take a long time."

"How about his current stuff, I know you've been looking into it. Found anything yet?"

I looked right into the eyes of my old friend. He smiled back and held my gaze. He was nudging, gently.

I pulled the bullet out of my pocket and handed it over. Timmy looked at me quizzically and rolled it over in his handkerchief before popping it in his breast pocket.

"Have you heard of a man known as The Coward?" I asked and he lost his smile.

"No. Is this relevant to Dyke..."

"How about 'The Portly Gangster'?"

86

This time he paused for a second, probably no longer but it was a noticeable hesitation, "No again and I repeat is this relevant to Dyke's killer?"

I shrugged. "I don't know. I don't think so but get the bullet checked out and let me know the result."

We sat in silence for a few moments. The park was peaceful, it was a true haven of tranquility and beauty in a dirty, smelly world. I stubbed my cigarette out and waited for Timmy's next question. When it came, it was a real disappointment.

"Have you found out anything else about the murder?"

I shook my head. "Nothing I want to share. So far everything is too sketchy, too many ifs, buts and maybes. If I do find out more I'll pass it on to you personally, you know that Timmy."

Timmy sighed and shuffled a little anxiously. "That may not be possible I'm afraid, Eezy."

"Oh?" I said, concerned at the tone Timmy had taken. Was this to be a stitch up, had he got me here under false pretences, milked me for all he could get only to truss me up and take me in? Normally I would have laughed at the suggestion but there was something about Tim's voice that made me wary. He was about to say something he didn't want to and even more so something that I didn't want him to.

"You see Eezy, I maybe not on the case much longer. Without knowing what Dyke's latest business was I have come up against a brick wall. So far all my investigations have come down to two people, you and Weeny Jung Ping, neither of which are giving me anything that my fuckin' secretary couldn't guess. Lieutenant Beech thinks that I am too close to you both, particularly you. I don't know how much Jake has told you but Beech doesn't like you one bit and because of our friendship he is going off me quickly."

He sighed a real deep sigh. "It looks like I may be taken off the case."

I shook my head. "I'm real sorry pal."

"Don't be, just you make sure that you solve it."

I looked out over the lake. A family was boating across the water causing the birds to scatter and the water to ripple. The kids were laughing and screaming and the father was splashing them with the oar. All the while, the mother was sitting back soaking up the sun. It was peaceful here.

Timmy stood up and looked at his watch again. "I'm gonna have to go, Eezy. Just one thing before I do."

He took out a piece of paper from his pocket and handed it to me. "It's a court order banning you from leaving the City borders. I'm sorry but Beech insisted. Don't make me have to lie for you okay? If you want to talk, and I'm not gonna push you, you know where to find me."

And he was gone.

Chapter Ten – Upstate

The landscape along the Hudson River from the City to Albany, the state capital, is among the most breathtaking in the whole of America. Alongside the many hiking and skiing trails there are miles of orchards, vineyards, pine forests and picturesque mountains lakes. It's a great area for fishing, for relaxing and for sheer enjoying the natural beauty of our fine country. It's not so great however when you've got the life of a young woman in your hands and the puzzle of a friend's murder hanging around your neck.

After Timmy had left Central Park I hung around for another hour or so, watching the boaters and the joggers go by. I took a walk back down The Mall and observed the street entertainers whilst eating an ice cream. I had planned to drive to Woodstock late this afternoon, well in advance of tomorrow's rendezvous. So far I had not told anybody of my plans and after the meeting with Timmy I was even more reluctant to say anything until I got there.

I followed Route West right the way up to Saugerties before heading west into the Catskill Forest Preserve. The drive took less time than I thought and I was soon checked into the premier hotel in the small town of Woodstock, which was a quaint, thirty-room inn that hadn't been renovated this century. It was called The Mountain Star and had a bar, a restaurant and a conservative casino although there was little else. It failed to even offer twenty-four hour room service, although I did find a complimentary packet of peanuts by my bedside and there was a bible in the bedside cabinet!

That evening, after I had eaten a meal of buffalo steak, mashed potato and chick peas, followed by Black Forrest Gateau, I telephoned Ava. She was a smart lady, loyal as a bulldog, and the least I could do was tell her where I was. For all I knew the police could now have a warrant out for my arrest.

"Mrs. Jameson, how are you, is Ava there please?...Yeah, it's Errol...Ava, how are you honey?"

"Errol, where are you? I've been trying to find you all day."

"What is it sweetheart, are you okay?"

"I'm fine, Errol, don't worry about me. I just need to talk to you, that's all. Are you coming in to the office tonight?"

"I'm away on business, baby. I'm upstate in a town called Woodstock. I'm afraid I don't know how long this is going to take."

"Woodstock! What are you doing there? Errol, if you..."

I explained the situation minus a few details but it only served to make her more agitated.

"Errol, there's been a man in to see you. He says he's been looking all over for you."

"What sort of man, who is he?"

"A Mr.Benjamin Wilson. He says that he wants to talk to you in a matter of extreme urgency."

"What's he like, sweetheart, is he a Fed?"

"No, definitely not. He's a little strange, effeminate even. Certainly not police."

"Does he fit the description of The Coward?"

"No, he's tall and thin, your upper-class gentleman, English country squire type. He was very polite, very well spoken and....and very strange. He was most insistent that he must speak to you as soon as possible."

I lit up a Lucky and inhaled deeply as Ava gave me his number. She'd run a check on him and came up with nothing.

"I don't know if I'll be able to contact him while I'm over here, I've got to tie up this end first. Don't worry precious; I'll be in touch as soon as I return. If he comes again try and get a little more out of him, tell him I'll coming back ASAP."

"Okay Errol."

"That's it...good girl. Has Hermeez been in touch today?"

"No not yet and I haven't heard from his friend Muchado either. I hope he hasn't taken exception to me for standing him up."

"Are Mike and Terence still there?"

"Sure they're here. Do you need to have a word?"

"No, just tell them I want them to keep working until I return, and if Hermeez gets in touch tell him to call me."

I gave her my number, "And the same goes for you Ava, if there's anything you don't like, give me a call. Promise me."

"I promise. Now, you take care Errol, you hear me?"

"Sure thing angel. Listen, any more visits from the police get straight in touch with Jake, he'll know what to do. I'll ring you again soon. Yep...you too darling, bye."

"Any messages for Black?" I asked the receptionist as I arrived back through the double doors and into the two-story lobby, with its dark, hardwood floor, plethora of potted plants and impressive antiques under dingy recessed lighting.

She smiled warmly and checked the messages tray. It may have been warm but it sure was stuck, I bet that smile stayed in place all day.

"No sir, I'm sorry," she replied.

I lifted my hat and headed for the stairs. A few moments later I found the third floor and ambled towards my room. The hair on the back of my neck stood on end and immediately sensed there was something wrong.

There was.

The room door was swinging on its battered hinges, the lock broken in two most probably by a powerful kick or makeshift battering ram. There was a breeze blowing in from the open window that led to the fire escape and down to the kitchens and goods entrance. The interior of the room could best be described as having been trashed. Everything that was breakable was broken and everything that could be knocked over had been. Drawers were hanging out of their chest, the wardrobe knocked so that it was resting on its side, and the toiletries from the bathroom were all smashed and scattered all over the room, which ironically gave a rather pleasant aroma to the chaos.

I had brought few belongings with me and after a quick check, they all appeared to be still there and relatively unscathed. My clothes had been tossed around and the contents of my bag had been rather hurriedly or hastily gone through but nothing was broken and nothing had been taken.

I went to the bedside and picked up the telephone. To my surprise, it was still working and after a couple of barely

91

perceptible clicks a honey sweet voice asked me what my request was. I told her about the room and within minutes the manager was knocking on the battered door with a couple of beefy security guards alongside him.

"We won't be needing them," I said, nodding at the gorillas. "Whoever has done this is long gone."

The manager agreed and waved them away before taking a full inspection of the trashed room. He was a tall, thin man dressed in a casual cream suit and straw fedora; he was in his early thirties with short graying hair, wide vacant eyes and a smile that crept slowly across his tired looking face.

"You must accept my most sincere apologies, Mr. Black. We will of course be looking into this most unsavory incident most vigilantly."

I nodded and accepted his apologies while lighting up a Lucky.

"Would you like one?" I asked.

"No thank you. I haven't smoked for twelve months now and unless there is another war in my fighting lifetime I don't suppose I ever will again."

I smoked alone, but we had a drink together and soon we were walking into the Catskills Suite, the premier room in the house. Harry, the manager, had okayed my upgrade as soon as we found out we had both served in the same military band of men in the Pacific. He didn't go into details and neither did I but it was clear we had both seen things we would rather not see again and it created a strange bond between us, like many of us ex-servicemen back in the real world. We didn't have to talk about it, Harry's little comment about cigarettes was enough and from now on I knew I had at least one ally in Woodstock.

The Catskills Suite was something else. Like the hotel lobby it was high-ceilinged with a fiercely polished hardwood floor and adorned with many old trinkets and paintings. There was an open stairway that led to a balcony which had a better view than the kitchens and loading bay and also led to the two bedrooms; underneath there was an extensive bar, comfy chairs and a marble fireplace with a well lit fire that cast haunting shadows in the subdued lighting.

Harry stayed for another drink, bourbon on the rocks, and said goodnight. It was just as he opened the door and was half way through that I asked him about The Coward. His reaction was the same as other people I had asked, one of genuine ignorance.

"How about The Portly Gangster?" I said.

"The Portly Gangster, sounds like..."

"Yeah, I know what it sounds like," I said, cutting him off with a serious tone in my voice, "but it's all I got to go on."

Harry shook his head and smiled a wry smile. "Sorry, Errol Black. I never even heard the name before and I have heard a lot of names. I'm not saying there is no Coward or Portly Gangster but in this job you hear lots of things, lots of names and lots of baloney. I'm afraid I never heard of anything like this."

I nodded. "Okay Harry, thanks again for the upgrade, you are a true gentleman. Goodnight."

"Yeah, goodnight," he said and almost closed the door. Before he did he stopped again, paused noticeably as if he was evaluating something in his head and finally he turned around.

I stepped closer and he whispered in my ear.

A minute later, he had gone and I was running a hot bath. It had been a long day and I was exhausted. A nice, long, hot soak would revitalize my body and make me sleep a good deal better. I looked around the vast array of toiletries on the white marble shelf, selected a bottle of honey and lemon bath salts and squirted it all under the powerful tap.

Whilst the bath was filling up I considered who could have trashed my hotel room and why. There were few people that knew I had made the journey and I was pretty sure I had not been tailed here from New York. That made it likely that it was someone that had been expecting me and so someone who was connected to The Coward. But that theory made little sense as I had so far fulfilled my bargain with The Coward and would be ready to meet him tomorrow night. Also, there appeared to have been nothing taken from the room so just what was the reason behind it? I was sure it would become evident in the days ahead so for the time being forgot about it.

As I lay back in the boiling hot water with my eyes closed, feeling my body shed its fatigue and relax, my mind was again wandering. I had just lost one friend in Dyke Spanner and now I was worrying that soon I would be losing another. Whichever way I turned it around there was no acceptable reason for Hermeez to be mixed up with Muchado. He must have owed him money. That was the only reason that added up, Muchado was a loan shark by trade after all. It would make the most sense that he had come looking for Hermeez for payment. But why had Hermeez needed to borrow money from a low life like Muchado, when he knew only too well that he could always come to me? We may have been hard up but there was always ways, better ways than going to low lifes like Muchado.

I turned the tap off and ran my fingers through my hair, feeling my cheeks flush in the boiling hot steam. There was a gentle drip drip drip as the steam hit the mirrored ceiling and condensed, dripping back down into the bubble filled tub.

Maybe Hermeez had not borrowed money from Muchado, maybe he had hired him to do another job? This was the thought that had been eating away at me for the last few days and one that I was frightened of believing. It was well known that Arnold Muchado was not just an ordinary loan shark, despicable trade though that was. He was much more flexible and could be hired for a number of jobs whether it be to frighten, to give a good beating or if the rumours be true, to kill.

I emptied my mind of the thought as I stood up in the bath tub and wrapped a big, fluffy towel around myself. I felt a little light headed with the steam and heat in the room so I swilled my face a couple of times with cold water and padded out into the suite. Fixing myself a drink, I toweled myself dry before heading through to the master bedroom, clicked on the bedside lamp and got under the covers.

Sleep came quickly but was fitful and full of vague dreams, all of which featured the mysterious, beautiful Marlow. Like most people when I wake and sleep has ended, I find it hard to remember dreams, particularly if they are really special, and this day was no different. I can't recall the detail but that was unimportant. At that time what was also unimportant was the fact that Marlow had surely duped me. In what way I was not quite sure, whether she had purposely lured me to The Dragon Bar that fateful night for whatever reason, or simply that she had failed to tell me that only a few nights before she had been sharing the bed of Dyke Spanner, my one time friend and partner. Or maybe something else that I yet had absolutely no idea about. Whatever the truth was I was certain that she had played me all along and probably cared little for me, but I was still determined to find her alive. And I would.

After a hearty breakfast of eggs, bacon, tomatoes and fried bread, followed by grapefruit and swilled down with three cups of coffee, I was ready to hit the muddy streets of Woodstock. It would prove to be back breaking and disheartening work, although I had very little to go on and could very well be barking up the wrong tree altogether.

I primed Harry for a few tips on who would be the best points of call for information gathering but found him less than forthcoming. It's not that he didn't want to help, he was just a little wary of any reprisals and when I refused to tell him what it pertained to he clammed up. My persistence paid off a little and he gave me the names of a few people around town that may be able to help but did not repeat the advice he had given me last night.

They didn't. Help that is.

I started at the constable's office in the Town Hall, at first on the precept that I was following up the break in at the hotel before going on to mention the names Coward, Daniels and The Portly Gangster. As I had been told by Harry to expect I got no joy and was asked to leave several times before I was physically escorted from the tatty, one floor, and wooden premises.

Doing the rounds of the Woodstock bars certainly took its toll and even though I devised several different ways of steering an aimless conversation around to the questions I wanted answering I never got a satisfactory one. At times I got the impression I was purposely being stonewalled, although in hindsight that was probably my own suspicion of this whole business and the sheer indifference of the people that I was questioning.

Local businesses fared no better. I found myself repeating the bizarre names over and over again, sometimes being laughed at and sometimes insulted. Very rarely did I get the impression that anyone was hiding anything and even on the odd occasion that I did, I was quickly shown the exit, with a note in my notebook my only real sign of progress.

I thought of what Harry had whispered in my ear just before he left the Catskills Suite and the effect it had appeared to have on him this morning. He was scared, of that there was no doubt, and I decided it would not be wise to start throwing the Tighe name into the many conversations I was having. I already knew a little about the Tighes, enough to know that they were not the sort of people you wanted to get on the wrong side of and I had to think of Harry. He only mentioned them because he couldn't come up with anything else, and now he wished he hadn't.

Chapter Eleven – Stanley Cortene

It was mid afternoon and I was sitting on a barstool in what looked like the sleaziest joint in the district. It was the only bar I could find that wasn't full of cowboys. I'm a liberal kind of guy; homosexuals, drug dealers no problem. As long as they don't bother me I won't bother them. But country yokel music, and bars full of putzs in tight jeans and boots with spurs on them, shouting, "Yee Haa!" That's where I draw the line.

So here I was in a bar that was much closer to home. It was a typical watering hole of the underclass; full of undesirables and layabouts. A fight would break out every half an hour, usually settled outside on the pavement. The barmaid had a black eye and a tattoo on her upper chest. She was chewing gum and wolf-whistling every incoming male customer. I would just drink my drink and mind my own business.

There was a short, stocky guy with thick clumps of black curly hair, sitting about three paces away. He had a bulge above his shoulder, making it obvious to guys like me that he was concealing a shotgun. He had Outfit written all over him. You could almost smell it. A big, heavily built guy with a shaven head was standing next to him, clearly his minder. They were wearing scruffy corduroys and tartan, woolen shirts with chequered flat caps on their heads. And they both spoke in harsh, Irish accents.

I asked the bartender to bring over the telephone, keeping my eyes on the guy with the shotgun. I dialed Jake's number and waited. Meanwhile the two guys were laughing and joking about something. They kept pointing across the room and then cracking up in hysterics.

"Jakey, it's Errol. How's things going?"

"Errol, thank god you called. Not good I'm afraid. You're gonna have to get you ass back to Manhattan pretty damn quick. I don't know what it is your chasing out there in the sticks, but everything's at stake over here, you hear me?"

"Calm down and tell me what's bothering you, will you Jake. I can't just drop everything and leave. I've got important business over here."

I noticed the two guys across the room calm down a hell of a lot and nudge each other as the door opened and in walked another man. He was tall business-like, wearing an all black suit. He casually looked around him and went and sat at the far end of the room. I knew that guy but I couldn't quite place him.

"Errol, are you listening to me?"

"Yeah, Jake, go on."

"It's that damn Lieutenant Beech. He swears he's got a witness to say that you were seen entering the Dragon Bar minutes before Dyke Spanner was blown away. That you were holding a smoking gun and that you wouldn't let anyone get close until you had made sure he was dead. Now I know this all sounds a bit like a fairy story, and I'm not quite sure just exactly how much of it holds up, but unless you can come up with something I've got my work cut out."

"What witness, Jake?"

"I don't know that, he won't put his cards on the table, but he sounds serious."

"So what's the story, I went into the Dragon and for no reason at all I cold-bloodedly murdered a close friend, a man I have known for most of my adult life."

"He wasn't a friend of yours and you know it. So do the police for that matter."

"Come on Jake, it's preposterous. There is no witness, don't you see and if there is no witness it'd be laughed out of court. In fact it wouldn't even get to court"

"Not if they pin a motive on you."

"You're going to bring up the Hermeez thing again, I just know it. Look maybe he had a motive but he wouldn't be that stupid and I certainly wouldn't be that stupid."

"Forget Hermeez. Let's say that maybe it was revenge, but for something else, nothing to do with bloody Hermeez."

I sighed, losing patience but still said, "Go on."

"Let's say that a couple of weeks ago a very dear friend of yours was killed in the same joint, by the very same Dyke Spanner. You maybe didn't go out to kill him, but let's face it you already had a thousand good reasons to do so. Maybe you went to talk and things got out of hand."

"Are you saying Dyke killed Woo Wang?"

"No. No I'm not saying anybody killed anybody, right. That's not my business. All I'm trying to do is tell you what is going on and to take this thing bloody seriously because the police are not messing about."

"What do you think though Jake? Do you think I did it?"

"Come on Errol, don't get snippy with me. I know you didn't do it, and even if you did I'd do my best to get you off, but you gotta help me. You gotta get back here and tell me what the hell is going on! You leaving town so soon doesn't help at all either. The police don't know yet but as soon as they find out that you broke that court order that's another weapon in their armoury."

"I told you, Jakey, I can't come back yet. Hell I pay you good fuckin' money to keep me out of jail. It looks like you're going to have to earn some for a change. Look I'm going to have to go..."

There was movement in the bar. The two guys in question had polished off their drinks and were heading determinedly across the room.

"Errol, don't you hang up on me, we've gotta talk!"

"Listen, Jake, talk to Weeny about it. He'll tell you exactly what happened. Just sort it out, I got to go."

"But Weeny's..."

I hung up and edged across the bar so I was a little closer to the action. I wasn't sure exactly what was going down, but it looked pretty heavy.

Shotgun sat down next to the guy in black. Muscles ordered drinks at the bar and joined them. All three men kept their hands on the table; a mob gesture of friendship. As soon as those hands moved there would be trouble.

I edged a little closer so to be within earshot and kept my head tucked down.

"Something's going down, and you know it," said the man in black down his nose, "I want you guarantee that it's got nothing to do with your boys."

Shotgun looked hurt. He was short, maybe five six, but his hundred-seventy pound frame was formidable. Big broad shoulders stretched his brown hunter's jacket tight. He had thick, black curly hair with bushy eyebrows and a scar on his left temple. Muscles next to him was a real monster; as big as a garage and a double one at that.

"She's gone again," Shotgun said to his goon with a smirk, "Which is terrible news, I'm sure." He then turned his gaze to the man across, "But what it has to do with me, I am not sure."

"You don't appear to be taking this very seriously," said the man in black with a scowl, "In fact you..."

Shotgun opened his palms. "Stanley, I give you my most sincere condolences. If I could do anything to help you, I would not hesitate. You know that is the truth, but..." he shook his head, "... what can I do?"

It was then that I realized who the man in black was. Stan Cortene was a legend in his own lifetime. He started out as a bagman in the '20s. Couriering dirty laundry for the East Combination - wire money, narcotics, booze; word was it didn't matter. He had a family early in life - nice wife, three little kiddies - and he would do anything for them. For years he was a reliable man; trustworthy and honest. The job would get done quickly and quietly.

Either the cops had nothing on him or they left him alone. Some said he bought them with his own money. It was a matter of honour - he was being paid to do a job and therefore it was his responsibility to see it done. Whatever the method he got the job done every time.

This impressed the boys in the East. A reliable bagman was a great asset and Charlie Lucky rewarded Cortene by offering him more. Soon he was Hammer for the whole New York City area, and was just as adept at this new profession. For years he served as the hit man before setting up his own outfit. He was now such a darling with the big boys, Luciani and Lansky that they left him alone. Of course he still helped them out when required and they in turn gave him his freedom.

He now ran a thriving mob north of the City. I'd heard he often still did jobs personally - most capos settled into respectability once they became the boss. It fooled them into believing they were legitimate businessmen despite the blood being still wet on their hands from getting there. And here he was talking business alone.

I took a guess the other two were from the Tighe organization; an Irish Protestant gang of racist thugs. Anyone who wasn't white, preferably from Belfast, fiercely anti-Catholic and married with twelve children was deemed suspicious. It helped if they drank ten pints of Guinness a night, looked like a hard up garbage collector and went home to beat the wife. They used to be big in this area, but they never really recovered from losing half their employees a few years back in a siege. The last few years had seen a shaky truce between the two mobs. Maybe today it was shakier than most.

Shotgun took out a silver box from his lapel pocket, opened it and offered a cigar to Cortene. Still looking angry, Cortene took one with a fat, hairy paw covered in gold and lit it up. I ordered another drink and listened.

"Listen to me Stan," began Shotgun, "I appreciate you coming here alone. You are welcome on my patch, anytime. All your boys are, you know that." He emphasized 'my patch' through gritted teeth. "But I know nothing of your problem, and that is the truth."

"That is all I wanted to hear," replied Cortene, looking out of place with the long, thin cigarillo in his hand. "Thank you for the bourbon." He stubbed it out and stood up.

"Just one thing," said Shotgun. "There's a new man in town. Shady character with big money, lots of influence but little ambition, so I hear. Call me."

Cortene nodded and headed for the door. He didn't quite get there however, before it was knocked from its hinges. The room went silent and everyone turned to see three heavily armed gorillas where the door had been. In the middle of them stood Dan Washington, the meanest, dirtiest cop in the East. He was holding a gun in each hand; both were nickel plated, one with a five inch barrel the other six. A grin filled his black face like a white scar.

Dan Washington made Ness's Untouchables look squeamish. He was a bad dude, respected and feared by good guys and bad guys alike. Nobody knew how many people he had killed, and nobody dared ask. Word has it Charlie Lucky offered him a King's ransom to switch sides, desperate to have a man like Washington on the payroll. In return big Dan killed a man for every grand he was offered. Lucky was getting nervous himself before they deported him back to Sicily.

Dan was a tall, handsome man. For a smoke he had a light complexion with a gentle nose and blue, alert eyes. His mouth sat under a thick, black moustache, which was twirled at the ends like a French chef. As dapper as ever he was wearing a well fitting brown suit, black tie and a red handkerchief ruffled in his breast pocket.

We'd met a couple of times but I don't think Dan recognized me. Stan Cortene was not so lucky; he was shepherded back to the table with Shotgun. There were so many pairs of hands in the air it looked like someone had asked for Spartacus. Dan just stood there, soaking it all up. And then the fun really began.

Shotgun lived up to his name, pulling out his weapon and cocking it in one fluid action. This triggered the melee as the room descended into chaos. Billiard balls sprouted wings and began flying; bottles and beer glasses did likewise. The first few blasts of gunfire came from Dan Washington and his boys, narrowly beating Shotgun and Muscles to the tape. That's not to say they didn't fire off a few shots in anger; quite a few punters had that pleasure. Although not all of them had the best part of their face blown off in return. That's what big Dan did to the gangsters.

Blood splashed onto the table that me and Stan Cortene sheltered under. I looked at his face and he looked like a normal man. He smiled back, but his eyes weren't smiling. Especially when one of Washington's gorillas appeared with a smoking gun.

"Say goodbye Cortene. You really shouldn't go causing trouble in a Tighe stronghold. Gang gunfights usually end with dead gangsters. Bound to end in tears."

He re-cocked the weapon.

I lifted the table from the floor and charged into the surprised cop, knocking him off balance. Shots were whistling

102

round my ears, but I was still alive. So was Cortene. He grabbed my arm and we rushed outside to a waiting Ferrari. Instinctively we both jumped in and the car sped away. The driver looked straight ahead and didn't say a word.

I sat there quietly for the next few minutes, just wondering what I had done. The cops face as I slammed him with the table stayed in my head; a look of surprise and disappointment. Meanwhile Cortene was in hysterics, having to cover his mouth he laughed so much.

"I don't know who the hell you are, but I thank you," he uttered after a while. "Very courageous, very courageous indeed."

"The name's Errol Black, I'm a private cop. I think I'll try and forget yours."

"Probably best, but let me tell you this...I'm a big fish. You probably know already if you're a good one. You saved my life. Why, I don't know and neither probably do you. That little piece of heroism that you just performed will not be forgotten by me."

He pulled up on a side street and looked me in the eyes. "I'm going to give you a telephone number. Wherever you are, if you ever need anything, I'll help you."

"Hold it," I said, putting as much of an edge on my voice as I dared. "I got a lot of friends that are cops. Whatever I did in there does not make me a wise guy. Hell, I even got friends that are honest cops. Okay, I helped you, but I sure as hell don't want to gain access to the 'only kill each other' club. You got it?"

Stan smiled. "Errol, I owe you my life, and I always, always honour my debts. Take it."

I took the piece of paper from him and put it in my inside pocket. Before I could say anything else Stan Cortene opened the car door. "Now you must leave, I've got important business to attend to!"

I got out of the car and off sped Stan Cortene. It would be the beginning of a long and complicated association with the family. If I knew then what I know now, maybe I'd have gone home there and then.

Chapter Twelve – A Twist in the Tale

The night soon arrived, and with it came the rain. Woodstock was not the prettiest of towns and when the rain came it all got worse. The roads, which were nothing more than dirt tracks with traffic lights, washed away. All that was left was a swamp, a dirty, smelly, sleazy swamp. Even the hookers wore Wellington boots.

It usually took much more than the rain to dampen the locals' vociferous activities. For the gangsters there was always work to be done and fun to be had. For the tourists the fun was to be had from observing the gangsters having theirs. Gunfights were not irregular, as I knew all too well, and were usually quite entertaining. Tonight, however, everything was quiet.

I called Hermeez but there was no answer. I would have liked to hear his opinions on a few things or just his voice but it would have to wait. At that time, I didn't know quite how long.

Even the hotel casino was restrained. It was still full of people. All smoking, drinking and clinking their chips. But the laughter and joy of winning were calmer. So were the wails of despair.

There were half a dozen roulette wheels, half a dozen blackjack tables, nine crap tables and a hundred slots. A long, mirrored bar ran the length of the far wall, with a thousand different bottles of liquor. There were heaps of unattached, beautiful girls from their late teens to their early twenties, all with their chests half showing. Most were circulating the casino in a predatory kind of way, others tagged onto a winning punter or a rich type.

I was neither.

I still scored a stunning redhead.

She was decked out in a clinging red suit with red gloves and lots of jewelry. Her lipstick was as bright as her suit. She was playing at one of the dice tables shaking her cupped hands with a wide smile on her face.

"Come on six, come on baby."

She threw a seven and deflated immediately.

That's when I stepped in. I wined her and dined her and then we went upstairs.

"What did you say your name was again?" she asked, whilst re-applying her lipstick. She was bent over the bed, her considerable breasts swaying.

"I didn't. It's Black, Errol Black," I said, thinking about Marlow.

"Errol Black," she mouthed it slowly. "That's a nice name. Do you want a drink Errol Black?"

"Sure, Remy Martin, no ice."

She walked to the liquor cabinet at the far wall. My eyes followed. Her milky body with gravity defying breasts floated gracefully across the room. Her legs were a long and smooth and she had a sweet, well pruned pubic patch, a couple of shades lighter than her lip gloss. She may not have been Marlow but she was one hell of a substitute.

She handed me a short glass brimming with cognac.

"Cheers," she threw her head back and the glass too. I did the same.

"I suppose I ought to cover up," she said, gesturing to herself. Her nipples were pink and erect, about as big as quarters but without George Washington's head on them, "I gotta go."

"So soon? Is my time up?" I said a little curtly.

The girl scowled and threw a high-heeled boot in my direction. It missed comfortably and I handed it back with a conciliatory smile.

"I'm sorry. Let's have another drink. Sit down."

She filled the glasses up again and perched on the end of the bed. "I don't suppose that I'll be seeing you again, will I?" she said, a little regret in her voice.

"I suppose not, but that's no reason to rush off," I sat up and reached out my arms.

Half an hour later, we were interrupted by the telephone. It was the duty manager; he had a call for me in the office and insisted it was urgent. It looked like she was right after all. I apologized and left.

I was ushered into the office and picked up the telephone.

"Errol Black," I said.

The line was dead.

"I'm sorry sir, the gentleman said that he could no longer wait. He did leave you this message, which I took the liberty of writing down."

He handed me a slip of paper, which said, "If you are ill don't tie your own bandages. The blood must be quelled immediately."

I thanked the duty manager and left the office.

It was ten o'clock when I arrived. I had plenty of time until the meet and I was pleased contact had been made. The Woodstock Country Hospital was nothing to write home about. It was situated in what looked like a converted old farmhouse. Dirt tracks led up to the entrance, with a colourful row of geraniums down the middle. The walls were brown and the air was dirty. I was expecting to see a herd of cattle penned in the gardens, but there weren't any. Gardens that is.

The reception was more of the same although beige now took precedence over brown. The waiting room was full of cowboys nursing various riding injuries. I waited in a queue but before I reached the front I felt a slip of paper in my pocket which hadn't been there earlier and a quick breeze. I casually looked around and walked into a corner whilst taking out the note and reading it.

It gave me directions to the Hospital Chapel on the third floor, which I followed and took a seat next to the only worshipper present on the second row from the front.

"Errol, I'm glad you hurried. Come on sit down."

I obliged, taking off my hat and looking at Weeny Jung Ping. He looked tired and worried.

"Not long until the meet. Are you fully prepared?" he asked.

"I think so. It has been an eventful day but yes, I think that I am now ready."

My friend smiled, his eyes were almost closed as he blinked his long lashes. "Yes I think it can be said that you have truly experienced the lower end of Woodstocks' vast talents. The

106

man Ferriby has now left town and taken his goons with him, but the same cannot be said of the other criminal elements. I do hope tonight's events will not get you noticed."

I shrugged. "Washington got himself plenty tonight. He has no need to worry about what slipped, especially when his own methods were rather unorthodox to say the least."

I suppose I should not have been surprised. Weeny Jung Ping had confirmed to me his brilliance as a shadow man many times before. That was one of the reasons that I selected him. I had absolute confidence that he would do the job better than anyone. The other was the continuing absence of my regular partner Hermeez Wentz.

"Thanks again for doing this for me Weeny. I appreciate it," I lit up a Lucky and sucked in the smoke. "Tell me, what else have you got? Have you got anything on The Coward?"

I asked the question sure in the knowledge that there would be more. Weeny Jung Ping was a master of detection work and it was clear to me that he was doing this as much for himself as he was for me. He was convinced there was a connection to the death of Woo Wang. And if it had become personal he would have covered every angle.

There was plenty. Although he wasn't keen to spill.

"Tonight, I will be your shadow. You never invited me in on the investigation and I never asked. Let's leave it at that shall we Errol?"

I shook my head. "No let's not Weeny. If you have information that maybe of help then spill it. You already know as much as me."

"You know how I operate Eezy, hell you and me are more alike than you realize. Leave it."

He was right. We were both stubborn sons of bitches that like nothing better than solving a case on our own, but I didn't leave it. I took out my gun and put it to the small man's head, cocking it so it clicked loudly just above his ear.

"Does this remind you of anything?" I held it there for a couple of minutes and then put the gun away. "Come on Weeny, if you know anything I think you owe it to me to spill."

Weeny looked up and smiled a mischievous smile. He made me laugh, not his silly grin but he was wearing a bloody dog collar for Christ's sake. He patted me on the back, surprising in his strength for such a small man and then extinguished my cigarette between his forefinger and thumb. "It's no smoking in here you know."

He gave me a brief summary of his investigation, from pumping his contacts back in the city to his time here in The Hudson Valley. He still had very little on The Coward, nobody wanted to talk and there was no previous form recorded to be found. If he was a gangster, he had kept his nose extremely clean or he was from out of town. Both were equally possible.

His findings were very similar to my own. I had dug around myself over the last couple of days and come out almost fruitless. It transpired that the Wyatt Earp was more of a Tighe haunt than one of The Coward; Weeny recognized several faces there but nothing that resembled the description of the Portly Gangster. There was always the chance that he was working in league with the Tighes but nothing really pointed us in that direction.

Just when I was thinking we had both come up against a brick wall...

"I was getting rather tired of acting like the curious tourist and was getting ready to call it a day when I spotted him."

"Who?"

"The guy that has been following me off and on for the last few weeks. He was right there in the Earp."

"So what did you do?"

"I followed him for a change. He led me to a ranch a little out of town between here and Hunter, real mountain country. Mr. Wang's pig and barley ranch was well known by the locals. They weren't quite as forthcoming as I would have liked but the rubber hose soon solved their coyness. I now know more about pig farming than I ever thought there was to know."

"And Coward, was he there?"

Weeny shrugged. "It is a pig and barley ranch but it is also a lot more. It is a palatial home with a lot of security but little manpower. Last night a man answering Coward's description was there for most of the night with no bodyguards, naked for all to see. I can't be certain but if you are asking me for my opinion then yes it is him and that is his house, or at least one of his houses."

He shrugged his bony shoulders and looked at me with a glint in his eye. "To guys like us, Errol, it would be like gate crashing a five year old's birthday party."

"I see where you are going Weeny, but I prefer to stay with the original plan. It is always good to have a back up and you have done well as always..."

Weeny nodded his small head gently forward with his hands pressed together.

"... but The Wyatt Earp is where we shall meet. There is still no solid reason for us to do otherwise."

"I may not agree but I will defer to you Errol. This is your game but I shall warn you of one thing..." His tone had softened. He was winding up for the finale, there was always a finale with Weeny, whatever you talked about he always saved the best until last.

"And that is?" I asked, rubbing my bruised face.

"I may not be certain that it was The Coward that was there on the ranch but I am damn sure that it was your Marlow."

Chapter Thirteen – The Wyatt Earp

I picked up the receiver and dropped twenty cents.

"Tim, it's Errol. I need some information."

"Why the hell should I do you a favor? You scratch my back sometime and then maybe, just maybe, I'll scratch yours. I warned you about leaving town. Christ, I believed you were actually gonna listen to some sense for a change. And what do you do, I bet your bags were even packed as we swapped pleasantries?"

"What do you know about the Tighe mob?"

There was a short pause. "Small time Irish mobsters. They're as big as they're ever gonna get. The families tolerate them 'cause they're sick motherfuckers, and don't mind who's brains they blow out. The old Dons have got used to living to a ripe old age and don't want some psychopathic mick to spoil the party. They're too fuckin' crazy to ever become really organized."

"Are they all Irish?" I dropped another twenty as the line began to pip. "Or do they take all comers?"

"Hold on a minute." There was a rustling of papers. "Yeah, they're pretty strict on that, although maybe things are changing. I heard a whisper that they were talking to outsiders. They desperately want to be big you see. Maybe they'll form an alliance; if they get any interested parties they could become the Tighe Triad."

I ran out of change and the line went dead. I could still hear Timmy laughing on the other end.

Entering the Wyatt Earp was like walking into a time zone. It took your eyes a few seconds to adjust to the dingy lighting at first, but when they did, it was hard not to appreciate its authenticity. There was a large room full of tables with felt coverings and sawdust and gravel on the floor; a huge, ancient bar that stretched out across the whole room with a full length mirror behind it that served to make the bar appear larger than it really was; four creaking ceiling fans laboring around lazily and making the barest of breezes; large wanted posters of outlaws and lawmen adorned the wood paneled walls, of Dillinger,

Holliday and Kidd; a vintage old duke box in the corner blasted out tunes from a bygone age; and a cast of characters to fill any wild west movie.

I was wearing a casual, brown felt suit, open necked without a tie with a light fedora and shiny brown boots. I had a Lucky flaming in between my lips, a well-disguised shoulder holster fully packed and a six-inch stiletto tucked down my sock.

The bartender was a tall, disheveled looking man in a white t-shirt covered by a leather waistcoat, frayed jeans and cowboy boots. He wore a ten-gallon hat big enough to swim the Olympic trials in and a stupid grin that was asking to be wiped from his ugly mug. There were a few other punters scattered around nursing their beers and singing along to the noise that was classed as music in these parts.

Nobody appeared to take any notice as I entered the bar although I felt a cold chill blow across the back of my neck. I felt strangely uncomfortable as if I was walking into the lion's den and found myself looking back at the door expecting, hoping even, that soon that too would be knocked off its hinges by the great Dan Washington.

I would have to proceed with caution. If Coward was indeed a regular of this watering hole then either he had managed to not draw attention to himself, or had been very persuasive in keeping mouths shut. What was the reason for this? Was Coward simply a publicity shy gangster, there had been many of those over the years, or was it something else? For the time being I would have to assume that I was firmly on his turf and proceed accordingly.

"What's your drink?" asked the bartender in a deep baritone voice that was as unexpected as it was cultured.

"Beer, thanks," I answered, and took a good look around.

It looked the kind of bar where everyone knew each other. Every head had lifted and taken a good look at me from when I walked through the door and quickly returned. The balls had not exactly stopped on the big pool table at the back but it was that kind of bar.

I accepted my beer in a frosted glass from the bartender and took it to a booth at the other side of the large room.

Several people came and went in the next half an hour. Every one greeted the bartender personally and most said hello or goodbye to the other customers. None looked like I imagined the Portly Gangster to look like and none were accompanied by Audrey Daniels or the dandy I had knocked out, outside my office.

Until now.

He was wearing a white suit with a pale yellow, open necked shirt and white fedora. His face was as round as a water melon and his nose as red as a beetroot. His eyes like tiny specks, his mouth narrow and ears baby-like gave the impression that his head was too big for his features. The rest of him was big too, he must have weighed at least three hundred pounds although he carried it well, his large stomach held at bay by a thick, black belt.

He strided through the door, with Daniels at one side and the dandy at the other, scanned the room and smiled when his eyes settled on me. He didn't hold eye contact for more than a second, ordered drinks from the bar and whispered something in the ear of his sidekick before coming over.

He stood over me offering a huge hand. I remained seated and he made a comic face at Daniels before joining me in the booth sitting right across from me.

"Mr. Black, may I take the opportunity to welcome you to Woodstock. What an honor it is to meet you at last and that's no lie. An honor indeed. How are you sir?"

I failed to answer and so the man continued...

"First of all, I must apologize for the rather cloak and dagger way I have gone about this but my patience was at an absolute end. I am not a gangster I want you to understand. Far from it in fact, although my late brother was quite accomplished in that particular trade. I may have learned a few tricks from him before he died," he said innocently before carrying on...

"When I have explained the situation you will understand I am sure you will."

He shook his watermelon head. "You've been proving a very difficult man to get hold of, I'm afraid. It seems that all the rumors and mystique about the daring, brilliant Errol Black are true. Too true..."

"Tell the kid to put his piece on the table," I interrupted. "Either he puts it right there, where I can see, it or he walks out of here. Alternatively I walk out of here."

"I don't think that you will do that, Mr. Black. Not before hearing me out. Audrey," he said and looked over his shoulder at the kid, "Why don't you wait in the car."

The kid scowled, gave me a 'you're dead' look and stomped out of the bar, kicking the sawdust as he went. The dandy looked at Coward who nodded and then he too left the bar.

"There is no need to be so confrontational Mr. Black, there really isn't. Audrey is a good kid, he is not here to cause you any discomfort or harm."

"Audrey is far from a good kid. Not only is he wanted in the City for a string of crimes, but I'm sick of the sight of him. You do know that he's been my regular little companion these last few days, what with breaking into my apartment and then my hotel room and all the while he's been sticking closer to me than my own hair. He's a goddammned pain in the ass!"

The Portly Gangster giggled. "He has been paying you close attention that much is true. Although you will soon understand my reluctance to let you out of my sight I am sure you will."

"He's lucky I haven't put a bullet in him."

"Come come, Sir. I was hoping this would be a friendly meeting. Let's not us start off on the wrong foot."

I smiled inwardly. After what he had been up to he was now worried about starting off on the wrong foot. The man was a card, I'd give him that.

"We already got off on the wrong foot Coward when you killed Dyke Spanner."

His face was filled with surprise and horror. "Be careful, Mr. Black. I would not go repeating such lies if I were you. I had nothing to do with the unfortunate death of the young man Spanner. Am I not correct in thinking that it is you that is suspected of such a crime, not I or anyone that I am involved with?"

113

He was right so I left it at that. I had no evidence at all to suspect that Dyke's murder was connected to The Coward and even if I did, I wanted to hear what he had to say. Not however before I knocked him back a peg or two.

"Okay, so we'll cross murder off the list, but how about kidnap? You admitted as much on the telephone and as I am sure you know I do record all my telephone messages."

The Coward raised his nose in the air and dabbed at his considerable cheeks with his handkerchief, unmoved by my threat. He took a measured sip of his drink and plucked out a long, gold cigarette holder, before filling it with a French Gauloise and lit it up. The smoke burned brightly and smelled foul.

"Ah yes, the voluptuous Marlow...so helpful. You are very much the hero aren't you, Mr. Black? I bet that you thought you could swagger into this bar, sling her over your shoulder and ride off into the sunset. Mmm, very interesting. She is in absolute first class health I assure you...And..."

I tried to interrupt, but the tone of the man's voice loudened, "You will get your chance to talk to Miss Marlow a little later. If you are cooperative, of course. She is, what they call my banker, my ace in the hole if you like. But before we get to your love life we have some very important business to take care of."

Again the man giggled, his flabby cheeks beaming out like a beacon.

I stayed silent and took another drink. I was damned if I was going to get into an argument with this clown. Not yet. Soon enough the truth would come out. I would just have to bide my time and play along.

"I don't take kindly to threats, Mr. Black, as has become crystal clear neither do you? So let's put all our threats, our anger and all of our macho bargaining aside just for the minute. You asked for Audrey to leave and he has. You have threatened me and I - in my haste - have done likewise. If you really believe me to be the perpetrator of the heinous crimes you allege then there is nothing to prevent you from shooting me down right now. You would probably escape as well a man of your talents. But I

114

urge you to hold fire for just a moment and let us talk like the gentlemen that we are."

I ordered another drink and the bartender brought it over promptly, once again leaving us alone.

"Okay, let's cut to the quick shall we. What do you want from me?" I said.

The man smiled and giggled like a child. "First, I must ask you one question and I would appreciate it if you give me a truthful answer."

I nodded.

"Are you here alone, like I requested? As you can see I am now here alone, so are you? I do hope so."

I took a sip of the beer. It was still cold and it slowed the perspiration on the back of my neck. I nodded and said, "Yes I am alone. Now I ask you once more, what do you want from me?"

The Coward pursed his lips, his big bulbous, purple lips and dabbed at the corner of his mouth with his handkerchief before tucking it back in his breast pocket. He looked at me as he said it.

"Okay, enough joking around, let's get down to business..."

His eyes widened with excitement. Two tiny specks on a mass of flesh,

"I will now tell you the story of the Hope Diamond. It is truly one of the most special and treasured gems that the world has ever seen. Named after a one-time purchaser Henry Thomas Hope, this particular diamond has an illustrious history most of which is shrouded in mystery, myth and make believe. Are you a diamond lover, Errol, are you? Surely a man such as yourself knows that it is the diamond that is a girl's best friend, although maybe you beg to differ?"

I said nothing, only I couldn't help smiling as this preposterous man, would-be killer, continued his tale...

"One significant part of the story cannot be verified, but is now largely accepted as fact. This is that the Hope is in fact a cutting from the more famous Blue Tavernier Diamond, a stone once owned by King Louis XIV. The Tavernier was discovered

115

many centuries ago somewhere in southern India where it was revered and worshipped for having mystical powers, probably due to it's unique color and size. It's not your average engagement ring diamond, no the Tavernier is a very special deep, indigo blue and is quite exquisite in its beauty.

"It was in 1642 that the Tavernier was brought to Europe by the good King Louis. In his haste, the silly man had the diamond cut from 113 carats to a mere 67.50 and the more famous Hope was created. It was so big, you understand, that it could be cut and still the result was quite incredible. Not long after it was cut the diamond went missing, probably stolen during the French revolution and in fact did not turn up again for quite a while.

"It is in this time that many stories, much of which I am sure are quite untrue, started circulating. The diamond passed from owner to owner, from sultan to king, from jeweler to thief. Nobody knows exactly where it was during the years that it was stolen but in 1830 when a diamond much smaller than the original Tavernier, but with a remarkably similar color and texture, was bought by Henry Thomas Hope, an English banker, the Tavernier had been restored to the world. Although from now on it would of course come to be known as the Hope diamond, rather an absurd name considering the fate that had befallen its owners to date.

"At the turn of the century it was purchased as a gift for a young lady, Evalyn Walsh McLean the wife of Ned McLean. Ned owned the Washington Post and the Cincinnati Enquire and paid an incredible $185,000 from the current owners Cartier. It is Mrs. McLean that still owns this incredible diamond and good luck to the woman but it is not there that the story ends."

He stubbed out his cigarette and took a long drink before wiping the corners of his mouth. He now had my full attention. I had a good idea where he was leading but I decided to remain silent and waited for his next move.

"So far, Mr. Black I have not told you anything that you could not easily have discovered for yourself. A few hours in the Central Manhattan Library for instance or perhaps a few telephone calls around the more knowledgeable scholars of our great nation. However it is not the Hope diamond that interests me."

"It's not?" I said in mock surprise.

"What it does not tell you in the history books, and this is probably because it is still as yet unconfirmed by the correct authorities, is that the Hope was in fact one of two cuttings taken from the Tavernier. It was the larger and I am quite sure the most expensive but for the true admirer of the essence of diamonds it was quite certainly the lesser beautiful stone."

The bartender once again replenished our empty glasses but this time we both ignored the man. I was quite engrossed in this story of unchartered history and Coward was an equally enthusiastic storyteller...

"Think about it, Sir. The Tavernier was originally 113 carats and the Hope is a mere 67.5. This does not mean that the second diamond is 45.5, as you are probably aware it does not work quite like that but it is still a considerable stone."

He closed his tiny eyes and took a deep breath, as if savoring the finest fragrance before breathing out and his lips trembled in ecstasy.

"A very fine gem indeed, Sir, a most wonderful gem and what is more its rightful owner is sitting right here."

I smiled. "Is that right?"

The Portly Gangster nodded.

"Can I have a look at this blue rock?"

His smile evaporated and a look of anger flashed across his oversize face. There was a pause, quite a long pause that must have lasted almost five minutes. All the time I stared right at The Coward and he studied my bland face as if searching for the diamond behind my eyes.

Eventually he broke the spell.

"The history of the second diamond is much harder to chart than that of the Hope. For whatever reason it was lost in time and what's lost is sometimes forgotten. But I did it. I found it, Mr. Black, and it took a good deal of my life. Not just a little searching you understand for that I would have hired a man such as yourself, no to find this diamond it needed a lifetime's dedication and that is what I gave it."

117

"What does this have to do with me?" I asked, looking at my watch, "If you found the diamond then everyone's happy."

"Ah well, yes indeed I did find it, Sir, but as things often are in life it was taken away from me. Stolen you could say and not in a night raid by some unsavory character. No the diamond was plundered from me by my own flesh and blood."

I repeated, "And what does this have to do with me?"

"We have now reached our endgame, Mr. Black. You have been a very good listener and now it is time for cards to be laid on the table as it were. Some years ago - how shall I put it? - you were witness to a very significant event. You must remember Sir; it quite irreversibly changed your life?"

"There's been a few cases that beat me - not many but every now and then it does happen and there are many reasons for that. A heavy cold or good beating, no way, but sometimes cases aren't meant to be solved. That said there are very few that have changed my life."

"You really are a character, by Christ you are. You make me want to offer you a deal. How about it Sir, do you fancy coming on board? We'll do what we have to do, and then you can become my personal detective. It'd sure be worth it, just for your little quirks and comments, I'm sure it would."

I looked at him with distaste. "Don't be sure I'm as crooked as I'm supposed to be," I answered. "Hell, you could probably pay me more money than I could ever earn, but I don't like you or your boys and I don't like your methods one bit. Get on with the story or I will walk!"

The man couldn't control his laughter. "A character, that's no lie."

He took a while, but soon enough calmed down, stopped laughing and began again...

"Well Sir, the incident that I have in mind did indeed change your life. The incident in question my good man is the closest you ever got to the big time. It was in all the papers, talked about on the news although your name and that of your associates was curiously absent. That was extremely skillful hiding, Mr. Black and you have my compliments."

I remained silent...

118

The Portly Gangster sighed a heavy sigh, which sounded like the deflation of a rather large rubber dinghy before continuing...

"You may as well quit the mask of innocence, Mr. Black. Of course you already know all about the Diamond because you are in possession of it, or at least you have access to it. I do not doubt that you were not fully aware of its unique history, its incredible value or indeed who it belongs to. But now, Mr. Black you are in full possession of the facts I think maybe it is time to do some real business. I will of course pay you very handsomely, very much more than the market value of the blue rock as you so eloquently put it."

He watched me like a child waiting for candy.

I shook my head. "I'm sorry Coward, you've lost me. I don't know anything about the damn diamond and even if I did..."

"The mask of innocence is very impressive, Mr. Black. Very impressive indeed, maybe you should consider a career in the movies when all of this is over. I have several very good contacts in the Hollywood industry I could put a good word in for you..." he held up a finger, "but it does not wash. This is where we come around to your friend, Dyke Spanner. He has told me all about it you see. How you were the last person to talk to my dying sibling before he was taken to the hospital. There was you, there was Spanner and there was your former boss. Now there is just you, as the others are both no longer with us."

I got to my feet. The Coward put a hand on my shoulder and shook his head.

"He refused to do business until you were present. He said that it was you that held the key to the diamond. That is quite understandable, but there was no need to kill the man. I could quite easily have had that arranged for you and still paid you your dues for the diamond."

"I don't know what Spanner told you but he was lying. I don't know a damn thing about any diamond and..." I leaned over the Coward and took his collar in my fist, lifting it high enough to make his face redder than it already was, "I did not kill him. But I have got a good idea who did. If he refused to do

119

business with you then that seems like a pretty good motive to me."

I relaxed my grip and started to walk away.

"I have a witness Mr. Black."

I stopped and turned around. The Portly Gangster was smiling widely and patted the seat. My eyes narrowed as a wave of anger washed over me. I took a deep breath and once again sat down.

"Yes indeed, you do remember Audrey don't you Sir? As you already know he is in rather a bit a trouble with the law enforcement boys but..." he opened his palms,"...deals can be done. You see Dyke Spanner refused to sell the diamond. You tried to persuade him but he would not budge. I don't suppose that you meant to kill him, but your attempts were repeatedly knocked back and it just happened. Audrey saw you do it..."

"Audrey is a no good murderous punk, he'd be laughed out of court."

"As did Miss Marlow, although I am sure she would not want to testify."

And it was now that his grin got wider and he beamed at me like a wicked child.

"So if you killed her also to shut her up," he sighed deeply. "Well that may be just enough to convince the most hardened doubter."

This time I got up and did not turn back. I heard Coward's parting shot which was, "Think about it Black. Don't be hasty there is a lot at stake here. I will be in touch."

But I was too mad to think straight and I just walked right out of the Wyatt Earp and kept on walking until I was too tired to walk any longer.

Chapter Fourteen – Liam Tighe

If anyone had been following me they would have had it easy as I was taking no precautions. I was way too mad to bother about double backing on myself or looking in shop windows for surreptitious tourists. My body was shaking and my mind was spinning which was not good news for self preservation and when I found myself down by the park I took a seat on a bench and smoked five Lucky Strikes. All that achieved was to give me one hell of a sore throat and a raging headache but thirty minutes later, I was back in the land of the living and began to contemplate the worsening situation I found myself in.

It was now patently clear that I had been set up right from the beginning. I was not certain who was part of the set up and who was an innocent bystander, or who had been used in the scam, but this whole thing went right back to the night when Claudia walked into my office and everything after was dubious.

I felt sure that Dyke had been killed by the Portly Gangster for refusing to sell the diamond, but I had little chance of proving this. Instead it looked like I would be chasing my own tale to avert being strapped to the happy chair and sent to sleep. Everything he said was right; I was on the spot with a motive a means and a track record to have carried out the murder myself. Add on a witness in Audrey Daniels who was eager to cut a little slack with the NYPD, backed up by the more believable Marlow and my bacon was in the fryer. With the only alternative to Marlow's testimony being her own murder, which was sure to be another set up to make it look like I had done her in as well. That was the ingenious bit; why else would I follow her here to Woodstock whilst under a restrictive court order not to leave the City. Her body would be cold and the police would be breaking down the door of my hotel suite before I had a chance to do anything about it.

Hell what a mess.

I got to my feet and hurried to the nearest bar that I could find. This time I did pay attention to my surroundings and was fairly sure that I had not been followed. This was another thing puzzling me, where was Weeny Jung Ping? I passed on that question and ordered a cognac but received a brandy. I shrugged and took a booth in a corner keeping a close eye on anyone who passed through the door.

The more that I thought about the meeting with Coward the more the mess got dirtier and dirtier. This was not just about the death of Dyke Spanner anymore and that was what scared me. This was now about a large chunk of my life that I had left behind ten years ago. It wasn't just the Shadow Man Detective Agency that I had turned my back on in 1935 it was one of the most famous gangland hits of the era. Me, Dyke and Terry had not supposed to be in the Palace Chop House when Dutch Schultz, Lulu Rosencrantz, Abe Landau and Otto Berman were hit and with skillful maneuvering and a lot of string pulling, we managed to not be there. Terry was dealt with in a way in which we had become accustomed and Dyke Spanner and I erased our presence. As far as I was aware there was not another person except Hermeez Wentz that knew we had been there.

Apart from one. The one that Coward failed to mention and therefore either didn't know about or was pulling a hell of a bluff. That one was the Irishman that I wanted to forget. The Irishman was called Liam Tighe.

The first time that I met Liam Tighe, I was left convinced that he was insane. Crazy as it sounds he was a remarkably likeable man considering he was an unabashed racist, sexist, violent thug. He appeared to live in a fantasy world where he was a cross between Nietzsche's Superman and Hitler's dream of the ultimate Aryan. No taboo was too risqué and no subject was not fair game for his narrow opinionated ramblings that although alone were disgusting, were delivered in such a comic way in that they regularly brought a smile to your face where there should only have been a scowl.

He was a small, squat man with a shaved head, his round face covered in light, brown stubble and his big, happy eyes dark brown. He usually wore a smart, black suit with a bright orange waistcoat underneath. This was kept out of sight and was his own tribute to his heroes of Ulster. He also carried a pistol in his pocket and was not afraid to brandish it at the most inappropriate of times.

I was manning the office of the Shadow Man Detective Agency alone. It was lunchtime and the others had gone out for a slap up meal, leaving me to man the telephone and read the newspapers unbothered. There was a knock at the door and in walked Liam Tighe. He was carrying a parcel and placed it on the desk, before looking suspiciously around him. He put his bottom lip over his top one and sunk his head into his shoulders before asking where Terry was.

"He's out for lunch," I said. "Can I leave him a message?"

Tighe lit up a roll-up cigarette and held it between his forefinger and thumb pointing inwards, sucking the smoke deep into his lungs with his eyes closed before putting his head back and exhaling.

He then looked at me and shook with laughter.

"Get your money on Eastern Purple today in the two-thirty. It's got Marcus on him and he's carrying six pounds less than last month when he fuckin' stormed home. He won by twenty lengths that day. Really, twenty lengths!"

He pulled a Racing Post out of his inside pocket and placed it on the desk. There was a red ring around the two-thirty race and he jabbed at it with his stumpy finger.

"That is the easiest money you'll earn all week. It's home and hosed believe me. It's going down in class to gain a bit more experience and then it will be going for the big ones later in the year."

"Have you backed it?" I asked.

He shook his head. "Nah, I'm not betting today," and he pulled a slip of paper from his pocket, unfolded it and held it towards me. "Look, I've got fifty billies here. Number five, five to one, ten bucks to win," He again laughed out loud, raising a fist in the air and shouted, "Fuck 'em eh? Fuck 'em all!"

I did put a few dollars on Eastern Purple but it would be the last time I backed one of Liam's hot tips. Every day he came into the office he was singing the praises of one horse or another, convinced the race was over before it had begun and every time without fail it trailed home well out of the places. But he did win money. Almost as frequently as his tips failed, he triumphantly held aloft a winning ticket from some other race in which he had backed on the spur of the moment or at random.

Another regular part of Liam's routine was his fantasy forays into the world of buying and selling. One day he would bring in a box of bulbs, the next day it would be drinking glasses and the next day bootleg liquor. He would then allow himself to be bartered down below cost on the precept that he was starting a new venture. Sometimes the demand would be there and there was real money to be made only his supply always dried up before he could make any. He would proudly regale you with his vision of a bright new future, of the Tighe empire that he was building, only to slope in the next day with the disappointing news that he couldn't fulfill your very first order. Unperturbed the next day would herald the bright new dawn of some other doomed venture.

The box that he laid on the desk that very first day was full of cigars, fine Cuban cigars and I bought the lot for a very reasonable price.

"Fuckin' Cubans, eh. Bastards!" he said and pulled a face as if he had sucked a particularly bitter fruit. "Not as bad as the fuckin wops though are they? Eh? Eh?"

He leaned a bit closer towards me, tucking his shirt back in his trousers as he spoke, "If it was up to me I'd take a few boys and go knock on all the doors of those fuckin' shit holes in the Lower East Side," he motioned as he was talking, "I'd say right you've got one hour to get all your shit together and be on a plane or a boat back to wherever it is you come from. Same goes for the niggers, the spicks, the Jews, the gooks and the fuckin Pope lovers. Send 'em all back to the fuckin' jungle or wherever it is they're from and if they don't go we should burn their fuckin' houses to the ground. That'll teach 'em, eh, for coming here and fuckin' our women."

I said nothing, shaking my head and sighing inwardly when Terry and boys returned. Forgetting about his tirade Tighe raised his arms and gave Terry Shadow a great big bear hug.

I then listened in amazement as he and Liam had a long conversation about how the Irishman was helping an old African

124

lady that lived in the ground floor flat of his tenement block. Incidentally, the flat was in the Lower East Side. He had been going round for the last two weeks, every day and cooking for her, buying her groceries and cleaning the flat. In the same sentence he denigrated blacks for being 'filthy, disgusting motherfuckers' and smiled fondly as he recalled the over proof dark rum that she had sent back from relatives that she had given him as a gift.

He went on and on and on and we were all convinced he was as close to a mad man as you can safely be but then we learnt to look forward to his visits. We disagreed with pretty much all of his politics, his views on the world and his attitude to women but yet he always brought a smile to our faces and never appeared to once threaten the real world.

Until one morning when the Tribune hit the mat and he was there for all to see on the front page.

Right until the last time I ever saw him, Liam Tighe denied that he did that terrible thing to that young girl and I guess I believed him. I shouldn't have, none of us should have done, he fantasized crazily about doing something similarly nasty every time we met, but when it had actually happened he broke up.

I think we would have offered our support whatever the financial situation. After all, Terry and Liam were real tight, and Terry was a kind hearted kind of guy in a strange sort of way. But when the family organization came knocking on the door and peeled off ten big ones and put them in Terry's greasy hand with a promise of much more to come. Well it kind of sealed the friendship and Liam was assigned twenty four hour protection.

That was what we were doing there that night at the Pork Chop House when Dutch Schultz got whacked. It now seems a hell of an irony getting caught up in a gangland hit whilst on the payroll to protect a body from exactly that kind of operation. But the contract out on Liam was not from anywhere near as high up and we had holed up in the Garden State for the last few weeks, so the location was purely coincidental.

And now I was forced to confront that day again. I thought that I could forget it, the day Liam Tighe fled to

Argentina, but now it was on my mind that he might just have fled with a little bit more than his family's stock of white powder.

When the bar closed up at two thirty I was about to get back in my rental car and drive all the way back to Manhattan, but I had had far too much to drink and I felt exhausted so I walked back to the hotel. I hoped that after a good night's sleep everything would be clearer in my head.

I stumbled into the hotel and made my way slowly up the stairs to my room on the third floor. Feeling well lubricated with too much alcohol and frazzled with the night's revelations, I took a blazing hot shower to clear my mind for sleep. It warmed me up and made my body feel a little better but I was still so tired, so very tired and was sure I would be asleep the moment my head hit the pillow.

Unfortunately, it did not get that far.

When I finished toweling myself dry and ambled through to the bedchamber, I felt a large arm around my neck and a heavily smelling handkerchief pushed over my mouth and nose. I tried to fight it off but one or two inhalations of the handkerchief and my strength drained quickly away and unconsciousness came a little quicker than I had even imagined.

Chapter Fifteen – Night Visitor

It felt like I had been sleeping for days.

I knew I was sleeping in a nice, warm, comfortable bed, but I had no idea where and no conception of for how long. Dreams can sometimes be guidance but not with me, I can quite often have three or four epic dreams in the space of a couple of hours. Whole lifetimes are lived on the grandest scale and minutest detail yet if I wake and take a look at the clock barely enough time to boil an egg has elapsed.

This time was no different. Ever since Claudia had walked through my office door, she had featured strongly in my vivid dreams, and then Marlow, and sometimes the both of them. They were the weirdest yet the most exciting dreams. The kind that make you really disappointed when you wake up, leaving you feeling that you have lost a chunk of your life forever.

I heard the chinking of keys. I awoke to see the door open and in walked the frame of a tall, beautiful woman. The lights were switched on and stood before me was Marlow.

I sat up in bed and rubbed my eyes. I couldn't believe what I saw; she was there as large as life, wearing that same dressing-gown from a few nights earlier. She had a huge smile on her face and came running towards me. Before I knew it she had her arms around me and was showering me in kisses.

I pushed her gently away and looked into her sparkling green eyes. "Marlow," I said. "Are you all right? How did you get in here?"

She smiled nervously and held the keys in her hand. "Oh Errol, I'm so glad you're here," she replied. "I thought that you'd never come."

I rubbed my eyes and sat up in bed, unable to take all of this in. I had so many questions I had to ask her, so many things that I needed ironing out in my mind and yet all that I could think about was how beautiful she looked and how much I would like to show her how I had missed her.

Marlow smiled, tears in her eyes, but she looked cold. "Are you all right Errol, did they hurt you?"

"I'm fine baby, don't worry, I'm fine," I said, and then took a few moments to clear my mind of hurdles before saying, "Marlow there's a hell of a lot of questions you need to answer and you need to answer them well."

She slowly caressed my hand and sniffled. Then she took a deep breath and nodded her perfect head so that her red, curly locks bobbed across her painfully sweet face. And then she began to answer the questions. I fired them thick and fast, one after the other and sat back digesting exactly what she had to say, how she said it and how she reacted to suggestions that I made.

I listened to everything Marlow said. I listened intently and I wanted desperately to believe her, but I was still extremely sceptical.

She insisted the original case was not a set up. At least not by her, she felt genuine worry for Claudia and wanted the situation clearing up. The fact that the trail led right to the murder of my former partner was a huge and unforeseen coincidence. She confessed candidly to being the lover of Dyke Spanner, although this was a separate issue to Claudia and to George Ferriby that she had felt no reason to tell me. Staying with that theme she strongly denied being the cut out for The Coward, as Woo Wang and later Weeny Jung Ping had insisted and also denied ever working with or for The Coward or Audrey Daniels or anybody regarding Dyke. As far as she was concerned he was her lover and nothing more. They met by chance at a show on Broadway.

But of course all these paths would eventually cross each other and that was when she began to tell lies. She was devastated when she found out Dyke had been killed and that she had been so close to the incident and went into instant shock, although that was not to diminish in any way on our night together she added hastily. Of course one burning question that I had to ask again was why Daniels had called at her apartment and why did she instantly get scared if she didn't know him?

"Dyke never fully confided in me. If you knew him as well as you say you do you would know that he wouldn't do that however good you were in bed. But he did tell me that people were after him, real bad people that wanted to kill him and if they saw me with him would want to kill me too. That must have been why that killer called me up and now it freaks me out even more.

"Dyke tried so hard to contact you, Errol. He told me you were business acquaintances and that he didn't want to see any harm come to you. Unfortunately, whenever he got in touch you were out, and wherever he went nobody knew where to find you. He tried, Errol, he tried desperately to warn you and that's certainly why he's no longer here. I'm sure it was his constant talking of you that led me to think about Claudia hiring a detective. You sounded like just the kind of guy she needed."

Marlow started to weep, resting her head on my chest. The more emotional she got, the more she began to convince me she was telling the truth.

"Take your time sweetheart, take your time. There's no rush."

I got her a drink of water and she gulped it down hurriedly.

"Was Dyke killed by The Coward because he was trying to warn me off?" I asked nonchalantly.

"Yes, I think so. They must have known that he was trying to approach you and they wanted to get him out of the way. He refused to do a deal with them. You know, a deal to hand you over for a king's ransom. And so...and so they sent a contract killer to send him into the big sleep."

Again Marlow could not control her floods of tears.

I lit up a Lucky with my small, metal-plated lighter and inhaled deeply. A thick cloud of smoke filled the room as I exhaled. Jeez I could do with a drink right now. Meanwhile Marlow was gradually composing herself again.

"Why didn't you tell me all this, the other night? Hell, you were so evasive, keeping everything close to your bosom. Then I could of thought things over a little better. Instead of being in this damned mess."

"I'm sorry, Errol, I didn't know what to do, I was frightened of what these people would do to me. If they could kill a man like Dyke, then they could surely get to me but as far as I could work out they were unaware of my link to either Dyke

129

or you. I don't know, I guess I thought that if you met me in Manhattan you could take me away from all this but first I needed to think. And that was when they struck and brought me here.

"You still could, Errol. The other night I was not in full possession of the facts but now after a couple of days here I think maybe I am. How could I get it for them? Me, being a mere innocent girl, but you, Errol. You could do a deal I am sure, you could sell this blue diamond and we could go and live miles away from here."

Marlow pushed herself close to me, rubbing her hand up and down my leg. She looked absolutely ravenous and I was so tempted to just forget everything and take her there and then. I looked at her beautiful face and our mouths met. We kissed passionately, but before it got any further she pulled away.

"You do have the diamond don't you, Errol. The Coward is right isn't he?"

I ignored the question and again moved closer to Marlow, kissing her luscious, red lips. She kissed me back, but then again pulled away.

"It's very important, Errol. He will not just give up on this. He has told me all about it. He has spent most of his life and he has covered the four corners of the world for this stone. He won't just give up on it and right it off you know that don't you? You must have it, you must have."

She looked at me, her eyes deep and hopeful. She reminded me of that little kitten she had back in the apartment in Brooklyn, all innocent and dependent. I knew, of course, she was nothing of the sort. She was highly independent and a very cunning lady.

"What happened when Coward's boys pinched you? Why didn't they kill you, like they killed Dyke?"

Marlow looked away and stood up. She made sure to avoid eye contact and dabbed her forehead. "Clearly they thought that I'd make good bait. It makes perfect sense doesn't it? They agree a meeting where you can rescue me in exchange for the diamond. That's why you came isn't it, Errol, to rescue me from their evil clutches?"

130

Or maybe you were bait for some other reason, lady. Maybe you were a foil for me to come and complete the second half of their big sting. I would travel all the way to Woodstock to murder the only living witness to my earlier killing of Dyke Spanner. Apart from wanted felon, Audrey Daniels of course, making his confession all the more believable.

I finished my cigarette and stubbed it out in the ashtray provided. Fumbling around in my trouser pockets, I realized it had been my last one. Marlow duly obliged, pulling a fresh packet from her gown pocket and offered one to me. I took the packet, and she lit one up for me.

"Sure it is sweetheart, that's why I came. So is that still the deal, I give them the diamond and we walk free together in the morning with a big bag of money?"

Again she sat down at my side, her confidence seemingly restored. She smiled and looked thoughtful for a while before again opening her mouth.

"That's the deal that they're expecting. I overheard them all talking, they said that a couple of days here in captivity and you would see sense. But like I said before, Errol, why don't we sell the diamond. Get rid of the pesky gem and then we can leave together, we can got to Hawaii, Tahiti, Australia even and start a new life together?"

I smiled and put a hand on her cheek, softly but with menace.

"There's one other thing that's been puzzling me," I said looking at Marlow's hands.

She recoiled slightly and moved away.

"How did you get in here? You being a prisoner and all, and yet here you are with a set of keys. Let me guess," I continued, winking an eye at an increasingly uncomfortable looking Marlow. "You slipped them out of the guard's pocket, while he wasn't looking?"

I chuckled out loud, and looked in admiration at Marlow.

Marlow put on a smile, not an all too convincing smile, but a smile nevertheless. She shrugged her shoulders and blinked her eyes. "You know me Errol, ever the opportunist? I just saw my chance and took it. Guess what, I've also got one for the front door. We can be out of here, Errol. All you got to do is tell me you got the diamond. Tell me you've got it, hidden away somewhere, and we can go."

She took a deep breath. "So, Errol, have you got it? Have you got the diamond?"

"Come to bed darling, we'll talk some more later," I urged and undid the tie around Marlow's waist. She pulled away and the gown swung open, displaying her magnificent body, covered only by a red, lacy basque. I licked my lips and smiled. "Come on baby, you want to get in here?" I asked, lifting up the covers making a space for her beside me.

Marlow looked confused. "Errol, I'm desperate for you, but do you think this is a good idea. Soon enough they're going to notice that these keys are missing. If we stay here we're simply wasting time. We can't afford to take any risks or we'll end up with nothing." She leant over towards me and kissed me on the tip of my nose. "Come on, brave soldier, tell me where the diamond is and we can leave together."

I sighed deeply and lit up yet another cigarette. It was time to raise the stakes.

"What if I don't have the rock?" I asked. "If I have absolutely no idea where it could be found. What happens then, you still want to go to Tahiti?"

A look of more concern filled Marlow's face. "Of course I do," she reassured, not a hint of happiness showing. "You know I just want to be with you. But Errol, you do have it don't you?"

"I'll tell you what I think," I stood up and began to dress myself hurriedly. "I think the money that that stone will bring is your main concern. Me, well maybe I'm a bit of a bonus, but certainly the loot is your main concern. You told me Dyke wouldn't do a deal with Coward, but what's to stop you? My ass for a piece of jewelry..."

` "Errol, how can you say this?" screamed Marlow. She rushed towards me and put her arms around me, clinging desperately onto my waist. "You know that it's you I want. You know I love you, I've loved you since the first moment I met you."

"Yeah, sure you do," I said, whilst fastening my belt. "Maybe you do, but then maybe you loved Dyke. He couldn't quite deliver what you really want, but I can."

I chuckled. "Or you think I can."

"Errol, stop this, you're hurting me. I want us to be together. That's what I want more than anything in the whole world, but don't you see, we must have the diamond - it's our passport out of this dreadful world."

"I'm sorry," I relented. "I know you're right. Don't worry I've got the diamond nicely hidden away. You want to know where I put it?"

Marlow nodded eagerly.

"Yeah, sure you do. Well, it's in a safety deposit box in the Financial District. There's a key in my lock-up, just off Broadway, you got that. It's been there a good number of years," I scratched my head. "As soon as I locate my shoes," I looked around the place stupidly, "we can get...er...out o...f here and get the plane tickets. Oh," I looked at Marlow. "I forgot, you'll have to change too, won't you?"

Before I'd even finished my sentence Marlow had dropped her gown to the floor. She slowly un-popped her basque and shook herself free of it, displaying the most beautiful sight in the whole world. A sexy smile filled her face and her eyes twinkled as she seductively caressed her shapely breasts before me.

"I'm sorry Errol," she whispered. "I can contain myself no more. I'm afraid we're going to have to risk it," She breathed heavily and started to unfasten the belt I had tightened only a moment earlier. "Come on Errol, I want you, I'm desperate to have you..."

Chapter Sixteen – Reunion

I awoke with a smile and I reached out to cuddle up to Marlow. At first not quite realizing, I reached out a little further, but she was not there. I sat up and rubbed my eyes sleepily. My first thought was that they had realized she had gone and had come in here to find her, but there was no signs of a struggle and I doubted that I would have slept through if that was happening. My next thought was that it had all been a dream, she had not really walked into this room last night only in my vivid imagination.

A shiver went down my spine and I reached out, fumbling for a light switch that wasn't there.

My head felt foggy, my mouth dry and with a nasty taste and my body ached. I found all this out as I threw the sheets back and slowly climbed out of bed, heading towards a floor to ceiling set of red, velvet drapes. My feet sunk into the thickly carpeted floor which tickled and soothed. I pulled the drapes aside half expecting to be confronted with a solid wall, only to see the moon shining through a thick, barred window. The sky was clear and the stars were all out illuminating a beautiful mountain landscape.

The moon lit up the room, revealing that it was quite well furnished with a bedside cabinet either side of the double bed, a dresser, a full-length wardrobe and a desk with telephone and writing equipment.

I found the lights and tried the telephone. It was deader than Dyke Spanner but a lot less mystery, as the expertly snipped cable under the desk gave it away. The door, that I imagined Marlow opening and sauntering through sometime in the night, was the only exit from the room. I guessed that it would be locked, but guessed wrong as it swung freely open at the first turn of the handle.

The cold night air hit me and knocked the surprise right out of me, which was a lot more pleasant than the fist that knocked the wind right out of me. It came from nowhere, putting me on my backside and was followed by a kick, which caught me right under the chin and put me on my back. I lay there for what seemed like hours staring up into the star filled sky, searching out the constellations that every child learns at nursery and then forgets forever, but was probably no more than a couple of seconds, before I was pulled back into the sitting position. I found myself face to face with an angry sumo wrestler of a man who patted me down before grabbing me by my neck and lifting me onto my feet. He then smiled a gap toothed grin and spun me around before gently shoving me back through the door.

I heard him say, "And don't wake me again before morning!" and the door slammed shut but was not locked.

I didn't recognize the man although I assumed he was one of Coward's goons. I was wondering just how long I had been held captive here. I was not wearing a watch and there was no sign of a clock so there was no way of knowing. By the look of the sky, it was still night out there and the feel of my chin it was not still the same night that I had been kidnapped. But why had I not had any further contact with the Coward? Was this all part of a plan to wear me down in the hope that I would become more forthcoming with the diamond? If so I should have expected another interrogation by now.

This led me to believe that my night visitor was not a dream after all which threw up two possibilities. Either Marlow had been used and then murdered by the Portly Gangster, with me conveniently out of the way so not to throw a spanner in the works. If this was the case then I would expect to soon be deposited into the hands of the police with a lot of damning evidence planted at the scene. The other possibility was that Marlow was in fact working alongside The Coward, either under duress or with compliance, and the information I gave her last night was now being checked out with me being held here as insurance.

I shook my head as the possibilities scorched my mind.

I stood up and put on a pair of trousers. If I was going to consider getting out of here, I wasn't going to do it in my boxer shorts. The trousers weren't mine and neither was the shirt and sweater that were laid out on the dresser but I put them on as well. Once fully dressed I got up and prowled around the room,

135

searching for anything that could constitute a tool or weapon to aide my escape.

I checked the drawers, under the bed, on the window sill. There was nothing that could tackle the bear of a man outside the room. Even if he wasn't armed and I hadn't been locked away after being poisoned by chloroform, I wouldn't have fancied my chances. Where was I going to run to anyway, I didn't even know where the hell I was?

Maybe it would have made more sense to just get undressed again and get back into the bed. But I had an uneasy feeling that if I did that I might just not awaken again and I was damned if I was going to lie down and die. Instead I took a couple of deep breaths, moved the dresser so it was right in front of the door and ripped the rather bulky telephone from the desk. I then opened the door and stepped outside.

This time I was ready for the cold blast of night air that hit me and I sucked it deep into my lungs. I was also ready for the sumo wrestler who quickly appeared in front of me.

I held up a hand quickly as the wrestler prepared to lunge.

"I need to use the bathroom," I said, and took a step backward into the open doorway.

"Listen to me Mister," he said, his impatience thickly laced on every syllable. "You need to piss you use the bucket. You need to take a dump you use the bucket. And if you interrupt me once more..."

I did interrupt him -and in a way that I'm sure he didn't anticipate- by swinging my other arm that held the telephone and smashing it into the side of his head. That sure knocked the impatience out of him and I further interrupted him by plastering his nose across his face with my head. That sure made my headache worse, although I didn't scream out loud like the sumo wrestler did.

I then grabbed him by the scruff of his neck and flung him through the doorway into the darkened room. I followed him in and slammed the door shut.

He had tumbled into the dresser and was lying in a heap on the floor. He quickly regained his composure, but not quick

136

enough to prevent me aiming a kick into the place where every man dreads being kicked. Either I missed the vital spot or he was stronger than I hoped, whichever he now got back to his feet and dived at me his big bear-like arms mauling as he lunged. We both flew backwards crashing into the wardrobe that fell on its side and landed in a heap.

The wrestler was first on his feet and swung a massive fist that caught me just under the rib cage and wracked my body with pain. As he swung, again I picked up a bedside cabinet and crashed it wildly into him. It must have been more solid than it looked; either that or he had a different pain spot to the rest of us, as he dropped to his knees and just stayed there. I lifted the small cabinet over my head and dropped it again into the wrestler, this time onto the back of his head, and he collapsed to the nice, soft carpet. He wasn't dead but would not be sumo wrestling for a while.

I left him tied to the bed with electrical cord and for a third time opened the door and stepped out into the night. The moonlight made me feel as vulnerable as the borrowed clothes did uncomfortable but it also gave me good vision in this alien of place. It appeared that I had been held captive in outhouse, one of many that were scattered around the main building. It looked like a typical country retreat owned by many celebrities, tycoons and gangsters alike and had all the views of the Catskills and the greenery that the City so lacked.

The main house was huge with two storeys above ground level due to it being on stilts. There was a large gravel forecourt where several swanky cars were parked and the many outhouses formed a semi-circle around it. A long, tree-lined driveway led from the front of the house and had many narrower offshoots that spider-webbed over the expansive grounds. The rest of the land was finely manicured gardens with colorful flowerbeds and huge shrubs and bushes.

It was difficult to appreciate exactly how big it all was as the land undulated and from standing level there was always a hill blocking your view. This was to my distinct advantage as there was always somewhere that was out of sight and on foot there would be many hiding places.

Feeling ridiculous, I crouched down and scanned the ground all around me, listening for the faintest sound and searching out the slightest movement. I felt confident that nobody would be looking for me for quite a while. I had gagged the sumo wrestler and he would hopefully not be found until morning. By then I would be back in New York City and the game would have changed full circle.

The whole complex was deadly silent and every footstep on the gravel made my heart beat faster. I quickly made it to the grassy area and hopped from tree to tree down the long, long driveway. It wasn't long before I was out of sight of the main buildings and my confidence quickly returned. I could see where the estate ended and the open road back to the City began, with only a ten-foot high fence, probably electrified, or a guardhouse to breach. I could not tell whether it was manned but would have to assume that it would be.

I took my chances on the fence, and to my surprise and great pleasure, it wasn't electrified. I quietly climbed to the top, swung my legs over and shimmied down the other side into the heavy undergrowth. I broke a twig as I landed in a bramble bush. As well as giving me a nasty cut, it confirmed that the guard-house was indeed manned as a pair of torch wielding, uniformed sentries appeared.

I quickly got to my feet and feeling the bright glow of a torch on my face set off running down the road as fast as my heavy legs would allow me. I kept on running and running and running. When I could run no more I stopped, bent over with a hand on my hip struggling for breath and looked over my shoulder.

There was nothing.

Smiling to myself, I took a deep breath and turned around, only to be blinded by a bright light and feel a terrible pain on my right side. The car screeched to a halt and a man got out. He helped me to my feet and it was only when I smiled at him and assured him that I was all right that I realized who it was.

I wiped my brow and sat back in the comfy passenger seat of Stan's car. My heart was eventually getting back to normal, but my mind constantly ran over and over the events of the past few days. I kept hearing Jake's words, "No more walking into homicides" over and over again. It awoke a perverse sense of humor in me. I looked over at Stan. He smiled back keeping a good speed up. I wasn't exactly sure where we were heading but it looked like we were deeper in mountain territory now, possibly as far north as the Adirondacks.

Stan carried on driving looking at the road all the time. "So," he said. "Errol Black, what's the story buddy?"

"It's a long one," I smiled. "A very long one indeed."

"Do you want to talk about it?"

I shrugged. "Why not?"

I gave Stan a story - not the real story - but a story nonetheless. I told him that I was on a missing person's racket and that my case had led me right to Woodstock, taking the utmost care to miss out any mention of the diamond. I told him about Marlow, she being the missing person, but I was careful not mention any names. He listened and nodded a few times, but I got the general impression that he wasn't all that interested. He certainly gave me nothing away.

"I could have killed you just now," he said calmly. "What were you doing out here? You're quite a way from Woodstock now, is this where you think the girl is?"

I shook my head. "Not anymore. Maybe I did. It doesn't matter anymore, now I just need to get back to the City."

"First you need to get freshened up, you look terrible. And you need a good meal and a change of clothes."

"I guess we're even now?" I ventured.

"Not quite," he said vaguely.

There was a long silence between us as Stan continued to drive. I wasn't at all sure where we were headed but it was a beautiful drive in the bright moonlight. I realized that I had not asked Stan one single question. He had questioned me for the last fifteen minutes without a second thought and I had not done the same, despite the odd hour and the strange coincidence of his knocking me down.

139

Stan noticed me looking a little curiously out of the window and looked across at me.

"I'm going to take you to my house," he said matter of factly. "Don't worry, you're not going to be a prisoner with us, but I'm sure there's a lot of things been going on the last few days that you just want to forget. You probably want a long, hot bath, or a dip in the whirlpool. We'll give you a good old traditional Italian meal and a comfortable bed for as long as you want." He paused and sighed, as if embarrassed with himself. "No doubt you'll want to call someone, eh? Whatever you need to do, that's fine. Don't worry, you can leave whenever you please. Anything you need you only have to ask. To answer your question, Errol Black, we are far from even, you have saved my life and I have run you over. In my book that is not a debt repaid but a debt deepened."

And at that he continued to drive well into the night.

We arrived at the Cortene household a good deal later. I was escorted into the house, shown to another beautiful bedroom, which I was told to use as my own and then given a very brief tour around the glorious house.

I bathed myself in the spacious bathroom, which was carpeted with Persian rugs and decorated with ornate furnishings. I had a little dip in the hot tub and then settled down for a soak in the steaming, bubble-filled bath. Feeling refreshed and relaxed, I lay back on the bed and must have passed out immediately. When I awoke it was morning; the birds were singing and sun was streaming through the drapes.

I sat up in bed and rubbed my eyes. I dressed myself in a brand new pair of pants and shirt and tie that had been so neatly laid out for me by the young, black maid and went down to breakfast.

The food was marvelous, just like my mother used to make for me when I was a boy. Unfortunately, I dined alone with only the maids for company attending to my every need. There were several vases of fresh flowers on the huge table but one stood out in particular. I had seen it before, not the vase, but the arrangement. The exact arrangement.

I mulled it over with another slice of buttered toast swilled down with strong, fresh coffee. To my surprise, I was then given a free rein around the house. Bernice, a short, plump lady who appeared to be in charge of the maids informed me that I would be left to my own devices. Mr. Cortene would be pleased if I would take lunch with him before I made my way back to the City. Of course I agreed. Well you don't refuse the Mr. Cortenes of this world do you?

After a walk through the grounds, I relaxed on my King-size bed and started to go over things in my mind. This was certainly an unexpected twist. Once I had climbed over the fence I had run like the wind without looking over my shoulder. There was absolutely no way that I could tell how far or for how long I had run but I didn't think it was far. That being the case then it was a hell of a coincidence that Cortene happened to be hurtling along in his Sedan at exactly the same time, in exactly the same place. There had to be more to it than that - I was sure of it - but then what solution could there possibly be? I had saved Cortene's life and I'm sure he was grateful but that was no reason for him to take any more notice of me than I had of him. Considering who he was there was less reason. No, it had to be a coincidence.

I thought back to the questions he had asked me on the drive over here. At first, he came across as highly curious but as I fed him the mundane tale of a PI on an upstate missing persons wild goose chase his interest faded. I wasn't sure if he believed what I had told him, to be honest I very much doubted it, but he didn't seem to mind and so we left it at that.

The preoccupation of all the Cortene's once we arrived back also puzzled me. Where was this traditional Italian hospitality? This wasn't how Jimmy Cagney did it. I suppose it was very early in the morning - five thirty when we had walked through the door - I had found this out the moment I walked through the door and the great old grandfather clock was chiming away. That said there seemed to be a lot of activity without me being involved. The maids were rushing around, the front door was never still and I could hear vehicles arriving and departing all morning. They were probably all going about their business like most mafia families did.

141

I was surprised to be left on my own and took advantage by snooping around the various corridors of the house. Every now and then I would bump into what looked like an extra from *Scarface* and they would merely tip their fedoras and pat me on the back. I was a regular hero although I was not sure just how long it was going to last.

Upstairs everything seemed silent. I don't know what I was looking for but for some reason I couldn't stop myself. There was something not quite right about all of this and my curiosity was growing. Checking each room as quietly and inconspicuously as possible, I searched for any sign or clue but as I have learnt many times when you don't know what you are looking for it is a lot harder to find it.

I came across a room with the door slightly ajar. Like all the others, I poked my head in and took a good look around. Shrugging to myself I thought just how silly I was being. What on earth was I hoping to achieve?

Just as I was about to turn around and head back downstairs I felt the hammer blow of recognition. Suddenly I remembered and when I thought about what it meant I wished that I hadn't. The feeling that comes across you when your mind suddenly locates that missing piece of jigsaw can either send a chill down your spine or a tingle of excitement. This was a mixture of the two but the chill was a great bucket of ice and the excitement was the kind of thrill a crazy would get before furthering his death wish on a treacherous ski slope.

I didn't really get time to cogitate my discovery. It was like one of those moments in your life that appears to be in slow motion, that later seems like hours and is in fact less than a second. I was still in the process of closing the door back to its original position when I froze. She was suddenly stood there right in front of me.

There was another door from inside the bedroom - I guess it was an en-suite - and she had just wandered right through it. The second hammer blow in a minute hit me like a thunderbolt. I must have looked like one of those far-eastern fish that constantly swim around the tanks in the downtown

142

aquarium with their huge mouths wide open and their ugly faces blank of any expression.

And she was smiling.

Without realizing it so was I.

And she was in my arms, all curves, scent and giggles.

Was nothing ever as it seems? I tried to think about what to do next but this embrace was taking all my energy. What did break it up was the appearance of the maid, Bernice, who looked shocked and frightened at the sight of me.

"Oh I'm sorry, Mr. Black, I'm under strict instructions not to let anyone in here. Mr. Cortene would not be very happy."

Before I could attempt to charm the maid into letting me stay, Claudia said, "Oh Bernice, you must let me talk to Errol. He's a very good friend of mine. We won't be long."

The maid stood up defiantly. "But Miss Cortene, I don't want to get into trouble. You need to get some rest and I am under strict instructions. Mr. Cortene was most clear."

I smiled at Bernice and put on my most charming voice, "Come on Bernice. Stan wouldn't mind if we have ten minutes. I saved his life for Christ sakes, I'm a regular hero."

That made her smile, but it didn't last.

A deep sigh and a look of worry still filled Bernice's face as she vacated the room. She shut the door behind her and I sat down next to Claudia.

"Oh Errol, it's so good to see you."

"I know baby. It's great to see you."

She held out her hand and I grasped it tightly.

I frowned. "So your secret's out. That's a big one Miss Cortene, a real big one," I said it a little curtly.

Claudia looked worried. "Oh Errol, please don't get annoyed with me. I thought you'd be really happy to see me again. You like the flowers I just know you do."

"I do like the flowers and yes I am pleased to see you darling, I am," I added, more warmly. "There's just a lot of things I think we need to talk about."

"You're right. There are so many things I must tell you, Errol. You're the only one, you know, the only one."

143

Claudia coughed a nasty, chesty cough and so I got her a drink of water.

"So where do we start?" I asked.

"I'm going to tell you everything right from the beginning. Hopefully, when I've told you, you can take me away from all this." She looked at me desperately and I smile reassuringly at her but my heart sank.

"Okay baby. Away we go, take your time."

"I am the niece of Stanley Cortene of the Cortene Organization. You must have heard of them in your line of business."

"Oh yes, I know the Cortenes."

"Several years ago I was romantically involved with Liam Tighe..."

As soon as she mentioned Liam Tighe my heart sank. There was that name again. Things were starting to come together. There may have been a thousand different strands at the moment but they were coming together. Before long they would be one tight knot.

"We were never accepted as a couple. Mixed-family relationships never are. And if you know the Tighes you will know that their reputation is far from being a good one. I kept getting told never to see him again, but we were close, you know?"

I nodded, not quite understanding where this was all leading.

"Anyway, it was a relationship doomed to failure. Both families did as much as they could to split us up and keep us apart and eventually they succeeded. Liam told me that we had to break it off. He said he was sorry and he loved me...but...we had to finish."

I squeezed Claudia's hand gently as she paused, obviously going over some pretty heavy feelings. She blew her nose, took a deep breath and continued…

"To start with, I thought my family interfered so much because it was Liam. I didn't really understand, but I managed to get over it the best I could. When Liam was accused of doing such a terrible thing to that young girl I thought maybe they had

144

been right all along. I'm well aware what our families are like, don't for one minute think I'm not, but Liam was different he was never really involved with the family organization. Well, that is what I thought.

"From then on every time I got remotely close to a guy my family intervened. He was never good enough for me, he was a scum bag or a waster, never good enough. My brother Mikey once killed a guy who was coming onto me," She shook her head at the thought, "stuck a knife into him nineteen times, one for every year of his life. It was awful..."

What a nice guy.

Tears formed in the corners of Claudia's eyes. I gave her an encouraging hug, but as I glanced at the clock on the wall she realized time was passing on...

"You must understand, Errol, I'm not like them. I'm a normal romantic, fun-loving girl who's just unfortunate to have drug dealers and pimps and god knows what else tucking me in at night instead of a normal family. I tried so many times to get away. So many times.

"Every time, I was brought back by Uncle Stanley or Mikey or Mario or whoever. They kept on telling me I was in danger if I was to leave, that I was the jewel in the family crown, much too delicate to be let out. They said that the rival families would be out to get me. I wasn't allowed to go to college alone, I was escorted there and back everyday, or dancing classes or anything. Whatever I wanted to do must be done here, at the family home." She looked deep into my eyes. "It was a nightmare, Errol, it really was."

I nodded, as compassionately as I could manage, and then she continued further...

"I have run away many times but this time I really thought I had got away. I managed to evade them for six months making a home for myself in Greenwich and finally made a few friends of my own."

"Friends like Marlow," I said.

"Oh my dear Marlow she will wonder where the goodness I have got to. I first met her whilst I was working in the Library. She was studying and asked for my help in locating a whole pile of study books."

She smiled and looked distant as if remembering a fond moment.

"I found the books, we got talking and then we went for some coffee. We must have spent most of the next week in each other's pockets, you know talking and dressing up and going out. Girly things. Sisterly things. She is the best friend I have ever had it was amazing how we just clicked..."

Amazing.

"It was Marlow that introduced me to George." She shuddered at the mention of his name. "It's kind of strange really that it was Marlow that got us together and in the end it was Marlow that so desperately wanted us to part. I guess she saw through him a lot sooner than I did and felt guilty that she had got us together."

She looked at me and smiled, taking my hands in her own and kissing them softly. "I'm glad she did it. If I hadn't been with George then I would never have met you, Errol, so it was worth it."

I pulled my hands away and lit up a cigarette. I had to do something; she was nearly making me blush.

She sighed deeply and continued…

"I should have known it was too good to last. Just when I was worrying about George coming back and for the first time in my life I had other things to worry about than my family, they appeared. I went to sleep last night dreaming happy positive thoughts and woke up a few hours later back here. A prisoner once again."

I looked at Claudia. She was radiant in spite of her distress. The tatty pair of old Levis and a huge, woolly sweater she was wearing did not detract from her beauty one jot. If anything, they enhanced her vulnerability, which made her all the more delicious. She noticed me watching and smiled what she probably took to be a seductive smile but came out more like a shy schoolgirl smiling at her older suitor.

"Errol, do you believe in fate?" she asked me.

"I guess so," I replied, not really thinking about the question.

"I most certainly do. I am sure that it is Fate that has brought us together. It was my destiny to walk into your office that night and for our lives to cross like they did. Maybe we are fated to..."

Her sentence trailed off and she was now lost in her thoughts.

For the next few moments, we sat in silence. It was hard to take it all in and I was sure Claudia was finding it equally confusing my being here. A few things added up: the secretive house lease, Claudia's wealth in spite of a poorly paid job and the whole veil of secrecy she had surrounded herself with. Other things were not so clear; just how Marlow came into all of this and whether there was a connection between my case and the Cortene Organization. I hoped to hell there was not but all of this would have been a hell of a coincidence if that was the case.

My thoughts were broken by the door opening. It was Bernice with an anxious look on her face. "Quick, he's here," is all she said before closing the door again.

I opened the door and found Bernice outside looking red-eyed. Stan Cortene was facing her, his face like thunder. It was clear that he'd just finished giving Bernice a good telling off, catching me coming out of his niece's room in the process.

"Get back in there Bernice and do what I pay you for! Remember, last chance!"

Bernice nodded dutifully, clearly upset and re-entered Claudia's bedroom. Cortene's glance then passed to me.

"I'm afraid that's my fault," I offered. "I just wanted to see Claudia."

"That much is clear," he said, and waited for an explanation. I gave him a quick one about how I had met her in the Manhattan Library where she had been working. How we had immediately struck up a rapport, sharing a love for poetry and classical music and became friends. It was all lies of course, apart from the poetry.

"I hope you don't mind," I said to Stan with an innocent look on my face.

147

Stan smiled, to my relief and patted me on the shoulder. "Of course I don't mind, Errol. Claudia will do well to have a few more friends like you. People like you, good people who care about others are very valuable. Very valuable indeed. It is the scum that has seeped into every walk of life that we must worry about, the evil that is strangling our great country and bleeding the great men and women dry. It is these evil fuckin' putos that I must protect my niece from. If anyone, anyone at all hurts my little girl in any way then I will kill them. I don't mind telling you that."

He stopped and stared right into my eyes. I said nothing but felt terrible, like I was being studied under the microscope. It should have felt better when he smiled but it only felt worse.

"You're a good man, Errol. I know you wouldn't ever hurt her, but from now on she needs rest and a lot of it. She's been through a hell of lot and she's going to have to recover."

Stan began to walk along the corridor. I assumed I was meant to follow him and so obliged.

"Errol, I would like you to take lunch with me. It is the least I can do. If you want to make a telephone call or twenty telephone calls, feel free and please accept my offer of a lift back into the City whenever you feel like it. Come on!"

He patted me on the shoulder again and headed down the corridor. On the way he carried on talking.

"I am pleased that you and my niece are friends. Very pleased. I hope you don't mind, I took the liberty of checking you out a little after our first meeting. I was intrigued. Hell you saved my life without a second thought when it would have been a good deal easier to just get the hell out of there. That is a pretty special person in my book."

"What did you find?" I asked obviously with a little too much trepidation in my voice because Stan laughed and said, "don't worry I didn't find any of your dirty secrets. No I was just curious you understand. I found out where you were staying in Woodstock, I paid your tab and left a good tip. I also found out a little about your case."

Bang!

"You did?"

Stan nodded and rubbed his lips with thumb and forefinger. His ice cool eyes bored holes right through to my soul and I just stood there with a silly grin on my face.

"Look, Errol I don't really want to pry into your business and I wouldn't expect you to tell me all about it when it's got nothing to do with me. Don't look so worried, okay. If you are going around telling people it is a missing person's racket that is fine by me."

"But. There sounds like there is a 'but' coming up somewhere."

"Isn't there always? No, this isn't really a but more of an if," he looked me straight in the eyes, his little pools of ice boring right through me. He sure was a class act exuding a malevolence that was unattainable with simple violence or threat, a malevolence that was entirely his own.

"The 'if' in question regards the Tighe Organization. I very much doubt that this will happen, but if on your investigations you come across the runt of the litter. If, he is back on American soil contaminating us all with his filth and depravity. If, he has dreams of coming upstate. Or even if he simply wants to come back to visit his mother's grave. If. Yes such a lot of ifs, but Errol, if any of these ifs come about," he paused, "I would appreciate it if you would pass it on, do you understand?"

I nodded. "I understand."

"Good," he flashed me a handsome smile and once again patted me on the shoulder. "Come on lets go get some lunch."

We ate lunch. It was fantastic; a real Italian banquet like you get in only the finest establishments in Little Italy only better. The long table was full. All male, all with hearty appetites and most likely all made men. I ate plenty, drank plenty, laughed at their anecdotes funny or not, told a few of my own, strictly not funny and as soon as it was over I was ready to be on my way. Stan had arranged for one of his drivers to take me back to the City. I had talked him out of it telling him it would make more sense for me to take a hire car and drop it off when I got there. The car was waiting outside the house.

149

"I don't know what to say Stan, you've been great," I shook his hand tightly. "Thank you, thank you a lot. And you look after Claudia, you hear me."

Stan shook my hand back. Very firm and strong. "Don't you worry about that," he said. "Come visit us sometime! I'll look forward to it."

"Maybe," I said and walked out of the house.

I got in the car and knew she was there immediately. I don't know if it was her scent or an inner feeling that I had but I knew. She leaned forward and put her head between the two front seats.

"Can we go now?" she asked.

I turned around with a cold look on my face. "We are not going anywhere Claudia. If I take you with me your family will probably kill the both of us."

"But what about Marlow, I must see her."

"Forget Marlow. She's not the friend you think she is. She probably isn't a friend at all."

"Errol, how can you say that? Marlow is my best friend in all the world."

"Marlow is a conniving, manipulative tramp. Just for the record, it was Marlow that was seeing your darling George. She probably wasn't the only one but it was her that I caught him with when you hired me. Not only that but she was also seeing a very good friend of mine who just happened to get murdered. Add me to that list and you get the picture."

"You slept with Marlow?"

"Yes, twice. Three times in fact and that's not all. She's involved in the case that I'm on and I don't mean the infidelity of George Ferriby. This is more to do with murder, kidnap and extortion and Marlow is in it right up to her neck."

"I don't believe you. Why are you saying these things?"

I put my hand to Claudia's cheek and stroked it gently.

"Sweetheart, I'm sorry. Really, I am but it is true. All of it is true. And I truly wish that I could take you back to the City but I can't. Please just get out of the car and go back inside. I'll be in touch I promise."

A solitary tear rolled down her cheek and she leaned over a bit more and kissed me full on the lips. She then opened the car door and got out before going back into the house. I drove off without looking around and my hard on didn't wear off until I hit the City limits.

I considered turning around and going back to Woodstock. I could search the redhead out from the casino and we could spend the day making sweet love with a couple of bottles of champagne and a jazz concerto on full volume. That is how I felt but I resisted and kept heading south towards the City. I hadn't felt this way since I left Casablanca and I wasn't sure who was making me feel worse. Marlow was incredible but it was Claudia that I was falling in love with. I was sure of it.

I didn't think I would ever feel like this again and for the last few days I had successfully convinced myself that I wasn't but when the car door slammed shut and she disappeared inside the Cortene house it was all released. It felt like listening to Dizzy Gillespie do a fifteen-minute solo whilst high on grass, the emotions came rushing to the surface and I was left feeling physically weak and lost.

I pulled over a mile from the City and got out of the car. Twenty push-ups followed by a one minute rest and then twenty more got me gasping for breath. I repeated this two more times, shadow boxed for a further ten minutes and then got back in the car.

Chapter Seventeen – Partnership

I dropped the car off at the rental office and walked the rest of the way. Terence and Mike were still standing guard outside the main office. They confirmed that there had been no sign of trouble. I paid them both a healthy bonus and asked them to carry on their security for a few days more. They happily agreed.

I could hear Ava's typewriter clicking away as I walked through the reception area. I let out a deep sigh and took her in my arms, giving her a long hug. She melted in my arms, every curve wrapping around me.

"Errol, I've missed you, are you all right? You should have telephoned me. I would have arranged some breakfast."

"Hey, hey, slow down sweetheart," I held her at arms distance and winked. "I'm fine darling. I feel tired but I'm still here and I've eaten already. What's been happening, are you okay?"

She relaxed her grip and smiled. "I'm fine now you're back, Errol. Mr. Wilson has been in here for you again. Four times in fact. He said yesterday that if you don't contact him urgently then there may be serious consequences."

"How did he say it? Aggressively? Threateningly?"

"No, nothing like that. More matter of factly. You know as if it was out of his control. He's a very nervous man, scared even, but not threatening at all."

"Why hasn't Hermeez seen him? Is he still not showing his face around here?"

"No, Hermeez has been around," she said. "But Wilson won't talk to anybody but you. He is most insistent."

I lit up a Lucky and inhaled deeply. "Okay darling, arrange a meeting tomorrow."

"In the office, or would it be better in a public place?"

"No, I think the office will suffice. He's not dangerous is he?"

"I don't think so, Errol, he didn't look like he could harm a fly. He's got a very creepy aura about him though."

"Okay darling, the office is fine."

I sat down on the couch, flicking through the weekend's Tribune. The news was pretty much as normal, except for a large article on the Cortene family. Of course, it wasn't a blow by blow account of their Mafiosi activities, more a sycophantic piece on their wonderful contribution to the community. How through many different fields they provided jobs and hope to a decaying society.

I tossed the paper back onto the table.

"What's the latest on the Dragon Bar murders? Is Beech still sniffing around?"

Ava sat down beside me. "He's been in a few times throwing around idle threats with no real weight behind them. Asking me where you were, what you were doing and how long you would be away. You know the usual Beech outbursts."

I nodded in agreement, a wide grin filling my face at Ava's absolute control and ability to frustrate the hell out of the police force. She'd had a good tutor.

"A few days ago he sent Tim Matthews round. He said that they wanted to check the firearms that we hold in the office."

My face changed. "Son of a bitch, did you check it out with Jake?"

"I rang Jake whilst Tim waited. He said it would be better to let them go right ahead."

I blew out a thick cloud of smoke and stubbed the cigarette out in the crystal ashtray on the side table. "And we came out clean?"

"Clean as a whistle. Tim said that there was no possibility of the murder of Dyke Spanner or Woo Wang being committed by any of the weapons here. Of course, this didn't satisfy Beech, he's been grumbling that you could still have the murder weapon with you. Or that maybe you've disposed of it."

I let out a gasp of air and smiled. "That sounds dangerously like slander to me. I hope you made him take it back."

Ava gave me a sparkling smile, showing off her beautifully whiter than white set of pegs. "I passed it on to Jake and he immediately sent a letter of complaint to the New York

153

Police Department. The next day Beech came in personally to apologize. Grudgingly, you know, quite clearly under orders, but an apology nevertheless."

I stood up and went over to the drinks cabinet, pouring myself a large Remy and a small tonic for Ava. She took the glass from my outstretched hand and gulped it down, eager to continue the story.

"How well do you know Weeny Jung Ping?" she asked me, completely changing the mood of the conversation.

I tried not to, but almost certainly did, look puzzled. "Very well, why do you ask?"

"I'm afraid this is the next angle. He too disappeared almost exactly the same time you went upstate. The police went to his shop for routine questioning and everything was locked up. Subtle as ever they decided to have a look anyway, and forced their way in. Tim wouldn't let on the full story, but it sounds like they found something in there which now leads them to suspect he may be the killer."

"Of Dyke and Wang?"

"So it seems. I don't know if they found the gun or plan, or what, but for the last week the papers won't leave it alone." She reached into her drawer and tossed me a couple of newspapers.

ANTIQUES DEALER LINKED TO MURDER MYSTERY. TONGS POSSIBLY RESPONSIBLE *-Today police revealed that a local Chinatown Antiques Dealer has been discovered to have links to the sinister Tongs network. The man, a Mr. Jung Ping, has disappeared from his lifelong place of residence in extremely mysterious circumstances and is now a prime suspect for the two murders committed recently that have been given the tag of The Dragon Bar Murders.*

I looked at another...

JUNG PING KILLS WANG? WHY?

I downed my drink in one and went back to the cabinet for another.

"Not for me, Errol," Ava said and turned around to look at me. "Well, could he have done it?"

"Weeny always used to tell me, 'Keep your friends close but your enemies closer'. Who knows…" I raised the glass and winked at Ava. "Anybody could do anything in this crazy world, you must know that by now."

Ava looked disappointed by my answer. It was as if she could see the cogs going round in my head but couldn't quite work out what it was they were thinking.

"Anyway, it looks that for the time being you're in the clear."

"I'm always in the clear, you know that honey."

Ava stood up and returned to her desk, looking at me inquisitively all the while. "Jake wants you to contact him as soon as possible. Just to check you're not in any more trouble. You want me to sort that out for you?"

Once again, I smiled my wide, toothy grin. "You're an angel, you know that? A beautiful angel."

"Just one more thing, Errol," said Ava, as I made my way through to my inner-office. "I know you're not going to tell me too much about this case you're on, but…you know, if there's anything I can be getting on with, anything you need me to do for you… you only have to say."

"An absolute angel," I uttered and continued through to my desk.

For most of the afternoon, I sat with my feet up on the desk thinking. I got through a couple of large packs of Lucky Strikes and the best part of twenty bucks worth of Remy Martin, but still nothing made any sense. I was pretty sure that the Coward would be paying me a visit quite soon. I would certainly have to make some arrangements for that. I also decided that if the office was a possible target, then it was no place for Ava to be. She was a fantastic detective but had no experience of anything so dangerous and I had no intention of putting her in danger. I would have to tell her to take some leave.

I was interrupted by the telephone ringing. I sighed, put down my empty glass, and picked up the receiver.

"Hello."

"Errol, you've got a visitor, shall I send him through?"

My heart began pounding as I held my gun in one hand and the handset in the other. I put it to my mouth, "Who is it darling, I don't want any appointments this afternoon unless it's Mr. Wilson or Timmy."

Before Ava could answer, I heard the door open and a head popped round. I sat back in my chair and let out a huge sigh of relief, dropping the gun on the desk.

"Hey, what are you going to do Eezy, shoot me?"

It was Hermeez Wentz.

"Thank you," I said down the phone to Ava. "Do you want to get off home now sweetheart. Lock the door behind you."

I turned and looked at Hermeez. "You know something my friend? Am I glad to see you?"

Hermeez hung up his coat, fixed himself a drink and pulled out a small box from his inside pocket. He placed the box on the table and smiled.

"I take it Ava has not told you."

I shook my head.

"You missed the service Eezy. After what you told me at the house I did not want to bring you back for a ten minute service in the grubbiest chapel in Chinatown."

He opened the box and pulled out a small, wooden urn with a bronze plaque. On the plaque, the name Dyke Harvey Spanner was engraved with his favourite poem underneath.

"I held Maggie's hand and we didn't shed a tear between us. Dyke's attorney, Timmy Matthews and a couple of old winos from the Dragon were the only other attendees. After the service, which lasted a whole fifteen minutes, his attorney pulled me to one side and gave me some news. Apparently it was Dyke's wish that you should take his remains and scatter them down by Jamaica Bay. I collected the urn this morning."

I picked up the small wooden case and studied it closely. I was struck at how light it was. That a man can be reduced to something so insignificant and something so shabby made me feel sad. That it was Dyke Harvey Spanner that was the man was

156

a little more palatable but melancholic nevertheless. Hermeez picked up on my turn of mood and tried to cheer me up. He ran into a couple of anecdotes about the drinks reception after the service which in normal circumstances would have made me laugh only now they didn't appear very funny.

"Ava did tell me something else," I said, uncertain just how I was going to approach this. Hermeez's reaction solved my dilemma. He held out both his hands in a gesture of surrender so I shut up and let him say his piece.

"I'm sorry, Errol. I shouldn't have lied to you about Marcia. You are my best friend in the whole world and I love you dearly."

"I guess I shouldn't have gone to see her but I was worried about you. I still am."

Hermeez's face took on a more serious look. "I'm not going to reprimand you mate, but no you shouldn't have gone to see her. It wasn't your place." He smiled. "She told me about what happened."

"If Ava hadn't told me about Muchado I wouldn't have interfered."

"You still should not have interfered, but I guess I should have expected it. Look, it's not what you think okay? I know how your mind works and I'm telling you you've got it all wrong. I'm going to say this to you, I don't have to but you are my buddy so I guess I will. First of all, I did not kill or pay Arnold Muchado, or anyone else for that matter, to kill Dyke. Secondly, I am not in any trouble. I know it looks bad with that thug coming by the office and I apologize for that but everything is fine."

He licked his fingertips and brushed his eyebrows back. I watched him do it and after a couple of minutes, I realized he had finished. I decided not to push it. Throughout our friendship, we had always trusted each other completely. Hell, we had to, we wouldn't have survived two minutes in Guadalcanal if we hadn't. Or the mean streets of Manhattan. But I still was left feeling a little short changed. When Hermeez told me he had nothing to do with the death of Dyke Spanner I had to believe him. When he told me he was not in trouble, I had to believe him. But it still didn't make it any easier. After a long silence, I

157

shrugged, flashed him a wide smile and patted him on the shoulder.

"Hermeez, let's go for a drink at Joes. We've got a lot to talk about."

I locked the urn in the safe and we left the office.

Joe approached the table to take our glasses and brought them back a minute later refilled.

Hermeez watched me pick up my glass and take a drink. I put it back on the table and looked at my friend.

"Are you ready?"

He nodded. "Yes."

I told him, omitting nothing. From the beginning, which he already knew I told him about the punk arriving on my doorstep, to the Coward's phone call, to the rendezvous in the Wyatt Earp and the fantastic tale of the Blue Tavernier diamond, to my kidnapping, to my run in with Stanley Cortene and the revelation about his niece Claudia. His face stayed calm and staid throughout. He didn't look afraid although I hoped he was, I certainly was. I felt better for having shared it but was not sure if I had done the right thing. Hermeez had been my closest friend for over thirty years but right now, everything was topsy turvy.

When he did speak, his voice was grave: "This is bigger than either one of us could have imagined, Errol. If we're going to see this one through we need to look after each other. Agreed?"

I nodded, "Agreed."

"First of all, do you think there is a diamond?"

I shrugged. "I don't know. I haven't had chance to find out but if there isn't then this whole thing takes another right turn. So for the time being yes I am assuming that there is."

"Okay, and you don't have it, right?"

"Right."

"So the question is, did Dyke have it? I don't know about you but my gut reaction says no. If Dyke Spanner took a diamond from the dying Dutch Schultz seven years ago, he would not have waited until now to do anything about it. It would have been sold years ago and the money safely deposited in one of his Swiss bank accounts."

"So, if not Dyke then there is only one person."

Hermeez drained his drink and nodded. "Our old friend Liam Tighe, who so far appears to have escaped the notice of your buddy the Coward." He waved at Joe to bring over more drinks. "Before we get onto the whereabouts of our elusive former ally we need to go right back to the beginning of this caper. Firstly, is Claudia Cortene a part of this scam? She set you off on the case so it's a natural assumption, plus she is the best friend of this Marlow and the niece of a gangster. A very fuckin' big gangster. What do you think?"

I shook my head. "I don't think she is knowingly involved in anything. She's vulnerable and open to manipulation. I think she's innocent."

"Okay, so Claudia's in the clear. What about Marlow? Why did she set you up to be present at the Dragon Bar the night that Dyke Spanner was iced? The obvious answer is to set you up for a murder that she knew was going to be committed. She then conveniently disappeared only to draw you in to another sticky situation. With the motive being blackmail to get the diamond. If she's not pulling the strings she is certainly doing a good job for the Coward."

"That's what blurs the issue. When I met Coward at the Wyatt Earp he intimated that unless I played ball Marlow would be killed and I would be up for two murders."

"But it didn't happen, did it? My guess is that between them they tried their damndest to bluff the pants off you. Her quite literally, the Coward using more traditional strong-arm tactics. She must be involved, especially after her cameo appearance at the Coward's ranch. And if she's involved there's every chance Ferriby is too."

That's when it hit me. The grinning bartender who liked to talk. "Diamonds is what I heard." George Ferriby, the cad, the woman beater, the would be ferry Captain. He was into dodgy dealings and the rumour was diamonds. I filled Hermeez in on the necessary.

"Okay, so we got Coward at the top of the pile. Alongside him we got Audrey Daniels, known hoodlum and cheap punk, plus an unknown dandy, plus Marlow and diamond dealer George Ferriby. What about the Cortenes? You say Claudia is not involved and I believe you but what about Stan? Is there not the faintest possibility that his knocking you over was a set up? Is there not even a possibility and here's a spanner in the works so to speak, that it was not Coward that pinched you but someone else. That someone else being the very man that picked you up?"

I thought about it. It was a possibility that I had not considered. After all, I had not real evidence that my kidnapping was anything to do with the Coward. The only significant event was the presence of Marlow, but I had no idea of who she really was. It was possible.

"I don't know. Sure, it's possible. But I think that if Stan Cortene is involved he would surely have shown his hand. What I do know is that the Coward is going to come looking for me. He wants the diamond and he thinks I've got it."

"So we've got to either get rid of him or find it."

I nodded. "Whatever else happens, we deal with when we have to. Right now, let's concentrate on the immediate. We find the diamond and we get the Coward with Marlow into the bargain. When this is all over we will also have Dyke Spanner's killer and we can all go back to being small time no good sons of bitches."

We agreed to work alone on separate parts of the case. Hermeez would track down Liam Tighe, last seen heading for South America with a whole stack of illegal money. He would pull in all his contacts and try to find out what he had been doing for the last five years. Meanwhile I would trace George Ferriby. Whether he was a part of this through choice or not he was certainly an important piece of the puzzle. He not only linked Claudia and Marlow to me, but was a rumored diamond dealer. That alone was enough to get my interest up.

Hermeez suggested that we close the office for renovations for the next week. Neither of us were comfortable with Ava being there alone most of the day when there was a good chance that Audrey Daniels and the Coward would soon be back looking for me. We couldn't afford to keep Mike and Terence there indefinitely and anyway the longer they patrolled with no action the sloppier they would get. Ava would take our calls at home and do whatever work over the telephone. That's what she did best anyway.

She could start by doing a little historical digging on the Blue Tavernier Diamond. There was sure to be something on it amongst the millions of pages in the Central Manhattan Library and while she was there, she could make discreet inquiries about former employee Claudia Cortene. I did not want to believe that she could be in any way involved in this but I had to look into it.

The only subject we did not resolve was the role of Weeny Jung Ping. Hermeez knew Weeny just as well as I did and could not believe that he had betrayed me. But neither could he tell me where the hell he was and in particular why he had not come to my aid, as planned. All the shit about him being printed in the press only made things more complicated.

As the evening progressed, the case was left far behind. Hermeez was simply carrying on his comic-strip lifestyle as normal. Me, I needed a break. Never one to take things too seriously, he wouldn't let the small matter of Mafia, murder and constant danger of premature death get in his way. It was all comfortably taken in his stride. It was a bit like the old days in a way. We were down at Joe's Diner being drunk and raucous without a care in the world. The only difference being that in the old days there really was nothing of any importance to care or worry about, they were all tin pot cases that you could solve in half an hour over the telephone. This was, of course, very different. But what the hell, we acted the same.

Our last, but possibly most important agreement was that we would both ring in at Joe's private telephone line every twenty-four hours. If we didn't both call in every single day then the other would go to Timmy Matthews with the whole deal.

Chapter Eighteen – Private Eye

I awoke the next morning not knowing where the hell I was. When I saw the empty bottle of brandy, my memory kicked in and it all came back. I took a deep breath and sat up prepared for the hammer blow to my head. It never came. I felt better about that. The hangovers were getting milder, but I was still dehydrated, so I took a walk down the hall and drank a liter of ice-cold water. It helped, so I drank another, then showered and shaved.

Feeling human again, I dressed in another set of borrowed clothes and made myself some coffee. Joe had kindly put me up for the night despite my drunkenness. His one request was that I didn't wake him until at least midday. It was eight thirty now so I drank my coffee and headed to a diner for breakfast.

I walked down the road and planned my day. The heat was mild but I was sweating from last night's alcohol. I stopped at the nearest diner, ordered bacon, eggs, tomatoes, mushrooms and two racks of toast. Half an hour and three more cups of coffee later I felt ready and headed to the East Village.

This time there were no freshly cut flowers neatly arranged in vases making the place look pretty. There were no flowers at all. Or vases. And the place didn't look pretty at all. I had managed to force a window open and slipped through without breaking anything. It was only when I was inside that I realized there was nothing left to break.

There was a 'To Let' sign outside the front door but even that had not prepared me for this. There was nothing left at all. Not only had all the furniture gone; every sign of human inhabitation had gone with it. I suppose all the bits and pieces are easily moveable but the carpets had been lifted, the walls stripped and the light bulbs removed.

I lit my Zippo and stood in silence for several minutes, taking stock of the situation. As soon as Claudia had left there must have been a big clean up operation. I came here looking for any trace of Ferriby and there was not a hint that the house had been inhabited by anyone in the last ten years. If I hadn't have stayed here with Claudia that night that Ferriby attacked her I would not have believed that she ever lived here.

I ambled up the wooden stairway and through to the bedroom. The room where she had straddled me whilst wearing only that skimpy little nightie and tended to my meager wounds. That too was empty; no bed, no dresser, no cuddly toys. I tried to picture us that night but my mind kept conjuring up images of Marlow with a knife and a wicked grin. I shook my head and began a thorough search of the whole house.

Every room was the same. There was absolutely nothing of any interest left at all. I would have checked the telephone to see if it had been disconnected but that wasn't left either. The cable had been snipped and was dangling limply half way up the wall. I sat down on the bare wood floor and smoked a cigarette.

Half an hour later, I woke up with a dry mouth and a cricked neck. I rubbed my eyes, yawned, stretched and got up. There was nothing for me here. Before I left I took a piss and flushed the toilet. It was only when I was half way down the stairs that a thought struck me. I had seen it in an old film before the war. I remember thinking at the time that it was the last place that you would think of looking. Although as the years went on and my love of books took me to new places every day I found that it was not such an original idea after all. Still, it was a long shot, but worth the look.

I ran back up the stairs and re-entered the bathroom. The toilet was still making a hell of a noise from being flushed a moment ago and the cistern was slowly filling up. I rolled up my sleeves and lifted the heavy porcelain lid off the cistern. It was high on the wall and there was nothing to stand on, so I had to stretch out my arm and blindly plunge it into the rising water. Splashing around with my fast numbing fingers I was soon disappointed. I would have preferred to get a stepladder and a flashlight and take a proper look but the result would have been the same. There was nothing there.

I dried off my arm on my jacket and replaced the cistern lid. For the second time I headed down the stairs and for the second time I had a thought that stopped me in my tracks. There

163

was a second bathroom. Claudia had mentioned it in passing on the night we spent together. It was located at the rear of the house and was not obvious as it was an outside bathroom that was not directly linked to the main house.

I soon found the second bathroom and had to kick in the door as it was locked. The back of the house was fairly secluded so I felt safe that I would not be heard although I didn't want to hang about to find out. The toilet smelled rank and was dried up. It had not been cleaned and didn't look like it had been used for years. Nevertheless, I did the same trick with the cistern and this time got lucky.

Taped to the side I found three keys on a small key ring. I didn't feel them at first as they were covered with a several layers of thick, industrial tape but my vigilance paid off. A little lower down was a small bag of cocaine. I pocketed the keys and the drugs and left the East Village.

The ferry people had not seen Ferriby for weeks. Apparently, he had only been doing some casual work and had proved unreliable, until one day he just didn't show. They hadn't seen him since. The recruitment officer told me there was few, if anybody, there who knew more than Ferriby's name. He had been a loner and kept himself firmly to himself. He told me to call by a bar in the Lower East Side, The Museum after dark. It was the only place he could recall Ferriby mentioning. I thanked him and put a folded five-spot in his pocket.

My next destination was the small diner in the Financial District. I was hoping the same bartender would be on duty and was disappointed when I entered the small room and found a tall, thin pleasant faced young man. I asked about the other bartender and he simply shrugged and asked what I wanted to drink. I sipped at the drink and asked him about George Ferriby. His face could not have been any blanker so I finished my beer and ordered a pastrami sandwich.

Two hours and several blank looks later I was on my way to Brooklyn Heights. The traffic was light and I made good progress, even taking into account the fact that I had double backed and swapped cars several times. I satisfied myself that I was not being followed but still parked two blocks away and did the final leg on foot.

This time I didn't have to break in.

But somebody else had. Nothing was damaged and the place was largely as the last time I saw it, but there were subtle differences. Every drawer, every shelf and every ornament was still there but in a slightly different place. Even the two abstract pictures hanging on the crimson walls were a touch askew. It wouldn't have alerted the police or even a casual visitor but I noticed it straight away. My mind was tuned into noticing such things. It was the same with my place the morning I returned home and Hermeez was there drinking coffee in my kitchen.

I shrugged it off for the moment and got on with doing my own thorough search of the apartment. I wasn't sure exactly what I was looking for. Was I expecting to find a clue regarding George Ferriby, Marlow and the Blue Tavernier diamond? Or was I simply taking an opportunity to snoop? Right then I couldn't have been sure but the simple fact that the first key fit the lock to the front door was enough.

I moved quickly and steadfastly checking every drawer, shelf and cupboard. Every item of clothing was a possible hiding place and I felt, probed and scrutinized for anything that was suspicious. When I had gone through the obvious, I stripped the bed, I rolled up the rugs and I moved the furniture.

Nothing.

I checked behind the blinds, on the window sills and in the bottom of the coffee, sugar and tea jars. There were two wine glasses and a couple of plates draining on the board. I looked closely but they had been well washed. The rest of the kitchen took a good hour to search thoroughly.

Nothing.

After replacing everything back to exactly where it was before I entered and finding nothing of interest I made myself a coffee. I was feeling hot and tired and needed a burst of caffeine to awaken my brain cells. The coffee did the trick and ten minutes later I was once again playing private eye, this time trying to fit the remaining keys into any available slots. They didn't fit any of the windows, the doors or the jewelry box on the dresser,

165

which was empty anyway. They didn't fit anything in fact so I put them back in my pocket and picked up the waste paper basket.

I found a roll of trash can liners in a cupboard, and laid a couple out on the kitchen floor. Careful not to spill anywhere but on the liner I emptied both the kitchen and bedroom waste paper baskets on top. Donning my thin medical gloves I perused the contents of the rubbish, finding a couple of Metro receipts, an old shopping list, several empty bottles and old newspapers and a variety of kitchen and cosmetic waste. I carefully scanned the newspapers for signs of interest but nothing was cut out or underlined. The shopping list too seemed innocent. I folded it up and put it in my pocket regardless.

It was only when I was putting the trash back in the bin that I found the one suspicious piece of paper. It had been screwed up and found its way into an empty tin of caviar. All that was written on the piece of paper were a series of numbers. The numbers resembled a timetable, the two-hour intervals and corresponding depart and arrival times immediately stood out. I put the piece of paper in my pocket also and then got on with making the apartment exactly as it had been prior to my entrance.

I found the second piece of the jigsaw a few minutes later. When I had left the apartment, I had noticed a car idling on the roadside. The driver was recognizable as the occupant of the apartment next to Marlow's. I had seen her there the other day and decided it was worth a few questions.

The usual Black charm fell flat on its face and the lady blanked most of my questions. This was after she had spent the best part of ten minutes closely studying my identification. She refused to even confirm that she lived next door to Marlow and after several attempts to dig out information I gave up.

When she drove towards a block of high class garages at the end of the cul-de-sac however, I was following every step of the way. I even managed to sneak past her unseen as the electric door was closing and made my way into the garage block. There was nobody else around so I started checking the keys in the cars that were parked there. There were six in total and the key fit the second one I tried. It was a red Studebaker.

166

It had Marlow written all over it. The upholstery was black leather, there was a spare pair of underwear in the glove compartment and her shade of lip-gloss was smeared all over the cigarette buts in the ashtray. But there was nothing that linked it to Ferriby.

I checked under the hood, I crawled underneath the body and I searched the interior with a fine tooth comb. The other item of interest was a parking ticket that had the district marked on it. It was not very much but it was all I had to go on.

Ten minutes later, I was once again on my way to the Financial District. I stopped at a call box on the way and telephoned Ava.

"Sweetheart it's me... Yes I'm fine honey. Listen I need you to do me a favour..."

I gave her the list of numbers and told her to check train, boat, plane and coach timetables. It was a long shot but I asked her to first check for Buenos Aires. If that didn't work it would be a long day but she was happy to do it. She told me she had an appointment with a Professor at the University later in the day. She had had no luck in the library. There was absolutely nothing on any cutting taken from the Blue Tavernier Diamond. It was not totally unexpected but she sounded a little downhearted. I cheered her up a little and she promised to keep looking. I said I would call her later in the evening and hung up.

For the second time that day I was out of luck in the Financial District. No friendly bartender and nobody with any information worth a dime. I listened to tale after tale that bored the socks off me and that made me feel tired. It was while I was drifting off listening to an old wino recount tales of drunken introspection that I had an idea. I patted the old guy on the shoulder, put a five spot in his top pocket and left the diner.

I found the place where the parking ticket was purchased and looked around me. It would be long and tiring work but I needed the walk to wake me from the rut I found myself in.

I started a couple of blocks East and worked my way through every bar, restaurant, shop, bench and passing person that was in my path. I described the people I was interested in, I

167

threw names at people, and sometimes I just talked. There were plenty of people who were happy just to talk to me. The hands went round the clock four full circles before I gave it up and I still didn't have any information worth a dime.

I stopped at a twenty-four hour joint for a porterhouse steak and a bottle of red wine before trying my luck at The Museum. It was a small, low-ceilinged joint with a bar that ran along the whole of one side of the room. A tired looking bartender was wiping glasses at the far end of the room. He looked up and dredged up a smile for my benefit.

"What'll it be, fella?" he asked in a friendly but wary voice.

"Beer, thanks," I said and dropped a five spot on the bar, looking around the near empty joint. There was a Juke-box playing soft rock tunes in the background, a couple of down on their luck drinkers staring into their half empty glasses and a young couple with only eyes for each other canoodling in the corner.

He brought the beer over and I dropped another bill. "And a little information."

"Are you heat?"

I flashed him my badge and he relaxed.

"You look like the kind of guy that hears things."

He looked from side to side and pulled himself a beer. "Go on."

"George Ferriby, tall blonde, ladies man. He drinks here right?"

The bartender pursed his lips and then took a long drink of his beer. He looked like he was weighing up his options as he emptied the glass in one go. Finally he said, "He used to but I haven't seen him for weeks."

"Tell me about him."

He pulled me another beer and one for himself. This time he only took off the top before talking. "Look fella if you want to know about George Ferriby you're asking the wrong bloke. All I know about him is that he likes a drink and he likes a lady even more. I don't know what he does for a living and I don't care. I don't know where he lives and I don't care. I..."

168

"I get the picture."

The bartender took the note from the bar and put it back in my pocket. "If you're going to act all heavy you might as well get it over with. It won't change nothing though," he said, with a note of resignation in his voice.

I held out my hand. "The name's Errol Black. I don't do the heavy too well so let's have another beer. What do you say?"

The bartender laughed a little ha ha laugh and shook my hand. "Pleased to meet ya, Errol, I'm Joseph and I don't mind if I do."

We talked socially for the next twenty minutes or so. Joseph was a nice guy, the sort that you meet in bars on every block in America. Hard done to, put upon kind of guys who have been dealt a bad deck in life's game. He had worked for twelve hours a day in the same bar doing the same mundane routine for the last nine years. It barely paid the rent. We talked about the forthcoming season and the chances of another Super bowl coming to the Empire State. He had to spend more time serving as the bar busied up but whenever he got a spare moment would come back and talk to me.

"You know, there is a guy who may be able to help you. Goes by the name of Jeff. Never did really warm to him but I did see him with Ferriby once in a while."

That caught my attention.

"Today's Saturday, right?"

"Right."

"I think maybe he usually comes by on a Saturday. Do you want me to give you the nod if he comes in?"

"That would be swell Joseph." I pulled out the five note and tucked it in his pocket. "A thank you, please keep it."

He smiled and walked over to serve another customer.

Two hours later I had learned very little else about Ferriby. Most punters were reluctant to talk but I got the impression that most simply didn't know anything about him. Nobody knew where he lived, the best I got was, "I think he lives with his girls." and he was interested in racing, but then so was half of America. So I was mighty relieved when a small, heavily built man with a shiny bald head strolled into the bar and ordered

169

a drink. Joseph poured him a gin and tonic and gave me a barely visible nod.

The small guy said something to Joseph and he laughed. He said something back and nodded towards me just as I headed over. The small guy looked around and his eyes met mine. They were full of anger and fear. He picked up the glass, tossed it in my direction and ran out of the joint.

"I'm sorry Errol, all I said was that you wanted a word."

I didn't reply. I was half way down the street chasing the fleeing G and T drinker. He was a fast runner for a small guy and he made me feel unfit as he started to pull away from me. We were heading down Fifth and whenever he passed a mobile newspaper stand or a hot dog seller, he tipped it all over and into my path. It was designed to slow me down and it worked. He needn't have bothered I doubt whether I would have caught him anyway.

We ran and ran and ran. Although he was widening the gap between us I just about managed to keep him in my sights. I considered pulling my gun and shouting at him to stop but it was highly unlikely he would take any notice and then what would I do? Shooting him in the back would not get me any information of Ferriby and would most likely land me in jail.

He turned a corner and disappeared down a side street. When I caught up he was gone. I found myself on a small side-street with a couple of closed shops and a private member's club. The street was empty. Not a single person was around. I tried the shops, rattling on the doors but there was no answer. I quickly weighed up my options and entered the club.

I was met by a burly doorman, who smiled and asked politely to see my membership card. I smiled and showed him my Private Investigator's license explaining that I was on urgent business. He shrugged, never losing his smile for a second and the shook his head.

"I need to see a membership card. Without it you don't enter. I'm sorry."

I rubbed my chin and decided to ask him about the bald man. He again shook his head and then repeated himself. Time was moving on and I was losing my patience so I tried bribing

170

him and when he shook his head for a third time I knocked him out with a right uppercut and strolled on in.

Inside the club I passed quickly by the receptionist, declining to hang up my coat and headed on in to the club. It was comprised of a large lounge bar area downstairs and a fitness center on the first floor complete with spa, sauna and gymnasium. I took a drink from a passing waitress and scanned the bar area. There was nobody resembling the bald man and so I quickly drained the glass and headed upstairs.

I narrowly avoided the rather annoyed looking doorman and a couple of his colleagues in the locker room. I ducked behind a six-foot cheese plant as he rushed by. There was an old man with a full head of white hair and a shiny tracksuit combing his hair. He smiled a toothy smile at me.

"Have you forgotten your kit young man?" he asked in a cultured, European voice, nodding at my empty hands.

Before I could answer he let out a laugh. "Or are you another bloody vandal, come to steal from our lockers?"

"What do you mean?" I asked.

"Just now," he replied, "some fuckin' hophead. Burst in here, not unlike yourself, sweating like he'd done an hour on the treadmill. Knocked me right off my feet and instead of apologizing and helping me back up he headed for the lockers."

"This man...bald, about five foot two, red shirt?"

The old man smiled again. "That's the one. Friend of yours is he?"

"On the contrary," I said and pulled out my PI license, holding it not quite open right in the old man's face before quickly tucking it away. "I am a Federal Officer. I am investigating a man of the name of George Ferriby. I believe that the man you have just described is a vital witness to my investigation."

The man stood upright and held out a hand. I shook it and he looked proud. "If there is anything I can do for you, sir, you just ask. I fought for this great country and I will do anything to help. Especially in the apprehension of lowlifes like Ferriby."

I looked shocked. I couldn't help it. "You know Ferriby?" I asked.

"Oh yes. The man is a lowlife and a scumbag. He runs illegal rackets for a sideline and he deals in illegal, knock off gear. On his evenings he goes to bars and he chats up young ladies, the younger the better and he takes them back to their flats and he fucks them. But before he fucks them he empties their purses and then he leaves them. Oh yes he's a really nasty piece of work is Ferriby. He acts like he owns this place, strutting round in his flashy suits, bragging about the pussy he has scored. There's a name for guys like Ferriby."

"There is?"

"Cunthounds, that's what we used to call them in the war."

"When did you last see him?" I asked.

"He hasn't been here for a couple of weeks. I hoped he was gone, long gone but he still keeps a locker."

"He does?"

"Yes, that's the one that hophead was trying to break into just now. Look, I'll show you."

He walked to the end of a long row of lockers and fingered one, number 21A. There were scratch marks along the edge of door and around the lock. I inspected it closely, examining the small key hole, and was satisfied that the bald man must have been interrupted. There was little damage done and with the right key it would be no problem opening the locker. My mind was wandering when the old man once again brought me back to earth.

"He took me to his lock up once you know."

That certainly got my attention. I sat down and the old man did the same. There was nobody else in the locker room.

"It was full of worthless pieces of junk. Paintings that were supposed to be originals, jewelry that was nothing better than seaside tat and piles and piles of designer clothes. I did find a nice pair of brogues though and this," he pushed his sleeve up and showed me a chunky timepiece. It was Rolex and tackier than a weekend in Vegas.

"Where? I need to know where the lock up is and anything else you can tell me about Ferriby."

172

The old man smiled. "I'm sorry young man," he said, "Georgie Ferriby never told anybody where he lived. Sometimes I doubted he had a home, he slept with that many women I guess he just lived with them. Probably fuckin' ponced his way through life."

"What about the lock up? Where is the lock up?"

"Don't know that either. You got to understand fella. George Ferriby is not your average lowlife. He lives in a constant state of paranoia and by the looks of it, it is well justified. He don't like to take nobody to his lock up. He always brings the gear to you, but with me he made an exception. I guess he thought I was just some harmless old soak. Nothing to worry about with old Arthur. Still he blindfolded me all the same."

"He blindfolded you?"

Arthur grinned a wicked grin and tapped the side of his nose with a crooked old finger.

"Couldn't fool old Arthur though. You see he didn't reckon on my ability to observe. You don't survive the Great War and three years in a cold, smelly old trench without developing a good sense of direction."

"Look Arthur, I would love to stand and chat with you," I said, a little exasperation creeping into my voice, "But I am a very busy man."

"You want to know where the lock up is?"

I nodded.

"Well, like I said, I was blindfolded but I am no fool. I may be old but I got good ears and I know how to use 'em."

I waited.

"I can't be certain but if I was a betting man, I'd say it is somewhere along the boardwalk. I could hear the old roller coaster see," he chuckled. "That old roller coaster is unmistakable. The wind was in my face so I guess it was on the East side, probably one of them wooden shacks that lines the whole drag." He smiled. "You knows where I'm talking about don't you?" and stood up. "Now I have to go. Good luck young man."

173

I watched him leave the locker room and fumbled in my pocket. There was still nobody else in the room so I put the key in the lock and turned. The door swung open and a wide grin filled my face.

Inside the locker, I found a small sports bag. I lifted the bag out of the locker and placed it on the bench at my side. My heart was beating quicker and quicker and I felt a little light headed as I unzipped the bag. It almost leapt out of my chest as I found my hands running over the cold, metallic surface of a revolver. Next to the gun was a wallet. I inspected it and found five thousand dollars in used notes and nothing else. I didn't need anything else; I already knew who it had belonged to. It was the wallet of the late Liam Tighe. I knew that because I had bought it for him.

Hermeez checked in at Joe's ten minutes before I did. I was calling from a public booth and was dripping from the early morning rainfall. Joe told me the same as he told my buddy, that Audrey Daniels had been sniffing around the diner. He had got short shrift from the regulars and Joe told me he had been tempted to give the kid a good beating. I was pleased he hadn't. If Daniels was back, it meant that I was still in demand and if anyone was going to give him a beating it would be me.

I met Hermeez for breakfast six hours later, after a fitful nights sleep on the hard boards of Claudia Cortene's old pad. My back was sore but I was feeling happy. I was anxious to share what I had learned with my partner and keen to hear just what he had discovered. I was sure the case was coming close to a conclusion but would never have guessed the twists that still awaited me.

Hermeez looked as dapper as ever. He was clean-shaven and wearing an immaculate beige suit, with black waistcoat and short fedora with a goose feather in the belt. He got to his feet as I arrived and smiled a warm smile before pouring me a cup of strong coffee and handing me the tray of freshly buttered toast.

We talked briefly for a few moments but it was clear to the both of us that we were anxious to get down to business.

174

Hermeez looked as excited as I felt even if he did keep it under a veneer of cool.

"You haven't spoken to Ava this morning?" he asked dabbing the corners of his mouth with a perfectly folded napkin.

I shook my head. "Is it about the diamond? Has she found out something?"

"No, not yet. She did take a telephone call from your friend though, the delectable Claudia Cortene."

I involuntarily raised my eyebrows. "She did?"

"Yeah, they're going for lunch today. Ava said that Claudia wants to meet up with you again. How are you fixed for dinner?"

I shrugged. "I don't know that that's a good idea. Getting mixed up with gangsters and their families is not always a good idea."

"It's never bothered you before."

I smiled. "You're right and I may have to speak to her again anyway."

Now Hermeez smiled. "When you hear what I have to tell you, you will definitely have to talk to her."

There was a short silence whilst we drank our coffee and munched our toast. I refilled both cups and decided that I would beat my friend to the punch.

"Liam Tighe is dead."

"You know?"

"Yup, and I know who killed him."

Hermeez laughed out loud. "You lousy son of a bitch. I get dressed up all smart to come and show off my detective skills and you piss all over my breakfast. Put your tail away and tell me about it."

I did.

Hermeez told me his side of the story when I had finished. Ava had come up trumps with the times I had given her yesterday. They had turned out to be flight times to Mexico, not Argentina. Tijuana to be exact and Liam Tighe was a passenger several times over the last twelve months. So was George Ferriby but Hermeez had not seen the significance of that until I told him my story.

175

Once he had located Liam in TJ, Hermeez had called up a few of his contacts and found out plenty. Liam had a pad down there, quite a palatial pad and had been living there quite openly. He was well liked and played quite a part in the local economy, sponsoring the schools and throwing money at numerous community projects. He was still overheard to espouse racist and prejudicial views but happily frequented the Hispanic hotels and was even dating a black girl for a while. This happy existence had all come to a sudden end only one week ago when his house was burned to the ground and everything in it perished including his life. He had been identified from a collection of bones and a period of mourning was underway.

Hermeez told me he had planned to go down and do some more investigating but now he wasn't so sure. I told him he should.

"Joe told you that Daniels is back. I think maybe I should stick around, you may need me here with you."

"I'll be fine," I said. "They won't try anything again, not yet. And when they do I want to have something to bargain with."

"The diamond?"

"Exactly."

Hermeez sighed. "But it looks like Ferriby is a better bet than Liam. I could go all the way to TJ and the diamond could be right here in New York. No, I think we need to find Ferriby and then we'll find the diamond."

"You're right. Tell Ava I will meet Claudia. I need to tell her about Liam and maybe see if I can pump her for a bit more on Ferriby."

But all I really wanted to do was see her beautiful face again. The very prospect made me feel lightheaded and dizzy. It was a feeling I was uncomfortable with but a pleasurable one. Ever since she had kissed me with so much passion and verve before walking out of my life, seemingly forever, I had been unable to get her out of my mind. I would now relish the opportunity to meet her again although the same problems would exist. Stan Cortene was a man I did not want to cross and I would have to tread very carefully indeed.

Chapter Nineteen – Benjamin Wilson

As it happened, there was soon to be another reason for Claudia Cortene to come back into my life. Hermeez always told me that most cases require a good deal of luck. Either luck or good fortune, which was largely the same thing. Tenacity and skill are essential requirements but it is luck that it the real vital ingredient. Our piece of luck arrived in the form of a sweating, rather frightened, yet very proud shape of Benjamin Wilson. I was waiting for him in my temporary office in the back room of Joe's Diner.

Mr. Benjamin Wilson was a slightly built man of medium height. He had black, glossy hair smoothed back. Wearing a black cravat with yellow flashes and holding a derby hat in his pink-gloved hands.

I followed him into the office and sat at my chair, lighting up a Lucky. "Please sit down, Mr. Wilson."

Wilson bowed like a prince over his hat, said, "Thank you, Mr. Black," in a nervous, high-pitched voice and duly sat down. He sat up straight with his hat and his gloves placed neatly on his knees.

I inhaled deeply before blowing out a stream of smoke above my head and asked: "Now what is it I can do for you Mr. Wilson? And may I ask, what are the serious consequences of me not doing it for you?" I asked with equal nonchalance.

He rubbed his palms together and began: "I do not wish to start our acquaintance off on a confrontational manner, Mr. Black."

He paused and smiled. "Maybe I was a little curt with your dear secretary." His voice was at almost a whisper and I noticed his hand shaking... "I was simply anxious to talk to your good person and it appeared time was running out fast with no sign of your return."

He shuffled a little in his chair, opting to move his hat and gloves onto the edge of the desk nearest to him. "I trust you underwent a satisfactory journey?"

I said nothing, eyeballing him throughout. It was clear this man was extremely nervous, but I was unsure just why. Again he attempted at pleasantries.

"Anyway you are back now, and may I say just what a pleasure it is to finally meet the great Errol Black."

I nodded in acknowledgment, making sure not to smile and display any more warmth than was required.

Wilson stopped rubbing his hands and placed them down on his knees, where his hat and gloves had been moments ago. "Clearly I am wasting time," he said a little more assertively, but still in a dull whisper. "I must introduce myself properly."

He let out a little exhalation of air and continued. "I am here representing a Mr. Liam Tighe."

Wilson must have noticed my ears prick up and this appeared to give him more confidence in himself.

"I am afraid my client Mr. Tighe has recently passed on."

"Passed on?" I interrupted. "So that's why you are in a hurry. If Liam has passed on, as you put it, then I bet it wasn't a peaceful passing in the night was it? So I guess whoever whacked the Irishman has got you in his sights."

"Ahem," said a slightly ruffled Wilson, wiping his mouth with a golden, silk handkerchief, which he quickly returned to the pocket of his trousers. "Yes, well let's just say that he is no longer with us. And as that leaves me without a client you are correct, I will indeed be moving on."

I stubbed out my cigarette, my attention much more focused on what Mr. Wilson had to say, and he continued articulately.

"For years I have been Mr. Tighe's legal advisor. He has confided many, many secrets in me. The one that concerns you, Mr. Black, is this…"

He looked in his inside pocket of his navy blue blazer and produced a small key, dropping it on the desk before me. It looked like a safety deposit box key, with a tag around the thin key ring bearing the number 10234.

Still I remained silent, waiting for my mystery visitor to continue. "He left me with the strict instructions that I was to get this key to a lady friend of Mr. Tighe's."

My heart missed a beat but I disguised my interest behind a smug smile.

"Very nice for you, now where do I come in?"

"Mr. Black, I am only a humble lawyer. I have no experience or inclination to start tracking down ex-lady friends of my clients."

He smiled a weak smile that accentuated the highness of his cheekbones. "Mr. Tighe was most insistent that I referred the task to a Private Investigator, namely your good self. You must take the key to the girl, let me say...discreetly. Nobody else must know anything about it."

I opened my drawer and poured myself a cognac. Those damn pills I took an hour ago were certainly not going to clear my headache, so maybe a drink would? I offered, and to my surprise, Mr. Wilson duly accepted.

I sipped at the drink gently. "If this whole thing is so important, why did you waste your own no doubt precious time waiting for me? Why not take it to another Dick, let's face it there's no real shortage of wannabe Phil Marlowes in this district?"

I could see Wilson did not quite follow the slang for detective, and so put him straight reiterating the question. Again, Wilson shuffled uneasily in his chair.

"I am afraid Liam was a great admirer of your work. He was quite clear about his conviction that you were a man who would not fail the task..." he paused and his eyes left my gaze, wandering around the room, "...under any circumstances."

I took another slug of cognac, swilling it around in my mouth thoughtfully, and Wilson continued: "You must get this key to the lady as soon as possible. Once you take the key off my hands and you sign this document," he fumbled in his brief case, "I will be on my way."

I finished my drink and picked up the key, tossing it from one hand to the other. I noticed Wilson kept his eyes firmly on the key at all times.

"I'm sorry Mr. Wilson, I'm afraid I'm a little too busy at the moment. You'll have to take this to someone else," I tossed the key back to Wilson and he fumbled it, dropping it on the

179

floor under the desk. He crawled around for a moment or two on his hands and knees and reappeared with a bright, red face looking extremely worried.

"You don't appear to understand, Mr. Black. Liam was most insistent that it was you that undertook the job. He had it written down on his will in capital letters that it must be Mr. Errol Christopher Black PI, of Manhattan Island, New York City. It seems you are the only detective… ahem or dick, that he held in any regard and deemed this very important."

I sighed and looked at a now very frightened looking Mr. Wilson square in the eyes. "Capital letters, eh."

Wilson nodded.

"But the guy's dead, you told me yourself. How will he ever know who finds the bloody lady to give her the key. Nope, I'm afraid you'll have to take it somewhere else."

"I am prepared to pay grandly for your services. A sum of ten thousand dollars for the completion of the task."

Sweat was freely running down the cheeks of Wilson, but he forced a smile nevertheless. "Ten thousand dollars, Mr. Black, as I am sure you are aware is a lot of money."

I smiled, rubbing my chin thoughtfully. "Ten thousand dollars eh? That is a very intriguing sum of money. Now do you mind me asking just why you are prepared to pay such an amount for such a simple job?"

Wilson shuddered a little as I termed the job 'simple'. He then picked up his glass that had been sitting on the edge of the desk untouched, and emptied it of its contents in one go.

"The intriguing sum of money, as you so succinctly put it would be paid from the deceased's estate, Mr. Black. I am simply conveying the information. Once you locate the girl in question and hand her the key you must accompany her to the bank and your fee will be waiting for you inside the deposit box."

He looked at me carefully and smiled. "I am sure you have been told everything you need to know, Mr. Black. Now am I safe in assuming that you agree to take on the task that I offer you?"

I could sense a little more self-assurance in Wilson's voice. He had stopped sweating so profusely and now looked genuinely more at ease.

"Yeah, you know I think you can Mr. Benjamin Wilson, I think you can. But I will of course want a cash advance on the ten big ones you understand?"

Wilson immediately reached into his inside pocket and pulled out a large, black leather purse. "Of course, how silly of me. How much shall we say, five hundred?"

I reached across and snatched the purse from the quivering hands of Wilson and pulled out a thousand in cash (the full contents of the purse). "This will do me for getting on with," I uttered, and threw the purse back across the desk.

As Wilson gathered his things together and once again stood upright I held out my hand. He shook it weakly and sort of curtseyed. He then put the key back on the table and turned away.

"Just one more thing, Mr. Wilson," I said as he headed for the door. "The name of the girl, the one I take the key to?"

"Ah yes," answered Wilson, the truest smile of the day now on his greasy face. "How silly of me. The girl in question...ahem," he cleared his throat, "...is a Miss Cortene...a Miss Claudia Cortene."

And he was gone.

Chapter Twenty – Dead End

I knew exactly where he meant and within twenty minutes, I had found just what I was looking for. The boardwalk ran all the way from Coney Island to Brighton Beach and was lined with wooden shacks. Most of them were used as beach huts, storing surfing and lifeguard equipment. Others had been converted into restaurants or cheap fast food stalls. Further along the boardwalk towards Brighton Beach, the area took on a more residential feel. There was still a large Jewish community here although that would soon be overwhelmed by the mass Russian immigration of the 1970s that spawned the birth of Little Odessa.

I found the shack that had been rented to George Ferriby after talking to an old timer who had lived in Coney Island since the last century. He knew all the owners, landlords and casual tenants of the last twenty years. Not all of them by name, but certainly by sight and a brief description was enough to awaken his memory of the jack the lad that dealt purely in cash and had not been seen for the last few weeks. He directed me to the hut that was situated between a seafood restaurant and a hot dog stall and thanked me as I slipped a five spot in his pocket.

The smell hit me as soon as I poked my hand through the door. It was held by an oversize padlock that's shiny exterior was out of place amongst the rusty hinges and rotten handle hanging limply by one screw. I made sure there was nobody paying too much attention as I fiddled lamely with the lock. It was a great possibility that the place was under surveillance and I did not want to be caught breaking and entering.

A young couple walked by, chewing happily on hot dogs, smiling sweetly at each other as they wiped mustard from their chins. I stepped back from the shack and lit a Lucky, smoking it quickly as the stream of people thinned out. I had come prepared and stubbed the cigarette out before severing the lock with the bolt cutters I had concealed in my overcoat. I slipped them back in my pocket and pushed the door open.

I quickly reached for my handkerchief and held it tightly to my mouth as the stench hit me. I had to close the door after me to avert any unwanted attention but was unsure just how long I could stand it. It was a smell I had experienced before but however many times you smelt it, it did not get any easier and was particularly unpleasant.

Still holding the handkerchief in place, I opened my eyes and flicked on the light switch. The place was less than twenty square yards in size, but was a veritable Aladdin's Cave. It was full from floor to ceiling in swag, ranging from bags of jewelry to old oil paintings. There was electrical gear stacked right to the roof and box after box littering the floor. Right by my feet, spread-eagled on a rather ornate oriental rug lay George Ferriby.

He was dead, of course and by the smell of him he had been for some time. He was laying in a dried pool of his own blood with a bullet wound to the neck and one to the chest. He had a rather surprised look on his face and his mouth was open.

I put on my thin leather gloves and searched his body. The bile was rising to my throat and it was pretty gruesome business but necessary. I found nothing more than an empty wallet and a packet of gum.

Next, was the highly unpleasant business of searching the lock-up. I did this quickly and thoroughly but it too proved fruitless and I was left feeling not only sick as a dog but very angry. Like ripples in a pond, the circles just kept getting bigger and bigger. I felt like every move I made I was led up a path and hit a big brick wall.

I left the shack in a hurry and didn't even bother to disguise the broken lock. Worrying about whether George Ferriby would be found before his body rotted away was the last thing on my mind.

Chapter Twenty-One – The Key

I was sitting on a barstool at Joe's with a Remy Martin in one hand and the little key in the other. I turned it over and over in my hand, thinking. There was always the possibility that I could try and find out where the key belonged myself. If I could do this, I could at least find out what it was that it led to. Assuming I could do this - find out where the key belonged (a safety deposit box somewhere) - would that contravene the deal that I had struck with Wilson? I could still get the key to Claudia, the only difference would be that I would know what I was giving her. Whether it was going to be a pot of gold or a bomb that would blow her face off.

Or a diamond.

I winced at the thought of the bomb and polished off my cognac. No, I'm afraid I would have to do what Wilson was paying me for. Who knows, maybe he was from the law and was checking me out for honesty? Beech had certainly done things stranger than hire out a mole agent in his time. And there was still the possibility of that bomb.

Yes, I must get the key to Claudia and then keep close tabs on what results. Who knows, maybe it was nothing to do with anything. Maybe the whole thing was a coincidence. Unfortunately, this was the least likely possibility of all the speculations so far. I had been involved with Liam Tighe, who had been with me, Dyke and Dutch Schultz the night he was murdered, as well as former sweetheart of Claudia Cortene. And so on. For all of us to coincidentally cross paths again in the middle of this winding, turning rattlesnake of a case would be sheer fantasy. Wouldn't it?

Tomorrow I would find out. For now, I would just make a call to Ava and call it a night. I picked up the handset and dialed the number.

"Ava, is that you sweetheart? Yeah, I know I'm sorry it's late darling. I've just got a couple of things for you to do for me."

I waited a moment as Ava got her writing equipment. "You ready... Right, I have left you a package in your mailbox. It is addressed for Timmy Matthews NYPD. I want you to take it to him personally, tell him it's from me and I want him to check it over the same as all the others. Yes, just say those exact words, he'll know what to do.

"And the other thing you can do right away if you want to. Give the station a buzz, don't talk to Timmy on this one or Lieutenant Beech, the duty officer will do, and don't tell them who you are... I know you do sweetheart just making sure. Tell him that there's been a disturbance on the boardwalk in Coney Island. You got that?" I gave her the address. "That's right. Tell him you've heard a lot of out of the ordinary disturbance, obstreperous noises, crashing and banging, that sort of thing and that they ought to check it out.

"You think you can do those things for me tonight? Good girl, I knew you would. Hermeez should be in touch in the morning with a message for me. If you can have it ready when I call. Okay sweetheart, I'll be in touch with you in the morning, you sleep tight and remember you're the best."

I leaned over the bar and held out my glass. "Are you still serving tonight Joe or just looking pretty?" I shouted, and he dutifully filled my glass.

"Don't you have a home to go too Eezy?" he retorted, a big wide grin filling his fat face.

"No, I'm afraid I'll be dossing down in the office tonight, as long as you're sure that's okay with you?"

"Sure it is. You know you can stay there as long as you want. Just don't keep the place tidy that's all I ask."

I smiled and patted Joe on the shoulder, before heading through into the back office. "Goodnight Joe," I uttered.

"Yeah, goodnight hotshot. I hope you're gonna catch some bad guys tomorrow, it'd be good for business."

And off I went into the office.

I awoke with a cricked back and freezing feet. I must have dozed off in the office chair with my sock-less feet rested up against the desk. The desk was a mass of papers, sketched ideas and empty brandy glasses and the ashtray was overflowing with stub-ends.

185

I let out a long, tiresome yawn and stretched my arms out. I would certainly have to either solve this case pretty quickly or find another nice young female to share a bed with. Many more nights shacked up in Joe's ram shackled old office, on an uncomfortable chair and it would be the end of me.

As I lit up a cigarette, I got a shot of pain in my back. I sat up straight, which only made the pain worse. Before I could do anything about it the telephone rang. I rubbed my eyes and picked it up: "Black," I said assertively.

"Errol, how are you doing buddy? Any progress?"

I let out a sigh and fumbled around the desk for yesterday's leftover pastrami-on-rye sandwiches. "Hermeez. I'm just about to get in touch with Claudia. Last night was more of a planning exercise. I'll be getting down to it today. How about you? I thought you were going to pass on any messages through Ava."

"I know, I'm sorry Errol, but this couldn't wait. I did what you said, I took a drive by your lock up and it was exactly as you thought it would be. The whole place had been turned upside down. It was difficult to tell where the break in ended and the looting began but you get the picture."

"Well that confirms pretty much what we already knew. Marlow is in it up to her pretty little neck."

"Yes, well that is the second part of my news."

"Go on."

"Maybe you can hear the shower in the background? I do not want to divulge too much over the telephone, but I have some very intriguing news for you. If I wasn't such a bloody professional, you would very soon be able to add me to your little list."

I took a deep intake of breath. "Hermeez, be very careful. Whatever you do, do not reveal who you are. She is a very dangerous lady."

"Sure. She is also a very, very attractive lady. Look I got to go. I'll meet you for lunch tomorrow say two o'clock at Grand Central. Until then I may be busy. Have a table ready."

"I'll be there, and just remember what I told you, be careful."

186

Before I could finish my sentence, the line went dead. I sighed and flipped the receiver back onto its holder, stuffing the rest of the pastrami sandwich in my mouth at the same time.

I wondered how Hermeez had found Marlow. My guess was that she had left a clue at the lock up but that would have been uncharacteristically sloppy. Whatever the reason he had done a good job and it could prove vital in cracking the case. In particularly I was curious as to whether she was in league with the Coward or was working on her own. I hoped he would heed my advice and be very, very careful and I suppose a little bit of me felt jealous that he was now likely to be getting intimate with her. She might have been a conniving, manipulative, and possible killer but he was right, she was damn attractive and a wonderful lay.

I finished chewing on the sandwich and went through to Joe's kitchen where he was currently putting on a pot of coffee. "Eezy you're awake old son. How about a nice thick, hot cup of coffee to get the old grey matter into gear?"

Normally I would have jumped at the offer of a coffee at this time in the morning, but I'd tasted Joe's creations before. His coffee was similar to his tea, which was similar to his broth, with was similar to his hot chocolate and so on. I wouldn't have minded but his hot chocolate was the worst in the district.

"Sorry Joe, I'm afraid I just don't have the time. I'm going to have to fly. Catching bad guys like you suggested, but first I think I'll take breakfast with a beautiful lady. See you later buddy."

"Yeah. Butter her a croissant for me will you? Butter it real slow."

As I mixed with the morning traffic, I was unsure on just how I was going to approach this. I had arranged, through Ava, to meet Claudia for morning coffee at one of the new trendy joints opening up around Times Square. Now, not only did I have the key to pass on to her, I had the information that two of her former boyfriends were dead. And to make matters worse, their early baths could both be a result of the case that I was

187

currently investigating. Add that to the strength of feeling that I was personally harboring it was going to be a tricky encounter.

I thought back to our last meeting. Claudia practically begged me to take her away from her captivity. Although I wouldn't admit it at the time, I would have liked to do just that. In fact, I would have loved to. But the truth was I knew it just wasn't practical. There was no way that it could have happened and when I walked away, I was walking away for good. And now I was going back and I didn't know how to approach it. I was getting a funny feeling in my stomach, a feeling that I didn't recognize and it made me uneasy.

I decided I would have to play it cool. Very cool to the point of appearing harsh. It would hurt me to do so, but it was the only way out of a very difficult situation.

As I was approaching the Cafe-Noir I noticed a disturbance along the avenue. There was a gang of smokes in a semi-circle, all dressed up in their Rastafarian gear, shouting and swearing. I couldn't quite see just who or what at, but I was curious and had a strange feeling come over me. I decided to go and investigate.

As I got nearer I could see a young, brunette girl stood in the middle of them with her shaking hands clasped together clutching her purse. She had tears streaming down her face and was cowering away from the ringleader, who was giving her a whole load of unrepeatable abuse. A few more steps and I realized the girl was Claudia.

She hadn't seen me yet and neither had the ringleader. The others had as they slowly began to move apart, leaving room for me to approach the ringleader. In one movement I grabbed him by the dreadlocks of his hair, pulled it right back and slammed his face into the parked car on the roadside. I lifted his head and again brought it down hard on the car bonnet, causing his nose to bleed profusely. I then let go of the man and pulled my rod aiming at one of the smokes, then another, then another. One by one they casually put their switchblades back in their pockets and moved away.

"I think this conversation is over, don't you?" I said to the ringleader, handing him my handkerchief to dab his nose.

188

He didn't say anything, just held out his hands showing off his white palms, and then slowly backed away. When he got a good ten yards away, he quickly turned and started running. I put my gun away and held out my arms to give Claudia a hug.

"Oh, Errol," she said. "I'm so glad to see you."

She held me so tight, tears freely flowing down her rosy red cheeks. I held her equally tight and buried my face in her shoulder. She was finding emotions in me that I had long repressed. I would have to pull myself together and snap out of it.

I took her for breakfast at one of the less sleazy places I knew. It had sickly, happy music playing in the background, but at least the tables were clean and the waitresses were polite. We ate croissants and drank coffee and all the time I had this heavy imposing feeling in the base of my belly. Maybe I was nervous about what I had to tell her? All the time she gave me a running commentary on how she was getting on better with her family, how much she liked my secretary and how much she had missed me. Eventually she had decided to take me up on my word and look me up.

"Oh Errol, it's so great to see you again, it really is. I don't think I could have stood it much longer cooped up in that room, like an animal at the zoo."

I smiled warmly at her and lit up a Lucky.

"Don't worry though Errol, it's not as if I've run away again. Not properly anyhow..." She paused. "Stan and Mikey are away on business in Havana. They'll be gone for at least a week and I squared it with Mario that I was coming to visit you, I-"

"You told him that? That you were coming to see me, you mentioned my name?" I said it a little too coldly but I could picture the scene at the family home and see my grave being dug in the middle of the desert.

"Yeah, he was fine about it, don't worry. If there's a problem he knows where to find me. Anyway, they've been so much better these last few days and I'm sure Uncle Stan thinks a lot of you, Errol. He wouldn't mind us spending a little time together, you know, doing what friends do, or maybe even..."

"Just hold on a moment! This is not a very good idea at all. Don't you understand Claudia, I think you're a great kid but you come with a responsibility that I am not up to."

I held up my arm to the waitress. "A large cognac!" I shouted. "The hell with it, bring me the bottle with a large glass!" And then I looked into Claudia's big, blue eyes. "This is not a very good idea at all, baby."

"But Errol, at the house, what you said."

Tears were beginning to form in the corners of Claudia's beautiful eyes.

The cognac arrived and I poured a large glass and downed it in one go. I coughed a little and held Claudia's hand on the table. "Look sweetheart, what I said at the house. I was trying to comfort you a little, you know. I was trying to make things a little better... And they are, you said so yourself."

I poured another glass and retook Claudia's hand in mine. "But the idea of you and me going away together. It's just not going to happen is it? You don't know anything about me."

"I know you're a hero, that you've saved me from something bad on two occasions. I know that you're handsome and charming. I know that you're kind, caring and sweet. I know…"

"You don't know any of those things. At the moment I've got too many friends that are dying or disappearing. I am a dangerous man to be around and to be blunt, sweetheart, so are you. I just don't want any harm to come to you, that's all."

I gazed thoughtlessly through the open window. "I've never been able to hold a relationship for longer than two minutes at the best of times, and believe me darling, at the moment this is not the best of times." I rubbed my forehead and sighed deeply.

Claudia began to weep. Not hysterically, or noisily, just single tears falling down her warm cheeks. Slowly at first, then more and more.

"Claudia, you're a great kid. And for the little time we've known each other we've got on well. But unfortunately there's a lot of things you don't know about. I'm not all those lovely things you think I am. I'm actually a bit of a scumbag. And do you know how old I am?"

"I don't care how old you are. All I know is that you are all those lovely things, you really are Errol, you are to me. And the case, I can help you Errol, you know I can?"

Suddenly she looked a lot more optimistic. Her eyes lit up and she looked at me with expectation and hope. I tried to avoid her eye contact but couldn't.

She was beautiful.

I creased my face up and rubbed my eyes painfully. "Even if we could be friends. Even if, in spite of all the mess that I'm mixed up in at the moment could be sorted out..."

"Or lovers."

I tried to ignore that last comment and cleared my throat, determined to finish what I had started to say. I ended up mumbling something, something like we could never have a future together because she was born into one of the families. I tried to remind her just what she told me back at the house. About her boyfriends, dead boyfriends, about Mikey and his deep hatred of any male that dared to go near her. I tried to make it clear that I could not possibly get involved with someone such as she, that it would be tantamount to suicide. All I ended up doing was hearing, 'Or lovers' going over and over again in my head.

I let go of her hand and looked away.

"Errol, you're not afraid of danger, I know you're not. I bet in your time you've been involved with more dangerous women than me. Stan likes you, you know that. And Mikey, I'm sure you could handle Mikey."

She moved closer to my face so I could feel her hot breath on my cheek, "We could be good together Errol, you know we could."

As I stared out of the window, many things were going through my aching mind. I remembered when she first walked into my office, and then at the house, how she nursed my wound and we talked the night away. Then I remembered Marlow, and how I felt about her. Brief images of Ava, of Maggie Spanner and the others also shot by. But it was Claudia that was doing this to

191

me, that much I was sure. It was Claudia who was making me feel the way I thought that I would never be able to feel again.

"We've got some things we need to talk about," I said in a businesslike tone. "A little bit of business to sort out."

"And then?" urged Claudia, licking her lips.

"And then...I'll take you back to your home and we'll never meet again!"

As soon as I said it I regretted it. I guess it was the last line of defense putting up a valiant effort. How long it would last I wasn't sure, but I certainly expected it to last longer than the next forty-five minutes.

Chapter Twenty-Two – Courting

I took her back to Joe's and sat her down in the office. I apologized for the mess but she didn't seem to take any notice. She was no longer crying or pleading but just showing more of a stunned, shocked look on her face. All the while I was feeling increasingly bad, my stomach now wrenching with guilt whenever I glanced in her direction.

Joe had looked up with a big grin on his fat face as we walked through the diner. He looked like he was gearing himself up for a bit of tasteless banter; some reference to the croissant witticism of earlier no doubt. Fortunately, he must have picked up on the atmosphere that followed us through the room and put to good use the crash-course in subtlety I tutored him through prior to his first date with Mrs. Joe.

I relieved Claudia of her coat and hung it on the hanger without saying a word. I pulled out a chair for her to sit on, and pushed it back in, before taking a seat myself directly across from her. All the time she simply looked down at her hands placed neatly on her lap, in silence.

I lit up a Lucky and very businesslike took out a key from my inside pocket.

"I've been instructed to safely hand over this key," I said quickly and abruptly before exhaling.

"To me?" asked Claudia in obvious surprise, her first words for a good half hour.

"Uh-huh."

Still she wouldn't look me in the eye, for which I was presently grateful, but perhaps I now had her full attention.

"By who?" she eventually asked.

I again inhaled a deep breath. "By a man acting on the behalf of Liam Tighe. He's dead. I'm sorry."

Claudia immediately reached for a tissue from the box on the desk and put it to her eyes. She dabbed her already reddened eyes and blew her nose loudly. It seemed more of a shock than a terrible upset, and she composed herself. For the first time since we left the cafe, she looked directly at me. Her beautiful blue eyes were now more mournful than ever, crying out for a helpful soul to take care of her.

I looked back strongly and seriously. Although I was feeling affection, I was looking and acting businesslike. It was a part of the job that I did very well. Hiding your feelings was a fine art and absolutely essential.

"I don't want it!" she shouted, picking up the key and throwing it at me, breaking up a thoughtful moment, which had lingered too long already. I caught the key in my chest and put it back down on the desktop, eyeing Claudia harshly all the time.

"I don't want anything more to do with him. It's you, Errol, that I want. You know it is. Please Errol, you..."

"Maybe you've got some idea where the key is for?" I asked, interrupting her.

Again, there was a short silence. We just looked at each other across the desk, calm restored. Claudia longingly, me... well as un-longingly as I could muster. Minutes passed and then Claudia tried a little smile. "Yes, maybe I do," she said. "We could maybe go together. I'll show you where it is."

I sighed a deep sigh and opened a drawer to my right. I pulled out a piece of paper with an official stamp on it and a little text. "Look," I said curtly, "my job is to get the key to a Miss Claudia Cortene."

I pointed at Claudia. "That I have done."

I pushed the contract over to Claudia, the key with it. "Could you please sign at the bottom," I indicated where, "to verify this."

I looked up at Claudia. Tears were once again forming in the corner of her eyes. I looked away. "Now if you decide you do not want to remain in possession of the key, you might like to take it down to the nearest police station. Or alternatively," my tone altered, "you could put it in an envelope and post it back to me."

"If you want the stupid key, you keep it!" shrieked Claudia, a solitary tear straying loose from an imminent downpour. "But unless you keep me with you, you can find out where it goes yourself. I'm telling you nothing!"

194

"Don't be so damn childish!" I said, raising my voice for the first time. "This is not a game, grow up a little will you!" I felt like a father scolding his child.

Again, I sighed and looked at my watch. It was still early but what the hell I needed a drink. I got up and searched the cupboard for a bottle of Remy. There was none left and all I could find was a half-empty bottle of Daniels. It would have to do. Claudia watched me closely, still desperately controlling her welling eyes, looking fearful after my outburst. She nodded sheepishly as I offered, and poured us both a drink.

"If you sign the form I'll give you an envelope right now. You can tell me where the box is located and leave the envelope on the desk on your way out. I'm afraid that's the procedure. I've gotta have your signature to show I've done the job. Otherwise I..." I stopped mid sentence realizing I had just told Claudia what she wanted to hear.

She surprised me, however, signing the document immediately. Without even reading it. Then sitting back, looking straight at me, cupping the glass in both hands.

"Remember the night you saved me from George?" she asked, taking a sip and the coughing.

I nodded. "Sure I do sweetheart. Now could you also sign just here?" I pointed to the top of the document with my finger, waiting patiently for the next installment of Claudia Cortene, femme fatale.

"The way we danced the night away, you with your patched up midriff, me with my patched up life."

It sounded worse than a line from Gone with the Wind but it still brought a smile to my stony face. I held my finger on the document but my thoughts were now firmly with Claudia.

"I wish that night had never ended," she continued, staring off into space with a contented smile on her face. "I was the damsel in distress and you were my dashing hero."

She took another sip, this time spluttering all over the desk. Still my mind wandered. My trance was broken by Claudia moving my finger from the paper before her, and duly signing her name on the dotted line.

"Errol," she said inquisitively.

"Ahem," I answered, checking over the contract and signing it myself.

"Why didn't you make a move on me that night?" It can't have been because of my family as you had no idea who I was then..."

I nodded in agreement.

"And it can't have been because of Marlow," she sort of smiled and sighed at the same time. "Surely you weren't saving your loyalty for her because guys like you don't do that do they?"

I smiled and thought back to the warm memory she was evoking in me.

"So why not?" she persisted. "Was it the paternal coming out in you? You'd stumbled across a mixed up naive kid and instead of bedding her you just wanted to look after her and keep her safe from the evils of the world?"

She said it candidly, knowing it could have been true but wasn't. She smiled at my smile. She was way off the mark and knew it, but sensing she was getting the upper hand it didn't matter.

"That's probably pretty close to the truth," I lied, an uncontrollable grin now filling my face. We continued to look at each other and remember that beautiful night. Contemplating what if... After all we'd both had a lot to drink and were both clearly attracted to one another. I was never one to be too fussy about who's bed I was sharing, and Claudia -she was young, beautiful and... and available.

I looked deep into her eyes. "Pretty close to the truth, but as you pointed out," I chuckled, "my midriff was damn sore."

We both burst out into laughter together. At first wildly, then we calmed a little and still laughed. We ended up holding our sides, giggling like kids, I was still laughing when Claudia reached over the desk and kissed me full on the lips. Without a second thought, I took her in my arms and kissed her back passionately, holding her tight as I did so.

We kissed and embraced for what seemed like hours. She certainly wasn't going to get away from me now. I was at last admitting to myself what I'd known deep down for a while - Claudia meant a lot more to me than I had let on, maybe a lot more than any woman ever in my life. Whatever the reality, I was enjoying the experience and simply wanted to prolong the wonderful feeling. She may have felt that she had won but we both had.

We were still locked in an embrace when the door burst open and in stumbled Joe, flesh hanging all over the place, dripping with sweat.

"Sorry to interrupt Rolly, but this is important."

It must have been, Joe kept an anxious look on his face in spite of his momentously bad timing, without a hint of embarrassment.

"'scuse me, miss," he said and nodded in the direction of the kitchen. I parted from Claudia, giving her a little peck on the cheek, before picking up the key and following Joe through to the other room.

"What is it Joe?" I asked my fat friend, sensing the worry in his thick, sagging eyes. Joe was a good friend. He had been ever since I could remember. Like the father I never had guiding me through my youth and corrupting me through my early manhood. Although he was always there and always willing to help, I never involved him too much in my business. There was no doubt he was a safe and trustworthy as a poodle - the only form of torture Joe would succumb to would be to hold a freshly baked pork pie under his quivering nostrils. Let the aroma fill him with ravenous hunger, watch him drool with desire, and then devour it before him. Promising him one if he divulged the secrets of the world - but after all he was only an honest bartender. Maybe asking him to put me up in the present climate was involving him a little too much. Even if he knew the full story I'm sure he'd be only too happy to help, but that still didn't alter the fact that I was not the safest lodger to have right now.

"There's a man in the bar, and he's screaming blue murder. Says he wants to see you and he won't take no for an answer. Says he knows you're here and he must see you." Joe blubbered it all out without even taking a breath. I hadn't told him why I was using his office, he didn't ask. But even Joe could work out that I wasn't taking casual calls.

197

"Did he say what his business was?" I asked, my fingers curling the trigger of my rod.

"Didn't say. Just that he knows you're here. When I told him he was wrong he got all snippy, shouting and swearing the odds," he paused and looked himself up and down. "He even called me fatso!"

I chuckled before realizing my insensitivity and patted Joe on the shoulder. He took a deep breath, "Errol it looks ugly. He's only a little, tubby guy but I don't like it. He could..."

"Joe calm down!" I again patted him on the shoulder, "I'll sort it. You go through to the office and take Claudia for a coffee or something. She'll argue but tell her not to worry. Tell her I'll see her tonight."

Joe smiled. His face was smiling but his eyes still brimmed with worry. I nodded and he was on his way. I then put my rod away, brushed myself down and headed through to the bar.

The morning throng was a little thinner than usual. People were idly chatting their lives away amongst the dingy, sleazy decor that made Joe's what it was. Sipping coffee, nibbling doughnuts, all oblivious to the banging noise they call Rock 'n' Roll blaring out of the jukebox.

Stood up to the bar was a small, stocky man dressed in a perfectly ironed suit and tie. He wore a wide brimmed fedora, a half-empty bottle of beer by his side and was generally scowling and waving his fist at the barmaid. He was too preoccupied to notice me as I appeared in the doorway and casually made my way towards him.

I sat down quietly on a barstool behind him. One of the very barstools that sent me plunging to a horrible fall the night before Joe's wedding. Still the man ranted and raged.

"Jake," I said loudly, tapping my brief on the shoulder. "Are you looking for me?"

The man turned around in such a way I already knew the expression before actually seeing it. "Am I looking for..." he hesitated a moment, lost for words. "Am I looking for..."

The following hour was filled by a great deal of histrionics and accusations, all from Jake towards my good self.

He was a little perturbed that I hadn't been in contact, that I hadn't bothered to ring - after all it is only courteous, he said. He spent what seemed like days filling me in on what I already knew, going over things again and again - why had Weeny left town? Was he involved in the murder, or possibly even the murderer? What the hell was I chasing in Woodstock anyhow?

I felt like a naughty schoolchild in his principal's office. I bought him a drink and apologized as humbly as I knew. Still he whimpered, running out of steam a little by now, that if he was to do his job to the full- keeping me out of jail - he had to know the facts, all of them. Thanking him again as he promised me Beech had nothing on me. The investigation was now centered firmly on Weeny. I was now only an accomplice or conspirator at worst.

The sun was shining warmly as I parked by the Crayfish. It was the best seafood restaurant in New York, located right in the beach area of The Rockaways. Claudia had a cigarette as I went inside to order a feast to take out. The waiter smiled and had my order of lobster, ciabatta bread and a chilled bottle of champagne, packed neatly in a picnic basket within minutes. I folded a five spot and placed it in his pocket as he handed me the hamper and a pair of crystal flutes.

Claudia had finished her cigarette when I went outside. She smiled at me and closed her eyes soaking up the occasion. I smiled back and blew her a kiss as the sun illuminated her form.

There was an old, wooden deck that led down to the beach. I carried the basket and Claudia skipped at my side. She slipped an arm through mine and beamed at me right the way to the sand. This was the only place to surf in New York but today we had it to ourselves. We found a pleasant spot and put the basket down. Claudia fumbled in her purse before changing her mind and zipping it up again. She looked up at me and giggled. I giggled too and we embraced in the warm sunshine.

We sat on the beach with our legs crossed. I opened the basket, pulled out the blanket provided and smoothed it out before covering it with our feast. We then demolished the lot in quick time without uttering a word. The sun had dipped behind the tall trees but the birds were still singing.

Claudia lit us both a cigarette and I poured the champagne. "To July 3 1940," I said.

"And to us," Claudia said, and we clinked glasses before drinking. The bubbles must have gone up her nose because she crinkled it in the most incredible way and blushed sweetly.

We cleared the debris, packing it back in the basket and then snuggled up on the blanket. The sun was now dying a slow and beautiful death leaving a deep scar across the clear sky. Claudia nestled her head in the crook of my shoulder and sighed a contented sigh.

"Have you ever been in love Errol?" she asked me.

I drained my champagne and felt a little giddy, thinking about her question and just how truthful I should be. "Yes, a long time ago," I said having decided that I would be totally truthful. "I was once completely in love, so much so that it physically hurt us to be apart. When we were together the rest of the world did not exist, there were no stars, no clouds, no sunshine, nothing. Just us. It didn't matter if we were freezing cold, ravenously hungry or without a dime in the world, we had each other and we were as happy as it is possible to be."

"What happened?" she said, bringing me right back to reality with that hauntingly similar voice.

"She betrayed me. One day I may tell you all about it," I said evasively. "But then one day I might forget about past loves and only be able to concentrate on current ones."

Claudia made a happy noise and kissed me through my clothes. I stroked her hair and prepared for questions of my own.

"Did you love Liam Tighe?" I asked and quickly followed up with: "You don't have to answer that if you don't want to."

For a moment, Claudia said nothing and then she started...

"I thought I did at the time, although I have since realized that it wasn't love at all. I worshipped Liam right from the very first time our paths crossed. I was a college student and he was driving for a courier firm. He delivered parcels to my school every day of the week. We got talking one day and he

200

dazzled me with his passion and ambition. Of course, I would later come to understand that for most of his life Liam lived in an absolute fantasy world. Hardly anything he said he would achieve, he ever came near to achieving, but as a young and very impressionable college girl, I didn't care.

"I found him attractive, adventurous and exciting. He was a lot older than me and from a similar background but like me he totally rejected his family and wanted to distance himself from them.

"It wasn't long before we spent every waking hour together. I would go to his flat after college and he would cook me the most wonderful meals. He would then pamper me and treat me like a princess. I never had to lift a finger; he cleaned up afterwards and served me drinks, whatever I desired.

"Of course it didn't last for long. The Cortenes and the Tighes being what they are they soon put a stop to our friendship. Stan swore that he would never ever sanction a marriage between a Cortene and a 'bog trotter', as he called them. He could be very abusive towards them and never seemed to realize that it wasn't marriage that we were after. It wasn't even a proper relationship as such."

She sat upright and looked out at the darkening sky. "We made love once. It was my first time. My only time. I didn't really enjoy it and to be honest I think Liam may have been homosexual. He only ever talked about women in the company of his friends. As you probably know, Liam was very, very different in the company of his male friends. There he enjoyed playing the rogue. He never actually said it to me but I think he knew I knew and I was happy just to remain friends.

"We just about managed to keep in touch. Sometimes it was only once a week and for only minutes at a time but our time together was precious and we relished every second. Liam broke it off once, he told me he loved me but that we couldn't ever really be together. It was true but we couldn't stop seeing each other altogether either. But it did all come to an end rather quickly. When Liam was accused of that terrible offence, he had to get away. He swore to me that he didn't do it and I believed him, I still do, but he had to get away.

201

"I think the answer to your question Errol, is no. I thought I loved him but I don't really think that is what it was. It certainly wasn't how love should be, it wasn't what I think I may be feeling now."

She nearly made me blush.

"When Liam fled the country did you keep in touch?" I asked.

She shook her head. "No. I was sad at first but I soon got over it. And before you ask Errol, no, I do not know what the key is going to lead us to. I think I may know where it is for but as to what will be behind the steel door, I'm as much in the dark as you are." She turned and looked at me. "Are you in the dark, Errol?"

And so I told her. I told her all about it, missing bits out, mainly the gory bits or the bits I needed to keep to myself, but basically I told her the whole thing. She listened in shocked silence as I told her all about her friend, the deceptive Marlow and the latest twist bringing George Ferriby into the story. I neglected to tell her my suspicions about Ferriby icing Liam Tighe or that I had found Ferriby dead, but apart from that, I was candor itself.

She took a moment or two to take it all in. I watched her throughout my monologue and she underwent every emotion imaginable. Everything I told her really was a surprise, either that or she was the greatest actress ever.

"Is there any possibility the key is not from Liam?" she asked me.

I shrugged. "It's possible but I doubt it. There sure is one way of finding out for certain. Claudia, listen to me, there's something I've not told you."

"Something else?"

"I only discovered this yesterday. I don't really know how to say this Claudia, so I'm just going to come out with it."

Her eyes widened and she looked at me fearfully.

"George Ferriby is also dead. I found him in his lock up yesterday. I think maybe he killed Liam for the diamond and then somebody, probably the Coward, killed him."

This time she did surprise me. I expected her to break down. Hell, her last two boyfriends were both dead and I had broke the news to her in the last couple of hours. On top of that, the last six months of her life was now on very shaky ground. Her best friend was a liar, a cheat and possibly a killer.

But she took it well.

She took several deep breaths, smoked the rest of her cigarettes and clung onto me like I was her last lifeline. And then she talked. She talked about Ferriby, she talked about Marlow and she talked about herself. She made a point about telling me that she never slept with him, almost as if this was essential information for our own coupling to blossom. She told me what it was that attracted her too him but that they were never going to sleep together until they were married. She really believed that it would not be long. She relied on Marlow to give her the benefit of her own vast experience and she looked at her as her sister and soul mate. She was brutally honest in her recollection and we both sat with tears streaming down our cheeks as it slowly sunk in that she had been duped from day one.

I didn't probe too deeply but it transpired that she had nothing to add to the body of information I was already grappling with. For that I was grateful, I didn't need anything else complicating matters and for now my next move was clear.

We took a walk along the beach as far as Jacob Riis Park and only stopped to turn around when we came across a pair of male nudists. Claudia went red in the face as soon as she saw them and buried her head in my chest. We both indulged in some much needed laughter and skipped back to the car.

The drive back to the City was somber. Claudia told me that she would be returning back to the family home for the evening. Stan was going to call and she wanted to be home to speak to him. I was pleased she was thinking so clearly. She promised me she would be back tomorrow and we would begin a life together and that nearly made me cry again.

I waited with her until the car arrived and waved her off thinking just how great being alive was.

Chapter Twenty-Three – Wild Goose Chase

The next morning was spent tying up a few loose ends. First, I telephoned my launderette to change the delivery address for this weeks order. In response, I got a whole pile of abuse and a warning that there would be no delivery unless I settled the bill pretty soon. Second, I posted my application for license renewal. That also had been pending for a while, and now Beech was off my ass I anticipated a smoother journey.

Next on the agenda was my meet with Hermeez. He had called in late last night but I had missed him. I was fast asleep in Joe's office and my buddy refused to wake me. I was intrigued to find out how he and Marlow were getting along, and sure he'd only be too pleased to tell me.

I parked my heap illegally by the sidewalk, displayed my 'NYPD on call' notice, and got out. It sure was wet today, raining cats and dogs. Battering the ground with some force. I proceeded ahead on foot through Midtown Manhattan. As I checked my watch, rain trickled down my cheek and splashed across the glass face.

It was one fifty two.

I pushed ahead briskly, casually glancing over my shoulder as I passed The New York Public Library. I took a right turn on 42nd Street where it was a little quieter. I progressed quicker, altering my pace measurably weaving in and out of canopies to stay out of the rain.

Straight ahead, three hundred meters down the street, was Pershing Square. At Pershing Square, Park Avenue lifts off the ground to circle the huge mass of Grand Central Station, probably the most famous railway station in the world and without doubt the most beautiful. Constructed from a basic iron frame but with the exterior of a fine cathedral the Beaux Arts design has been regularly featured on celluloid. Again, I looked at my watch - one fifty seven - glanced in the reflection behind me and continued on towards the terminal.

The interior of Grand Central is even more impressive than the outside. The main concourse is truly one of the world's great open spaces, stretching 470 feet long and 150 feet high.

The ceiling is painted with a unique representation of the winter night sky, with 2500 stars sparkling out back to front. The beautiful marble corridors appear to go on forever, giving Grand Central a whole world of its own.

I arrived at the Oyster Bar right on time. I took off my fedora, gave it a good shake down, casually brushed down my slacks, straightened my tie and entered the building. Immediately a small, black waitress rushed up to me, relieved me of my trench coat and headwear, doing the same for another man behind me, wearing similar attire. She then ushered me to my table. The man sat two tables to my right.

The place was reasonably busy. Glancing around, there was no sign of Hermeez. I ordered a seafood salad and a bottle of crisp, white Chablis. The man across ordered smoked haddock with a glass of Zinfandel. Ten minutes later, Hermeez appeared in the large, wooden doorway with a scowl on his face. He was dripping all over the thick, carpeted entrance, smiled politely at the waitress, and made his way over.

He sat down quietly, a somber look on his handsome face. Looking straight at me, he said, "Errol, I apologize for being late. I've had a hell of a morning."

I poured a glass for Hermeez and smiled warmly as the waitress returned, carrying a whole pile of succulent seafood salad and two dinner plates. A moment later, she re-emerged with a drab looking haddock for the man across.

"What are you looking so peachy about anyways?"

I guess I was just one big smile. I couldn't help it, it didn't matter how much I thought about the case and what a big fuckin' mess it all was, I just kept breaking out into a great big smile. I let Hermeez stay puzzled for a moment longer and then I told him. By the end of my tale he was smiling too, but not as widely as me.

"That's great news about you and Claudia," he said. "I'm really happy for you."

"But?"

"But now I got to tell you my news and it isn't half as good as yours." He sighed again. "It has been one hell of a day, it

205

really has. I am sorry Errol, I am afraid I have lost her. She gave me the runaround."

I laughed out loud between spooning a mouthful of squid. Hermeez looked shocked, hurt almost. "You lost her? What did she do? Did she hide under the bed, whilst you were out buying parachutes?"

"This morning she was there," he looked down glumly at his empty plate. "When I awoke this afternoon she had disappeared. What can I say Errol? I am sorry."

I glanced over at the man across. He was gulping down his wine quickly, dribbling it down his stubbly chin. He looked over and our eyes met. His were filled with tension. Instantly he looked away nervously.

"Okay you lost her. That in itself doesn't matter," I continued, sucking out the juicy flesh of an oyster. "But it was worthwhile, yes? You did find out something worth knowing?"

"Oh yes!" answered Hermeez. "I have found out a great deal of interesting information. But..." he took a sip of Chablis, "nice wine," he said before filling his plate with seafood, all the melancholy of a moment ago seemingly disappeared. "But when you hear it..." he shook his head. "Well... maybe she'd have been useful to hang on to."

"I'm listening," I said, just as the man across clicked his fingers to catch the waitress's attention. As he did so his jacket swung open revealing a holstered piece.

"Did you see that?" asked Hermeez

I nodded, "He's..."

"He's drinking Zinfandel with smoked haddock."

I paused for a chuckle before returning my attention to Hermeez. "He's been following me most of the journey here. I'm not sure where he picked me up but I remember his from as far back as the Brooklyn Bridge lights."

Still in disgust Hermeez eventually said, "Don't worry Errol," whilst cracking open a crab's claw and sucking out the white meat. "He has got no chance. Zinfandel with white fish, I ask you."

Over the next half an hour, I listened as Hermeez Wentz told me Marlow's story. All the time we kept close tabs on the rookie to my right, who gulped down more and more wine, whilst making himself all the more obvious. Hermeez made a hell of a story out of it all. Comical, thoughtful; it was like a chapter from Gone With The Wind. Slowly and methodically, he described how he managed to track her down from the distinctive scent of perfume at the scene of my trashed lock up. She was staying at the Hilton Hotel and bought the perfume from the hotel perfumery. He told me how he earned her trust and respect through his boyish charm and an ingenious cover story, so that she'd tell him anything. He sounded the true professional, doing a job thoroughly and having a good reason for everything he had to do. Hell, he even had me believing the deep soul searching he underwent before sleeping with the broad. The sacrifice of guilt, of corrupting a woman's emotions for honour and the sake of a dear friend.

"Once I was booked in at the Hilton, I realized that I would need a good cover story to approach her. Something that would enable me to talk openly to her and for it not to seem queer that I would want to listen to what she had to say."

"I'm surprised you didn't just wow her like you usually do with the ladies."

"If it wasn't such a delicate and important situation I would have Eezy," he smiled. "She is a looker isn't she?"

I smiled. "So what was your guise?"

"New York Times journalist and prospective unauthorized biographer of the soon to be Governor of New York State and top crime prosecutor Thomas Dewey. I played the role low key, interviewing several guests in the lounge, taking lots of telephone calls and plenty private conferencing with the manager. It cost me, mind you, but it worked. It wasn't long before Marlow sent a bottle of champagne and two glasses to my private table. She soon followed and we sparred for the next hour or so, teasing and testing each other without giving too much away.

"Of course she was interested in what I was writing. She had noticed the way the waiters and distinguished guests were all falling over themselves to talk to me, and the way I listened before jotting it all down in a notepad the minute they were gone. She guessed I was a detective, a policeman even, but it was the mystery that intrigued her. She said she had always been drawn to detectives, particularly lone wolf types. She found them exciting and dangerous and that was a big turn on.

"I was surprised by how candid she was. We had barely finished our first glass of bubbly and she was already laying herself bare. I told her my cover and she swallowed it without batting an eyelid. She made a point of praising crusading journalists equally as high as detectives.

"I told her my subject matter and that really got her interest. Thomas Dewey was a perfect figure to write a biography about, she went into quite some detail about him, surprising me just how knowledgeable she was. I went into my pre-planned spiel about the structure of the book, who I would be concentrating on and the issues I would be raising. I made a point of keeping the subject of Arthur Flegenheimer low key. Sure I would delve into their very public feud, the rumors that the Dutchman was going to personally hit Dewey and that that possibly contributed to his own slaying. But I didn't want to overplay my hand. At this point, that would be like telegraphing my real intentions on Trans-Continental but I got the subject out in the open in a muted way. I was intrigued how she would react, whether she would shy away or take the bull by the horns.

"By now we were into our second bottle of champagne and Marlow wanted to talk of nothing else but my book. She was acting sexier and sexier as the night went on and I was finding it difficult to keep my concentration. Then she dropped her bombshell and I was brought right back down to earth. One moment she was blowing smoke rings through her voluptuous red lips, the next she told me she had been the mistress of Arthur Flegenheimer and that if I paid her $10,000 she would give me enough information on Tom Dewey to make my book a bestseller.

"I could not believe what I was hearing. I had barely got into my routine and had not yet dare mention the questions I really wanted to ask her and here she was telling me just what I wanted to know. I stalled on the money for obvious reasons but

208

I made it clear to her that I was interested. She accepted this, after all it was highly coincidental that I had stumbled onto such a scoop and who did carry that amount of cash on their person? I ventured a joke and answered Dutch Schultz and she liked it, inviting me back to her suite to continue our business.

"Hell I didn't know how to play it now. I know what you had told me, that she was one dangerous lady to be alone with but I found myself drawn in like a fly to a spider's web. I was desperate to find out more, to quiz her on the diamond and find out what the hell was really going on, but more than that I was desperate to kiss those beautiful red lips.

"Back in her suite we got more comfortable; shedding our coats and Marlow fixed our drinks. I took the end seat on her sofa and she sat on the other side swinging her legs onto my lap, caressing my chest with her stockinged feet. She told me that she would accept a small advance on the ten big ones and she would give me enough to be going on with. Was I interested? Of course I was interested and I emptied my wallet, getting a little embarrassed as a rubber dropped out. She immediately picked it up, smiling to herself before placing it on the coffee table and lighting a cigarette.

"For the next hour or hours, I'm not quite sure how long it was, she told me more about her life with New York's Al Capone. She made it sound like it was more of an equal arrangement, she insisted she was not just his bitch and she got just as much out of it as he did. Hell, do you doubt it, she is one woman that is not going to be second best in any relationship? I listened as she mocked Schultz's young wife, the lovely Francis reveling in telling me how they often made love under her nose. She insulted his henchmen. Abbaddabba Berman was the only one she respected, the rest were just monkeys, she said and would have walked off a ten-storey building if Dutch asked them to. She even talked pretty scathingly about the Dutchman himself, saying he wasted the opportunity that he had to be the City's numero uno. If he hadn't have been so damn obstreperous he could have cut a deal with Luciano and taken a piece of the Syndicate. Instead he let his Zionist principles get the better of him and got landed with a life on the fringes, keeping her on the fringes with him.

"She talked solidly for a very long time and hardly any of it referred to Dewey but I just let her continue. When she got on to the subject of Schultz's killing she got a little emotional but it stemmed mainly from the fact that she was not looked after. Because she was only his mistress, whatever their real relationship was, she ended up with nothing. She was not mentioned in the will, was known to nobody that mattered and so was left empty handed.

"And then she mentioned the diamond. A big, blue and extremely beautiful diamond. She didn't know its history but she knew that the Dutchman had it, he had promised her that it would be hers, but somebody had killed him before he got around to giving it to her. Now she got quite tearful so I comforted her and she let me. Before long we were making love in her over size bed and I was feeling like I had gone to heaven. The diamond was forgotten but not for long.

"When the morning came she was back to being the hard-headed businesswoman. However hard I pushed her she refused to talk any more about Dewey, Dutch and especially the diamond. All she said is that she was determined to retrieve it. After all she was the rightful owner and she would make sure that she got her birthright. When I challenged her she spat out a bitter diatribe, she said that every keeper of the diamond that did not merit its ownership had suffered a nasty death. She said that it almost had a mythical power and would never bring happiness to the undeserving. As far as she is concerned she is the rightful owner and will not rest until she has it back.

"We spent the rest of the day together and as the hours passed by she mellowed again. We had a very pleasant time and once again ended up back at her suite in The Hilton. I had batted very carefully as far as the diamond and Schultz were concerned. I wanted to take my questioning a step further but wasn't sure how to approach it."

My friend smiled a wry smile. "When I had worked it out it was too late."

210

He laughed, filling his glass again and stealing the last of the king prawns. Hermeez was simply all wrapped up in his own melodramatics. Somewhere along the line, however, I had a funny feeling it wasn't all as it seemed. Hermeez made it sound like a super job, the master at work when all the while I got the feeling he'd been led a line. That whatever she told him she wanted to tell him. That she did so on her terms and not his, simply making it look like he'd pulled the strings. Maybe I was wrong, but I got the feeling Hermeez had been taken for a sap.

We'd now been in the Oyster Bar a good hour and a half and the man to my right was getting edgy. He'd been looking over at regular intervals for the last fifteen minutes. The waitress came to clear the plates away and take any more drinks orders.

"Thank you sweetheart, that was very nice," I said. "Now do you want to bring over a bottle of bourbon and would you be so kind to ask that gentleman over there if he wants to join us? Thank you."

Hermeez smiled as the waitress disappeared, searching for a bottle of bourbon. "So there it is Errol. I am sorry I lost Marlow, but it was a worthwhile exercise. An enjoyable one also."

"Yeah, you did a good job, mate, a good job," I said even though I was feeling a little put out at Hermeez's sloppiness. "Now I'm going to go to the bathroom in a moment. You take care of Mr. Incompetence over there and meet me at Joe's tonight."

"You got it partner. No worries," laughed Hermeez, letting out a huge guffaw as the confused looking man pulled up a chair.

When I returned to my car, there was a confused looking police officer by its side. He was knelt down peering through the side window, his helmet placed precariously on the roof.

"Is this yours, officer?" I asked the startled man, knocking the helmet into his shaking hands. "Now I appreciate you..."

"Excuse me sir," interrupted the officer, arrogance restored. I stepped back, offering him the floor.

211

"Do you realize that you're illegally displaying an NYPD sticker in your..." he paused, "...vehicle?"

I shrugged. "I'm on important business. Private investigator, don't worry about it. You got a problem contact Timmy..."

"What is your name, sir?" asked the officer, interrupting me for a second time, before pulling out a notepad. "I'm afraid I'm gonna have to book you for this. It is a serious offence you understand?"

I sighed and pulled out my car key, putting it in the lock.

"Your name sir, what is it?" persisted the police officer, holding his pencil threateningly.

"You want to learn a little respect officer..." I inspected his badge, "...officer Jarvis. Now I've told you I'm on sensitive business and I'm sure you've got a lot better things to be doing. For the record the name is Errol Black, now if you don't mind I'm going to be on my way."

I could feel my anger rising. Twice now I had been interrupted by this supercilious, snotty nosed kid. Controlling it I opened the door and threw in my hat and coat.

"Don't move any further sir! I'm warning you. Turn around slowly with no sudden movements."

I couldn't believe what I was hearing. I looked around to see the pimply police officer, gun in hands, taking aim. His hands were violently shaking, but he had a determined look on his face, his nostrils flared and teeth gritted.

I held up my arms limply and turned my body full around so we were face to face. All the time I was grinning uncontrollably, surprised at the boy's persistence. I could see the sweat running freely down the acned cheeks of the young man. He must have only been eighteen, twenty two at most.

"As you will not co-operate sir," he stammered, edging towards me and putting a hand inside my coat, "I'm gonna have to take you in."

His hand ran over my holstered weapon and stopped. I could almost feel the increasing rate of his pulse, the worry on his young face intensified. Before he could say anything else I gave him a short, sharp knee to the groin. He let out a deep squeal, dropping almost to his knees.

I looked around the empty street smiling before I gently took his sticky paws away from my trench coat. Easing his handgun from his unresisting grip, I re-holstered it. A quick jab thudded into the side of the man's jaw, putting him out cold. I held him firmly around his shoulders so he didn't fall, and placed him neatly on the sidewalk, his back leaning against the wall.

"Can you please get this man some assistance?" I shouted to the news vendor down the street. "I think he's drunk."

I shrugged, flashed a wide grin and fixed up the engine of my baby. Jeez, what was the NYPD coming to these days? In the days if Bob Curtain a couple of tickles, like the one's I just dished out, would not only hasten up the imminent journey to the station, but get you as good hiding to boot. I gave the unconscious policeman one last look before mixing with the late afternoon NY traffic.

Chapter Twenty-Four – Bequest

Hermeez drove sensibly and safely through the early evening traffic. The avenues were packed, every lane a mass of loud horns, flashing lights and stressed drivers. I looked at Claudia, seated behind me in the back seat. She looked back, a picture of happiness.

As we slowly made progress towards the Ambassador Hotel, my curiosity was growing. For too long I'd been on this case. Chasing all over the place. It was certainly long overdue that it was solved, and I was well aware that it was only the Benjamin Wilson windfall that was keeping it going. Then I could wrap up five years of history and wave good bye to a heap of spooks. And bury the ghost of Dyke Spanner for good.

I was flung at the door as Hermeez swerved suddenly to avoid the car ahead. He immediately reeled off a torrent of abuse. My first thought was that it was a crude attempt by the Coward to recapture me. Retaliatory gesturing by the other driver, however, eased any such worries. Mopping his brow, Hermeez lowered his gear and continued slowly.

"Ahem. You all right in the back sweetheart?" he asked, chuckling embarrassedly before turning to me. "Teach you to sit up front."

Ten minutes later we arrived at our destination. Hermeez slowed the car down gently to a standstill outside the main entrance. He already had a fifty-dollar note sticking out of the window as the little mustachioed man came running to the car, closely followed by the burly doorman. Discreetly the man whisked it from Hermeez's grasp and smiled greasily.

"You can wait just down there, sir."

The man pointed to the VIP drop-off area. "I'm afraid ten minutes at the…"

Another fifty,

"Take as long as you need."

Hermeez parked up and killed the engine. I opened the door, brushed down my trench coat and straightened my hat. Claudia got out and stood by my side. "Okay this is it, partner," said Hermeez in pure New Yorkian. "Be careful in there. Don't you worry I'll be watching your ass. You can count on me."

I slapped him on the shoulder and slammed the door shut. I couldn't deny that I was feeling a little trepidation. Since our luncheon at the Oyster Bar Hermeez had been visibly on edge and that in turn put me on edge. I couldn't help thinking about him and Marlow together and the image bothered me. It wasn't exactly jealousy, I was firmly in love with Claudia by now, even if I didn't admit it to myself, but it bothered me nonetheless. I wasn't sure if I was feeling let down by my buddy or by Marlow. I had no right to feel either, after all Hermeez was only doing what he did to assist me. Or maybe that was what was really bothering me. Maybe I was sceptical as to what Hermeez's real intentions were. He still refused to elaborate any more on his acquaintance with Arnold Muchado, clamming up whenever I broached the subject, and yet he was most insistent that I kept him firmly informed on this case.

I tried to put this all to the back of my mind. At least for the moment. Now wasn't the time to be getting more uptight than I already was.

We strode on through the main entrance and confidently made our way to the reception area. It was a long mahogany bar with various signs above. All polished and shiny with two overlarge cacti in clay pots at each end. By the check-in counter was a heavily bearded man of South American origin. He was arguing vehemently with the attendant, who's grasp of Guatemalan was clearly no greater than my own.

We marched past and stopped under another sign.

"Good evening sir, what number please?"

I stood over it, Claudia supportively by my side. We were in the sanctuary of a private cubicle with bullet and sound-proof walls. There were no windows, just a door -two feet thick solid steel -that could only be activated by a computer. When we wished to leave we simply pressed a red button on the keypad on the wall and waited for the delectable young assistant to assist us.

The room was small, maybe eight feet by eight. It contained a table and two chairs, solid and varnished, a telephone with no outside line and the small keypad on the wall. It was how I imagined a war cabinet room to be, minus the drinks tray of course. The only other thing was a clock. A cute little novelty, carved in the shape of King Kong that ticked loudly.

I could feel the sweat on my brow as I hovered over it. The loud tick of King Kong rang irritably in my head. It was not as large as I expected, what the attendant called a "medium-sized" box, but it was in the maximum security quarters. I took off my hat and coat and handed them to Claudia. She passed me back a small silver-plated hip flask, so I took a big gulp. It tasted foul, but what the hell.

I gave the flask back to Claudia and rummaged in my pocket, pulling out a small chrome key. Turning it over and over in my sweaty palm I could feel my heart beating heavy. I turned to Claudia. "Are you sure you want to stay, darling? Just in case something goes wrong?"

"I won't leave you, Errol."

I smiled and turned to the safety-deposit box on the table. One quick turn of the key and the lock released. I reached out, my hands trembling a little, and lifted. It was a lot heavier than I imagined but a touch more force and the lid was up. I looked into the box, then across at Claudia and back at the box.

When we arrived back at Joe's Diner that night there was a whole entourage waiting for us. The usual illegal poker game was making slow progress in the smoker's corner. Most punters were keeping a watchful eye on the barstool seating Timmy Matthews. Next to Tim sat my faithful secretary Ava Jamieson. They were chatting away quite happily. A bottle of red wine next to Ava on the bar was almost empty. Filling their glasses very attentively, as Joe always is to a visiting officer of the law, was my friend the landlord.

Before I even managed to get through the door I was accosted by a hack. Investigative reporter for the New York Post and very keen to assess my knowledge of the increasing organized crime in the law. It goes without saying that he was sent packing story-less, but he did leave a card and raised my suspicions of just what he really wanted from me. Why would a Post reporter want the views of a humble New York PI on such a subject? He dropped a few lines about a shadowy organization emerging in the City and the lack of an arrest for the ongoing homicide investigation of detective Dyke Spanner. Maybe he would later be worth twenty cents?

"Here they are!" announced Joe theatrically, as myself, Claudia and Hermeez walked through the door. "Look who's here Eezy, shall I grab another case of bourbon from the cellar?"

"Errol," Timmy Matthews cut in, breaking my thoughts of Joe hauling a case of bourbon up from the cellar -the last time he tried he was laid up for a fortnight nursing a sore back. "How about we have a little chat over there?" He pointed to a quiet corner.

I nodded ushering Claudia to the barstool the other side of Ava. Hermeez had already pounced on Tim's, who hastily grabbed a bottle of Jim Beam from Joe and an extra glass.

"It's been a while. I thought maybe you'd have called me?" said my barrel-bellied buddy, filling the glasses.

"You've been in good contact with my secretary." I nodded at Ava across the room, who was guarding Claudia from the amorous clutches of the Diner's regular crowd. "Maybe it's not the proper practice for suspects to fraternize with investigating officers."

Tim creased his haggard face into a look of hurt. "Come on Errol, don't you start on me already. You've done yourself no favors, no favors at all. Beech isn't happy." He lit up a cigarette and threw me the packet. "You never did do yourself any favors with that son of a bitch."

"So how's the investigation Tim?" I watched him closely. "Did Weeny Jung Ping kill Dyke?'

Tim looked worried. He mulled it over and rubbed his forehead uneasily.

"Errol, listen to me." Suddenly he looked serious. "Really I should take you in for questioning. If it was Beech here and not me you would already have the bracelets on."

"What's stopping you?"

Tim sighed. "Do you really need to ask me that?"

My face softened and I waved for Timmy to continue...

"I have received an anonymous tip off. Normally we would ignore it, but because of the circumstances I can't."

"The circumstances being the NYPD's finest haven't got a fuckin' clue who has been going round shooting people."

Tim smiled at that.

"What did it say?"

"It said that one Errol Christopher Black was the accomplice of Weeny Jung Ping in the killing of Dyke Spanner. Ping hit him first and you finished him off, hence the two type of bullet wound we found in Dyke."

Now I was surprised.

"It was a male. He refused to give any more details than that but he insisted he had evidence that would lead to conviction, he had a material witness and he would soon be in contact with further instruction."

I lit another cigarette from the stub of the last one and chuckled.

"One other thing. It was the same man that put us onto Weeny in the first place. You know I shouldn't really tell you this, Errol. Bullshit aside, I'm trusting you a lot further than I should." He inhaled his cigarette deeply. "When we busted into Ping's shop we found a whole heap of shit in there. Not only weapons, but bomb making equipment, classified papers and the whole deal. Real hard terrorist shit."

He smiled and downed his bourbon. "I don't know if he whacked Dyke or not. To be quite honest I've got no fuckin' idea. But whether he did or not, he's in, or involved in, something big. I always knew Weeny Jung Ping was involved with the Tongs, hell maybe even a leader but you know the Tongs. They keep themselves to themselves and they get left well alone. Not anymore. This is big. Hell, we've got enough just from the shop to put him down for a long time."

I looked my friend over. He looked tired, as if he'd been chasing this goose for way too long. "So why are you here Tim, if you're not going to take me in? If you, or Beech's boys think that it's Wang, which incidentally I don't think that you do, then pull the son of a bitch and charge him." I lit up another cigarette and exhaled. "Or do you want me to solve this little thing for you?"

"Well what the hell have you been doing this or the last few weeks, Errol?" he exploded. "Something to do with Dyke, I know that much. I'm pretty sure you wanna see the killer in the dock just as much as I do. Otherwise, you wouldn't keep sending me firearms and ballistics to test at the lab. To keep you updated the bullets don't match and the last gun you sent me is a no no as well."

"Maybe not for the killing of Liam Tighe."

"You know that Liam is dead?"

"Check the gun Tim, I think you may be pleasantly surprised. Just don't tell Beech it came from me."

I poured us both another drink. "What is the official version on Liam anyway?"

"Nothing concrete. To be quite honest with you it's been kept well out of our hands, him living in Mexico and all. The Department naturally assumed it was his own family. That they had eventually caught up with him. You know the Tighe Family have long memories and Liam did take their entire stock of China White."

There was a short silence between us. Timmy studied me closely, beads of sweat had congregated around his eyebrows. He wiped them with the back of his hand. "And George Ferriby," he said. "Was that you as well, Errol?"

I said nothing.

"He was killed with a different weapon to Dyke. Just in case you're interested. Are you?"

I still said nothing.

He looked me square in the eyes. "You aint been in the office much lately, Errol. And whatever it is you have been doing, you've been keeping it to yourself." He couldn't help but glimpse over at the lovely Ava as he said it.

"Oh that's nice," I snorted. "Now you're plying my secretary with drinks. I never thought you would have done that Tim.'"

"Come on Errol, don't give me this bullshit. You know Weeny Ping better than most people. When we find him Beech is gonna cook his ass. Maybe yours too."

He sighed. "Why don't you tell me where he is?"

I remained silent, sipping my drink.

"For God's sake Errol," Tim erupted again, his red cheeks flapping. "I've given you a hell of a lot. Just give me a little back, that's all I ask."

I looked Tim straight in the eye. He was looking old; old and tired, his eyes sagging, heavy lines underneath. I told him so and he waved his arms irritably.

"Okay Tim," I said. "Listen to me now. You know better than anyone the way I operate and you're going to have to respect that a little longer. I'm giving you my word right here and now that by the end of the week you will have Dyke Spanner's killer in your cells. With a bit of luck you'll have George Ferriby's also. I'll hand over the murderers personally. Now all you got to do is keep cool and keep smiling." I squeezed Tim's cheek and he pulled away slapping my hand. "In the meantime you try and find Weeny Jung Ping. I don't know where he is I really don't. You try real hard and when you've got him maybe you could give me a call. I'm sure you don't want to see the wrong man go down again."

"Oh come on Errol, Beech would never..."

"To hell with Beech. He wants a result more than you do. Different reasons, I grant you, but he needs it and you know it. This is for you Tim, not Beech and not the fuckin' department. It's for you."

Tim scratched his nose. Studying me intensely before refilling the glasses. "So you're saying you really don't think Wang killed either of 'em?"

"I'm saying nothing more," I slapped Tim on the shoulder. "You'll get your plaudits, just let me speak to Wang, you must have some idea where the little yellow bugger's hiding."

At last Timmy smiled and raised his glass. "Errol, you're as impossible as ever. Cheers!"

We spent the next couple of hours chewing over old times. Claudia was the only real outsider amongst us, but she fitted in famously and Ava looked after her real swell. I talked briefly to Timmy about the Coward. He appeared to be none the wiser but was happy to listen to what I had to say. When I changed tack and turned the tables he quickly got frustrated by my evasiveness and gave little away.

I managed to find a moment alone with Ava whilst we waited for Joe to change a barrel.

"She checked out today," she said, meaning Marcia.

I nodded letting her continue without interruption.

"Before she did she was visited by twice. One meets the description I gave of Muchado."

"And the other?"

She pursed her well-glossed lips and sighed. "It was Hermeez."

When the clock chimed twelve times Hermeez escorted a rather drunken Ava home and Timmy Matthews sulkily caught a cab. I informed Joe that I would be taking Claudia to a hotel for the night and he bid us goodnight. I'd booked us a suite at The Hilton.

The short drive to the hotel didn't take long. Throughout the journey Claudia wouldn't leave me alone - running her hand up and down the inside of my thigh, softly kissing my neck. She was unrecognizable as the timid little girl I thought I knew. Of course, this would usually have been great but I still had a hell of a lot to think about. Despite her magnificent efforts, I still couldn't take my mind off the sealed envelope that was in my pocket.

I parked up in the basement car park and killed the headlamps. Claudia immediately crawled over from the passenger seat and sat astride me. "Are you gonna take me upstairs and have your wicked way?" she asked, a silly grin plastered all over her drunken face.

I kissed her passionately on her red painted lips, opened the door and lifted her out. I checked everything over and followed her onto the concrete area.

"Come on," I said linking her arm. "Let's get you to bed."

221

The reception was only a short stroll from the car park but took a good half and hour. Every few steps Claudia would stop, pin me against the nearest pillar and do the most amazing things to me. Letting out a girly giggle whenever somebody walked past, therefore alerting them even if they hadn't noticed. We finally arrived at the entrance and I checked in.

I looked at Claudia and smiled. The hell with it, the envelope could wait until the morning.

I put the key in the lock and turned. The door swung open displaying a large, airy room, thickly carpeted in warm maroon with a four-poster bed and a sunken bath.

Claudia immediately headed for the king size, four-poster bed and began taking up different provocative poses. I took off my shoes and walked over to the large window in the far wall. Looking out through the thick glass there was the most spectacular view over Liberty Island. The statue of Liberty stood commandingly over the floodlit city. I pulled the drapes tightly closed and went through to the bathroom.

When I returned to the bedroom, I found Claudia curled up on top of the duvet, fast asleep. She had a contented look on her sweet, attractive face. I sat by her side stroking her silky brunette locks for a short while before carefully undressing her down to her underwear. She possessed a lovely petite body, maybe not film star proportions but the curves were in all the right places. Her small, but well shaped breasts looked beautiful in the soft peach cotton enclave of her brassiere. Gently I maneuvered her into a comfortable position and tucked the silk sheets snugly around her. I was just about to reach for the sealed envelope in my inside pocket when the telephone rang.

"Yeah," I said holding the receiver accusingly.

"Mr. Black, I have a message that there is a visitor waiting for you in the hotel bar."

"Ahem, what is the name of my...visitor?" I asked, checking that Claudia had not stirred.

"I'm afraid I do not know the answer to that, sir. No name was given."

The line went dead.

I sighed heavily and slowly lowered the receiver.

222

My mind was racing. Could the visitor be Hermeez, or even Timmy? Maybe he'd found something for me. No, they were both half pissed and would definitely have given a name. Maybe it was Coward or at least one of his monkeys - they'd finally caught up with me again. I knew only too well that they eventually would, but was hoping to have everything sewn up by then. So well sewn up in fact that they would have no option but to leave well alone.

Maybe it was someone else?

I checked over Claudia once again and locked the door on my way out, leaving the 'Do Not Disturb!' notice hanging. The elevator was empty and a couple of minutes later I found myself in the entrance to the Short Bar. It may have been late but there were people littered all around the large, decidedly un-short bar. Couples chattered away happily, business men in dark suits and groups of drunken people partying. I quickly scanned the tables, but couldn't see either anyone I recognized or anyone on their own.

I went to the bar and ordered a bourbon. When it arrived, a man sat a couple of barstools down with his back to me. Looking around there was no sign of anything improper so I walked over to the man and tapped him on the shoulder. When he turned around I almost fainted.

Chapter Twenty-Five – Stranger in the night

"The hell you did!" I shouted at the man across the table. "You let me walk right into this whole mess and then left me to it. You didn't give a damn whether I lived or died."

The bottle of bourbon on the table was taking a battering. Already half-empty in a matter of minutes. We were now sat at a table in a quiet corner of the bar, well out of earshot.

"Errol, everything I told you was true." He held out his hands. "I just missed things out. I always have and you wouldn't expect anything else, you're just the same. There were things I didn't feel I needed to tell you and there were things I didn't want to tell you. Hell, you know the business we are in. When it came to the crunch I just didn't have any choice."

"You always have a choice." I shook my head. "I'm sorry, I'm having a little trouble understanding all this. Are you saying you didn't know that I was going to be pinched by the very people I had you protecting me from? Did it take you by surprise? What happened, did you get sloppy, did you have too many drinks and forget all about me? Come on Weeny, I want some answers."

Weeny Jung Ping's eyes darkened and he fixed a stare on me that despite his raggedness was pure malevolence.

"I didn't get sloppy," he asserted. "And seeing as you appear to be in the mood for accusations, I did not kill Dyke Spanner or Woo Wang."

I watched Weeny as he spoke. His initial anger had now subsided. He looked a shadow of the man he used to be. His face thin and gaunt, devoid of any colour. His hair thinning increasingly, and his eyes, they looked dead. He had never been a bulky man, but by his own proportions he looked weak and had visibly lost a lot of weight.

He inhaled his cigarette deeply, like it was the only lifeline he had.

"Errol, the truth is that they got to me. They got to me a while ago but I thought I could handle it and so I brushed it off and carried on doing what I have always done. I thought that with you on board we could beat them at their own game."

224

"Excuse me, waiter," I shouted at the dumb looking man who was idly collecting glasses. "I want a large pack of Lucky Strikes...please," I added as an afterthought.

Weeny again began to speak but I waved him down, "What does Coward, we are talking about Coward aren't we?"

He nodded.

"What does the son of a bitch have on you?"

Weeny looked away. "More than you think."

I said nothing.

"You know what he wants and you know what he is prepared to do to you to get it. What makes you think he isn't doing it to me as well? I am sure you have read it all in the newspapers. Only I don't have the get out of jail free card that you do. All I have to do is to leave well alone, let them get to you and thus to get what they want." He finished one cigarette and quickly lit another. "But I can't do that can I? They killed a dear friend of mine so being what I am I throw it back in their faces and I refuse to cooperate. Only next time, they kill two more and put the squeeze on my whole operation."

He looked me square in the eyes, like he was pleading an old buddy to throw him a lifejacket. The waiter interrupted with the cigarettes. I lit one up and listened.

"Even then I didn't leave it. I couldn't could I? I didn't really believe he would fit me up satisfactorily but if he did I was going to fight it."

"What happened?"

"Muang. That is what happened."

Muang was Weeny's youngest sister. He told me how she had recently been seeing a nice young Chinese man. Weeny was protective of all his family and with Muang it was no different but they got on well. He appeared the perfect gentleman and treated her with great respect. Within days, they were spending every waking hour together and Muang had fallen head over heels in love. It all happened so quickly Weeny did not have time to stop it before he realized what was happening.

"When Muang left home I had no idea what she was getting herself into. She left in the middle of the night leaving me a short note. 'Don't worry!' it said but that is exactly what I

225

started to do. I tracked her down and that was when I discovered who it was she was really seeing. It killed me but I did not know what to do."

"So what changed?" I asked, pretty sure of what the answer would be.

Weeny talked vaguely of the Coward. Although he hated him deeply I got the feeling he held a grudging respect for him also. Like the old adage honour among thieves, mutual respect amongst gangsters is just as common.

"He has got no record, if you ask around the local firms you will always get short shrift. Do you remember what it was like at Woodstock? Right in the middle of a piece of prime Tighe territory you still got the feeling that it was Coward running the show. The man is an absolute phantom and a hell of a lot more fearsome as a result.

"You know that he is reputedly the elder brother of the Dutchman?"

I nodded.

"I don't know if that is true. Maybe it is, maybe it isn't but either way Coward is not planning on going down the same way. Maybe he seems a lot bigger due to his absolute secrecy and ability to operate in the dark. Whatever you do Errol, do not underestimate him. Whoever he is, he is extremely well connected and probably right to the top. The Tighes have long been a spent force. In fact, most of the Irish are declining and the great Jewish gangsters of old are on the wane too. Luciano may think he is the undisputed King of New York and maybe even America, but there was room for Dutch Schultz and there is room for Phillip Coward."

His eyes glazed over again. "But I didn't always think like this. The more time went on the more Muang's abduction ate me up. When Woo Wang first passed me the information about Dyke and the diamond I wouldn't have believed it would lead to this."

"You still haven't told me what happened."

"I got a warning that if I didn't cooperate then it would be Muang's life next. Coward wants that fuckin' gem so much it doesn't matter what he has to do to get it. They made it clear she

226

would suffer. Always messages; telephone messages, notes, words in ears, never in person."

Tears filled Weeny's eyes. "The thing is, Errol, I love my dear sister more than I love myself. I didn't know how much they'd got to her... brainwashed her. I thought she was the unsuspecting victim."

He filled his glass and gulped it down in one go, his thin neck accentuating the liquid as it went down. "In the end it was probably her that telephoned the police to frame me up."

The word 'me' made me wince.

"For years I saved her, I compromised my friends, I made sacrifice after sacrifice and look how she repaid me..."

Tears rolled down Weeny's cheeks and he shook uncontrollably. I finished my Lucky Strike -my third- and held out a hand. Weeny held it tightly, a grip you wouldn't have believed the little man had in him. For a few moments, we sat silently holding hands and then Weeny composed himself, wiped his face and smiled.

"Two days ago I took her back. They did a good job on her she fought like a trooper, but she's safe. I took her to a safe place and in forty eight hours time she'll be on a plane, with or without me."

I looked at the clock on the wall. It was late - two thirty - but the Short Bar was thriving. Before I even raised my arm, another bottle of bourbon was on the table. The waiter smiled a sickly smile and went back to washing glasses.

"I'm sorry but I got to ask you this."

"I know, you want to know what happened at Woodstock. But Errol, I have just told you. I had to make a choice and I am sorry you came second. If it's any consolation there are few people in this world that you would come second to, but in spite of all that she has done she is my sister. And I kind of figured that you would survive, after all you still hold all the aces."

I nodded, watching Weeny closely. He appeared to have made a speedy recovery. Now talking quicker and louder, with more bounce.

227

"It wasn't me that killed Dyke, although I may get the chair for it," he added. "I'm afraid I don't know just who it was but I think you know a man who does. I haven't even met him face to face whereas you are practically his drinking buddy."

We sat for the next ten minutes or so in silence. I was desperately trying to take in what my former friend had told me. He just sat slumped in his chair. His thin face looking desolately glum. Occasionally he would raise the glass to his colourless lips and gulp down wolfishly before returning his gaze somewhere over my left shoulder.

Eventually, it was Weeny Jung Ping who broke the silence, "Of course you don't have to believe any of this, Errol, although it would make it a little better if you did."

Again, there was a long silence.

"And when you sprung Muang, what then? Why haven't you been in touch?"

"Errol, it is late, you are tired. Think a little more before you talk," he smiled. "The police arrived on my doorstep and I was forced to flee. A double homicide suspect, fugitive from the law and no doubt top of one or two other hit lists."

I looked lost, shrugging my hands in the air. "So what happens now, Weeny? Have you got one more chance to hand me over for a passport to Brazil?"

A look of genuine hurt came over the Chinese man's face. Hurt and shame. He slowly shook his head. "My business in New York is now at an end. I care only what happens to my family. And my friends," he added a little hastily. "I have never been interested in this diamond." He paused. "If it does actually exist at all. It has taken a great deal of effort to find you, you cover your tracks very well." He reached out and touched my shoulder. "I just wanted to square things up...and... and tomorrow I give myself over to the police."

I was surprised but kept my face stolid and impassive.

"...and if I go to the chair, so be it."

There was a long pause. Our eyes never left the other's for a second. It was Weeny that cracked first.

"At least I know my sister is now safe. And if I know you rightly, Errol, you'll crack the case. Maybe not for me, and I

228

can't blame you for that, but for Dyke, and for the sake of honour and maybe a little bit for yourself."

At that, Weeny Jung Ping got up from his barstool and walked slowly from the Short Bar.

I remained seated on my own for a good while longer. Still the pianist tickled the ivories, and still the beer drained slowly away. And all the while old Father Time went about his business, making it 3.32 before I let out a big yawn. It had been a long day and it was now time for some rest. The sealed envelope would have to wait a little while longer. It was after all addressed to a Miss Claudia Cortene, even though she point blankly refused to have anything to do with it.

As I got to my feet and slung my trench coat over my tired shoulder, I reflected on a fruitful day. A good deal had happened this rainy, bitterly cold Autumn day and I was now pretty confident of having a happy reunion with Lieutenant Beech by the end of the week. Tomorrow would of course be a big test - would I hear from Timmy after all, and would the secret contents in my inside pocket turn out to be everything I hoped they would be?

The waiter bid me goodnight and I slowly trudged out of the Short Bar, into the elevator and waited for the doors to close. The lift was surprisingly full for this time in the morning, so much so we almost had to hold hands. An older lady dressed in a purple, full length dress with her gray hair cut in a bob, winked at me. I smiled back and looked down at my feet as the elevator began its slow climb.

I was suddenly feeling very tired as I made my way along the corridor. The ride up had taken longer than expected, the doors opening at every floor to let someone stagger out. My head was feeling heavy and the world around me was drifting. When I reached the room, I fumbled with the key, managing to fit it into the small keyhole at the fifth attempt. The door swung open and I tumbled in feeling more and more disorientated. Could it be the alcohol? -it certainly appeared to have affected most other people tonight. Had I drunk that much? I wasn't sure just how much we had consumed.

The room was dark so the lights stayed off.

I slowly undressed, tossing items of clothing all over the room, not caring where they happened to land. I had just enough energy to amble over to the washroom, fill a tumbler with water and wash my stubbly face. The ice-cold water splashed over my eyes several times, before I turned off the tap and got into bed.

Claudia was fast asleep under the covers, just as I had left her earlier. She murmured quietly in her slumber, nothing comprehensible. I pulled the duvet up tight around my chin and closed my eyes. Steady shots of pain jutting across intermittently. I closed my eyes tighter and tried to go to sleep.

I awoke suddenly in a cold sweat. The sheets stuck grubbily to my back, making a tearing sound as I peeled them off. I sat up sharply resting my back on the headboard. My head felt like I'd done ten rounds with Joe Louis. I rubbed my eyes irritably and slowly opened them. It took a moment or two to focus, the light making them sting. As that gradually wore off I looked at my watch. It was ten thirty three.

There was no sign of Claudia next to me! The other side of the bed was neatly made up. I could hear the shower in the bathroom and the sweet humming of a lady. I noticed my clothes were all folded up in a pile on the side of the bed and a steaming mug of coffee was beside me on the dresser.

I smiled and sat back relaxed. The coffee was hot. Hot and thick, just as I liked it. Sun streamed in though the large window, the curtains tied back as far as they would go. Old Lady Liberty smiled at me and I winked back at her, remembering the old woman in purple last night. I don't know why, but suddenly I imagined her as the Statue of Liberty, in that gaudy dress, coated in thick make-up. I shook my head trying to shake the crazy thought from my mind.

Claudia wandered through, only a small pink towel covering her assets. Her masses of shiny, brunette locks placed up on her head. She smiled sweetly, and then frowned before heading over to the cabinet. Searching through the drawer, she eventually pulled out a small container that rattled, before taking out two tablets and swallowing them down whole.

"You're finally awake," she said, giggling and came and sat by my side. "I thought maybe you could do with it," she pointed at the mug in my hand, not looking me in the eye.

"You're a sweetheart," I said, kissing her forehead softly. She looked real beautiful, leaving little to the imagination. I adjusted her towel as it started to come undone, so to protect her innocence.

Claudia looked surprised. "I didn't think you'd mind," she said smiling, "not after last night."

I laughed. "Last night, do you remember much? Was it good for you?"

Claudia looked puzzled. A little embarrassed, her cheeks reddened then she smiled. "I was okay wasn't I?" she asked as if afraid of the answer, "you weren't disappointed?"

Again, I laughed and Claudia jumped to her feet and walked across the room. Hiding her face from me she softly said, "I did make an effort Errol, maybe I'm not too experienced but I want to do is make you happy."

"Okay, okay. Stop right there sweetie," I chuckled. "I'm being cruel here..."

"No you must tell me you..." she interrupted, now holding the towel tightly around her.

"Claudia listen," I held up my hands, "last night, when we arrived back here..." I could see her cringe, "nothing happened okay. You fell asleep and I couldn't bring myself to interrupt you. You wouldn't have wanted it to be like that anyway."

"Really?" she said, and I nodded.

Claudia breathed out a huge sigh of relief. "Thank God for that, I couldn't remember a thing. I thought maybe I'd..."

"Shush, shush." I opened my arms and held her against me.

We both got dressed in silence, smiling cheekily at each other like kids. Slowly and meticulously, I attired myself in my working clothes from an overnight bag. Crisp, white shirt, black trousers and socks. I left the trench coat off for the moment, adjusting my jacket perfectly. Claudia took a little while longer, doing something great with her hair and lightly painting her face, creating a beautiful picture. I used the time well, munching breakfast and mulling over my next move.

"Are you going to open the envelope today, Errol?" asked Claudia, a little unsure.

"I guess that's up to you honey. It was left to you in the will. I got my money," I said referring to the $10,000 in used notes that were left to me in the safe. "The next move is up to you."

Claudia shook her head. "I told you yesterday, Errol. I want nothing to do with it. Whatever there was between me and Liam... it finished a long time ago!"

I nodded in agreement.

"But if it's gonna be a help to you Errol, on the case, you should open it."

The rest of the morning was hectic. I got in touch with Ava who informed me that Mr. Wilson had sent me a postcard, several postcards in fact from all over the world. The guy was spreading the net far and wide. I then got a call from Timmy; he was in unusually high spirits and gladly informed me of the capture of one Weeny Jung Ping. I could have ten minutes with him if I got over to the station pretty damn quick. When I declined the offer he hung up on me, calling me a 'goddam son of a bitch.'

Although Claudia was getting pretty caught up in the case I felt it was unfair to involve her any further. Still, I was apprehensive of just how quickly we should progress despite our acceptance of a few home truths. She wanted to stay by my side but I ignored all her protests and dropped her off at Ava's promising her dinner that evening. I also urged her to ring her family regularly and let them know she was fine. The last thing I needed was the Cortene's back on the scene when things were coming to a crucial stage.

I then stopped at my temporary office at Joe's Diner. My next move would be a visit to my apartment in the Bronx. It had been a while since I'd been 'home', not deeming it a safe area with everything that was going on. That was sure to be the first place they looked. I felt pretty sure that they would have had a man there 24 hours a day, maybe they still would. However, it was long overdue that I returned to clear up a few things. I arranged to meet Hermeez there in an hour. I figured it would always be safer in numbers.

Before I headed off there I had just enough time to open the elusive envelope. I felt a sensation of excitement fill my body as I thought of what the contents may hold. It had taken a lot of restraint not to open the bloody thing right there and then at the hotel, but in spite of what I had told Claudia I wanted to do it alone. The initial disappointment was replaced by increased curiosity. But with Hermeez breathing down my neck and the simple fact that it was addressed personally to Claudia, I withheld. There was of course the possibility that it was nothing, maybe just a little windfall or a memento for an ex-sweetheart. Although with a ten grand fee simply to deliver the key, I dismissed such thoughts.

I lifted up my trench coat and fingered through the pockets, trying to remember just where I'd left it. At first I thought maybe I missed it due to the excitement and my hurried search. I checked and I checked again, at first not realizing the inevitable outcome.

I sat down with one of Joe's awful coffees, drinking thoughtlessly, searching desperately through my mind for an answer. When had I lost it? - the chat with Weeny, the packed elevator ride during the night? The realization hit me like a sledgehammer: the disorientation, the immediate drowsiness and the uncharacteristic sleep in till gone ten. It seemed pretty likely I'd been drugged, but by who? Weeny? He had given himself up, Timmy already told me, and, I sighed. I had already declined to see him.

I parked my heap two blocks away. Making sure I was alone, I got out of the car and locked her up. It wasn't really necessary - if someone wanted to take her they would. Some chance, I thought, and strided out on the slippery sidewalk. The rain poured down heavily, bouncing high off the avenue.

The neighborhood looked the same as always. Gangs of smokes loitering on every street corner. All huddled up proudly wearing the latest designer gear and more gold than you could find in the Federal Reserve. Thick clouds of smoke billowed up from their heads into the grim, dark sky. Litter strewn all over the sidewalk like a whole stack of rubbish skips had been lifted up in a big crane and turned upside down. Left to scatter aimlessly over the graffiti ridden estates.

I soon arrived outside my flat and looked around for any sign of impropriety. From nowhere I felt a firm hand on my shoulder and swung around.

It was Hermeez.

"You okay?" he asked, not his usual merry self I noticed.

I nodded. "Is everything all right?"

He grabbed my arm and physically pulled me over into a forested area at the side of the apartment block. "I've checked the place out. As far as I can make out there's one in the flat and one just over there." He pointed at a stationary vehicle thirty yards on the street. Inside there was one man, seated in the passenger seat, carefully studying a newspaper. I recognized him as the man from the Manhattan Bistro.

"Have you checked the contents of the envelope?" he asked almost anxiously.

I looked my friend over. He was dressed the same as usual. Immaculately as ever. He had sweat dripping from his face.

"It sure is raining hard." He brushed the sweat off, sensing my stare. "So Errol, has Liam left us a trail to the diamond?"

"No, I haven't opened it just yet," I said, not quite lying. I looked back at the car. "Are they armed?" I asked stupidly.

Hermeez didn't answer immediately. "Oh yes," he eventually said, "but it's not a problem. I thought you were going to open it last night. Why then are we here if you haven't opened it? That is the object of the exercise is it not?"

His persistence was irritating me a little. "Look, we'll talk about that later, okay?" I lit up a cigarette and inhaled deeply. "Just trust me okay?"

Hermeez nodded slowly without looking me in the eye.

"Are you ready?" I asked and smiled.

The atmosphere that had been building since we met was quickly lifted. Hermeez snatched the Lucky from my mouth, stamped it out and smiled. "Sure I am Eezy. We do not want to go giving them smoke signals, though eh?"

Checking carefully that there was nobody around Hermeez weaved in and out of trees till he was as close to the car as was possible, whilst still being concealed. He leaned with his back against a small bricked wall, maybe ten yards from the blue Chevette. I, meanwhile, brushed myself down, stood up tall and began a slow stroll towards the entrance of the block. I looked straight ahead, apparently oblivious to the shiny motor car until...

The familiar clicking of a handgun being cocked. "Hold it right there dipshit! Turn around slowly, no sudden movements!"

I held my arms in the air at my sides and slowly turned around. I couldn't help but smile as I saw the haddock man, gun in hand attempting to look menacing with a pink plaster stuck right across the bridge of his nose. He scowled as nastily as he could manage and waved the gun about restlessly.

"Get in the car, Black, you're coming with me."

I put my hand on the door handle, but before the door opened there was a thud, and the gun toting man slumped forward. The grinning face of Hermeez Wentz looked through from the other side. He took the key out of the ignition and carefully placed the newspaper over the unconscious man, before joining me at the entrance to my apartment.

"Okay Eezy, you sure will be all right alone?" asked Hermeez, looking from side to side.

I flashed him a confident smile and slapped him on the shoulder. "You just be ready, okay, like I told you. If it all goes to plan I'll be out in fifteen minutes to half an hour and we drive away."

Hermeez nodded and disappeared chameleon like into the background. I straightened my collar and proceeded forward into my apartment. Almost as soon as I entered, I was once again greeted by the cocking of a weapon. I turned slowly, hands in the air to find not one but two men facing me. One I didn't recognize - he was a small, stocky man with fair hair. He had a young face and a shiny handgun. The other had a smile as wide as his face and was wearing an undersize suit. It was clearly straining to hold in the bulk of the man's frame, fraying at the seam around the inside leg.

"Mr. Black, so nice of you to pop in sir," said the large man, "do sit down."

I looked around, found a stool - one of only three seats in the joint - and duly sat down. The place looked pretty much the same as I'd left it. I noticed there was a half-empty jar of coffee on the work-surface and a pile of take-away food wrapping. I took off my hat and looked at the fat man, who was slumped unceremoniously in the only comfy chair. The fair headed kid was behind him, on his feet. He paced back and forth nervously, switching the gun from hand to hand.

"I hope I didn't keep you waiting too long," I said, a hint of humor in my voice.

The fat man chuckled, his spotty bow tie wobbling as he did. "Oh, I expected nothing less from you, sir. You are a man that does just as he pleases, I am sure." He looked over his shoulder at the kid. "Where are your manners Audrey, get Mr. Black a drink, he must be thirsty."

The kid scowled, put his gun down on the work-surface and opened a cupboard. I could just about make out the contents. "You can put that right back where you found it. Do I look like a bloody Russian?" I commanded as the kid pulled out a bottle of vodka. He looked directly at me, a look of menace, but did as he was told as the fat man nodded. Next, he pulled out a bottle of Scotch Whiskey and filled two glasses.

"Oh, you not drinking with us Audrey?" asked the Coward as he passed over a glass, not one of mine I noted. The kid failed to reply, opting to retrieve his pistol and hover around in the background, eyeing me throughout with distaste.

"Now sir, I do hope you are here to talk business. Much as I like your company my patience does have a limit and I have traveled a long way to meet you."

"Last time you wanted to do business you threatened to frame me for the murder of Dyke Spanner. You set me up to come all the way upstate to Woodstock so you could frame me for another murder, and then you had me kidnapped before I could chew over the pros and cons of the situation. Since I got back to the City, somebody has started their own hotline to the police and one of my friends has been arrested. What on earth makes you think I would do a deal with you now?"

He shook his head. "This has been most unpleasant business, most unpleasant indeed. I do apologize, sir for all the inconvenience that you have suffered. Most wholeheartedly, I apologize, but I must protest. You really have got me all wrong. None of those things that you accuse me of are true."

"Is that right?"

He nodded.

"So who telephoned the NYPD? And maybe I dreamed it, but I sure as hell can't get the taste of chloroform from my mouth."

"I have said this to you before, Mr. Black, but seeing as we are about to conduct some very important business I will tell you again. Firstly, I am not a gangster, nor am I a criminal. Check me out with your police officer friend, Sergeant Matthews and you will see that I have an absolutely exemplary record. I will tell you a few other things as well. I did not, nor do I know who did, kill your friend, Dyke Spanner. He was very courteous and amenable to me at all times and assured me that the diamond would indeed be mine, for a good price of course. Neither am I fitting you up for this or any other murder. I suppose in my haste I may have given this impression but it was pure jocularity and maybe a little bit of bluffing on my part, and for that I am sorry. Think about it Mr. Black, why would I want to put you in jail when there is a healthy transaction for us, $20,000 for you and the Blue Tavernier for me?

"On the subject of Mr. Ping." He flung out his arms and shrugged. "Weeny Jung Ping has been a ruthless Tong leader for many years. He is responsible for some terrible crimes alongside his mentor Mock Duck. Have you thought maybe it is Ping that is double-crossing you? And what of your partner, Mr. Wentz? I hear that he had a cross to bear with Spanner. Are you really sure that he is not responsible?

"If anything, Mr. Black, you are closer to organized criminals than I am. Like I said, I have a clean record. I am

237

unfortunate in that I am related to the late Arthur F but you, you choose to fraternize with the Cortenes, the Tighes and the Tongs."

"Okay so we're being open, then answer me this. Why did you kidnap me?"

"The simple answer is I didn't. Who exactly did you see when you were taken? My guess is nobody, least of all me or any of my staff. And who did you see once you came around? Once again it was nobody you see here. Would it by any chance be the lovely Miss Marlow?"

My face gave him the answer.

"I will give you a friendly warning, sir. Miss Marlow is a loose canon. I have to admit I have had dealings with her in the past but I know her capabilities. Not only does she sleep with people to get her own way, she kills them if she doesn't. It was most likely her that took you in Woodstock and with the sole reason to get her hands on the diamond and keep it for herself. For some insane reason she thinks she deserves it."

"I don't buy it," I said, "Why did we have to meet in Woodstock if all of this is true? And Marlow, she maybe be a bad egg but a killer, no."

"Woodstock is my home. It is also a very good place to meet and see if you were serious about doing a deal, which I think maybe you are. And if you really don't believe me about Marlow ask around amongst your 'friends'. She is the original Tiger to Virginia Hill's Tabby."

There was a long pause in which Coward smoked a couple of Gauloise and I did the same. Eventually I smiled and his face lit up. He let out a little giggle. "Let's get down to business. Am I right in thinking you now want to do a deal?"

The kid watched me anxiously as I threw back the whiskey, coughed a little, and held up the glass. "Why else would I be here?" I replied shaking the empty glass.

Coward gestured with his large, flabby arm and once again Audrey visited the "drinks cabinet". I snatched the glass back from his firm hand and waited for Coward to speak.

"I thought as much," he sighed. "It would be most out of character for you to simply return home unawares. After all the trouble you took to evade my boys this last week." He laughed an ironic laugh. "Most out of character."

"He didn't come to do a deal, he finally tripped over his own clever ass!" shouted Audrey loathsomely. "He's not half as smart as either of you two like to think."

Coward frowned. "Oh Audrey do be quiet." He turned to me. "So rude isn't he?" He offered by excuse limply dropping his wrist, before turning back to the kid. "I wasn't by any means blaming you or any of the other boys for Mr. Black's continued elusiveness." He smiled. "I was simply pointing out the professionalism of the man we are honored to accompany. This man is a true master of his trade. Yes, you should watch and learn from our Mr. Black..."

I sat back silently as the accolades rolled on.

"...and a great entertainer, oh yes, a truly interesting man, by God. Now please remain silent whilst we talk," he added patronizingly. "We have some very important business to resolve."

The kid stomped off out of sight in the direction of the bedroom. Watched closely by the Coward who raised a bushy eyebrow. He looked glued to the chair, his lower body not having moved an inch. His mammoth upper body hung heavily, yet dressed perfectly.

"He's a wild player young Audrey," I said aloud. "A bit of a hot head."

The fat man brushed it aside. "Oh yes, I suppose he can be a little excitable..." he said, "an invaluable employee, however. Like yourself, Mr. Black, he too is excellently adept at his chosen career." He sipped gently at his drink, his bright red cheeks shining with pride. "He's been with me since he was a boy," he glowed. "Very much the livewire in his youth, but I took him under my wing and through hard work and a lot of patience, channeled his immense talents."

He turned to face me. "Don't worry about Audrey," he assured. "He's a good boy at heart."

A short silence followed before once again we got back to the subject of importance...

239

"So, Mr. Black, what may I ask, is the deal that you have in mind? I don't suppose you have brought it with you?"

I shook my head. Coward shrugged and lit another cigarette.

I grinned a wolfish, toothy grin and began, "I think over the last few weeks I have come to appreciate just how much this little rock means to you."

"Oh yes, by God, it is a fine specimen. Unique in its beauty, unique in its worth. Nobody, Mr. Black, can overstate just how much I desire to have my hands on it. I will of course have the $20,000 ready for whenever you desire, in cash of course."

"Of course."

The fat man looked at me, his eyes were wide with excitement, his face shaking with anticipation. "Am I right in assuming you now have access to it? That you have dug her out of wherever it is you have hidden her and that you can bring her to me soon?"

"In return for the $20,000, plus a small favor, I will indeed bring her to you. Well to be frank it is quite a big favor, but nonetheless."

The fat man's face dropped. All the built-up joy and anticipation was replaced by frustration. "Come, come sir. $20,000 is an immense amount of money."

I stood up suddenly and picked up my hat. "You've tried pinching me once, and it didn't work. You've tried fitting me up and it didn't work. Whatever you say I know that you have not ruled out killing me as well and you know what, that won't work either. Now, if we're going to do business we do it on my terms or not at all," I said loudly.

Coward held out both chubby hands. Shocked by my short temper he waved me back down gently, a pained look on his meaty face. The kid had reappeared in the background, maybe hoping to be called into action. The portly man however was most apologetic, and soon returned his mood to one of excitement and hope.

"I do apologize, sir, by God I do." He paused. "But you must forgive me if I am a little anxious." He opened his mouth

240

wide, showing his white teeth, before continuing, keeping a close eye on Audrey. "After all, sir, you have once before refused point-blank any sort of deal and now in spite of my friendliness you continue to hurl insults at me."

"Look if you don't want to trade, I'll be on my way." Again, I got to my feet, ignoring Audrey's advances.

Once more, the Coward relented, first waving the kid away like you would swat a fly, before gently urging me to retake my seat.

"You appear to be a little too demanding in your present position, sir, by God you do." He smiled. "However, I am sure you are a man of your word..."

I nodded solemnly.

"And I understand, though not necessarily relish, your conditions and practices. Whatever favour you require I will grant you."

The kid sighed in disgust. "Why the hell are you letting him dictate the terms? If I wanted I could pop him off right now," he shouted aiming his handgun, before making a 'pop-pop' sound with his lips. "He's nothing more than a punk. No deal, you hear me, no..."

My fist connected with the kid's jaw mid sentence, sending him sprawling to the polished oak floor with a thud.

Coward creased his eyes shut, wincing as Audrey hit the floor. He made no attempt to move, simply looking up as I examined my fist. "A little rash, sir, I think. The boy was..."

"The boy was a pain in the ass. Now it's quieter and unless you're going to shoot me," I eyed the tiny silver pistol the fat man now held in his left hand, "we should continue."

A big happy grin once again appeared on the man's face. He peered over his knees to check that Audrey was out cold before asking, "Okay sir, what may I ask is the bargain? Is it more money you require, I have lots of that."

I shook my head and a look of surprise filled the fat man's features. "A private detective that doesn't want more money, you never fail to surprise me, you really don't." He let out a shrill laugh. "So if it isn't money?" He squeezed his flabby lips together questioningly.

"I want a fall guy, maybe two fall guys. Tell me, are you familiar with all your boys?" the last word hung in the air dirtily.

The fat man lifted a heavy arm, the flesh hanging against the tight suit. The arms were way too short. He scratched his head, a look of nobility now on his face. He sniffed discreetly before fiddling with the spotty bow tie below his chins. "Yes, I do believe that any task on my request is to be undertaken by a personal friend. Why do you ask, sir, surely not to mock at their inadequacies?" He raised an eyebrow and smiled. "Believe me, my men rarely fail to satisfy. Not all my..." he paused, "...adversaries have your guile sir."

"I'm sure they don't," I replied. "But satisfactory or not, there's one or maybe two of your boys running around, who've done some naughty deeds. One of which interests me." I hardened my tone. "And if you want the diamond I want them trussed up and handed over. How about young Audrey here, he seems pretty handy with his toy, maybe he's my man?"

"Oh no, no no sir, you mustn't get over zealous." His sudden look of consternation was replaced by one of deep thought. He rubbed his bear-like paws together before slapping his knees. "If I remember correctly you are already acquainted with your one and only desired scapegoat, are you not?"

"I guess I am," I said. "I want him, if not the diamond gets lost again and this time it won't ever be found."

Soft murmurs drifted up from below the Coward's knees. Quickly he checked to see the kid rolling over, who was coming round, however still only semi-conscious. He edged his feet away from the kid's head, as if avoiding a nasty insect.

"However for me to hand over a prospective killer Mr. Black, well..."

"That's the deal!" I said abruptly. "I don't care whether he actually did it or not. Take it or leave it, but just in case you are thinking of using that thing," I nodded at the little silver pistol in his grubby hand.

"Oh, no no no sir, self defense I assure you," he replied indignantly.

"Well just in case you are," I smiled. "The diamond dies with me. As far as you're concerned anyway, so just think on. I'll be in touch."

"I'm sure you will, sir, I'm sure you will."

I strode out of my apartment, giving a groggy but conscious Audrey a little kick in the ribs along the way. Within a minute, I was sitting in my car going over the next move. I noticed an old Bluebird parked twenty feet back. Its occupant had long, dark hair. Hermeez appeared from nowhere and got in the passenger seat. He had a strange look on his face, almost as if surprised to see me.

"You were longer than I expected," he said. "A moment longer and I would have come looking for you. How did it go?"

I looked him over. "To plan," I answered, squinting in the rear view mirror. The other car had started up.

"And just what, may I ask, does 'to plan' mean exactly?" he spat, never afraid to speak his mind.

I fired up the engine and pulled away from what would always be home, closely followed by the Bluebird. I don't know why but I thought of my mother. It was a while since I'd seen her although we did try to keep in touch -Thanksgiving, birthdays, a couple of other times a year. She was a fine lady, beautiful, smart and the most loyal, brave person you could ever hope to meet. She'd got me out of so many scrapes as a boy, never once sacrificing her personal ethic. 'To protect your family and friends is paramount. No matter what they do, or what adversity they face, you must stay strong and loyal. Good bonds will always be rewarded and are priceless.'

I reflected on the many lectures I had received as a kid. They didn't all get a good audience. Very few in fact would have been given any appreciation at all when given, but in time they sunk in. She was a creature of honor; a fearsome lady to oppose, but one you could always rely on. I would give her a call. Soon.

Hermeez brought me back to the present.

"What the hell is going on, Errol? Why are you being so secretive?"

243

"You ask too many questions, Hermeez. Leave the questions to me and everything'll be just fine."

The Bluebird had disappeared.

Hermeez leaned over the steering wheel, hauling it towards him. The car veered nastily towards the sidewalk, mounting the sidewalk. It stopped just in time to avoid a passing suit, leaving a skid ten feet long behind us. I slammed my hands on the dashboard and looked over at Hermeez.

"What the hell did you do that for?" I shouted.

"Are we doing this thing together, or not?" he demanded. His face was a mixture of anger and confusion. It was an unusual moment between us. An atmosphere hung nastily in the air, the horns and flashing lights of other cars, the heavy drum of rainfall on the roof, were not there. For a long while, we looked at each other, his dark commanding eyes not giving. My own stare was one of searching, probing, with no answers forthcoming.

The Bluebird re-emerged behind us.

I sighed and smiled, feeling a little suffocated by Hermeez's intensity. "You know me Hermeez, I like to do things my own way. You don't usually have a problem with that."

"Doing things your way I can live with. Knowing you for so long I've had to, but... if your way means not trusting your best, and probably only, friend in the whole of this world." He sighed deeply. "Is this because of Marcia?"

I said nothing.

"Come on, Errol, talk to me. I have told you that there is nothing to worry about."

"Tell me again. What was Arnold Muchado doing in our office?"

"I'm not going to answer that but if you think…"

"What the hell am I supposed to think? The man is a fuckin' lunatic. If we get in any trouble, we help each other out, that's the way it's always been. I've been straight with you on this case all along but right now..."

He stared unblinking at my gaze. I looked conciliatory at him, before directing my gaze at the hectic traffic. As the rain poured down I remembered when I first saw that look. It was a moment after Hermeez took a bullet in the shoulder, and went on to shoot himself and half of the unit out of ammunition at the Battle of Edson's Ridge. It was the second and near successful attempt by the Japanese to break our perimeter on Guadalcanal. They were stopped just short of the airfield and I later heard several people explain their failure with one man's actions.

That man was of course Hermeez. He hated everything about Guadalcanal, seeing it as a nasty, poisonous morass. He hated the crocodiles, the red, furry spiders, the lizards as big as panthers and the whole turgid swamplands covered in slithering creepy-crawlies, rats and crabs. He even hated Spam and dehydrated potatoes, which put him at a real disadvantage.

He hated it all, but in spite of his loathing for this most beautiful of islands he was the only thing that got me through it. Like many of the thousands of American casualties, I got a dose of malaria early in the campaign and several times thought I was going to die there. My buddy would not let that happen. Time after time he saved mine and many other's lives. It was something I had never forgotten. Maybe, until now.

I turned the key in the ignition. The engine turned over but did not spark. Still Hermeez stared. As I tried a second time and the engine fired, he opened the passenger seat door and got out. I wound down the window, but he continued to walk the other way, hands in pockets and head down facing the ground as the rain poured on.

"The diner, tonight. Be there, Hermeez, be there!"

I telephoned Claudia at Ava's from the hotel to cancel dinner. I was in a foul mood and had way too many things to think over. In a matter of a few moments I managed to alter her 'can't wait to see you' real excited mood to one of glum rejection. I promised to meet up for a drink at Joe's later that evening, but she insisted on pointing out that I had earlier promised dinner. She said she had remembered something important to tell me. I told her later. There was a knock on the door. She persisted. I hung up.

"Who is it?" I shouted, heading towards the door curiously.

"Room service," came the predictable reply.

I hadn't ordered any. "Just a moment," I countered, positioning myself just behind the door. When it opened I would be in the perfect position to disarm or disable whoever it might be. "Okay."

The door opened and a trolley was wheeled in. In one movement, I slammed the door closed and flung my arms around the trolley-pusher. Our two bodies tumbling to the floor. We wrestled around on the soft carpet and I managed to wrench off the fake hotel service cap, revealing long, silky red locks.

I stopped struggling and rolled over on to my back laughing. The trolley-pusher shook her hair free and smiled sweetly. She must have left the Bluebird a while back. It was not in the hotel car park. I had checked.

I got to my feet and walked over to the drinks cabinet. There were only miniatures so I mixed a few and handed one over to the room service lady. She took the glass from my grasp and sat down on the edge of the bed, the same bed that Claudia had slept so sweetly in twenty-four hours earlier.

"I thought it was you," I said, searching in my shirt pocket for a cigarette. "You're a lousy tail," I laughed.

She pulled a fresh packet of Luckys from her trolley and tossed them towards me. A lighter followed and I lit one up.

The trolley girl stood up, six feet of sheer beauty. Slowly she slipped out of her uniform revealing a shiny black dress that sparkled. She then pulled out a stick of lip-gloss, shook her beautiful hair back and applied it to her pouting lips. When they had a good coat of blood red gloss, she smiled, thrusting out her shapely breasts.

"So sweetheart, what's the story?" I said to Marlow and slumped back onto the comfortable bed, waiting for the dramatics to begin.

"I was afraid I was never going to see you alive again..." she began in a melodramatic, whimpering tone.

I reached forward and gave her a gentle slap around the face. "No, no, no," I said. "We've had enough of the fairy story. Tell me what really happened."

246

Marlow looked hurt. She held a cuddly toy belonging to Claudia in her angelic hands, playing with it clumsily.

"What are you saying?" she squealed. "You were there, you know what it was like," she cowered. "After all, it was to rescue me that you were there at all, wasn't it, Errol?"

I sat up and Marlow quickly continued.

"After I left your room that night I was again captured. They did terrible things to me..." She raised an eyebrow, stopping her monologue only to catch breath, "I bided my time and then I..." she hurriedly continued, sensing my patience nearing an end, "I took my chance the same as you and somehow I got out."

She went into a long and detailed tale about how Coward had chased her, capturing her before finally she escaped his clutches. "And now we are reunited, love has found a way through for us." She paused for a drink before continuing, "Dyke told me where you lived right at the beginning. I have been waiting there for days, desperately holding onto the grim hope that you might some day return." She smiled a truly happy smile, "and you finally did. I don't know how you managed it, Errol, getting away from..."

I slammed my glass down hard on to the bedside table. Marlow stopped dead, opening her big, brown eyes fully and looked timidly across the bed. I simply shook my head smiling wolfishly.

She paused for a moment before changing tack...

"Should I continue?" she asked with a cheeky smile, that despite my protests, set tides flowing deep in the base of my belly.

"Not unless you want another red cheek," I answered. "Try something else, we've got all night."

"I do love you, Errol, you must believe me."

"I don't have to believe anything. Now are we ready for act two?"

Marlow looked down into the contents of her drink. "I'm sorry, I never meant to lie to you, they made me you see," she added.

"This sounds a little better, who made you lie, precious?"

"The Coward. He told me if I didn't entice you there that they'd kill me like they killed Dyke. He thought that once you were on his patch he would force you to give up the diamond." Tears filled Marlow's eyes, well rehearsed tears no doubt, but still tears all the same.

"I'm listening," I grunted.

Marlow wiped her eyes, taking care not to smudge her makeup and continued.

"When you refused to cooperate they sent me to your room. They said I had to coax it out of you."

I grinned recollecting the method.

"This is the truth, Errol, honestly it is. I wouldn't lie to you again."

"My, my," I uttered, shaking my head. "So that night was all a sham... you were under orders to get the diamond, and I thought..."

"Oh, Errol, they made me do it, just like they're making me do this."

I looked surprised. Marlow's eyes lit up again, now confident her story was working.

"Yes, they have sent me here again. It is almost certainly my last chance. If I don't give them the location of the diamond they'll kill me. Maybe they'll kill me anyway," she said it all in one breath.

I took the Lucky out of my mouth and stubbed it out. A look of sheer surprise now on my face. I looked around the room with my mouth wide open in absolute disbelief. Marlow's eyes followed me. You could almost see her brain working away inside that perfect little head of hers. Still I remained silent as if dumb-struck, before..

"Errol, what is it?"

I swallowed heavily, before dropping my head into my hands, shaking it desperately. Eventually I looked up. "Are you saying the diamond is not where I told you? Are you sure, did they look properly?"

It was now Marlow who looked surprised. She took a moment, looking at my shocked face and then back down at her drink. The pause was only a few seconds but appeared to take

248

forever. There was the most beautiful woman I had ever met frozen. Like one of those models photographed for magazines.

Her stunned silence was interrupted by another gentle slap across her cheek. Her eyes thinned and she stared at me, all the lost innocence drained away.

"You want a third try?" I asked not able to contain my grin.

"You were always forceful, Errol," she whispered, accentuating the huskiness of her voice. "You always liked being in charge." She smiled. "You wanna be forceful with me now? Tell me what a naughty girl I've been?" She stretched out her arms, showing off her amazing body, before lying out on the bed.

I rubbed my forehead and sipped my drink. Marlow was truly performing tonight. Her eyes never left mine. So dark and sensual. She curled up like a Playboy Centerfold, pushing out her bosoms and holding her firm taut legs together, bent at the knee, well aware that her figure hugging dress was riding high above.

I pulled out another Lucky and put it between my lips. Before the flint of the lighter could do its perpetually mundane job the Lucky was no longer there. Tossed away by the soft, silky fingers belonging to the hand of a woman. Marlow sat astride me, just as Claudia had done only twenty-four hours before. I could feel her hot breath on my cheek, her pouting lips only an inch away from my own. She was breathing heavily, watching me closely with those big, brown eyes of hers.

I lifted her up and sat her down facing me. Running a hand gently down her cheek, I smiled wickedly and said, "Enough Marlow. I'm tired of all the games. I want you to tell me what really happened before I do something I regret. You can start right at the beginning by telling me just why you set me up to be at the Dragon Bar the night Dyke Spanner was murdered."

Her face softened and she nodded. "It all started a long, long time before that night at the Dragon Bar," she said in a voice I didn't recognize.

"I'm sure you have spoken to your partner," she said. "Or should I say the intrepid reporter." She laughed until tears formed in the corners of her eyes. "Did he really think that he was fooling me with that pathetic story?"

I shrugged never taking my eyes off Marlow.

"So you took Hermeez for a sap, but he enjoyed himself in the process."

"Did he? We didn't sleep together. We just talked. I'm sorry, Errol. I know he is a friend of yours, but if that's the best he can do he should stick to doing chores for Arnold Muchado."

That did get a reaction. I quickly stood up before Marlow held out her palms defensively and continued, "You didn't know right? I've seen him, he runs around after Arnold like a little lap dog."

"Go on."

"The things I told him are true. I was expecting him to convey them back to you, but to explain things properly I have to go right back to the beginning."

I wasn't sure if it was just another act, one that I had yet to experience, but she seemed to take on a more sincere tone and I listened carefully as she told me the whole story...

Chapter Twenty-Six – The death of the Dutchman

"I was the mistress of Arthur Flegenheimer for three years. One of several, I dare say, but I always convinced myself I was his favourite. During that time, he treated me like a princess and in turn, I would do anything for him. Yet I always knew he would never leave Frances and I would never become his wife.

"One thing Arthur did promise me was that if anything were to happen to him I would be looked after. Not through his estate as that would have been impossible to arrange without questions being asked. The security he had in mind was the Flegenheimer Diamond as it was named, the very same diamond that you have come to know quite a lot about over the last few weeks. Arthur attained it in a deal many years before and always insisted that it was really mine, a symbol of our love. He already had more money than he could ever spend.

"When he was killed..." She said this with no show of emotion, I noted. "I expected a man to come around with a parcel and bring to me what was rightfully mine. I knew Arthur always carried the diamond on his person, never trusting banks or safes and the fact that he regained consciousness several times in hospital led me to believe that he would not let me down. I waited and waited and waited but the man never came.

"I was of course distraught. Not only had I lost the love of my young life, I was now left virtually penniless and without what was always promised to me. I quickly realized that the diamond must have been taken during the assassination, but how was I to discover by whom, and even if I did I was not in any position to do anything about it.

"So the years passed by and the injustice of it all grated more and more. Sure, I used my initiative to make a good life for myself but still there was something missing. I wasn't exactly living a life of poverty but until I got the diamond I knew I would never be truly fulfilled. And that is when I met the man known only as the Coward.

"The Coward, I would later find out, was the illegitimate half brother of Arthur and for some reason he had it in his mind that he was the rightful owner of the diamond. He claimed

Arthur stole it from him a long, long time ago and had refused to accept him as his brother. A moment in his company and it became absolutely clear he was a fanatic about it. We forged a friendship and I agreed to help him in his quest to search it out.

"Through contacts that I dare not question, the Coward assured me that none of the gunmen had taken the diamond from Arthur. I would later discover he is tight with Charlie Luciano and Albert Anastasia, and he was convinced that none of their men had found such a stone. So that left only three other men, the members of the Shadow Man Detective Agency. It had taken a long time for Coward to track these men down as the only other people present when the shooting took place but he did it, and he also discovered their names.

"Of course, Terry Shadow, the founder of this small time agency, was now dead but the other two were both alive and well. They were of course Dyke Spanner and Errol Black. You were missing, Errol, so Coward decided that Spanner was the man that would lead him to the diamond. He quickly became acquainted with him and urged me to do the same. We would then swap stories and ensure we got the truth from Spanner. The only problem being I soon fell for the man.

"Whatever your differences and Dyke did not try to hide them, he thought a lot about you, Errol. Whenever he talked about you his eyes sparkled and he spoke with great respect and admiration. I liked to listen to him talk about you and he made me desperate to meet you. Meanwhile he was playing a dangerous game.

"Dyke confided in me that he had no idea who had the diamond. He certainly didn't and he was sure that you didn't either. In spite of this, he decided that he would play along with the Coward with the intention of bluffing him and taking a lot of money from him. The best way he knew how to do this was to stall for time by insisting that he would only do business once you and he were together. Amazingly, the Coward bought it. He spent a good deal of time wining and dining my lover whilst I fed back whatever stories he asked me to.

"Dyke didn't care about the diamond; all he was bothered about was money. But he realized just how much it meant to me and it was he that let me into the secret of Liam Tighe, the other man present when Arthur was shot down. Dyke didn't say as much but it was pretty clear that he thought it must be Liam that had the diamond. He had the opportunity and the motive, added to the fact that he fled the scene of the crime and was never seen again. He took some persuading but eventually Dyke told me where Liam was now living.

"I got in touch with an old friend from my days with Arthur."

"Ferriby?" It was the first word I had said in the last half an hour and Marlow simply nodded.

"Yes, George Ferriby had always been a rogue but I felt I could handle him. He was interested in diamonds and for the right price would do whatever I asked of him. We decided it would be worth befriending Liam Tighe's ex-girlfriend to see if there was anything else we could find out before meeting with the fugitive. When George went to Mexico he was only supposed to talk to Liam, negotiate even, but it all went wrong and Liam ended up getting killed."

"I know."

Marlow nodded. "I'm sure you do. But we still didn't get the diamond. George came back in a terrible state, he was furious with the whole mess and had got it into his head that Dyke had double-crossed us. I pleaded with him to see reason but he wouldn't listen, he wanted to meet Dyke and have it out with him and he said if he wasn't happy with the result he would kill him."

"So that's where I come in?"

"Yes. I was afraid that George would be good to his word, after all he had already killed once. That was when I hatched the plan to send Claudia to see you. Although I had only befriended her to get as much information as I could about the Flegenheimer, we really did become close. She reminded me a lot of myself maybe ten years ago and I felt responsible for her, especially as she was oblivious, to whom George Ferriby really was.

"She had fallen head over heels for George and was going to get badly hurt. They had only been seeing each other two minutes but to her it was the real thing. George used to

253

laugh at her calling her a stupid kid and lots worse but she was blinded by love. It amused him that she was connected to one of the families and he was taking her for one hell of a ride.

"And I was terrified for Dyke. It was all I could think of, if you were tailing George there was no way that you would let him kill Dyke and at the same time you would rid Claudia of him. And with a bit of luck I would get to meet you into the bargain. Only it didn't work to plan. Somebody shot Dyke before we even got to meet him," she smiled at me, a smile full of sadness yet brimming with hope, "although I did get my wish and I did meet you. And you were even better than I had imagined."

"Who killed Dyke, Marlow?"

She shrugged. "I honestly don't know. Maybe the Coward discovered he was being played for a fool. It wasn't George. That I do know. If I had to take a guess I would plump for Coward's gunslinger Audrey Daniels but Dyke made no secret of the fact that he had many enemies."

"Ferriby's dead, do you know that?"

"Yes. After Dyke was killed and Claudia kicked him out he went right off the rails. He became paranoid about everything and started living very dangerously. I don't know who killed him either but again there are many candidates."

There was a silence as I refilled our glasses and then Marlow continued.

"The Coward got in touch immediately after Dyke's shooting. He was furious that I had been seen with Ferriby, and insisted that I started pulling my weight. He suggested that I get closer to you and I of course agreed. He still knew nothing about Liam Tighe and therefore I was at an advantage. It was his idea to coax you to Woodstock where I would be used to make you crack and give him the diamond, only I knew you didn't have it."

"What makes you think I have it now?"

"I know about Mr. Wilson. Liam Tighe left the diamond to Claudia and you opened the safety deposit box. You do have the diamond, Errol, I know you do."

At that moment, the telephone rang out making us both jump. I told Marlow to stay exactly where I could see her and keep silent. I picked up the receiver.

254

"Errol, is that you?"

It was Claudia.

"Hello sweetheart. I'm sorry I'm a little busy right now, can I call you..."

"Oh Errol, come back to bed darling!"

As she said it, she pressed her finger over the telephone and cut the connection. She then took the handset from my fist and threw it on the floor before peeling off her black gown. Before I could say anything, she had dropped her bra and panties to the floor and was rubbing her soft fingers up and down my neck.

"Come on, Errol," she panted, tugging at my tie. As always, it was neatly tied up in a Windsor, giving a little more resistance that the orthodox tie. "I'm tired of all these questions. We can talk some more in the morning."

I pushed her away gently. So not to make her stumble and lose her sitting position over me, simply keep her at arms length. A puzzled, almost frightened look came over her intense face as I reached for my holster. I watched her all the time, admiring her sheer sensuality, even more sexy in fear.

"You shouldn't have done that Marlow," I said, but my voice was weak.

To her relief I simply unstrapped the leather shoulder belt that holsters my weapon and tossed it on to the floor. I was now completely naked from the waist up with the most beautiful woman in the world on my lap. She curled her nose up and lunged to kiss me on the face; arms and hands traveling all over my hairy body. Again, we stopped by me lightly pushing her away.

"Don't stop now Errol, you want me so much you're gonna burst," she declared, knowing that she was spot on.

She was right. God damn was she was right.

But I hesitated. I thought of Claudia; sweet, beautiful, innocent Claudia who would do just about anything for me. She was the girl that I loved and she was the one that really loved me back. Marlow would never love me. She would probably never love anybody but herself. What must Claudia be thinking now I wondered but the thought simply filled me with dread. It didn't last long.

I looked at Marlow and sighed. Lives were at stake here.

Marlow was truly surprised by the sheer force I flipped her over with, from sitting above me onto her back. I pinned her lithe, struggling body down, holding her wrists in each clenched hand and her legs slightly parted by my full weight. She looked up at me, now struggling with less urgency, more rubbing herself against me, and again a big smile appeared. "That's the way, Errol, you know you want to."

She began to laugh, but the giggles of victory were soon replaced by moans of pleasure as I lowered my mouth to her neck. The gentle sighs and simpers rang in my neck as I slowly edged down the oasis of beauty that was Marlow.

I awoke for the second time. It was seven thirty and I could hear the shower. It stopped and before I properly got the sleep out of my eyes, in she walked. Only a towel around her dripping body and another wrapped around her head. She held a small handgun in her left hand.

"You really should wake up earlier," she said sweetly, tightening the towel around her breasts and perching on the far corner of the bed. "The early bird catches the worm. You know the old saying?"

I sat up, resting my back on the headboard, pulling the quilt up to my waist.

"Oh, don't be shy Errol, please. Not after last night." She frowned. "It's a shame things are as they are but..." She stood up and dropped the towel, "...that's just how it goes."

I sat in silence, watching intently as Marlow slowly dressed herself. Teasing me with her sheer magnificence, she slid on her silky, black panties before swapping them for navy blue. Then, a matching bra, with stockings and suspenders. She stood there, over me, after doing in reverse what politicians would pay thousands of dollars for, and sighed. The handgun held firmly in her left hand.

"Do you want a coffee, Errol?" she asked.

"You're not working for Coward are you?" I said, not waiting for an answer. "Not for them under duress, and not with them."

Marlow half smiled, looking at myself and then the lump of metal in her hand.

"Is that what you used to kill Ferriby?" I asked nodding at the gun.

She smiled wickedly. "Come on now Errol, let's not spoil things. We were getting on so well."

"Don't flatter yourself sweetheart," I retorted. "You're nothing special."

"You can resist me about as much as I can you." She smiled. "You know that as well as I do."

I said nothing, which seemed to upset Marlow.

"I do love you Errol. In your own way I know that you love me also but if I have to..."

"What, you'll shoot me down?" I interrupted.

She held the gun uneasily, touching her wrinkled nose. "Just tell me where the diamond is and we can stop all the unpleasantness. I told you everything you need to know last night. You now must realize that the Flegenheimer Diamond belongs to me. It certainly doesn't belong to Claudia Cortene and I think you have already been handsomely rewarded. Just tell me where it is!"

I fumbled on the bedside cabinet, knocking off a tumbler of water, which splashed down on the lovely carpet. Marlow let out a shriek before pulling out a pack of Luckys and tossing them over. I lit one up and inhaled deeply. She looked extremely agitated as I exhaled, impatient to the point of hysterical.

"Maybe I don't know where the diamond is. Everybody seems to have got it in their head that I do, but hell, maybe they're wrong?" I held out my hands and puffed on the cigarette. "So Liam left his old girlfriend a little something but it wasn't the diamond. He didn't leave her the diamond because he never had it himself. None of us did. Both you and Coward are looking up the wrong tree and the only one playing games is the late Dutch Schultz. He would have never left a priceless diamond to a cheap tart!"

257

"How can you say such things?" whimpered Marlow her face a mask of anger and despair. "I love you. You love me. If it wasn't for me the Coward would have already killed you."

I laughed a good old chesty laugh and shook my head condescendingly.

Trembling now and with tears running down her cheeks, Marlow raised the gun. "Where is the diamond Errol? It's the last time I'm going to ask you. Coward may have offered you $20, 000 but I am offering you your life."

Casually I took another drag of my Lucky and blew out a thick cloud of smoke. "I very much doubt that my life is yours to offer," I answered.

"I love you but I'll kill you if I have to." Slowly her violently trembling arm moved and pointed the gun right at me. "Don't make me do it Errol, tell me where it is and it'll be all right."

I remained defiant. Holding the burning ember between forefinger and thumb, squinting as I sucked the last life from it. She was barely three feet away from me now. Arms held out in front of her, with the gun shaking. Her usually immaculate face was tarnished by dried tears. Wearing the most incredible lingerie, she looked even more beautiful than usual. Despite the usual arrogance having drained away, I could see the anguish in her face. Indecision; could she do it after all? Could she pull that trigger? I was in no doubt that she could, and probably would.

In the short time I had known her, Marlow had displayed her talents to the full. Switching roles from damsel in distress to lady-killer with the utmost of ease. She was a woman who knew exactly what she wanted all of the time. Was our situation different? I considered it for a while. Maybe she really did love me in her own inimitable way, but even if she did it wasn't strong enough to stop her killing me. Marlow was out for herself and would let nothing get in her way.

Her finger curled nervously around the trigger, and she began to sob uncontrollably. No longer the silent streams flowing down her high cheekbones, giving off the desired effect without too much effort. No, she was now going the whole hog - maybe they were even real, right now I didn't really care.

"Last time... Errol... I mean it." She could barely manage to get out the words, as her finger applied more pressure.

I shook my head and flicked the stub into the ashtray. My sudden movement broke the détente and as her finger overbalanced, squeezing the trigger its full recoil. She closed her eyes and screamed.

The short, sharp clicking sound of the firing pin hitting an empty chamber was clearly not the expected outcome. Immediately her eyes opened, now in desperation and shock, and she pulled the trigger again and again and again. Still no gunfire and the gun dropped to the carpeted floor.

I reacted quickly, leaping out from under the thick, heavy duvet and grabbed Marlow. Tossing her on to the bed like a rag doll she yelped with pain as her head hit the board at the end of the bed. Holding a hand to her throbbing head, she watched me fearfully. I reached a full arms length in between the mattresses and pulled out a tin, followed by my own 9mm handgun.

"I knew the gun was empty, I was just..." A heavy slap across the face stopped her pathetic pleas.

"Oh no," I said somberly. "I think I've heard enough for the time being." I shook my head and smiled my toothy grin. "You surprised me sweetheart, I'll give you that. It was fifty-fifty, but I'd have bet against." I put my hand to her wringing cheek and stroked it gently. "You really are a dangerous lady to know."

I put my gun down on the bed and opened the lid of the tin. "Don't even think about it," I said curtly, unable to resist a chuckle as Marlow eyed my own gun hungrily. She immediately put on a look of innocence and hurt, before peering curiously at the contents of the tin.

"Ammunition," I answered, without her actually asking the question. "Luckily, the pellets I took from your little weapon," I smiled at her worried gaze, "fit nicely into my own."

One by one, I filled up the little holes for the bullets and clicked the breech closed.

Chapter Twenty-Seven – Big man in the clouds

By the time I could get through to Ava, it was almost lunchtime. I washed and shaved at the hotel. I was still wearing yesterday's clothes. They were a little ruffled and shabby but would have to do until I could get back to Joe's Diner. I'd forced a smoked mackerel down about an hour ago. The hotel breakfast had already finished and that was all I could manage.

Ava picked up the telephone immediately.

"Hello sweetheart, it's Errol."

"Errol, where were you last night? That poor girl came back in floods of tears. I hope you've not..."

"Ava, listen okay, I don't have much time."

"Okay," she calmed down. "Fire away."

"This afternoon I want you back in the office. Open for business as usual. Any cases of interest note down the details and I'll be taking appointments next week."

"But..." she sounded confused. "I thought the office was dangerous. You said..."

"I said it was being refurbished and now it's been finished so I want it opened for business, okay?"

There was a short silence. "What about the case, Errol? Have you solved it? Is this whole mess finished and done with?"

"Not on the telephone, precious okay? Just do as I ask, open for business and I'll take care of the rest."

"Okay Errol, is that all?"

"No, just one more thing. Is Claudia still with you? I need to talk to her."

I could hear Ava sigh and again there was a pause. She was usually the most professional person you could ever hope to meet and to employ her was a dream; her telephone manner impeccable. Right now, however, she was clearly flustered.

"She's not here right now, Errol. Shall I tell her to call you at Joe's?"

"How about telling me what's going on right now?" I retorted.

Again Ava sighed. "It's probably nothing Errol..."

"Let me be the judge of that sweetheart."

"It's just last night like I told you, she was very upset. First you cancelled dinner and the..."

"Get to the point!"

"She called you at the hotel... she said that you were with another woman. She was dreadfully upset Errol. She ended up spending a lot of the night with Hermeez..."

Someone else I had stood up last night, I thought glumly. "They had a lot to talk about, conversing most of the evening. Then she came back here for the night, still very upset."

"So they had a few drinks together and he brought her back. What's the problem? For Christ's sake he's my best friend."

"Oh well it's probably nothing Errol, it's just... well he picked her up again this morning." She said it bitterly, as if her own hopes had been dashed. "She seemed very secretive; I don't know why I just got the vibes, okay? And they drove away quickly. She was supposed to meet me for coffee and hour ago and never showed."

"Okay sweetheart. Thank you for keeping me informed. Now you just do as I ask okay, I'll be in to see you later."

I hung up the telephone and rubbed my forehead.

When I arrived at Joe's Diner, I got the whole story again from my loyal friend. He seemed unconcerned, but duty bound to inform me. I patted him on his meaty shoulder and pinched his chubby cheek. "Don't you worry my old mate, everything's going to be just fine."

"Are you all right, Errol? You seem a little tired. Are things getting to you a bit? You should slow down a bit you know, no offence mind, just a little advice."

"Don't you worry about me. Get the bubbly on ice. Soon we're going to have a celebration. Do you mind if I use the telephone?" I asked, quickly changing my tone.

My fat friend stood back, his arms in the air. "Everything's just as you left it. Help yourself."

I thanked Joe and made my way through to the temporary office in the back room. It would be my last day there I thought joyfully, and I wouldn't miss it one little bit.

261

I propped my feet up on the cluttered desk and picked up the handset. Dialing with one hand, I loosened my tie with the other, instantly thinking back to last night. I reached over for the fresh bottle of bourbon on the edge of the desk as the phone connected through. You're a diamond you old sod, I thought about Joe, a God damn diamond.

"Hello I need to speak to Stanley Cortene please," I said politely down the phone, whilst pouring myself a healthy measure. "Oh, I think you'll find him if you look hard enough. Tell him it's Errol Black."

There was a short pause. I could hear a conversation in the background. And then...

"Black?" came the rough voice of the don. "Are you in trouble?"

I took a big gulp of bourbon. "Can we meet someplace, I've got something very important to tell you? As soon as possible."

Again there was a pause and a muffled conversation. "Seven o'clock tonight. The Empire State Building."

The line went dead. Slowly I replaced the handset and finished my drink. I hope you're right, I said to myself, I really do.

A quick change of clothes and I was once again on the move. A pair of gorillas had been tailing me ever since my meeting with the Coward. They were young, pretty and cute, but no doubt keen hotshots from twenty yards. It was nothing out of the ordinary, quite expected in fact, but I wasn't quite ready just yet. Where the hell was Hermeez? He wouldn't have any trouble losing them. I didn't have time to try anything at the moment so I took them with me. But soon they would have to go.

"Any problems, sweetheart?" I asked Ava, propping my hat on the hat stand. She remained silent and I pulled up a chair. "Seems like you've got everything up and running again. Sorry about the short notice, but..."

"Errol! Shut up!" shouted Ava. I could see she had been crying.

"What is it precious?" I asked, rising to my feet immediately and taking my young secretary in my arms. "I didn't upset you did I? You know I'm busy darling, it doesn't usually bother you."

"Errol, stop!"

I held her at arms length and looked into her eyes. Her long face was sun burnt and her badly applied makeup was all smeared. "Does this mean the wedding's off?" I laughed.

A small smile appeared on Ava's worried face. "Come on, it's not too hard is it?" I urged and her face cracked from a brief glimmer of a smile into one filled with sorrow.

"Oh Errol, I'm so sorry," she whispered.

On the desk was a letter. Ava picked it up in her shaking hands and held it out for me. I took the letter and looked at Ava for explanation.

"I was so suspicious, I didn't know what else to do..." she spluttered as if in justification.

I said nothing.

"I looked through her room," she continued, her head now to the floor in shame. "And this is what I found. It was in a worn, brown envelope. I'm sorry, Errol, I couldn't help but read it."

I held the letter in disbelief, before I could begin to read it Ava again hugged me, crying uncontrollably. "How could she do it Errol, how could she do it?"

A few moments passed. I held my closest ally in my arms warmly. Comforting her, combing her thick hair with my fingers. Eventually she calmed down a little and I made her a coffee. I sat her down in a comfy chair, poured a handsome measure of spirit into the coffee and handed it to her. I then sat down to read the letter. In silence apart from the odd sniffle.

My Dearest Claudia,

If you're reading this I suppose I must be dead. Firstly I must tell you I love you and I always have. I'm sorry the way things worked out. We were never really meant to be together, you're much too good for a petty criminal like me. Maybe in the next life, eh?

I never really was much of a letter writer - you know that - so let's get down to business. I have hired a Private Investigator to get this letter to you. If he's as good as he used to be you'll be all right. You could do worse than keeping him with you along the whole ride. No doubt the vultures will be out, and he'll help you to what is yours.

Everything is quite simple. I want you to enjoy what I never could. Don't refuse it because of your high morals, accept it as a gift from your darling Liam. It will enable you to escape your family once and for all, giving you the independence to do just as you please.

Be careful and enjoy. Love you always.
Liam xxx

At the bottom of the letter was an address and a number.

"Blanchard et Cie," said a more composed Ava, "It's a bank in the Swiss quarters. It deals predominantly with long term bequests and has many vaults."

Before I could speak, a large bourbon appeared in front of me. I downed it in one.

"I telephoned the bank ten minutes ago," continued Ava. "They said a young girl by the name Claudia Cortene had just left with a man answering Hermeez's description. I was of course checking on their safety and the clerk was only too helpful."

I looked blankly at the empty glass.

"I knew she was no ordinary girl. I'm not naive Errol." She paused. "I did think she was different though. I thought she really cared about you."

"You're jumping to conclusions sweetheart," I asserted, my best smile beaming out. I walked over to where Ava was sat and gently massaged her shoulders. "You've done a first class job, as usual, but you're wrong. Just leave the deductions to me."

"Come on Errol, she's walked out on you, and with your best friend." She turned to face me. "I'm sorry Errol, I really am. But you've got to wake up to it."

264

"She'll be back." I got my hat and headed for the door, the phone ringing. "You're wrong Ava. You did the right thing but you're wrong."

The two boys were both asleep when I reappeared from my office block. I walked up to the blue Chevrolet and tapped on the window. Instantly they jumped to attention, looking shocked and unsure as to what they should do. I stood grinning at them from the sidewalk and motioned for them to open the window. The real dense looking one obliged.

"Yeah?" he stuttered.

"On the ball, as ever," I sneered, holding my hands out as he grunted and pulled his weapon. "I've got a message for you boys for Coward."

They looked at each other in puzzlement and sighed before turning back to me.

"Okay," the blonde one said in bewilderment. "What is it?"

"Have either of you boys got a pen?" I asked.

A couple of minutes of frantic searching later I was handed a pen. I scribbled down an address on the underside of a Joe's Diner beer mat and passed it through the window, putting the pen in my pocket.

"Tell him to meet me at this address tomorrow night," I said. "Tell him to bring the necessary. You got that?"

"You want the boss to meet you tomorrow night at this address," he nodded at the slip of paper satisfied.

"Ahem, eight o'clock. On the dot."

"The boss meets when he wants, not when you or…"

"Eight o'clock," I repeated. My tone left no room for queries.

The man nodded like a scolded child.

"Can you remember the rest, or do you want me to write that down as well?"

"No, no, no. It's all right." He rubbed his meathead, trying to reawaken his few brain cells. "Okay I got it," he said happily. "He needs to bring the necessary."

I nodded patronizingly.

"Perfect." I clapped a round of applause.

"What's the necessary?"

"We don't want to overdo it now do we? Just you remember that for now, okay?"

I held out my hand and shook both of the stupefied gorilla's paws. "Now I'm afraid I'm going to have to lose you two for a while," I smiled. "And after tomorrow I don't suppose I'll interest your boss anymore. Goodbye fellas, it's been a pleasure."

At that, I walked down the sidewalk to my parked car. Ten minutes later, I was mixing with the busy New York traffic, having left the blue Chevrolet behind some two miles away in a heavy traffic jam.

I parked up on a side street on the outskirts of Manhattan. The area was quiet, not a sound except for the heavy downpour. I waited ten minutes until I was satisfied that the two goons were lost, and then got out. Hurrying along the main street were the many inhabitants of downtown Manhattan. Becoming busier by the minute, a collection of many differing cultures. You could now eat anything in the world within a two hundred meter radius. You could equally hear a handful of different tongues within the same distance.

Little Swiss was one of the many territories claimed by outsiders as their own. First, came the Sicilians and Little Italy, then the Chinese community and Chinatown. Now the city was no more than a miniature world. It was three o'clock. I needed to make a telephone call.

"Good afternoon officer, can you put Tim Matthews on please?" I waited patiently as the duty constable rushed off to find my friend in the force. I was sitting in a top-end drinker's bar on Fifth Avenue. There was a constant buzz of conversation. No one noticed me, or took any notice of what I had to say. The bartender sleepily poured me a drink, deciding reluctantly to leave the bottle and disappeared back into conversation at the other end of the bar.

The line crackled and I found myself listening to another officer.

"I'm afraid Lieutenant Matthews is unavailable at the moment. Can I be of any help, sir?"

"I very much doubt that sweetheart. Tell Lieutenant Matthews that the date has been set. Tell him to ring this number..."

"The date has been set..." repeated the female as I gave the number of the call box I was speaking from. Before I could finish there was a familiar gruff, 'Give me that phone!' and I was listening to my friend.

"Errol, is that you? Do you mean what I think you mean?"

The bartender ambled back over and placed a receipt on the bar next to me. Hovering bothersomely, I tossed him a ten-dollar bill so to be left in peace. I didn't mind paying for the drink, but before I'd drunk it?

"Yes," I grunted.

"Well come on, what's the deal?" he questioned impatiently.

"Tomorrow night," I answered. "At this address." I repeated the same address I had earlier written down on a beer mat. "Small-scale, Timmy. No sirens, okay? I don't envisage too much trouble. Bring two sets of bracelets."

"Two sets?"

"Two sets. And get Weeny Ping's release forms ready. Eight-thirty, don't be late."

I hung up the receiver and smiled.

The remainder of the day passed quickly and uneventfully. I did a couple more checks to lose any hangers on and I was pretty sure I was alone. My only real concern was what Ava had told me. She was easily led to conclusions without thinking them through but then there was no doubt the evidence she had shown me was pretty damming. Claudia and Hermeez - could they have run away together? Done a runner with the booty, leaving me, their closest one, in a whole pile of shit? On the facts known, it would be hard to refute. Time would tell. For the time being I must continue to go with the plan.

267

The plan was to be at the Empire State Building for seven o'clock. After a hearty meal at one of Manhattan's more classy food joints, it was time to go. Without my loyal buddy at my side it was now firmly left to me. Not a responsibility I was afraid of or even approached with hesitation. But there was a lot riding on my next move. If I happened to be wrong there would be terminal repercussions. Alternatively, if my little lady in the office happened to be right the end result would be similar.

I passed quickly through the early evening Manhattan bustle, arriving at the lobby to the Tower in good time. It was a magnificent piece of construction, towering high above the increasingly impressive Manhattan skyline. From the top everything was so small. Tiny cars drove along tiny roads, driven by millions of shuffling insects.

The Empire State Building is easily the most evocative symbol of New York. Despite construction beginning only three weeks before the stock market crash of October 1929, and continuing through the ensuing Depression, the building proceeded speedily, and was completed well under budget after just fourteen months. It stands 103 stories and 1472 feet tall, making it the tallest building in the whole world.

Where would be the best place for a meet? We would certainly prefer the ensuing conversation to be a private one. Away from prying eyes and more importantly prying ears. At least I was sure that I was alone. Quite a substantial part of the afternoon had been spent ensuring this. And I was certain the head of one of the families would be only too careful. In the toilets? -always an important venue for covert deals. The restaurant on the top floor, in a corner table, maybe? Even the elevator was a possibility. I gave all these careful thought before rejecting them. Our meet would be in the public viewing gallery. What better place to be unseen and unheard than a busy, public place?

I smiled warmly at the attendant, who duly saluted and pressed a button on the side of the elevator. Almost immediately, a bell rang and the door slid open. I entered the small, enclosed room and pressed the button for the public gallery. Several other people followed me into the cramped space. None of them I recognized, or wanted to.

As the elevator began its speedy ascent to the pinnacle of our culture, I eyed the walls. Even in such a treasured symbol of Americanism the graffiti lurked. The dirty walls were awash with bright colored splashes. From obscenities of the intellectual underbelly, such as 'fuck off' or the equally enlightening 'Stacey is a slag' to the young romantics 'Will loves Hill'. Illustrated graphically and without embarrassment. When we reached the top I straightened my tie and stepped out.

There had been a time when the public viewing gallery was completely open air. Adding to the incredible views was the crisp, night air brushing against your cheeks. The noise was dim, but could be heard. A dull concoction of New York life on extremely low volume. Now the gallery was open enough to feel the breeze, but was surrounded by a twelve foot high fence. This simple alteration singularly halved the city center suicide rate. Personally I preferred the open air but tonight? Well, I could live with the carpets and rubber plants.

There was a tap on my shoulder, followed by, "Lovely view, eh?"

A middle aged, reasonably built man stood forward, so he was next to me, shoulder to shoulder. He was wearing a dark suit covered by a trench coat with a wide brimmed fedora and a warm smile. His hands were held in his pockets.

"It sure is," I answered as a group sauntered by. "I'm glad you came."

Stanley Cortene pulled a hand from his raincoat and held out a box. "Cigar?" he offered. I duly accepted and lit it up. "How could I refuse the hero that saved my life? Had anyone else..." he continued indicating with his hands for me not to interrupt. "Had anyone else have interrupted one of Mama's spaghetti marinaras..." He spat out the end of the cigar, "I'd probably have thrown them over that fence there."

I exhaled a thick cloud of smoke unflinching. I was simply being warned not to mess the man about. He was busy and so was I. I took the polite warning without reaction and

269

looked briefly into Stan's icy eyes. "Before we start I have a little good news for you."

Stan rubbed his hands. "That's swell. I like good news, shoot."

"Liam Tighe is dead."

"That is good news."

"Yeah. He was murdered in his home in TJ. The cops down there don't know who did it and don't much care."

Stan puffed happily on his cigar, before turning towards me. "I appreciate the information Errol, but you didn't drag me all the way up here to tell me that the little Irish runt has been exterminated so we should move on."

I nodded and took a deep breath. "I have something to ask you," I said firmly, looking around the gallery nonchalantly. "Two things in fact."

"Don't worry Errol, I'm here alone. We're friends right, I'm visiting a friend." There was a short pause. "I guessed you would have. Let's hear it."

Slowly, I began to stroll around the three hundred and sixty degree gallery. Stan duly followed. We stopped and leaned on the rail, facing the north of Manhattan Island. To our right stood my favorite building in the whole of New York, the shimmering Art Deco masterpiece that was the Chrysler Building. Beyond that was the vast expanse of Central Park and further still the Hudson River, flowing beneath the George Washington Bridge that joined New York to New Jersey.

"I guess I'm calling in my favour, if you like," I said.

He coughed a little, before digging out a handkerchief and wiping his mouth. It had the expected result. When all the heads turned back around, and we were once again alone, Stan smiled. "Go on."

"And some more as well."

"I'm intrigued," admitted Stan, again stopping to take in the breathtaking view. "Try me."

I sucked nervously on the cigar. So far so good, now I'll hit him with it.

"I appreciated you allowing Claudia to visit," I said, watching his every move. "She means a lot to me."

"You're a good man, Errol, you treat her well. What's the point, are you asking me for her hand in marriage?"

"Not quite." I chuckled although maybe that is what I really wanted to ask him. "All I'm asking is for the leash to be relaxed a little."

Now it was my turn to prevent interruption before Stan could air his disapproval. "I'm not trying to tell you how to run your family, I wouldn't dare."

Stan didn't say anything, he just glared. His eyes were angry, but I figured he was still attentive to my thoughts.

"Look," I said matter of factly. "You know she's not cut out for family life. Give her a little room, that's all. You could buy her a house. She's very fond of me, you know."

"And you are of her," stated Stan firmly.

"Of course I am," I sighed. "But that's not my meaning. I'm not asking permission to date the girl. That's our business." Stan raised an eyebrow. "Just cut her a little slack, that's all I ask. Give her a chance to make up her own mind. If she decides I'm an asshole that's fine."

I felt a firm hand on my shoulder. "I don't know just what Claudia has told you, Errol, but she's not a prisoner. She is a young lady with her own mind, and to some extent her own life." He paused. "There'll be no interference from me unless she asks for some, or unless she's in danger. And then my interference will be swift and final."

I sighed. It had been a good try, but it seemed Stan was not even up to admitting it. But before I could again speak...

"I trust you, Errol. You'll look after her at least, if not settle down and marry her... and if it's Mikey you're worried about, I'll handle him. You're too good to be gunned down by that son of a ..." He paused. "He's got a nasty temper on him that one. Don't worry he's under control." He again reassured me that the hot headed brother would be warned off. That we would be given the freedom Claudia craved and, according to Ava, had stolen. For the time being I felt relieved.

"But enough of this unpleasant talk. What is it you have really come here to ask me?"

271

Stan's eyes looked at me with warm affection. Like you would stare at an old friend. He was not old, maybe late forties, and was still extremely well presented. A little short maybe, but solid as a rock. His attire was immaculate and within that tough exterior was a human being. Unlike the leg men, the contacts and the killers, he was a man with a family he loved, and a great deal of good living to do. However, in spite of all these merits I was sure that he wouldn't hesitate to kill, if he decided it was the required action. Momentarily I questioned my next move but I had to press on.

I finished the cigar and pushed my nose through the fence. "I want to talk to you about a man known as the Coward. Do you know of him?"

There was a short silence as a group of tourists barged past. The city was looking beautiful tonight. Lit up in all the colors of the rainbow, shimmering under the strong light of the moon.

"Go on," is all he said, but I was now reluctant to say what I had come to say.

"I'll take that as a yes," I said, stalling for time.

Stan smiled, putting his face right to within an inch of mine. I could feel his eyes boring through me and it felt uncomfortable. Again, I began to walk slowly around the viewing gallery.

Stan pursed his lips together and opened his palms. "Errol, I know a lot of men. I probably know more men that you will ever know, now are you going to tell me what this is all about, the excitement is killing me?"

I smiled. "I may have to kill him," I said.

Stan stood in silence. The viewing gallery had thinned out a bit. There were still plenty of customers, reveling over the beautifully illuminated skyline, but where we stood, we were almost alone. There was not a soul within hearing distance

"Is this the same Errol Black that insisted he didn't want any part of the 'only kill each other club', I think is how you so eloquently put it? And now here you are asking my permission to kill a member of the club. That is what you're asking me isn't it, Errol?"

"I don't think I have another option. It looks like it's going to have to be him or me and I'm quite fond of living right now. Look, he wants something from me that I don't think that I can give him. If everything I hear is true then it's only a matter of time before he gets to me."

"So you want to get in there first?"

I nodded.

Stan slowly shook his head but before he could speak I interrupted him. "Look, I don't know what else to do. I think that I love your niece when I never thought that I would love again. It feels like I have been given a second chance when I never thought I was going to get another one. I want us to spend our lives together and live until we're old and gray. If you won't say yes for me say it for Claudia."

Stan smiled a cold, dead smile. "Errol you're a private eye. How did a man like you get involved with the phantom?"

I shrugged.

"Still don't want to tell me, hah? I don't blame you, there's a lot of things I wouldn't want to tell you. Did I tell you that I checked you out?"

I nodded. "You did," I said calmly, although I felt anything but calm.

"One thing I noticed," he continued, "is that people close to you have got into a habit of getting killed. Rather an unhealthy habit; your boss, your ex partner and of course your very good friend, Liam Tighe." He paused ever so slightly before continuing: "I'm sure there were plenty killed in Guadalcanal. And now you want to start killing people, yourself."

"It's like I told you, if I don't kill him he has me killed. It's that simple."

Stan sighed. "You ask for a lot, Errol, you know that? But if you don't ask you don't get. I like you, I like you a lot but if you're going to be the man that makes my little Claudie happy you're not the man that shoots villains down in cold blood. Do you understand what I am saying?"

Stan patted me on the shoulder, but it wasn't a friendly pat. "I'm sorry Errol. You're going to have to give him what he wants. I cannot and will not sanction a killing that may have unforeseen consequences for my own and many other families. I repeat you are going to have to give him what he wants."

"And if I can't?"

Stanley Cortene turned to face me. It was the first time that evening he'd looked me in the eye, and the last time he ever would. "You will not kill the Coward. Do you understand Errol, you will not kill the Coward?"

I nodded at the don.

"And similarly, he will not kill you, or arrange to kill any of your friends."

He reached inside his jacket and pulled out a card. "Errol, I'm going to give you a telephone number. Call it any time of night or day. I want to know a little information. When the phantom leaves you tomorrow, call it! If you come good there will be a nice nest egg for you and my niece, something that will give you two a great start in life together."

He held out his hand and I shook it firmly.

"Goodbye Errol Black, you look after Claudia, you hear me. It would be a real shame for us to meet again in different circumstances, a real shame."

And at that he turned around and slowly walked away. His stocky frame disappearing slowly into the distance. The elevator doors closed and it would be the last time that I would see Stanley Cortene.

I waited ten minutes further before entering the elevator myself. I was now sure he wasn't coming back and that I was in the clear. For the time being anyway. Stan had failed to kill me once again and so I rightly thought we had an understanding. That all the talk of honor and debt was true, not simply a movie myth. If, however Claudia did not return soon I would be sure to be paid a visit. A debt of honor would go so far, but the disappearance of one's niece would certainly override it. I took a last breath of night air before descending down into the city below.

I drove back to the hotel. It would be my last night there. Tomorrow I would be back at my flat in the Bronx. The case that had dominated so many lives over the last few weeks would be over. The ghost of Dyke Spanner would eventually be laid to rest one way or another. Timmy Matthews would probably get a promotion, the Coward would get his comeuppance, Weeny Jung Ping would be released in a blaze of publicity ...and Errol Black PI? I would either be very rich or very dead.

I made two telephone calls; one to a house in Chinatown, the other to an old friend of mine. That would be my insurance. I hoped to god that I would not need it but the way things were going I wasn't sure. The day had been a long one. Most of the required jobs had been accomplished. Everything was set up for tomorrow night, apart from one major detail. The meet with Stanley Cortene had gone reasonably as planned. The big setback was of course the news from Ava.

I sat back in the Short Bar, listening politely to the English couple who insisted on sitting at the same table. They had pulled up a pair of seats, claiming I was looking a little sad and lonely. The man, an ageing, portly chap with no hair had spent the whole of the last hour telling me about the marmalade business. He was the Managing Director of an important marmalade company. They were visiting New York for the annual conference. For over an hour, he had explained in intricate detail the inside workings of marmalade administration.

But I hadn't heard a word of it. My mind was firmly on Claudia and whether my meet with Stan had been a waste of time. A spectacular waste of time. I was in no doubt that the letter Ava had found was the one that had disappeared. The envelope was the same, the writing being identical. Had Claudia taken it intentionally without telling me? Was she secretly planning to run away with my dissatisfied partner, using the bequest as finance? Was she the reason that I had felt so rotten that night? Had she poisoned me to make sure she would be able to make the switch unseen?

I almost laughed out loud at the ridiculousness of the questions that kept popping into my head. There was no chance that any of them were true, that much I was sure. But I couldn't shake the feeling of maudlin that had crept over me. Just where had they disappeared to?

"Another drink, Eezy? On Mozza's marmalade of course."

"Yeah, sure. Thanks Ian."

"No problem at all squire, no problem at all."

"Sante!" said Ian, holding up his glass. "That's French you know," he whispered as if a state secret. "We have to be able to speak a dozen languages in marmalade you know."

Suddenly the bar broke out into music. Ian leapt to his feet and began to dance with Mrs. Robinson. The rest of the inhabitants of the Short Bar joined in also. Nobody seemed sure just what they were dancing but gave it a good attempt anyway. My thoughts of Hermeez and Claudia were interrupted by young Miss Robinson. She grabbed my arm and pulled me as hard as her minute frame would allow, in the direction of the frolicking marmalades.

"Come on, Eezy. I promised a whole crate of Mozza's for this song. Thought it would cheer you up!"

Ten minutes later, I sat back down, exhausted by the gyrating and moving of the smitten teenager. Once again my thoughts went to Claudia and Hermeez. Any minute now they'll stroll through that door. Big grins filling their cheeky faces. All smarmy and pleased with themselves, sure they'd taught me a real lesson. Alternatively they might be on a flight out of here. Arm in arm, with only a small bag each and of course a box.

I shook my head violently, as if to shake the thought away. It simply wasn't worth contemplating such an outcome. The loss of my girl, my best friend and the diamond all in one foul sweep. And to cap it all it would probably finish off with the loss of my own life.

I remembered how Hermeez had been acting these last few days. Easily irritated when kept in the dark and so anxious to know what was in the envelope. He had been sloppy, making blunders which were totally out of character. Added to this was his secretive behavior regarding Marcia and Muchado. Just what had he been hiding? He wouldn't trade friendship for the diamond, would he?

Ian 'Mozza' Robinson slumped back in his chair, laced in sweat. "Bloody great that Eezy, bloody great." He again leaned

276

over to me, his putrid stench following him. "You're gonna have to watch it buddy, I reckon young Matilda there's got an eye on you." He then let out an appalling guffaw before singing out loudly, drowning out the pianist.

I waited patiently in the Short Bar for a further two hours. Enduring three more jaunts to the dance floor with the increasingly hopeful marmalade heiress. Eventually I decided to retire quietly to the quarters of my room. It was my third and final night in the hotel and only one of them had been spent with Claudia. There was still no sign of her, and no sign of my best friend. Maybe they would be waiting for me in the suite? It was a rather hopeful thought, but I clung to it eagerly nevertheless.

The elevator ride elapsed quickly and soon I was stood outside my room for the last time. I fitted the key in the hole easily this time and turned. Expectation was quickly dashed as I pushed open the door to find an empty suite. The mini bar was sickeningly full, the bed neatly made up and the towels replaced for fresh ones.

I sighed deeply and slumped into a comfortable chair. The drapes were open and once again, the beautiful view of Liberty Island was on show. I took off my hat and tossed it aside. Ten minutes later I put it back on, pulled on my coat and headed out into the night.

Chapter Twenty-Eight – Laying to rest

As I sat on the boardwalk watching the waves lashing the rocks, I considered that my life had come full circle. Since I witnessed the death of Dutch Schultz ten years ago and subsequently turned my back on any form of mob work I had simply been treading water. It may not have been my choosing, not in the beginning, but the facts were there to see. I was now back right where I started, only this time I didn't have Terry Shadow or Dyke Spanner to fall back on. I had to face it, I was mobbed up to the eyeballs whether I liked it or not.

Tomorrow I was going to meet a notorious gangster with the intention of selling him a priceless gem. I was going into the meet with the official sanction of an even bigger gangster. If I couldn't get that gem then it was sure to end in a bloodbath and even if I did, the ending was unlikely to be a happy one.

I never had any intention of killing the Coward, but then that wasn't really the point. I simply wanted to test the water and thankfully, Stan Cortene had come up trumps. He had given me a license to get out of this whole mess without getting myself killed. So long as I could come up with the Flegenheimer Diamond.

As far as the diamond went, I really was right back where I started. I never got my hands on it in '35 and it was starting to look like I would never get my hands on it now. I couldn't blame Claudia for wanting to find out about her bequest, but it all contradicted what she had said earlier. Hell we all had a right to change our minds, I was well aware of that, but did she have to do it at such a crucial time? And did she have to take on my partner with her for company?

It struck me that all I wanted was for this to all be over. To forget about the diamond, the Coward, Dyke and all the rest of it. Then I could disappear with Claudia and we could be married and have children and live happily ever after. It was a fanciful thought but one that I was going to cling to until things were proved different.

I lit up a Lucky and watched the birds on the water. It amazed me just how they kept such a perfect formation without talking to each other. If it was humans there, they would need a good coach and several years of choreography classes before they could take to the air so gracefully and beautifully. One squawked from miles away and suddenly they all took off in one swift movement, gliding through the air in a perfect v shape, getting smaller and smaller as they headed out to sea.

I stubbed my Lucky out on the beach and pulled the urn from my jacket. I had collected it an hour earlier from my office safe before driving over here. It was almost two in the morning but it felt like the right time to do it. Dyke never paid too much attention to the conventions of day and night and so I don't think he would have worried too much about being cast into the sea with only the moon and a few seagulls to watch over him.

I took off my shoes and socks and rolled up my trouser legs to just above the knees. There was a crisp breeze blowing off the ocean but the temperature was mild. Holding the urn in one hand and my hip flask in the other, I padded down the beach and waded slowly into the waters stopping for a swig of brandy from the flask at regular intervals.

In a way, I was a little proud that Dyke had wanted me to be the one to send him on to the next world. Whatever had happened between us we had once been friends, close friends with a great deal in common. We were both men with great ambition and a will to succeed that highlighted our flaws as human beings. We were both selfish sons of bitches with a phobia about commitment and a disliking of soft cheese. Somehow we had both got caught up in this thing without really wanting to and without knowing just how to get out of it. Dyke no longer had a choice, but I did.

The water lashed at my ankles and I thought I heard a car pulling up on the road that was set back from the beach. I searched out through the darkness with my well-adjusted eyes, but saw nothing.

I thought back to Marlow's story and wondered just how much of it was true. I could easily see just how Dyke had been taken in by her, she was a very persuasive lady. Apart from a few timely pieces of luck, I too would have been taken in. She operated with an effortless ease and it was only my gut instinct in

279

emptying her handgun that had kept me alive. I figured that most of what she told me that night was probably true. It made sense and if I had have been in possession of the diamond she would have got exactly what she wanted. She was desperate to tell the story to someone and who better than the person that you are going to kill in the morning. You get the satisfaction of telling the whole tale without the danger that arises from coming clean.

The Coward, on the other hand, had been less than truthful right from the beginning. It was clear that he had attempted to set me up for Dyke and Woo Wang's killings to blag me for the diamond. When this didn't go to plan he hedged his bets further by enticing me to Woodstock to kayo Marlow and strengthen his hand so that he would no longer be offering a large wedge but would be offering me life, rather like an old Roman Emperor. When that too failed, he came up with the cash, but I was in no doubt that he would expect to take it from my bleeding corpse at a later date.

The water was now up to my knees and the hip flask was empty. I put it back in my pocket and turned around so I was facing the beach. The boardwalk seemed a long way off with a mass of black, foaming water to cross between me and it. Its dimmed lighting, that was covered with bugs and moths, shone out in the distance. I thought I saw another flash of light out there; a torch maybe or the burning ember of a cigarette, but it disappeared as soon as it appeared and I put it down to my imagination.

I turned back around and faced the ocean. Trying to remember a few words of comfort or religious salvation my mind went blank. Instead, I said a little prayer of my own and unscrewed the top of the tiny urn. I looked inside and smiled.

"Goodbye old friend," I murmured aloud, holding the urn out high above my head.

It was then that I felt a warm sensation on the back of my neck. I turned around, broke into a great big smile and launched the urn and its contents high into the air. The ashes were scattered all around us, there was a loud very audible plop followed by a glint of light and a smaller less audible noise.

Five minutes later, we were back on the beach, wet from head to toe and now shorn of our clothes. We made love silently under the moonlight and kissed each other all over for what felt like days and days but was in fact only hours. When it was time to leave, we did so in her car, which was waiting on the roadside.

Chapter Twenty- Nine – The Flegenheimer Diamond

I slept for most of the next day, getting up only to eat, shave and bathe myself. It was a long time since I had indulged myself in such slovenly behaviour but it felt good. My body felt refreshed and invigorated and ready for anything.

Evening soon arrived. And what a beautiful evening it was. There was a sensational sunset emblazoned across the sky. Slowly the blazing orb disappeared from view leaving the clouds stained orange and red. It shone out warmly, halting the swift onset of dusk, keeping the day alive a little longer.

The avenues were busy. I had been driving for almost an hour, with my mind wandering throughout. All the time the descending sun caught my attention, leaving its incredible trail behind. Nothing could be more mesmerizing than the unstoppable, perpetual collage that was forever left in its wake.

I parked up my heap, routinely locked her up and headed up a short graveled path. I was outside a small, but well kept detached house. There was a small tidy stretch of lawn at the front and a bright red door awaiting me. A big doorbell was affixed to the wooden door, inviting guests to press its gold button. I duly obliged before checking my watch. It was nineteen hundred hours.

There was a clattering from inside, followed by a quiet expletive. The door was opened and I was faced by an attractive, but overly made up woman. She was a good height, maybe five six with bleached blonde hair. Golden earrings dangled from her delicate ears and she wore long false nails. My eyes lowered down to her slim, shapely body, covered by a tight figure hugging dress. She had large jutting breasts complimented by a waist as thin as your wrist.

"Errol, how good to see you!" she exclaimed in her Southern trawl, throwing her arms around me. "Come in."

"Thanks Maggie, you're looking great," I replied, and I meant it. For a recently widowed lady on her way towards middle age Maggie Spanner looked truly superb.

I was shown into the well-kept house and the door was closed behind us. The hallway was heavily decorated; a thick carpet comforted the feet, whilst the walls were adorned with a mixture of artistic images and framed parchments. All of which were courtesy of the late Dyke Spanner, a keen amateur artist and common winner of investigative accolades. We made our way through the hallway and into the large living room. The venue of many coffee mornings, gossip exchanging circles and of course Maggie's beautician services.

I took a chair by the window, whilst Maggie went to the drinks bar. Peering through the semi drawn drapes, I satisfied myself that we were alone, and sat back.

"I was starting to think you were avoiding me, honey," came the familiar, overfriendly voice of my chosen host.

I reached and accepted the glass she held out, before sitting herself on the edge of the three-seat sofa. "You know me Maggie. Always throw myself into the case. I couldn't afford any added complications." I smiled. "You always knew I'd come back."

"I was surprised to get your call all the same. It's been three weeks since Dyke died and I've not heard a peep."

"I'm sorry about that, sweetheart. How are you shaping up?"

"Oh I get by. I suppose I half expected you to keep a low profile for a while. It may seem strange to others but it makes perfect sense to me. Don't think I'm putting a guilt trip on you Errol, I didn't expect you at his funeral and I do understand. You've been good to me, real good. I guess two funerals in the space of a fortnight are pretty hard going and I have to say this was the least upsetting of the two."

She was referring to her father's funeral. It was only a few weeks since they had buried him back in Alabama and that was the funeral that I had accompanied Maggie to just prior to Dyke getting shot. Dyke had refused to go on the grounds that her family had never once come out East to visit. It was a callous thing to do and I agreed immediately to go with her, despite the fact that we knew there would be no end of rumors about the two of us. Once I had checked with Maggie, and she decided she

283

could live with it, I took a perverse pleasure in riling my old sparring partner.

"I had all his other friends around one by one," she said. "Not that there were many of those." She paused and gulped her own drink. "And I got the policy through last week. There should be enough to look after me for a while."

I sat listening. There was not a trace of upset or loss in her voice. She was emotionless and businesslike, just as she had always been. Just as she had learnt she had to be.

Dyke and Maggie had been married for fifteen years. Naturally, they met on a case and Dyke swept her off her feet with his tales of adventure and excitement. This was a real buzz at first for the young impressionable trainee hairdresser. Pack in her dead end job in a tiny hamlet in South Arkansas and follow her own James Cagney wherever he may go. He was everything she ever wanted, everything she had dreamt of; brave, dashing, full of excitement, and of course rich. Filthy rich. Maybe he didn't flash it about. Always insisting he would never leave his home right here in Chinatown and would always tend to his thirst at the local Dragon Bar. Still in spite of his scruffy image and even scruffier office, Dyke was never short of money.

Soon, however, the magic wore off. There were cases that Maggie couldn't help with. Dyke got onto bigger and bigger things. Either she wasn't allowed to travel with him, or wasn't even told. Night after night she would be left on her own in their reasonably plush house. The stories he would come back with would at first be enough. Keeping the life of adventure alive. But eventually stories weren't enough.

Dyke ended up spending more time away from home than he did with his wife. For him the business would always come first. He was a workaholic and a public servant. Anyone who couldn't accept this suffered. The money was a great comforter. Maggie might not have had the fairytale marriage anymore, but she had enough money to buy whatever she wanted. And she wanted a lot.

Shopping sprees would last weeks. Clothes, furniture, new dining rooms, Maggie bought the lot. And when shopping failed to satisfy all her needs, she would join a new club. Every

284

sports coach from golf to tennis had had the pleasure of Maggie Spanner.

Despite the many rumors to the contrary, I never did join them. At first it bothered me, nasty sniping behind our backs. It wasn't my own reputation I was bothered about, that was never lily white, but Maggie suffered greatly. I suppose I should have put people straight, but Maggie always stopped me, she was happy to let people think exactly what they wanted. We were happy just as friends, bloody good friends, but friends all the same. I realized I was more important to her as a friend the further and further she drifted apart from her husband.

They ended up barely knowing each other. Their marriage became a convenient arrangement. Dyke would always love the little girl he saved from poverty. And Maggie in return would be forever thankful. She was a smart lady, well aware she was onto a good deal and rarely even considered a split.

I finished my drink and Maggie promptly refilled it. Doing the same to her own glass. "This isn't a normal visit, is it Errol? I can tell that you have got something up your sleeve."

I smiled a nervous smile.

"Have you got some news? Some skeletons to clear up?" she asked.

I rubbed my hands together. "I have indeed. Tonight is going to be a good one. We have a few visitors, a nice mixture of characters. We're going to have a bit of a party, a few drinks, nibbles, that sort of thing..."

"Oh good, I've got some pies in the oven."

I nodded approvingly, "...and then at the end of our get together I'm going to tell you all a little story."

Maggie's face straightened some. "So you have solved it I presume? I always knew you would do it, Errol. Dyke always said you were a good for nothing son of a bitch, but I knew that wasn't so. You have so many talents."

She didn't ask me who did it, I noted.

I raised my glass. "To Dyke," I proclaimed, eyeing Maggie heavily.

"To Dyke," she repeated eventually. "And to your ending of this whole sordid caper. I do hope it's a good one. My publisher's been screaming for an end to my book all week."

Again our glasses were filled and Maggie disappeared through to the kitchen. There had been no sign of my best buddy all day. After this morning, my hopes had slipped, but a small hope had remained. That was all but evaporated now. Unless...

I surveyed the room in which I was sitting. There was a black, leather sofa for three in the middle of the homely room. Another chair like the one I was sitting in, was situated at the western wall by the large open coal fire. Across from the fire was a solid wall cabinet full of cut glass, an untouched china dinner set and more awards. A big leopard skin rug sat in the middle of the room. In the corner between me and the wall stood a large, cuddly teddy bear. It was a big, brown fury creature standing two feet tall with a proud look on its face.

Maggie returned, a fresh coat of lip gloss shining from her delectable mouth. She stood behind me and slowly massaged my shoulders. It felt real nice, like all the worries of the world were slowly being prized away, leaving a warm contented sensation. Her soft fingers were replaced by a warm breath on the back of my neck. I could feel the goose bumps all down my spine as she softly kissed my tender flesh. I sighed and leant my head back in approval.

That fateful day, when I stumbled across my dying colleague I made a quick decision. To stay well away from the Spanner household. It was well known that Dyke and Maggie were not the most monogamous of couples. Anyone found to have an involvement with the widow would have been a suspect. Which was exactly what happened.

I knew I would always be able to return when the dust had settled, and the real killer was behind bars. In the meantime, Timmy Matthews would keep me informed. They had of course visited the house early in the investigation but it had been fruitless. Timmy knew as well as I did that Dyke was a brain man. Everything he knew was stored in his head. Predictably there was not a scrap of useful information to be found. And from Maggie? She pretended to be upset, but was also of no use. I made the decision to finish it all here not long ago. It was a perverse thing to do but it seemed very apt and Maggie was always a lover of a good yarn.

The teddy bear in the corner smiled wickedly.

"Hello," I said, sitting upright. "I'm afraid you're going to have to put that on hold sweetheart. It looks like our first guests have arrived."

Maggie smiled before preening herself in front of the mirror. The car came to a halt outside and a number of people got out.

"Are you ready for the dramatics to begin, sweetheart?" I asked, as Maggie again glossed her beautiful lips.

"I'm ready," she answered a little nervously. "Errol, you promise we're safe don't you?"

"Like I told you on the telephone sweetheart, just follow the script. As long as you do that everything will be just fine. If you get in a muddle follow my lead. Now are you sure you're going to be alright?"

She nodded.

"Good. You sit down there, honey. I better answer the door."

Maggie sat down in the corner as I stood up. There was a sharp knock on the door. Three firm taps followed by a pause and another three taps. I brushed myself down and opened the front door.

The smiling face of the fat man greeted me at the doorstep. Behind him, stood four other people. Two were bound and gagged, one carried a cocked weapon and the other stood staring at the floor nervously. I raised an eyebrow in surprise before ushering them all in.

"Come through. Join the party," I instructed.

"So kind sir, so very kind. Audrey put that gun away, we are guests."

Slowly they all made their way through the hall. I closed the door and followed them in. The Coward was already slumped in the armchair by the fire. The two men that were trussed up were carefully maneuvered to the side of the sofa, the nervous woman squeezed onto the other half. Audrey stood up, his gun now re-holstered and a scowl fixed to his baby face. I pulled up a stool from the dining table and sat down by the door.

"Here we all are," I began. "I thank you all for attending. Your host tonight is the beautiful Mrs. Spanner." I gestured at Maggie, who was already on her feet pouring drinks. "Before we continue any further," I now aimed my speech directly at the Coward. "Why the extras? The invitation was for your good self, young Audrey here and Mr..." I nodded at the killer of Woo Wang.

"My sincere apologies sir," began the Coward. He was as usual dressed in an undersized suit, a spotty bow tie and with a silk handkerchief protruding from his breast pocket. "Would you be so kind as to let me explain?"

"Of course." I smiled, looking at my watch. "You are early after all."

Everybody now had a drink in their hand, except for the captives. The other man was looking cool and calm, his eyes were relaxed. The killer on the other hand was close to making a struggle. His terrified eyes stared deep into my own, before darting across the room, first at Audrey then at the Coward.

I avoided his gaze, concentrating mainly on the fat man. As always he had a wide smile on his jovial face. He sipped at his bourbon before setting his glass down on the mantelpiece.

"You must indeed be wondering why I have brought with me two captives sir, am I right?" He emphasized the word two.

I smiled, nodding slightly. An answer was not required.

"I do hope you will not feel any less of me. Your friend has come to absolutely no harm, I must assure you."

Again I remained silent, gazing briefly at Hermeez before returning my attention to the Coward.

"I was, how shall I put it... cashing in an insurance policy, so to speak. You see you are not the only brilliant operator in this fine city of ours. The most brilliant maybe, but not alone in your brilliance." He paused and glanced at Hermeez. "It was suggested to me that it may be in my interest to keep a loose surveillance on your movements. I am sure you wouldn't have expected anything else, am I right?"

I smiled.

"Of course it is nigh an impossibility to keep tabs on Errol Black twenty-four hours a day. His subordinates however are not all so careful and so Mr. Wentz too became a subject of my spies."

"Did your surveillance prove fruitful?" I asked trying to keep the anxiety from my voice.

"There was nothing sinister in my actions, I assure you, but if I could attain my most prized possession on the cheap, as it were. Well why not? I am sure that you understand."

"I trust by your attendance here that you were not in luck?"

The deep long sigh followed. The Coward looked distant, thoughtful even, before once again he grinned uncontrollably. "I'm sure you understand my vigilance, sir. If you yourself were suddenly in the position to attain your half of our soon to be done deal for free..." He held out his bear like paws, "Well. It was worth a try. The end result being another lift in my deep respect for you, sir. To have let your partner slip through your own itchy fingers, only to lead my men to the stone would have been nothing short of sloppy. It would have been most out of character. I am now even more convinced of the brilliance of Errol Black. I truly am." He shook his head in accepted loss. "Such a pity you're untouchable, it really is."

I finished off my drink in one go. Maggie had disappeared into the kitchen, so I held the empty glass in my hands. "And what, may I ask, do you now intend doing with him? Those handcuffs look most uncomfortable."

Hermeez looked at me. His eyes were smiling although his face stayed expressionless. I was uneasy with his appearance here. He should have been with me all the way, not shunted in on the game right in the middle of the first battle. I avoided his gaze, choosing instead to look at Audrey, who appeared to have his own plans on that subject.

"I will of course release him into your care, sir. No doubt, you have your own ideas on what he deserves. I must however inform you that he was picked up with his bags packed and on route to the airport. I do believe he was walking out on you sir,

289

but that is of course your business and not mine. Do with him what you will...after of course I have my hands on my most prized possession."

He rubbed his hands in anticipation.

There was a look of disappointment on the face of young Audrey. He took the sensible option of staying quiet but his melancholy shone out. Meanwhile all eyes rested upon me. Maggie interrupted, carrying a tray full of hot pies, nachos, potato chips and various other nibbles. The Coward wasted no time in diving in.

A few moments passed and the stand off continued. "Why don't you untie Mr. Wentz, Audrey?" I said. "Ungag him as well. If he murmurs a single word you have my permission to shoot him." I paused as the young assassin carried out my orders. "Hermeez," I turned to my German buddy, "why don't you just stand in the corner and keep quiet?"

There was general pleasure from the other members of the party. Audrey and the Coward looked at each other and smiled. The woman looked smugly at Hermeez, before returning her gaze to her lap. The Coward himself was highly amused. He laughed out loud. "You truly are a character, you really are. And in the wrong profession, that I am sure. You would have made a truly great criminal Mr. Black, by god you would."

There was another refilling of the drinks. Only the still bound and gagged killer was looking glum. He sat with his head slumped forward and his shoulders sagging. Audrey now felt comfortable enough to sit sown, and joined the other two on the sofa.

The Coward raised his flabby arm and closely inspected his watch. "Time is passing on. Are we now ready to do a deal, sir? I think we are."

I sighed and shook my head. The smile on the face of Phillip Coward was replaced by a frown. I accepted the cigarette Maggie held out for me. She leaned sexily over me to light it, earning the daggers from the other woman.

"You are forgetting I fear that we have one more outsider amongst us. Maybe you misunderstood the deal." I inhaled deeply. "But as far as I can remember, it did not involve Miss

290

Marlow here." I nodded at the beautiful woman across, who immediately pretended she was not there.

"Let us not be too hasty sir," protested the Coward. "Miss Marlow here is present as a personal guest of my own. She has been…" he rubbed his chins, "…very helpful these last few weeks. I thought, as she is almost as anxious as myself to savor the beautiful Flegenheimer diamond, it would only be courteous and proper for her to attend. She will be absolutely no bother, that I do promise you sir."

"I'm sure she won't," I replied, looking firmly at Marlow. She was wearing more conservative clothes than I was familiar with. A short black skirt showed off her splendid legs, whilst she wore a businesslike white blouse and ladies blazer. She looked timidly into her lap, avoiding my gaze, as if it would kill her.

Maybe it would, I thought sardonically, recalling our last meeting. She had pleaded for her life, like a terrified animal, swearing she would do anything I ask. She would work for me, take the next plane out of America. She even offered me money. Of course, I ignored all her ridiculous pleas, casually filling my weapon with ammo. Tears no longer came from her eyes. They were part of her repertoire, part of her library of theatrics. It was a beautiful moment. Her eyes, all red and cold were now acting true. Genuinely fearful for her own life. The femme fatale all but drained away from her.

But here she was again. Obviously taking absolutely no notice of our parting shot, which incidentally had nothing to do with firearms. I had put my gun back in my holster, got Marlow's clothes together and put them in her arms. She stood frozen. Still not quite sure what would happen next. Had she been reprieved? Would we both walk away from the hotel alive? A prospect which for the last few hours had seemed most unlikely.

Whilst shepherding her to the door I played my royal flush. She was not to be used as target practice after all. I assured her that I was not yet a cold-blooded murderer, a fact that surprised her. Maybe, judging by her own standards, she thought the devil was in us all. I bluffed her with my innocence. She was to leave. To leave New York, the diamond and most importantly of all, my life. I was giving her a chance, and opportunity to save herself and to disappear. If however she did not, if I was ever to come across her delectable, sweet face again, I would have to reconsider my assertion. As yet, I was not a killer, but she certainly had the ability to change that.

She briefly looked up as I stubbed out my Lucky. Maybe she wanted to pick out another and light it up for me. Maybe she was surprised by her own audacity. Defying my warning she was once again in pursuit, but now hiding behind the substantial defenses of the Coward. My gamble had indeed paid off.

"Okay, she can stay," I asserted, earning even more plaudits from my chosen guests. "But I must warn you. She wants the stone for herself. When we do the deal, be careful. Turn your back and you may just find a knife in it."

"Okay sir," began the Coward after once again checking his timepiece. "I think everything has now been taken care of. Are we now ready to do a deal, I'm sure we are."

"You know what? I think we are."

The look of sheer excitement on the man's face was incredible. His big, friendly eyes were watering with anticipation, his cheeks warm and glowing. He rubbed his paws together constantly, as if they had just come out of a freezer. The consensus we had reached also appeared to have united the other members of the party. Audrey had lost his silent obnoxious attitude. A sense of excitement had now replaced Hermeez's cool indifference. And the other two; Marlow and the killer, their own laps were for the first time that evening not the center of attention.

There was a short silence, broken only by the chimes of the grandfather clock, stood proudly by the southern wall. It rang eight times. I finished my drink and began...

"As most of you will know, we are gathered here today to do an exchange," The Coward grinned uncontrollably, barely able to contain his glee. "Contrary to popular belief, the item in question, the so-called Flegenheimer Diamond, has not been in my possession of late. In fact it still isn't effectively."

There was a deep sigh. The fat man had a look of confusion plastered across his colorful features.

"I knew he was bluffing, let's kill him right now!" shouted Audrey. He sat down again when he noticed Hermeez Wentz, gun in hand. Hermeez had edged from his position of solitude towards the hat-stand in the corner. From my own jacket he found it and was now holding it in his right hand.

"Come, come sir. Now it is you who are forgetting the deal. A straight exchange as agreed. We are both honorable men."

"Please bear with me. I would be much obliged it you would quieten your friends." I eyed an increasingly nervous Audrey. "I was speaking literally. The deal is on, as planned. Hermeez, please put that away, we are all gentlemen here. There will be no need for unpleasantness."

The Coward piped up. "You do have access to the stone? A courier perhaps? Always popping up in the movies, those fantastic little men and their mopeds. This is your riposte, your grande finale, am I right?"

I shook my head. "When I said that the stone was not in my possession..." I emphasized the word 'my', "I meant exactly that. I was merely attempting to show the shortcomings of your own ...investigations."

The Coward looked around the room and shrugged. "We got here in the end; I say we got here in the end."

"It would appear so," I agreed. "I suppose in a way it was a blessing that we crossed swords three weeks ago. It was that which prompted me into action. There was no deal on offer then, because I did not have what you desire so very much."

The Coward nodded his head vigorously. "So very fortunate you escaped," he mused. "And so very typical. I presume you now are in such a position?"

"Why else would we be here?" I asked rhetorically, noting his first confession of guilt. "Mrs. Spanner here has seen to that." I nodded at Maggie who had returned with a tray in her arms. Sitting on the tray, glinting in the light, was the majestic Flegenheimer Diamond.

It was a truly magnificent gem. Its deep blue color as spectacular as it was unique. Although not huge, it was certainly

293

the largest diamond that I had ever held and would probably be worth enough to buy a small island on today's market.

Or a life or two.

There was a sudden silence in the room. Maggie walked right through, ignoring the advances and placed the tray down in my lap. Cupping the sparkling gem in both hands I was the envy of the party. I beamed a wide smile as the diamond glinted in the light.

"As you can see, I now am in such a position."

All sets of eyes stared, mesmerized as I tossed it gently from hand to hand. They were truly entranced by its presence. There was no sound, no movement except the occasional blinking of eyes. I had in my hands the contents of the Bank of America, to these people the Holy Grail. These people had given their lives to chasing after it. All four corners of the earth had been searched. Years had passed. And here it was, before them, tossed from side to side by a deadbeat punk private dick.

The Coward made a kind of gurgling noise. Spittle dribbled from the corners of his mouth. He did not wipe it. He didn't reach for his handkerchief, excuse himself, or clean up his little loss of etiquette. He even failed to register the occurrence. Continuing to simply stare. Eyes wide open, blinking only sporadically, as if he didn't dare allow it to leave his sight.

I stopped tossing it and smiled. A good two minutes of silence was rudely interrupted by Marlow. She sneezed again and her cheeks went crimson.

"Bless you my dear," said Coward, his lips barely moving. His eyes still firmly on the diamond he licked his lips, wiped away the spittle and took a sip from his drink. It was as if the whistle had been blown on a game of sleeping lions. People began breathing again, scratching their little itches, blowing their noses and drinking their drinks. Still, however, there was no talk.

Marlow had an interested look on her face. She had clearly never seen the stone before, despite her claims to be its genuine owner. Probably seduced by its legend, the reputation of wealth not only of money but of company. She eyed it cunningly. Maybe planning an ambush, I thought. What would be more her? Pull a gun, make a grab for the diamond and start a chase. It was unlikely but possible. The only certain thing about Marlow was her absolute selfishness. She was in all this for herself and herself only. Dyke, the Coward, Errol Black - they were all pawns in her chess game. Pawns which she would like to use to attain access to the Queen. I smiled at her knowingly.

Phillip Coward on the other hand -if that was really his name- was a different league. He was a man who had devoted his life to this quest. He finished off his drink without moving his eyes. He then launched into a mumbling monologue. Not a bit similar to the selfish Marlow, or the ruthless killer Audrey, and not the slightest resemblance to the gangs of New York. This man cared little for the power games with mobsters. He had no time for Sicilian family ways. For controlling gaming houses, narcotics and women. He was a collector. It really was as simple as that. Okay so he was below the law. He was not afraid to do just what needed to be done. He increasingly controlled a league of bandits and criminals. Temporarily married to the Tighes or the Cortenes or the Manganos. It really made no difference; he was not a Don, not in the traditional way. His one true love in life was collecting. This much could be read by his mesmerized face, by his sheer enthusiasm to attain. When the Flegenheimer Diamond entered the room he would have done anything for it. Killing his mother, his daughter, even one of his boys, would be a small price to pay.

For the first time his natural articulacy deserted him. He stuttered through the grande quest for this most prized artifact. Telling the world with true emotion how he had tracked down the stone for twenty years from Cairo to Shanghai. From Ottawa to Broome. It was to him a great adventure and there were exciting tales to be told. But when the diamond eventually returned to America only to disappear in the Bridge shoot out, his fortunes dropped. Not only was it widely presumed that it was now firmly in the hands of the families, locked away in an untouchable vault, his health suffered. For four years, he was in and out of hospital, not knowing if the next breath would be his last. All the time he dare not divulge the full story to a soul. There was a whole entourage of people around the sick man, not one of them trustworthy. Delicate feelers were put out, long shot

295

chances fleetingly showed themselves; a sighting in an antique shop in London, and auction in Paris, but none were accurate.

When the Coward finally recovered his full health, he knew only too well his priorities. Everything was tested, everything was tried… and the whole big sleaze began. The one thing the Coward overlooked was the role of Dyke Spanner.

"May I…?" he tentatively reached out his arms. They were trembling at the prospect.

I pulled away shaking my head. Cradling the diamond protectively in my arms. "Soon it will be yours forever. I'm sure another minute or two won't hurt?"

The Coward nodded and again sat back in his chair. He had now regained his composure and was ready to complete the deal. Timmy Matthews was due in ten minutes. By that time, we would be ready and waiting. But first the story was incomplete.

Coward put on a quizzical look. "Before we exchange…"

"You want the final chapter," I finished his sentence. Before he could even agree I finished off the story.

"All the time my men searched for you it was Spanner that had my baby," he laughed. "The cunning fox, by god. And I thought he was going to warn you off. Give you a warning to go to ground."

"A sly old devil, Dyke Spanner. Always was one step ahead of the rest."

I described how it must have been Dyke who walked away from the killing of Dutch Schultz with the diamond. Instead of trying for a quick sale, he put it to bed. The diamond was worth more than Dyke could ever earn, but it would also bring more heat than he cared to be under. Like any sensible criminal he would wait, whether it took him five years, ten years or a lifetime. In the end, of course, it cost him his own life.

Ten years after the event along came the mysterious man known as the Coward. He was gradually edging in on the truth and would sooner or later find out. To make it appear as if he was warning me off was Dyke's master stroke. Giving his old friend a bit of friendly advice, confirming the discovery of the incoming vultures. This would of course have only one conclusion. Erase himself from any suspicion and confirm that the diamond was my secret. Once the word was about that it was me and not Dyke that robbed the dying Dutchman our fate was sealed. A few words in the right ears and the story was complete. Escalating uncontrollably throughout the underbelly of Manhattan. The lines between myself and the Flegenheimer were now unbreakable. Ingenious as it was despicable in its treachery, it was a plan that worked. The only drawback being the bullets in his belly from the soon to be arrested shooter.

"What an appalling place New York is!" exclaimed the Coward. "Everyone's a traitor, a rat or a skunk." He paused, thinking carefully. "And still you will avenge this man, despite the fact he hung out your soul? Would money not be a better deal?"

"Take the money, Errol. The lousy traitor doesn't deserve your loyalty," shouted Audrey, now appearing to show respect and empathy. It wouldn't last.

"The deal remains the same. Dyke Spanner may have sold my name for a dollar, but he was shot down unnecessarily. And what's more he was killed by a punk. If detectives get killed by punks there's not a hope left for any of us." I nodded at Maggie who filled the glasses for the last time. "No, the deal remains the same. The killer of Woo Wang and Dyke Spanner for the stone, plus the cash adjustment that we discussed earlier. Take it or leave it."

The mention of Woo Wang caused the nameless to look up in terror. He had been sitting quietly, the delectable Marlow on his left and the blonde killer Audrey on his right. He had the look of a condemned man about him and if he really was the killer of Wang he deserved everything he was going to get.

Sweat poured from his shiny forehead. He had been uncomfortable throughout the whole exercise, shifting about nervously in his seat. Adjusting his tie continuously. Maybe he was under the impression that the Coward would help him wriggle out of it. Another few thousand dollars and his liberty would be spared. Sweat marks grew under the arms of his cream shirt. He looked hopefully at the Coward, every last drop of hope and pleading were in his eyes but the Coward dismissed him with a shake of his head.

The Coward sighed resignedly, before nodding his head. "I'm afraid the time has come."

I caught the eye of Hermeez Wentz. He still held my own gun in his hand. Throughout the proceedings, he had remained absolutely silent. Stealthily he had maneuvered towards the coat stand, but since had not made the slightest movement. A brief glimpse into his eyes was all I needed. I felt a little guilty for doubting him, although there were still things that needed ironing out. Did I not refute everything Ava had told me? Did I not insist on his loyalty to the end? No matter in life or death, did I not insist he was straight? Of course I had. I had always known there was no traitor in Hermeez Wentz... although still I doubted him.

That one moment, however, was enough to assure me that for tonight at least he was on side. It was a time that we would always remember, a confirmation, a pat on the back. Nothing need be spoken. I knew from those eyes he was ready. Nothing would go wrong, I was positive of this, but if it did Hermeez would be ready. As always, he would be there.

The nameless suddenly stood up. He was bathed in sweat, his thinning hair plastered to his scalp. He was shaking uncontrollably and had a terrified look on his face.

"Please," he screamed. "I will..."

Before he finished his garbled sentence, he clenched his fists and lunged at the fat man. There was a squeal from Marlow. All the tension that had gradually built up was now being unleashed. The killer tumbled to the floor, tripped by the outstretched leg of Audrey, the blond Satan. He landed heavily, his nose crashing heavily into the carpeted floor. Before he could move again his arms were held tightly behind his back. Audrey gave him a kick to the solar plexus and a back handed thud to the shoulder blade. The killer groaned before passing out. Audrey stood over him, one foot gently pressing down into his neck, grinning widely. "I never did like the slitty eyed son of a bitch!" he proclaimed.

"Do sit down Audrey," instructed the Coward. He had flinched and grimaced his way through the exchanges. "You have a dirty mouth, sit down!"

298

Once again he eyed the diamond eagerly, his hand pressed firmly together before looking into my eyes. "Here, sir, is your man. He has signed a full confession to the slaying of Wang and when he comes to his senses, he will take the rap for Spanner also. There will be no embarrassment I assure you. If there are any other outstanding homicides that your friend Lieutenant Matthews would like clearing up then..." He pursed his lips and gestured with one of his huge paws. "When the New York Police Department search his apartment they will find plenty evidence of his guilt, certainly enough to convict."

I nodded. "And the other?"

The Coward handed me an envelope. I checked it and smiled.

"Like I said sir, the time has now come." He nodded to the unconscious man, dabbing his mouth with his silk handkerchief. "You now have your fall guy, you also have your cash adjustment. And now..." he tentatively outstretched a meaty arm, "may I?"

Maggie looked at me. I could see in her eyes she was questioning me. Was this it? Was the man sprawled across the leopard skin rug my holy grail. Was he the killer of her husband, the man she once loved, but in the end didn't even like. She was extremely curious to the degree of being questionable. But in spite of all this I could see that she just wanted an end to it all. A great deal had happened throughout the last twenty-one days and she didn't know the half of it, but now she was free and to enjoy her liberty, it all had to end.

As the Coward got within an inch of the diamond, there was a loud ringing sound. It was the doorbell. Maggie Spanner immediately set off to answer the bell. She had played her role perfectly. Ignoring the bad blood from Marlow, and the discomfort of the subject, she had acted the perfect hostess. And she had done so with such dignity. Despite the fact that she was no longer in love with Dyke when he was murdered, she still cared for him. To remain silent and be so polite throughout the whole proceedings was a mighty fine effort.

I caught Marlow studying me as I watched Maggie disappear. She had remained remarkably still, not daring to

299

contribute to the conversation. I wondered just what she was feeling as I held the diamond in my hands. The exchange was close to being complete and still there had been no offering. Maybe she planned to do her work once the Coward was in possession. But what intention would she have on me? At first, I had suspected she would urge him to exert his muscle. Maybe demand my execution. Only then would she be able to sleep easily at night.

On the other hand, maybe she had me down as weak. I had allowed her to live two nights ago, when a self-defense plea would have been a good bet. And I had made no intimations to threaten her today, despite my grave warnings. I suppose she would have been quite justified in this opinion. Alternatively, it was possible that she had feelings for me. That she simply wanted to make sure I walked away from this alive. Once I was safely out of the equation, then she could tackle the phantom, and we'd all be happy. Time would tell.

Audrey got to his feet. He looked at the Coward, holding his gun readily. Coward returned his glance with a look of indifference, and then looked to me for an explanation.

"Nothing to worry about," I assured them. "In ten minutes time the exchange will be complete and you can walk away," I looked at the shiny gem, "with this little baby for company. Do sit down Audrey, please."

The young man again looked at the Coward before duly sitting down. He slipped his gun inside his jacket, holding it out of view. Meanwhile the front door opened and there was a brief muffled exchange.

Timmy Matthews stumbled into the cluttered room. Attired in his full-length raincoat and fedora hat, he appeared the typical storybook detective. Round of belly and sharp of wit, and a face as old as an Egyptian Mummy.

Maggie immediately fixed him a drink and relieved him of his hat. Throughout this little ceremony not a word was spoken. Timmy stood in the middle of the room, towering over the fallen angel, he simply looked. His expression was initially one of surprise and then of curiosity. Slowly he examined everybody present in the room, before smiling widely.

"Well, well, you've certainly assembled an all star cast here, Eezy. Where do I start? It looks like a crooks gathering."

"Pleased you could make it Lieutenant Matthews," I introduced cheerfully. "I hope you brought your cuffs."

"Mmm," answered the thoughtful policeman. "I'm just deciding who it is that's gonna wear 'em. Any volunteers?" He smiled again surveying the room. Eyes sweeping left to right. Smiling warmly at Maggie, nodding at Hermeez, stopping momentarily on Marlow before carefully studying the Coward and his sidekick. Not for a moment did his eyes rest on the diamond, which was now glimmering on the carpeted floor.

His manner was a lot more encouraging than of late. No longer did he appear tired and in need of a rest. Much more alert and willing to participate in the deadly game I was playing. His patience was holding strong, no demands or accusation; he simply waited for the next prompt. After all, he would get all the glory. It would all be handed on a silver platter.

"Good evening, sir," piped up the Coward. "Detective Matthews?" He held out his chubby hands, awaiting confirmation.

There was none.

"I don't think I've had the pleasure."

"Oh, my name is unimportant. Actually we were just..."

"On the contrary," I interrupted, putting a friendly hand on the Coward's arm. "Phil. You are very important, as is young Audrey here." I followed Timmy's glance over to the uneasy minder. A smile was glued to his haggard face. The phantom glared in incomprehension.

"I think our business is complete, Mr. Black," he said through gritted teeth and once again reached out his arms. "I'll take the... blue stone and be on my way."

"Come, come, have another drink. It's early," laughed Timmy clearly enjoying himself, despite not knowing why.

"That's right. Maggie, get Phil here and Audrey another drink will you? And don't forget Miss Marlow..." I saw it all click

301

in Timmy's face. She was the broad from the Height's, he was saying, that's why I've got two sets of bracelets.

"After all, how can you leave just yet? As we were all discussing, Tim's sure to want us all down at the station, aren't I right Timmy?"

"Yeah, sure," he stuttered, trying his best to be convincing. The Coward looked at Audrey. Audrey looked at the Coward. His hand inside his jacket wavered. An ever so slight shake of the phantom's head halted this. They instead both beamed out wide smiles, masking their confusion.

"To give our statements."

There was a silence. Nobody was quite sure if it was their turn to speak up.

"About the murder of Woo Wang, and how we can all categorically state that it was this man here." I pointed at the still unconscious nameless, shaking my head. A dumb look painted on my face, I said, "Funny how people forget things. But now we all remember. This is the man who shot Wang, no doubt about it. Isn't that right?"

"Absolutely!" said Audrey, eager for an input. "The son of a bitch!"

I nodded approvingly.

Timmy Matthews nodded his head in absolute disbelief. He looked directly at the Coward, then at Audrey. "Is that so?" he uttered rhetorically. "And you are all willing to come down the station and make statements to this effect?"

I looked at the Coward plainly. In one movement, I pushed the Flegenheimer towards him. It now rested next to him, brushing his left leg as he shuffled in his chair. A look of sheer ecstasy now filled his chubby chops.

"I say again, you are all willing to make a statement that this man killed Woo Wang?"

"Oh yes, Lieutenant," exclaimed the Coward. "We realize that it is our duty as American citizens. We must not shrink the responsibility of the honest man, who simply wants to live in a better world. You do a grand job sir, if I may say so, a job we are all extremely proud of. And if we can be of any assistance then we must offer our humble services." He licked his lips, rubbing his toes over the diamond.

"As Mr. Black has said, it is this man that is responsible for the Dragon Bar murders. Both of them, in fact. He killed both Wang and Spanner."

So off we went to the police station. Maggie Spanner was thanked and I promised her I would soon be in touch. Hermeez was not required, and so promised to meet me later at Joe's, for a debriefing. I hoped he would be there, but my uneasy feeling would not shift. The rest of us squeezed into Timmy Matthew's patrol car. Myself and Tim in the front seats, and an eminently more uncomfortable Coward, Audrey and Marlow in the back. The nameless, hands cuffed together, was clumsily squashed into the trunk. There was no chance of fitting four in the rear seat, three was a push with the fat man in the middle. Beaming like a king with the Flegenheimer Diamond hidden away inside his jacket.

"Which one is the other set for?" whispered Timmy as he drove through the evening traffic. "I could arrest the broad for illegal activity, the fat guy for procuring young boys, and the kid... well, take your pick from twenty shootings last night."

"Patience," is all I replied. Tim gave me one of his flabbergasted looks, but this time he was willingly leaving it up to me.

It didn't take long to wrap up the statements. Timmy had telephoned ahead and true to the Coward's word, the killer's apartment held all the necessary evidence. To make matters smoother he confessed to everything, once he got round to being interviewed. Twenty minutes later, we were all stood in the police station reception area. For the first time that evening, the Coward had let go of the blue rock, allowing Marlow a proper look at the priceless gem. Her excitement was almost at the level of his. Her eyes all glazed over as she rolled it over her soft, dainty hands. Inspecting its every detail, marveling at its truly beautiful finish. I slipped away to make a quick telephone call, but was back before anyone noticed I had left.

Weeny Jung Ping had been released. The charges of murder had been dropped in light of new, definitive information. He was to remain under investigation for illegal activity with a criminal organization and was urged to reside at his usual address. Tim Matthews had slipped him a one-way airline ticket on the way out.

The nameless hit man, a Mr. Flute, was now the sure thing murderer. Three statements said as much and the amount of damning evidence was overwhelming. Professor Coward and his young student Audrey had been going over a dissertation in an alcove. They had both seen the shooting clearly, but had been too frightened to do anything. Until now, that was, when their sense of duty and obligation to the good had surfaced. Miss Marlow had been shopping outside. She had seen Flute running out of the Dragon Bar, a smoking gun in his hand. She had heard the shot and watched as he sped off in a car, which was later found blood-stained and abandoned.

The weapon had been found, and the man's prints matched up. All three witnesses marveled at how quickly NYPD justice kicked in. The right man was in the cells, I knew that for sure, but the method was unique. Everything was completed quickly and without question. My three friends now assured that I was simply ensuring my half of the bargain. They would the walk free with their dream accomplished.

Dyke Spanner had been notably ignored from each of the three signed statements. I had intimated to Tim that to adjoin the admission would only cause problems. Naive as it was, NYPD law would not be able to pass a double identity so smoothly. The sergeant informed the Coward and his entourage that they would be required to re-attend to discuss that murder. We all knew they would not.

"It is truly magnificent," mumbled Marlow to nobody in particular.

"Yes, it most certainly is Miss Marlow, by god it is!" agreed the Coward, watching her closely. "Now if that is all sir, we will be..."

"Of course Professor you may leave. And thank you very much," said Timmy, looking nervously over to me.

304

The Coward and Audrey smiled at each other. I shook both of their hands, even enduring a sort of bear hug from the fat man.

"And so we must leave sir," he began. "It has been most superb to have done business with you. I do hope that we will meet again, by god I do."

I simply nodded, a smile plastered on my face.

"Okay." He looked around the room. "Miss Marlow are we ready?"

Marlow looked up and handed him the diamond back. All three then headed towards the exit. The Coward and Audrey were out of the door when I stepped across, in front of Marlow. She looked at me in fearful surprise as the door slammed shut. Before she could respond, there was a set of bracelets attached to her wrist and she was being led through into another room. Timmy stopped short, leaving us together.

"Errol, what is going on?" she asked helplessly, tugging at the handcuffs.

"Don't do that sweetheart, you'll hurt your precious wrists."

She looked at me mournfully. Her beauty shone out from her petrified face. Big brown eyes welling up with tears.

"I did what you asked, I signed the statement," she pleaded. "Why have you let the other two free and kept me here? I do not understand."

"I'm sorry darling. I didn't want you to feel left out, so I invented a story for you as well. The statement is probably going through the shredder right now..."

The dam burst, tears now streaming down her high cheekbones. She was definitely distressed. Was this one more game? Would I frighten her to death and then release her; a final warning. Or was I to be true to my word. That way she would not get out of this room alive.

She edged towards me. She didn't believe that I would kill her. Despite my influence with the police, I would not go that far. To kill her under their noses, with no witnesses to lie. Even Errol Black would not do that. She would appeal to my better nature. The nature that had taken her to bed not two days ago.

I stepped aside, avoiding her advances. "You see a statement from a murderer would be no good. For one killer to finger another holds no water in this town. I believe you honey, and so does Timmy, but there's enough to convict Flute already."

She stopped. "But I'm no killer, Errol, I'm..."

"Sure you are angel, you killed Dyke. You filled him full of lead and left him for dead right? To confuse matters more you even used two different firearms. Don't worry, the police won't need them."

She put her handcuffed hands to her forehead. Clearly shocked by what she heard, there was no rehearsed response. "Errol, how can you say such a thing? I could not have killed Dyke. You were there when it happened! You were watching me in the restaurant."

"That's true baby, I certainly was. And that is exactly why I know that you killed Dyke. You planted me there as your alibi, only to kill him anyway. You had the opportunity and the willing."

I lit up a Lucky and for the first time offered one to Marlow. She accepted, sucking on it desperately.

"You see honey, Mr. Flute was an amateur. A no good punk. It's only the NYPD's incompetence that's kept him on the streets until now. There's no way he could have killed Dyke because he wasn't good enough. Dyke Spanner was a lot of things, but an amateur was not one of them. He would never get killed by a punk. He couldn't let one get close enough. He was far too good."

"Then how was I supposed to get near him?"

It was supposed to be a question of defense. But it was exactly the response I had wanted.

"Because you weren't a threat, sweetheart. You and Dyke were lovers, just like you and me. Hell, I nearly made the same mistake." I thought of the empty gun, taking it from my jacket pocket and holding it up. "Guess what? It matches up. Yes, this is the same little baby that killed Dyke."

There was a short silence. Marlow was truly lost for words.

"Maybe he was close to figuring out you weren't who you said you were. You couldn't risk him staying alive to uncover you. That would ruin your plans to get the diamond. And nothing stands in the way of that. You probably arranged to meet him for a last drink. Maybe your intention was to call it all off and never see him again. Only he'd already figured it out and you had to kill him. On the other hand, maybe you'd planned to kill him all along. Hell, I can't blame you. He was an arrogant, know it all son of a bitch. I thought of shooting him a few times myself.

"Once he was dead, you would wait for me to arrive on your doorstep and snare the stone. It was a great plan, a truly great one. The only drawback being Dyke had it all along. So you killed the guy too early."

"What are you going to do, Errol? You can't hand me over to the police. I'll hang for this."

"Oh I don't know precious. If you're on form, I'm sure you'll bargain it down to twenty years, maybe fifteen."

"But Errol, you can't. What about us? I love you."

I studied her face. Sighing at just how pretty she was.

"Maybe you do, sweetheart, maybe you do. If you get the years, I'll be here to buy you dinner when you get out. If you hang, I'll remember the good times."

I left the room. Timmy rushed over as I made my way out of the police station.

"I heard all that, Errol. We'll take care of her now."

"I'm sure you will, Lieutenant," I answered.

"And Errol... Thanks."

I nodded at Timmy and hailed a cab.

When I made it to Joe's Diner it was gone ten. Marlow and Flute would be locked up in a cell and Weeny Wang would be on his way to Rio. I felt relieved that the whole business was finally wrapped up. Dyke Spanner could now rest in peace, and I could get back to being a good for nothing son of a bitch.

There was a loud cheer as I entered the watering hole. Joe hugged me, a bottle of champagne in one hand, a bottle of bourbon in the other.

307

"I wasn't sure which..." he explained.

Ava Jamieson and Jake Wiseman were deep in conversation. They both looked up and smiled. Ava nodded and mouthed 'I knew you'd do it, Errol'. I winked back at her. Jake took his hand from her knee and headed over.

"Well done Errol," he said. "Come here..."

Before I could say anything, he too was hugging me. "You did it."

Joe handed me the bottle of champagne and nodded to the stairs. "Hermeez is up there. Said he wants to talk in private."

I nodded, patted my buddy on the shoulder and ambled up the stairs.

Hermeez was stood in the doorway with two empty glasses in his hand. He took the champagne from me and poured us a both a glass, raising his in the air. "Congratulations Rolly, you solved the case."

I tasted the bubbly. It tasted sour.

"Joe said you wanted to talk."

Hermeez nodded and looked at his feet. "I'm leaving town, Eezy."

I said nothing.

"Tonight. We're on the night train."

He looked up and our eyes met.

"We're gonna start a new life together. Marcie and me, we're leaving it all behind. All the history, the bright lights, the grime, the celebrity lifestyle and the mobsters. All of it."

"Hermeez, I know. You don't have to go."

He looked rueful and nodded his head. "Yes I do. I've danced with the devil too many times. The Agency is all yours, Errol."

There was a long silence. Maybe five minutes of absolute silence. Sure there was noise going on downstairs but it was all blocked out. For the moment, there was just me and Hermeez.

"I'm sorry I lied to you, Eezy."

Hermeez went on to tell me about his double life, which had been consuming him for the last six months. He had always kept in touch with Marcia and they found themselves getting closer and closer. It was only the barrier that Hermeez had erected around himself that stopped them from falling back in love sooner. But it didn't stop them, not for long anyway. I could hear it in his voice, he was head over heels in love with her again. Maybe he always had been.

When he finally drew up the courage to admit it to himself, and to Marcia, that is when his problems really began. Marcia's years in California had been a real roller coaster, but neither of us realized just how far she had sunk. She descended into a world of drug addiction and crime, perpetuated by each other and tried on two occasions to take her own life. She found herself seriously in debt and with no way of getting out of it.

Hermeez helped her kick her addictions and gave her all the support and affection she needed. But he couldn't give her the money as he didn't have it. He should have asked me but he was afraid that I would talk him out of his reconciliation. He was wrong. I would have actively encouraged him, but even I would not have got my hands on the kind of money he needed.

When Arnold Muchado took over the debts, Marcia and Hermeez's problems were really beginning. They had three options: Marcia joined Muchado's stable of high-class hookers, they both died nasty deaths, or Hermeez did a few chores for the gangster. The third option was the only one they would consider. So Hermeez became Muchado's lapdog, running errands for the gangster and not asking the questions he should have asked, or getting paid the money he should have been paid. He broke the code and he got nothing for it. Apart from Marcia.

"She's trouble Herm. She always has been and she always will be. She'll hurt you again."

"No. No she won't!" He said it as if he was more sure of that than anything else in the whole world.

"And Muchado is now going to leave you alone?"

"The debt is repaid so he's gonna have to. Anyways he won't know where to find us. Nobody will."

I looked at my buddy. I could feel my eyes filling up but I just let them. He smiled at me and then looked away, his face a mask of embarrassment.

"Just what did he have you doing for him? What does a loan shark and a pimp like Muchado need a private eye for?"

Hermeez shrugged.

A cold chill swept over me. A sinister thought formed in my mind, a thought that I dare not consider. Before I had chance to consider it I found myself saying: "You shot Dyke Spanner."

His face said it all. I had picked the wrong killer.

"I'm taking you in."

Hermeez shook his head. "You're not going to do that," he said, before telling me just what happened.

"I found out that he was in trouble. Serious trouble. It wasn't just this diamond thing with the Coward, he had enemies everywhere. Everywhere. Muchado let it slip one day that there was a contract out on him. It wasn't one of his and he didn't seem bothered either way whether he lived or died. I think he found the whole idea a little amusing.

"What was I supposed to do? A man that I hated, who had been responsible for the worst chapter of my sorry life, a man that I knew cheated not only on his wife but on every friend or colleague he ever had, was going to be killed. Probably a couple of bullets in the back of the head. He wasn't big time, so I don't suppose he would even merit the honor of knowing who it was that was to kill him. No," he made a gun with his thumb and forefinger, "bang, bang to the back of the head and he would be dead. What should I have done, Eezy? Should I have let it just happen?"

I said nothing.

"No, I thought not. So I put all my personal feelings aside and decided I wouldn't just let it happen. I would do the right thing and go and see the son of a bitch. Guess what? He threw it right back at me. He told me to get out of his face and leave him alone. He was heading down the Dragon for a beer and didn't want to be bothered by a sorry, yellow kraut. I began to walk away. Hell if he was gonna get himself killed then fine, I owed the bastard nothing, except maybe a bullet or two of my own.

"I nearly got away as well, only now he turned right around and started to follow me. He started on the insults again, you know more of the ancestry shit. I was Hitler's little

310

descendant, I was a sausage eating slob. I was a fuckin' foreigner who should be repatriated to my fuckin' fatherland. I kept walking.

"Then he started on Marcia, calling her a whore and a slut. I stopped and faced him. I was going to punch the bastard's face in. I think he sensed it and he stopped coming forward, instead calling you now. You didn't get the heavy treatment, you were just a sap. A sap for putting up with me and sap for being my partner. But most of all you were a sap for falling for my wife. He said that Marcia had seduced you, 'She offered him that sweet pussy of hers and he lapped it up.'

"I knew he was speaking the truth. For once in his lousy life he was telling the truth and I didn't want to hear it. I suddenly felt dizzy and a little tingly all over my hands. It was like I wasn't in control of my own body. Have you ever felt like that, Errol, you know where it's like you're watching yourself doing something? I think it's when you can't cope with what is happening and you're real close to the edge.

"I took out my gun and shot him, just once. Then for some reason I took out my spare and shot him again. That just seemed like a sensible thing to do at the time. The next thing I can remember I'm at your house the next morning waiting for you to arrive back from Alabama. I was going to tell you all about it but I couldn't. Instead I buried my head in the sand and pretended nothing had happened.

"When Marlow left me the other night she took my bait."

"She took your gun?"

"Yes. The murder weapon became hers. I knew she was on to me and it worked like a dream. She's killed before, Errol. She will kill again if she gets out."

He was right. I knew he was right.

"The second weapon went to Ferriby's shack. You missed it but the police will have it by now. You did a good job Errol, you should be satisfied."

I put my gun on the table and held out my hand. Hermeez shook it and grimaced.

311

"I'm sorry, Errol. I broke the code. No gangsters, no hoodlums, no Outfit. I broke the code and I am truly sorry. Now you have done the same."

I shook my head. "I love Claudia."

"Yes, I am sure you do. Don't forget I love Marcia, I always have and I guess I always will."

He then picked up my gun and looked thoughtful.

I bowed my head and closed my eyes. I was almost willing him to do it! Hell, it was nothing more than I deserved! He may have broken the code, but what I had done was far worse!

There was what seemed like days of silence. It was broken by the door closing. I looked up to find my gun back on the table and Hermeez gone.

That night we eventually spent together. Not in the luxury of a five star hotel, but in my own apartment. We made our own romance, acting like children on a first date. We ordered pizza from the takeaway and drank our way through a good bottle of wine. Smoochy music drifted around the bare room and after dinner, we danced. When the record finished we kicked off our shoes and headed for the bedroom.

Suddenly, all the coyness and fear disappeared. We indulged in the most beautiful lovemaking. Only the squeaks of my mattress invaded our moment of togetherness. Claudia was perfect throughout.

When we finished for the second time we relaxed. Cuddling up close under the duvet, reliving in our minds what we had just done. It was only then that I thought of Marlow, and only for a brief moment.

Playing with the curly tufts of hair on my chest, Claudia began to talk. I was only half listening, but she continued regardless. She told me how she had found the envelope after I had gone. She had tried to tell me on the telephone but I had been too busy. She did not say it bitterly or even defensively. What we had just done had made everything right. She just wanted to tell me the story.

She'd got in touch with Hermeez and they decided to check it out. I had disappeared and maybe they could help me by giving me a surprise. Not for one second had they thought of doing anything but try to help me.

I smiled and kissed Claudia warmly. I knew she was telling the truth. Of course, her bequest had not been the Flegenheimer Diamond, just the small matter of $10 million. She offered to buy me a new car. I failed to answer her generous offer. Deciding instead to roll over and make love once more. After all, this would be the last night I would spend with Claudia Cortene.

The next morning I received a telephone call. It was from the new police Captain Timothy Matthews.

"You are one sly son of a bitch."

"Timmy, what makes you call at such an hour?"

"What makes me…Last night we made a couple of arrests."

"I'm very pleased for you, you'll make Captain yet."

"I just did."

"Congratulations. What happened?"

There was a chesty laugh.

"Just after I booked Flute and the delicious Marlow, we got a call of a disturbance just around the corner."

"Very interesting Timmy, but you get disturbances every night of the week."

"Yeah, but not involving the people that were involved in this one. They were arguing about some diamond or other. Hundreds of witnesses saw it all happen."

"Timmy, what can I say?"

"The only problem being the crooks had a little disagreement."

"Oh?"

"Yeah, the young one was most displeased. He calls the fat one 'a stupid motherfucker'. And shot him down dead before turning the gun on the pair of goons they were arguing with. They all ended up dead except for two smart looking guys. Turns out they work for the Cortene Organization. They got the

313

diamond, but I booked them for firearms offences and all of this happened right in front of Beech."

"So you've got three murderers in one night eh, must be a record."

"Damn right, Eezy. And you, my friend have got a case of bourbon. It's on its way to your place. Cheers!"

Epilogue

I never did find out who killed George Ferriby. Or his friend, the one that led me to the locker in the health club. He too was found shot to death a couple of weeks later and the murder was never solved.

A little like the killing of Dutch Schultz, there were many possibilities and many red herrings. The Dutchman is widely accepted to have been a casualty of his own brashness and lack of tact. His very public spat with Thomas Dewey leading to the decision for Charlie Luciano to order the hit. This never did ring true to me. After all why would Luciano order the killing of Schultz when it would automatically lead to himself taking the Dutchman's place as Public Enemy Number One? Which is exactly what happened. I guess I am in a unique position, with the knowledge I have, and it is this that lead me to think that maybe it was the Coward that ordered the killing of Schultz, his own half brother. And it is this decision that set the whole series of events in motion that ultimately led to his own death. It's not one that you're going to read about in the papers but to me it is the most likely.

Claudia Cortene went on to become a very successful woman. She broke free of her suffocating family when Uncle Stan was killed in a drive by shooting, a month after I last saw him. The last I heard she was making it big in the world of fashion, living mainly in Milan but jetting all over the world and earning lots of clean money. She is yet to marry after telling me that she would never walk down the aisle. That was just before she walked out on me the morning after I told her why Hermeez had left New York. It seems she could easily forgive me for cheating on her, but not for cheating on my best friend. She has a point.

I did cross paths with Hermeez again but I guess that is for the next chapter. Unfortunately, we never made up. I never stopped loving him as a friend and I figure he felt the same. Otherwise he would have used my gun in Joe's spare room instead of just thinking about it. He still figures largely in my dreams, usually as the guiding light when I find myself overwhelmed by monsters or attacked my faceless killers. He helps me and he saves me, often, and then he just walks away.

Timmy Matthews was on holiday when I took the call. It was long distance from a mutual friend of ours that was now living in San Diego. He said it was all over the newspapers down there after they exhumed the body of a local celebrity. He was to be flown home to Ireland and re-buried on consecrated ground. Apparently, it was protocol to give the remains a cursory autopsy before packing it up and loading it on the airplane. It had caused quite a sensation down there and he just wondered if we had heard about it. We had not. Fancy finding an extremely precious, dark blue diamond in the remains of the man's stomach. And it was genuine too. Thought to be a cousin of the more famous Hope Diamond and worth a great deal of money.

When I put the telephone down, I could almost see the sparkling eyes of Liam Tighe smiling down on me.

It was the end of something big...

BIOGRAPHY

Simon Swift has been writing for as long as he can remember ...

A voracious reader from an early age, he fell in love with the adventures of hardboiled detectives Sam Spade and Mike Hammer. A Humphrey Bogart season of black and white movies introduced him to film noir.

After reading Politics and Philosophy at The University of York, he embarked on a 12 month odyssey of adventure, traveling the world. Alongside his odd pair of clean clothes and his stack of paperbacks, his most treasured possession was the notebook, which contained the chrysalis of his own hardboiled novel.

Many years later, the result was Black Shadows, a crime novel which blends fact and fiction. It attained a gold star on Harper Collins' Authonomy in January 2010, on the way to becoming the all time top ranked crime novel and generating a record 1000+ reviews.

He is currently putting the finishing touches to the sequel, The Casablanca Case. In the meantime, Simon passes the time teaching primary children in a challenging area, playing football with his two young children and being a dedicated husband to his lovely wife.

As well as his family, his amazing job and writing, Simon loves most sport and giraffes.

Lightning Source UK Ltd.
Milton Keynes UK
UKOW021050080212

186880UK00001B/93/P

9 781907 954085